WONDERS OF THE SPIRIT

WONDERS OF
THE SPIRIT

William Porter

ISBN-13: 978-1-944662-83-7

Affirmation Press Publishing date: 03/30/2023

Cover Design by Michael Scott, MASGraphicarts.com

Acknowledgments

This book would not have been completed without the assistance and support of my wife Yvonne and our daughters.

Also, the following individuals were instrumental in the final production of this work:

Michael Scott: Front and Back Cover
Mary Louise Smith: Drawings in Figures distributed throughout the book.
Diane Henderson: Editor
Drew Becker: Publisher, Affirmation Press

Table of Contents

PART I: PRELUDE TO THE TRIP

CHAPTER 1
The Windy, Snowy City

Foundation Scripture: Luke 15:4,5

4 What man of you, having a hundred sheep, if he loses one of them, does not leave the ninety-nine in the wilderness, and go after the one which was lost until he finds it? 5 And when he has found it, he lays it on his shoulders, rejoicing.

While they enjoyed their time in church, the Manleys and the Mints looked forward to later in the day when they would get together and entertain each other, usually at one or the other's homes. The couples often hung out together, and, while Maggie was not aware of it at the time, she found herself putting into practice the message the pastor delivered during a special service on Saturday evening.

The minister's message that night was titled, "The Wonders of the Spirit." Pastor Henry began by saying, "The main theme of my talk today, people, is our privilege as believers to be especially sensitive to those who are less fortunate—particularly those among us who have lost their way. They may have strayed off the straight and narrow path by no fault of their own but because of the circumstances of life.

"Even Jesus says in a parable that if ninety-nine sheep are accounted for, we should go after the one sheep that is lost. And that's one of the 'Wonders of the Spirit' that I often talk about. What I'm saying is that the Holy Spirit will lead us to go after and assist that person who needs help the most. In some cases, we must crucify the flesh and be more concerned with others than with ourselves."

The minister then went on to give a rather brief but effective message on the wonders of the Spirit. Eventually, the service ended, and the Mints traveled home afterwards.

On the drive, Maggie said to Fred, "You know, honey, that was a nice sermon tonight. I can identify with the challenges Pastor Henry said all of us have. But I must admit it's difficult for me to get my mind around that last expression he made, 'wonders of the Spirit.' I mean, I know that we as humans have a spirit and, because of that, we can connect with God, who *is* spirit. But how can that translate into our practical experiences, those everyday life type situations that often confront everybody? He really didn't talk about that at all."

Fred replied, "Well, Mag, that is a difficult subject to tackle, the spirit I mean. And you didn't even mention another part of our makeup that the minister talked about, which is the physical. That part of us is familiar to people, and that's because we deal with our physical self every day with the five senses that we all have.

"Let me tell you this, Mag, you're familiar with *your* physical self, aren't you? That's why you spend so much time putting on makeup every morning!"

Maggie responded contemptuously, "Now is that supposed to be funny, Fred? You do know that's being sexist, don't you?"

Without giving her husband an opportunity to answer, she continued, "Anyway, I pray that at some point the practical aspects of these 'Wonders of the Spirit' the pastor talked about will be revealed to me."

"Well, be careful what you pray for is all I've got to say," Fred replied.

Maggie did not realize at the time how much those verses of scripture at the beginning of the minister's sermon resonated with her given the personal challenges she had. At some point, she would become aware of how the minister's message might be applied in her life to overcome issues confronting her.

On Sunday, Maggie had a strong desire to attend a local basketball game. It would be a challenge to 'crucify the fresh' as the pastor had promoted in his sermon the previous evening. Despite the inclement weather that was forecast for later in the day, Maggie really wanted to go to that basketball game.

Before arising from bed on the morning of the game, Maggie said, "Fred, I think we need to add some spice to our life—to do something different."

"Well, Mag, what do you have in mind?" Fred asked.

She replied, "You know the season tickets we have for the Bulls include two pre-season games, and one is tonight downtown. So, what do you say?"

Fred replied, "Well, Mag, you know what the weather will be like later. A storm system is supposed to be coming through."

Maggie answered, "Since when Fred has the weather kept you from doing something you really wanted to do? Come on, let's do it! Let's go to the game."

Fred relented and said, "Okay, then. I'll go. Let me call Gates and see if they want to come along. But you know how those two are; he and Courtney never reject something we want them to do with us."

Maggie looked at him, smiled, and said, "I know, Fred. That's why I asked you to call 'em!"

The unpleasant weather should have been enough to prevent them from going out. But Maggie was persistent in encouraging Fred to attend the game and wanted Courtney and Gates to come along with them.

Fred accommodated his wife. He contacted Gates about coming along with them to the game prior to the regular church service on the day of the game, that Sunday morning. Gates reciprocated and told Fred he and Courtney would love to come with them.

The Manleys and the Mints looked forward to their usual time together at one or the other's homes later on Sunday evening. After attending church *on this* Sunday however, instead of either the Mints or the Manleys acting as hosts to their usual Sunday evening get-together, the Manleys had agreed to attend a basketball game in downtown Chicago with Fred and Maggie.

Soon the Mints and Manleys were downtown at a hotel that Maggie had reserved and looking forward to attending a preseason professional basketball game early that evening, then coming back to the hotel to chill for a while. They did not anticipate staying at the hotel overnight, but Maggie made reservations for an overnight stay just in case they needed it. They were afforded that option because Gates knew the hotel's owner.

Because the weather had gotten increasingly worse—much worse than even Maggie had foreseen—they decided not to risk being on the roads so late and chose to stay overnight. The hotel was conveniently located not far from the arena.

Maggie had arranged to take a shuttle from the hotel, the Downtown Suites, to the arena where the Bulls played their preseason games.

After the game, it was still early, so the wives encouraged Fred and Gates to go out and get to snacks to see them through the night. It was windy, cold, and snowing as Gates and Fred set out for a local convenience store. They decided to pick up enough snacks to last not only just for the night but also into the next day or so in case they needed to remain at the hotel even longer.

As they roamed around the store, Gates said, "You think the girls would like some pink lemonade to go along with these chips and other snacks? We already have some sandwiches and cookies in the room, and there's a gift shop in the hotel where we can pick up odds and ins. I think that'll tide us over for the time we'll be stuck in the hotel, which will be a short one, I hope."

Fred replied, "Probably. But Maggie likes to drink wine on occasion."

Gates said, "Well, look what I got here in this bag my friend. It's some Manischewitz Concord grape wine. Courtney and I drink that often. I picked it up when you were over there getting those chips."

"You know, Gates, for as long as we've known each other, I never knew you to drink wine," Fred replied. "Now beer? That's a different story."

Gates replied, "Yeah, Courtney and I have both consumed that beverage—beer, I mean, on several occasions—in moderation, of course!

"Anyway, I've had wine before, you just haven't seen me with it in *your* presence."

"Okay, then, I think Maggie would like what you got," Fred said, giving his approval for Gates getting the wine.

As they were heading towards the cashier, Gates commented, "Well, I think we have enough odds and ends. What do you think, Fred?"

"Yeah, I think it's enough," Fred replied.

Gates added, "Wait a minute. You see those books over there, Fred? I didn't think they sold books at a convenience store, but there they are."

Fred replied, "Yeah, I see. Maybe I can place my book there. I'll come by here another time and see about that." He added, "You think anybody would buy my book if I had copies here?"

Gates replied with the intentions of encouraging his friend, "Why not? It's a good book. I've read it. I especially like the part where you talk about how you and Maggie met. By the way, congratulations on that book."

Fred corrected him, "Well, Gates, it's not quite finished yet. What you read was only a part of the manuscript—the part that dealt with our time in college. I still have some work to do on it, but the deadline for getting it out is almost here."

They finally arrived at the cashier, and Fred paid for all the items.

As they were headed out the door, Gates commented, "You know, Fred, the way that snow is coming down outside, we might not be able to leave the hotel for another day or so. To tell you the truth, we might not even make it back to the hotel right now!"

Fred replied, "Gates, we don't have a choice. We walked here and that's the only way we can get back. But you know how the weather is in Chicago this time of year, so why did in the world did we let the girls talk us into coming downtown to see the Bulls play in the first place? It would have been just fine if all of us had stayed at our house or yours back in the suburbs and watched the game on TV. Besides, that's what we do a lot anyway when we come together on Sunday evenings during the season."

"I don't know the answer to that question, buddy!" Gates responded.

Fred continued, "And you know what, Gates, it's only a preseason game. Personally, I'm only interested in seeing the team play after the regular season starts, not these pre-season games."

Gates replied, "Well, I know what you mean, Fred. But your guess is as good as mine about why they wanted to come down here tonight. You know we end up doing what they want us to do anyway. But usually things turn out fine like when they convinced us to travel with 'em to Florida to visit Sandra's friend Erin. Even though we didn't get to go to the Island of Love like Sinbad intended, it was a nice trip."

"You're right, Gates. But anyway, that's water over the dam, you might say. Let's pay for this stuff and head back to the hotel."

As soon as they opened the exit door, Fred and Gates were met with a fierce wind. After they left the store, the two men fought the biting gusts and blinding snow as they trudged slowly back to their lodgings.

"Hey, Fred, this wind is ferocious." Behind the ski mask he had put on, Gates struggled to shout to his friend over the roar of the wind. He continued, "If I had known it would get this bad before we left the hotel, I would've never come out tonight, not in this weather."

Fred replied, "Well, the conditions weren't nearly this bad when we left the hotel. But we have no choice now but to keep our heads down while trying to navigate our way back. And do you hear that wind? I mean, it's howling to the point of sounding like a song the way it's whistling out here—and these snow flurries!"

"Yeah, and the temperature is probably below freezing," Gates replied.

"Uh-huh!" Fred said.

After that, they stopped talking and concentrated on getting back to the hotel.

Ed's Convenience Store was only about a three city blocks down the street from the hotel. Although short in distance, the walk seemed much longer because of the weather. The normally crowded street was now void of any foot traffic at all, except for the two of them! At least it was a straight shot back to their lodgings.

FIGURE 1: A Walk Amidst Snowy Conditions

Fred and Gates barely managed to hang on to the bags they were carrying and to remain upright as they negotiated the wind, snow, and icy surface conditions. No one else had braved the weather by foot, and the streets were almost empty of traffic. Only occasionally did they see a vehicle slowly moving along on the icy road.

After a few more minutes, they finally had made it back to the hotel.

CHAPTER 2
Discussions

Foundation Scripture: Psalm 3:5

Trust in the Lord with all your heart. And lean not on your own understanding,

Fred and Gates were relieved to be back at the hotel—finally. They were anxious to get out of the cold, wind, and snow. Upon entering the lobby, they noticed empty seats in front of a large fireplace.

Fred said, "Let's go over there and thaw ourselves out before going upstairs with the girls."

"That sounds good to me," Gates agreed.

They went over and sat in front of the fireplace and took their place on two cushioned couches.

Gates said, "Um, these couches are more comfortable than I imagined. And that fireplace is really putting out some heat. It feels so good on a night like tonight. Yeah, I could stay here for a while."

"Yeah, Gates, you know they're waiting for us, so we shouldn't stay too long. But this reminds me of that fireplace in the lobby of the resort we visited down in Miami. Of course, it wasn't needed there. I mean, it was Miami for cryin' out loud. A fireplace in Miami? I mean, a fireplace almost anywhere in Florida is probably just to provide an atmosphere of relaxation.

"But down there in Miami how cold can it get? And speaking of atmosphere, look at that photograph above the fireplace of a snow-capped mountain. They should have had a picture of ocean waves rolling onto the beach. A picture like that would certainly make us feel like we're in Miami!"

"I hear you, Fred, but if you look out that window, you'll know that we're not in Florida. It's snowing like crazy out there!" Gates said.

FIGURE 2 Ambiance in Front of a Fireplace

"I hear you, Gates. You can't dismiss the weather here in Chicago on this cold wintry night. But inside the hotel here, that fireplace just adds to the ambiance," Fred replied. "And another thing, this fireplace is really puttin' out the heat that we need right about now! So, let's just sit here and thaw ourselves out before heading upstairs."

Fred and Gates sat there for what must have been at least an hour with the packages from the store placed down on the floor beside them. They began discussions about all sorts of things. But their main purpose was to warm themselves before taking the merchandize they had purchased to their suite.

The concierge, who happened to have been working late that night, went over to Gates and Fred and asked, "Would you two like some hot chocolate? That would help to warm you up. I see you both are shaking from the cold, and it probably will take a while before you heat up."

"That's nice of you, young man. I think we both could use something like that to provide even more heat to these cold bodies," Gates said.

Soon the hot chocolate arrived, and they remained there for several more minutes, talking about the weather, their wives, and the nature of relationships.

Fred and Gates continued to sit in front of that fireplace, rubbing their hands together to generate a little more heat to their bodies. Forgetting their wives were waiting for them, they sat there enjoying the warmth and listening to the crackling sound of the logs burning.

Fred asked, "Gates, I know you're a minister; maybe you can answer this question for me. I think me and Mag have a good marriage, but sometimes when we're together it just doesn't seem like she's there with me. It's like she's somewhere else. Do you have the same feelings with Courtney sometimes?"

"Sure! Just the other day I was in the kitchen doing something—I forget what it was—but I remember asking her a question," Gates replied. "Let me get a little closer to this fireplace," he added. "Anyway, what I was saying was that she was over in the chair in the living room, sitting there watching TV. I know she heard me, or at least I think she did. The point is she was looking at TV, and it was as though I wasn't there. And she never answered my question. I don't believe she even heard me!"

"Didn't you get irritated about that?" Fred asked.

Gates replied, "Well, I used to. But after years of being with her, I realize Courtney is a focused woman. You know that's what our spirit is all about, don't you?"

"No. What do you mean, Gates?" Fred asked.

Gates then elaborated, "Our inner man, as it's sometimes called, or our spirit pays attention to different things at different times. With Courtney, sometimes her spirit is somewhere other than with me, even when I'm right there with her.

"In other words, I can be next to her, but because she's doing something at that moment or is maybe even in deep thought that doesn't involve me, she'll be totally focused on that thing. That's when she kinda blocks everything else out of her mind, including me.

"Let me tell you this, Fred, and I hope it makes you feel better. In that situation, my first thought was that she was ignoring me just like you said that Maggie was not paying *you* any attention. But Courtney blocked *everything* out of her mind, including me, because she was concentrating on something else—on whatever she was watching on TV in that particular case.

"As her mate I must understand that sometimes she needs her space. And I realize I should give her some rope, you might say, and let her do what *she* wants sometimes, without my interference. You just have to trust God that your mate is still with you when it counts. I know the woman loves me, so I don't worry about it. Check it out in 1 John 3:16, and remember it's not the familiar scripture in the Gospel of John. Anyway, I don't even try to understand everything she does, so I wasn't bothered that she didn't respond to my question."

"Um, that's interesting," Fred replied.

Gates saw that he could share more wisdom with Fred about being focused, so he continued, "You know, Fred, one of the 'Wonders of the Spirit' that I often talk about is being able to live with someone like your spouse and understand some of the actions they might make. Yeah, it's all a matter of understanding who you're committed to."

"Well, that does make sense," Fred replied.

Gates wanted to drive home a point that he thought was much more significant in dealing with interpersonal relationships, and that is the spiritual aspect of it all. He continued, "You know, Fred, as a pastoral assistant, I don't speak much from the pulpit. But I do a lot of mentoring or, better put, advising. As you know, Pastor Henry pretty much controls the services each Sunday, and I don't mind that at all.

"But let me say this. The spiritual aspect of all our lives is much more important than what we all make it out to be. That's why I get so much satisfaction out of advising, talking to people about their personal concerns. I mean, ordinarily our focus is on the physical part of our beings, and we often fail to realize that the core of our existence is our spiritual part. And, oh, that spiritual part can really be amazing sometimes—what I mentioned before as 'Wonders of the Spirit.'"

Fred replied, "Yeah, I understand that, Gates. You know I've been listening to the same sermons you have, and Pastor Henry brings that point around just about every Sunday regardless of what his topic is. But how does this relate to my question about Mag? As I said, sometimes she seems to be in another world when she's around me. Why is that, Gates? And how does what you're saying—something about the spirit—relate to Mag's responding to me, or I should say *not* responding?" Fred demanded.

After giving Fred's question some thought, Gates answered, "Well, Fred, it relates in this way: There are some things in our spirit that only God and each of us know about. I mean, the time you were telling me about when Maggie seemed to be somewhere else mentally when she was right there with you—well, in fact she *was* somewhere else, that is, her spirit was somewhere else, and God allowed and sanctioned it. There are some things that are meant for only you and God to know about. The essence of her being wasn't there with you at the time."

"Well, thanks a lot, buddy," Fred responded facetiously. He continued, "So God allows us sometimes to be detached from one another?"

Gates replied, "Well, I didn't mean to be harsh, but let me break it down this way. You remember when you two first met back on the campus of MCCU at the social after that basketball game?"

"Boy, do I remember!" Fred replied with excitement in his voice. "That girl was all over me then; she couldn't keep her eyes off me. Well, to tell you the truth, I couldn't keep my eyes off her either. I mean, I guess it was love at first sight for the both of us."

Gates saw this as an opportunity to explain further to Fred about the workings of the spirit part of our beings. He said, "Okay, Fred, you hit the nail right on the head so to speak. When you two first met, both of your spirits were perfectly in sync with one another. And you said it: you couldn't keep your eyes off her, and she was totally consumed with you at the time as well. Based on what you told me, Maggie had her two roommates there too, but they were not allowed in that space—your and Maggie's personal as well as spiritual space. Well, the same is true for all of us individually; there are some things meant to be known only between you and the Master. That's why we can pray to Him by ourselves, and He understands our problems when anyone else might not understand, even our spouse. Now all that involved the spirit part of you two.

"Believe it not, you and Maggie probably didn't pay as much attention to each of your physical presences. Let me ask you this, and it'll drive home the point I'm trying to make. Could you tell me some things about Maggie's attire that night? I mean things like what she was wearing, how her hair was fixed, her earrings, things like that?"

"Well, before you answer, let me tell you this. You *were* attracted to each other initially by your physical presence, but those physical attributes were not what *kept* you two together. The connection of your spirits did that. Yes, the both of you being in one accord *spiritually* is what did the trick. In other words, you liked the way she talked, what she talked about, and for that matter, what she didn't talk about.

"Now, Fred, be honest. You're not attracted to someone who just talks too much when you first meet, are you? Yeah, one thing that attracts men to women is their curiosity about what they're withholding from us. That's true physically as well if you know what I mean. Anyway, that's what Maggie did; she didn't reveal a lot to you, a lot of spirit, that is. So, you ended up wanting to know more about her. That's what made you two want to continue to see each other, and, as they say, the rest is history."

"I guess you're right, Gates," Fred replied.

"Well, anyway, Fred, that same spirit is within her now as it was when you two first met," Gates continued. "It's just that everything in her spirit didn't come out at that time, and it may be coming out now.

"But, anyway, that spirit doesn't connect with you sometimes when you're together. Is that what you're telling me?"

"Well, yeah, Gates! That's exactly what I'm telling you. And all of what you have said makes sense," Fred admitted. "By the way, to answer your question, no, I do not remember what Mag had on that night. But that spirit, that personality, as you said, is what did it for me. And I was eager to know more about that personality—what you call her spirit.

"And you're right, Gates. I understand now, the difference between the ability of our physical bodies and our spirits to connect with one another. And it's still working now. There are times when our spirits *do* connect but not during the times when she has something else on her mind. Then she pays me no attention!"

Fred made that last comment partly in jest and then said, "Now, it's probably time for us to head upstairs to our suite and see what the girls are doing."

"Yeah, I guess you're right, Fred. We've been here for quite a while. Let's go on upstairs. Besides, I'm warm now," Gates replied.

So off they went to their suite where Maggie and Courtney were waiting.

CHAPTER 3
Return To the Room

Foundation Scripture: 1 Peter 2:25

For you were like sheep going astray, but have now returned to the Shepard and Overseer of your souls.

Having thawed themselves near the lobby's fireplace, Fred and Gates took the elevator up to the second floor. They arrived at their suite and upon entering received a big cheer from their wives.

"Well, well! Look what the wind blew in Courtney," Maggie said making fun of their husbands. Maggie was being facetious because of the length of time they had been away.

"Blew in?" Gates responded in a sarcastic tone. "You know, girls, I hope you're kidding by saying that the wind blew us in. I mean, the weather out there is no joke. It's windy and cold, plus snow flurries came up since we left, and we had to walk back in all that stuff!"

Maggie continued, "Now, Gates, don't sound like you're offended; it still doesn't account for why it took you two *that* long to do what you had to do. My goodness, you were gone for almost two hours!"

"Mag, it's all my fault," Fred said. "I was the one who caused us to be away so long because I suggested that we sit near the fireplace in the lobby and chat a little when we first got back to the hotel. If we had come straight up, we would've been here a lot sooner."

Gates weighed in on the issue. "Yeah, girls, the weather is awful out there, so Fred recommended that we warm up by that fireplace before we came up. And one other thing… I told Fred that if I had known that the weather would be this bad, I definitely would not have gone outside walking in the first place. Yeah, I guess we should have driven down there. But I guess that wouldn't have been good either, because the roads are too slippery to drive on.

"And I repeat: Fred is right. It took us so long because we decided to talk a little in front of that nice fireplace downstairs before coming up," Gates confirmed.

"Okay! We hear you, Fred, and you too, Gates," Courtney said.

Gates continued, "In a way I'm glad we went out because do you know what I got in the bag?"

Courtney replied, "Okay, you've explained why it took you so long. So, what *did* you get, Gates? What's in the bag? And it better be good!" Courtney added in a joking fashion.

That's when Gates pulled out the Manischewitz Concord grape wine that they picked up at the convenience store.

When the wives saw that, their demeanor changed drastically. Maggie looked at Courtney and said, "You know, I think we can forgive them this time for being out so long."

"Yeah, you two, you may have gone astray for a while, but you're back to the ones who really care about you. You two know that!" Maggie concluded.

"We do know that, Mag. Both Gates and I know who to come back to," Fred replied.

"That's good, but I must say, you two hit the jackpot tonight," Courtney said. "We can really warm up now with this wine. You guys bringing this back got me to change my opinion about you being out so long—at least mine anyway."

Courtney also said, "Hey, Maggie, that Manischewitz grape wine is the real thing, girl! Gates and I drink that quite a bit at home. It makes you feel so relaxed; don't it, honey."

Gates replied simply, "It does."

Maggie didn't want to let the fellows completely off the hook, however. She said, "Well, we still wondered where you two got to. You know it's dangerous out there in those streets. But I'm satisfied; you answered the question. You just wanted to chat a little in front of that fireplace."

While both she and Courtney raised all kinds of questions about why the fellows were out so long, Maggie also was curious about their conversation after they had returned to the hotel. Maggie then asked her husband, "Hey, Fred, you said you two had a chat. Well, what did you talk about for so long?"

Fred answered, "Just this and that, Mag."

Then Gates was more forthright regarding their discussion. He said, "Well, Maggie, if you really want to know, we discussed relationships between men and women. Now that's something you'd probably be interested in. Am I right about that?"

"Yeah, I would be, Gates," Maggie replied. Then she asked her husband, "Well, Fred, what about it—about your discussion concerning relationships I mean?"

Fred reluctantly responded to Maggie's question. He said, "Well, okay, Mag. We mainly talked about how some marriages seem to flourish while others seem to get caught in a snag."

"So, do you think our marriage is in a snag, Fred?" Maggie asked.

"Now, Mag, I think you're taking this all too seriously. What happened was that we were just trying to get warm, being so cold and all because of our walk from the store," Fred replied.

Trying to change the tone of the discussion, Fred looked at Gates and said, "Hey, Gates, why don't you tell the girls what we really got into in our discussion?"

So that's what Gates did. He said, "Well, Maggie and Courtney, we talked about how some marriages become stale, and sometimes couples take each other for granted."

Then Maggie interjected, "Well, Fred, did you tell Gates that I take you for granted?"

"Oh no, Mag. You're the best thing that's ever happened to me. You know that."

"Good answer," Maggie replied.

At that point Courtney looked at Gates and said, "Well, Gates, what about you? Do you think that I take you for granted?"

"Are you kidding me? My answer is the same as Fred's, Courtney. You're the best thing that's ever happened to me," Gates replied.

Courtney responded by going over and giving Gates a kiss on the cheek. She said, "Now that's what I want to hear, honey."

Somehow, the fellows never got a chance to mention their detailed discussion about the role of the spirit in people acting the way they do, especially when they become married.

As the night grew later, the two couples sat on couches in a common living area between the two bedrooms in the suite. They remained there having more pleasant discussions about a variety to topics while listening to smooth jazz and the winter winds outside in the Windy City.

After their discussions, the couples ventured back to their bedrooms to complete their packing for a midday departure from the hotel when they would head back home to the suburbs south of the city.

All the wind and driving snow did not prevent everyone from having a good night's sleep.

CHAPTER 4
Checking Out!

Foundation Scripture: 2 Timothy 4:2

Preach the word! Be ready in season and out of season. Convince, rebuke, exhort, with all longsuffering and teaching.

At daybreak, Maggie arose first to check out the weather and was amazed the wind had calmed drastically and the skies were clear. The snow flurries driven by the wailing winds were now a thing of the past. The piles of snow the winter storm had dumped on the city remained as the only evidence of the horrendous weather. The snow-covered surface of the sidewalks below glistened beneath a bright, shining sun.

Fortunately, most roads were cleared by the snow plows working throughout the night. Beyond the roads, the snow-covered surface presented problems for anyone on foot everywhere else.

After roaming around their part of the suite, Maggie finally went over to Fred and tried to wake him. "Fred, Fred!" she shouted. "Get up and let's get ready to have breakfast. The weather conditions have improved so much that we might be able to leave earlier than we thought. I'm in no rush though."

Still half asleep, Fred replied, "Okay. Maybe we can leave later this morning. But first I'm looking forward to a good breakfast."

"Okay, that sounds fine. But again, I'm in no rush. We can check on Courtney and Gates later." Maggie said.

About an hour after Maggie and Fred had dressed and prepared their belongings for a midday departure, they went to the dining area to have breakfast. Maggie had called Courtney earlier to let them know their plans.

After a few more minutes, when Maggie and Fred got to the dining hall, they found Courtney and Gates already there.

"Good morning, you two. We're surprised to see you here so early," Maggie said.

Courtney responded, "Surprised to see us? It's you and Fred who are a little late!"

"Well, whether we're late or early, when I called a while ago, I thought you two were still in bed," Maggie said.

Courtney replied, "Gates and I are early risers. I thought you knew that, Maggie and Fred. Anyway, the weather is so much improved from what it was last evening, so I think we could head out a little early."

Gates repeated what his wife suggested, "Yeah, we talked about that, and it suits me fine to leave early." He continued, "How's that with you, Fred?"

"I'm fine with it. But we all know we have to get an okay from Mag," Fred replied.

Gates said, "Well how about it, Maggie? Are you good to go early this morning?"

Maggie replied, "I know I said we could leave earlier because of the improved weather, but after thinking about it, I don't know why all of you are so eager to get back home. I love it here in downtown, especially now that the weather has cleared up. To tell you the truth,

I wouldn't mind going over to the skating rink. It's right outside. You can see a few skaters having fun out there now.

"I know you all want to get home. Listen, we don't have to do any sightseeing or anything like that, but at least let's spend our remaining time here on the premises of the hotel and just relax."

I agree with you, Maggie," Courtney said.

"Thanks, Courtney, for agreeing with me," Maggie said. "Just look outside. The sun is shining so brightly, and I just love all the snow. The reflection of the sunlight off the snow-covered surface is just blinding.

"By the way, have you two ordered yet?"

Courtney responded, "No, Maggie. We're just going to grab something from the buffet."

"Well, Fred, I guess we can do the same," Maggie replied.

"Fine with me," Fred responded.

Before long everyone had their breakfast in front of them.

FIGURE 3 Breakfast Ambiance in The Hotel Dining Hall

They all consumed a scrumptious breakfast. In the middle of the meal as she sat there gazing out the window, Courtney said, "Like Maggie mentioned, I just love all the snow."

Maggie said, "You know, Courtney, being from Flint up near Detroit, we usually get snow during the winter, but I don't remember ever getting as much snow as we've had down here in Chicago. It seems like ever since I've moved here with Fred, there's been so much snow in the late fall and winter."

Courtney asked, "Now, I wonder why we get so much snow here in Chicago, Fred? I know one time you mentioned that you took a geography course at MCCU, and you said the instructor talked about the reasons Chicago gets all this snow as well as a lot of wind, I might add. I guess that's why it's called the Windy City. So how about it, Fred? Why is that?"

Fred reluctantly responded, "You guys are trying your best to put me back in school. But, as I remember, Dr. Schilling, my geography instructor, said that Chicago, being situated right on Lake Michigan, usually has a lot of moisture in the air from all the evaporation from the lake.

"During late summer and early fall when the air is still warm, there's a whole lot of evaporation going on, making the air what Dr. Schilling called moisture laden. There's a lot of moisture in the air, that is, invisible water vapor. Well, at this time of year when fall transitions into winter, cooler air from Canada starts to come into Chicago from the west and north, and it crosses the moisture-laden air that's over the lake and creates snow here in the Chicago area.

"Now without getting into any more detail, did everybody understand what I just said?" Fred asked.

Maggie, Gates, and Courtney just shook their heads, seemingly not comprehending a lot of Fred's explanation.

Courtney said, "Okay, I guess I got my answer."

Maggie said, "Enough of that technical stuff. We just have to deal with whatever season we might be in—both in and out of season. That's what it says in the scripture.

Courtney asked, "Now I want to hear more of what you two talked about last night. Gates, I don't think you really answered my question when I asked you then. I know you all said you were just warming yourselves up from being outside in that bad weather. Let's go over here to the fireplace, where you two were last night, and finish that conversation."

Off they went to sit on the couches in front of the fireplace.

After they sat down in front of the roaring fire, Gates began, "Okay, Maggie and Courtney, not to repeat everything that we said, but I made the point to Fred that when we participate in interpersonal relationships, more of our spiritual being is involved than most people realize. You all remember in the scripture where it talks about the fruit of the spirit?"

Everyone nodded their heads in agreement.

Gates saw this was a time to elaborate. He said, "So, ladies, this is what I was telling Fred. I told him the fruit of the spirit that is found in scripture helps define the spiritual part of every believer.

"Let me give you some examples. The love that we have for one another and how patient we are and how understanding we are of others' viewpoints—all these are unseen parts of our being that are spiritual in nature. They are our spirit manifested in that kind of behavior, spiritual fruit, or you could say spiritual qualities that help define us as people.

"And those spiritual qualities are what holds us as couples together. Even though we may be attracted to another person initially based on their physical appearance—how physically attractive they are—it's not the physical part that keeps a couple together. Because we get so accustomed to our physical presence that often we can take each other for granted. But it's the spiritual part that causes a couple to have an enduring relationship through thick and thin as they say.

"But I'll tell you, those spiritual qualities I mentioned, those are the things that keep a marriage together or any relationship for that matter. But these are the qualities that also make for a vibrant and happy relationship—even sometimes when you don't feel like having those emotions. And that, you guys, is one of the 'Wonders of the Spirit' that I talk about so often. So, yeah, that's some of what I told Fred."

"Okay, Gates, I'll accept that," Maggie responded. "You two had a deep discussion on the subject, it seems. Well, anyway, everyone, I think that's a good place to end."

Maggie continued, "Yeah, I think I'm about ready to hit the road. Let's go upstairs and get everything ready to be packed into the van; then we can take off."

Everyone agreed with Maggie, and they all did what she suggested. Soon the two couples checked out of the hotel and left the downtown area to return to their homes in suburban Chicago.

CHAPTER 5
Wayward Spirit

Foundation Scripture: Matthew 26:41

"Watch and pray, lest you enter into temptation.
The spirit indeed is willing, but the flesh is weak."

The drive from downtown Chicago to Central Heights in the suburbs south of the city was a pleasant journey for the Mints and the Manleys. Everyone seemed to enjoy the snow-covered scenery all around them, but the roads were perfectly clear, and they encountered no problems driving.

Since Fred was from the Windy City and familiar with driving in the snow, he ended up behind the wheel in the rented SUV instead of Gates, who was from Hawaii. Gates and Fred sat in the front seat while the girls rode in the back, carrying on conversation the whole way.

After an hour's drive in moderate traffic, Gates returned the SUV he had rented back to where the vehicle was picked up. He got his personal car from where he had parked and drove Maggie and Fred to their house. The Mints thanked Gates for bringing them home and said their goodbyes to the Manleys. After that, Gates and Courtney continued to their house, which was not far from where the Mints lived.

As Maggie and Fred approached their front door, Fred said to Maggie, "It's so good to be back home, huh, Mag?"

"It sure is, honey," Maggie replied. She continued, "I can't wait to see what later this evening has in store."

Fred was not sure what she meant by that, but they proceeded to enter their home. A refreshing aroma of peacefulness met them at least for the moment.

This time was almost divine to Maggie, again alone with the man of her dreams. Once the door had been closed behind them, she said, "Honey, come on over here and give me some sugar."

Fred followed the command and they embraced. Maggie gave him a kiss, the kind she felt had not occurred for such a long time. Then she said to him softly, "You know I love you so much, Fred. And what I implied back at the hotel I really didn't mean it. I know you don't take me for granted."

"Oh, Mag, you haven't been this sensual in a while. And by the way, what did you mean about you can't wait for this evening? Are you anticipating something?" Fred asked.

"Oh, Fred, don't you know this is our anniversary? I mean, this was the day we first met. Remember, Fred? When we met at that social after the basketball game at MCCU?"

"Yeah, you know I *do* remember that, Mag," Fred replied. Then he said, "But I figured that anniversaries are reserved, at least in our case, for the date we got married."

Fred continued, "Anyway, as far as this evening is concerned, I hope you didn't plan anything special because I have an important meeting scheduled with my publisher at 7:00 back in downtown because, as I'm sure you recall, my latest book is due to be published in a few days.

"I didn't tell you, but I also had to arrange a trip to Las Vegas for tomorrow to talk about marketing opportunities. The publisher and I will take an early flight in the morning. And I'll be out there until

Saturday. They seem to really be high on this book. They think sales potentially could go through the roof. Aren't you excited for me?"

Maggie just stood there speechless. Finally she found the words to respond. "Fred, tomorrow is Wednesday. You'll be gone for four days—until Saturday?" she asked. "Why didn't you tell me all this? I was planning a special night tonight and had plans for the next few days."

Fred replied, "Mag, I don't mean to make you upset. I wanted everything to be a surprise."

Maggie replied sarcastically, "Well, it certainly was that—a surprise, I mean!"

Although she was completely shocked by Fred's sudden travel plans and upset that they wouldn't be together, Maggie was happy for him. Fred's excitement about his book was infectious. Trying to conceal her disappointment that her husband wouldn't be with her for this important anniversary, she said, "Sure, Fred, I'm happy to hear that your publishers feel the book will take off. I want nothing but the best for you."

Maggie continued, "Well, at least let's have a nice dinner later this afternoon before you leave for your meeting tonight."

"Okay, Mag, let's change and relax a little before that," he said.

Relax? Maggie thought. *I don't know what he's talking about. I'll be doing the cooking. And shoot! I'll have more than enough time to relax after he leaves on this trip of his.*

Maggie remembered the pastor saying in the morning sermon that one of the wonders of the spirit is our ability—though the Holy Spirit—to understand and adjust to one another's actions. Well, it was all Maggie could do to understand her husband's choice to be away on such an important day in their lives!

After much inner reflection, Maggie managed to adjust to Fred's unforeseen plans and tried to respond to him as lovingly as possible.

"Okay, Fred, you go in the living room and chill for a while, and I'll have the food ready in an hour."

"Okay, Mag, you do that. And I love you so much."

Despite her earlier disappointment, Fred's last comment made her feel much better.

Fred added, "Mag, thanks for your understanding." He added, "I'm going in the living room and watch a little TV until the food is ready.

Maggie replied, "Okay. I'll let you know when I'm finished." She went into the kitchen to prepare dinner. She wanted it to be as romantic as a meal could be in the late afternoon.

Maggie was in the middle of her meal preparation when she decided to take a break and check the call history on the kitchen phone. As she prepared to scroll through the numbers, she found that Freddie, the fellow with whom she was romantically involved during a difficult period of her marriage to John, had called and left a message while they were away in Chicago. She had continued to see Freddie even after the flames were reignited with Fred after John's passing.

The message indicated that he needed to talk with her and wanted her to return his call. *What in the world?* she thought. She listened to the other messages she had and then returned to preparing dinner.

Maggie was almost finished cooking when she decided to take a peek at Fred to let him know their special dinner was almost ready. But she noticed that instead of watching TV he was intently reading something; she assumed it was the manuscript to his soon to be published book. To avoid disturbing him, Maggie returned to the kitchen to finish preparing the meal. She hoped he would be finished with whatever he was reading by dinnertime.

Maggie was passing the phone when it rang.

Though the ringtone was low, Fred heard it too. Briefly interrupted from his reading, he thought, *I wonder who that is?* Then he said aloud, "Probably those doggone telemarketers calling the house."

Maggie quickly picked up the phone. "Hello. Who am I speaking with?" she asked.

A voice on the other end answered, "Hello, Maggie. It's me, Freddie. I'm so glad to hear your voice again. How have you been doing?"

Maggie said almost in a whisper, "Freddie, what are you doing calling here? You know how I don't like being called at home by some people."

Freddie interpreted her words as an insult and replied, "Okay, now, I'm 'some people,' huh?" He continued, "Hey, Maggie, if this is a bad time, I'll let you go."

That was a perfect opportunity for Maggie to end the conversation, but the flesh part of her, camouflaged as her spirit, still enjoyed hearing his voice. It was a *wayward spirit* to be sure.

She replied, "Freddie, you have me on the phone now, so you need to finish what you started."

"Well, well. Look who's talking," Freddie said. "The last time you came to my condo, it was me expecting us to have a special night, but instead you were telling me that you were married and wanted to end our relationship. Now, Maggie, you didn't finish what you came there for at the time, did you?"

Maggie had to consider her words. After a moment's thought, she told him, "Freddie, that was different. And, besides, you're lying," she added with a louder tone of her voice, temporarily forgetting that Fred was in the other room.

Then, in a quieter tone, almost a whisper, she tried to correct him. "Freddie, don't play with me. You know at that time I really wanted to see you. But you refrained from seeing me that night because of the dream you had. You remember that? The dream you had about your wife and kid being killed in a car accident. Also, since that time, I thought you had developed a relationship with Sandra."

Then Freddie replied, "Yeah, me and Sandra are still friends. And I must say you have a good memory, Maggie. Now wouldn't it be great to finish what I failed to do that night? I remember it was snowing, and the wind was howling so much. Yes, it would have been a special evening. But you know, Maggie, when I had that dream about my wife and kid being killed, I just couldn't get over it at the time."

Freddie continued, "But it's been a while since then. Maggie, I'm sure you haven't forgotten the time we had in Florida when all your friends came down to celebrate Erin's new position down there working under my cousin Sinbad.

"But what I remember most about that trip was when you described to me the dream you had. It seemed so real. You know, even though it was only a dream, I remember when you told me how we snuggled up next to each other on a blanket as we sailed on the ferry toward the Island of Love."

Maggie thought, *That man is talking about the dream I described as though it was real! He needs to realize that it was only in my dream that we made that trip! I only told him about it because it was just that—a dream. I'm just glad I didn't tell the others about that part of the dream.*

Maggie reminded Freddie of his other love interest on the trip, saying, "Now, Freddie, like I told you before, you had developed a relationship with my friend Sandra on that trip to Florida. You know as well as me that it all started when you helped her from the stage that night when she made an emotional speech. Remember? Yeah, you helped her back to her seat."

"I remember, Maggie," Freddie replied. "And by the way, I was shocked to find out that it was you who Sandra was with that night.

It's kinda funny now, but it's interesting how we both reacted when we first saw each other with your husband sitting beside you. I guess we tried to conceal our past relationship as much as we could.

"Anyway, I haven't seen Sandra much since we've been back from Florida," Freddie said.

Maggie responded, "Well, yeah, Freddie, and that's because she's spending a lot of time these days over at the casino in Winsor. She seems to love the atmosphere over there. I haven't heard from her in quite a while myself."

At that moment she heard Fred call from the next room, "Mag, I thought you were preparing our meal. Who's that you're talking too? I thought I heard my name."

Maggie put Freddie on hold without telling him who it was that had called her, and then answered Fred, "Okay, honey. It's just a telemarketer on the phone that I'm trying to get rid of."

Fred replied, "Well, okay then. It seems like you're pretty friendly with that telemarketer. Just tell the lady that you're busy."

Maggie replied deceitfully, "Okay, I'll tell her."

Moments later, Maggie returned to her conversation with Freddie. She lowered her voice again to barely a whisper and said, "Hey, Freddie, I can't talk now. You have my number."

Freddie replied, "Maggie, were you talking with your husband? I heard it when you told him that you were talking to a telemarketer. And not only that, but apparently, now I'm a woman! Now, ain't that a bitch!"

Maggie replied with a bit of anger, "Oh, Freddie, don't talk to me like that. Watch your language. The next time you call, just make it after midnight, and I'll be sure to put the phone on silent. Bye."

With that, Maggie's conversation with Freddie ended. She went back to where Fred was and said, "Hey, honey, the food will be ready in just about ten minutes."

"Okay, Mag. And, oh, we need to put a hold on the numbers of these telemarketers," Fred reminded her. "Anyway, just call me and I'll be ready to eat."

"Okay, you just go back to your reading, and I'll let you know when everything is ready," she told him.

For several days prior to their trip downtown to see the Bulls play, Maggie had prepared for *this* day, the day *after* the game. She wanted it to be special because on this date she met the love of her life, Fred, at that social after the basketball game at MCCU. Her original plans for tonight had to be altered because of Fred's meeting with his publisher, so she would have to make do with an afternoon dinner. She also understood and accepted Fred's career aspirations as an author.

Over the next several days, Maggie would be without her man. She could only hope that the fire she had at one time for Freddie would not reignite, given his recent communication with her.

Soon the food was ready, and Maggie set the table with her best China, a white tablecloth, and a lit candle in the center. She wanted nothing else to illuminate the room. She felt the dim glow of a single candle provided an intimacy she so much desired and an atmosphere similar to the experience they had at the soda shop on the night when they first met.

"Hey, Fred. Everything is ready," Maggie finally told him.

"Okay, Mag. Let me freshen up a little bit, and I'll be right in."

Yes, the late afternoon dinner would provide Maggie with *some* sense of fulfillment, knowing that the man of her dreams would be right there in her midst. Within hours, however, Maggie was alone again to ponder her thoughts as she would be during the coming days while Fred was in Las Vegas.

Maggie expected Fred to call after his meeting with the publisher, but she remembered that his meetings often went longer than she would expect. And this time it was no different—apparently.

Maggie had just changed into her nighties when the phone rang slightly after midnight. She answered, knowing who would be calling at that late hour. Why, it would be her husband, of course, telling her he was running late in his meeting and would be home soon.

But no! Maggie had forgotten *that* was the time she had suggested that Freddie call. When she answered the phone and heard that foreign voice, she surprised herself by being content about who was on the other end of the line.

"Hello, Maggie. I did what you said, and I'm calling you right after midnight," Freddie reminded her.

Maggie replied, "Oh, Freddie, I'm surprised you'd call back so soon after we talked earlier. But you're right. You did call when I asked you to. But as before, Freddie, this might not be the best time because my husband is late coming home from a meeting he had downtown, and he should be here any minute."

Freddie responded, "Well, he's not with you now, is he?"

Maggie answered, "Well, no."

Before Maggie could say anything else, he said, "So we can talk. Do you know, Maggie, I'm interested in more than our phone conversation? I really would like to see you."

"Now, Freddie, again, you seem to forget that I'm a married woman," Maggie replied. "You know what it's like to be married. And remember, it was you who called off our being together that night when I came by to see you because of the dream that you had. And not only that, but you *did* develop a relationship with my best friend Sandra."

Freddie replied, "I know, Maggie. But a lot has changed since then. My wife and I are no longer together, and it's gets so lonely around here at times. And I haven't met anyone else who could satisfy the need I have to see someone—someone like yourself."

At that point Maggie heard a noise at the door and quickly surmised that it was Fred. In panic mode, she said, "Hey, Freddie,

I gotta go. My husband is returning from his meeting. And he's getting ready to walk through the door right now. And listen, over the next several days he'll be out of town, at least until Saturday, so you can call me anytime during that period."

"Okay, Maggie I…," Freddie started, but Maggie ended the conversation before he had a chance to finish.

"Bye now," she said. And with that, she hung up just as Fred was entering the room.

Now inside, Fred said, "Sorry I'm late, Mag. It was a late meeting. By the way, I just got a glimpse of you hanging up the phone. Another telemarketer, huh?"

Maggie replied, "Yeah, Fred, a telemarketer."

Because of the late hour, Fred and Maggie didn't have a chance to do anything other than to prepare for bed and get a good night's sleep before his scheduled flight early in the morning. Just prior to going to bed, Maggie said, "Honey, you know I'm going to miss you over the next several days. What am I supposed to do around this house until you get back?"

Fred seemed not to remember that her niece Mary did most of the work at the day care when he said, "Now, Mag, you know that you have responsibilities over there at the day care."

Maggie replied, "I know, Fred. But you know Mary has been doing more and more of the work lately. But you're right. I guess I could go in and check up on things more."

Fred replied as they both got into bed, "There you go, Mag! Yeah. Go over there and do some checking up on that girl. I know she does a good job though."

Fred added, "Hey, Mag. I'm setting the alarm for 5:00. That'll give us enough time to get up and dress and even have a little coffee before you take me to the airport. I'm already packed and ready to go."

Maggie replied, "Okay, honey, I'll fix a little something to eat before we take off. Night!"

"Goodnight, Mag," Fred responded before they both fell into slumber.

The blaring alarm clock went off at 5 a.m. As Fred awakened, he discovered Maggie was already in the kitchen brewing coffee and, based on the aroma he detected in the air, preparing a little breakfast. He arose quickly, got dressed, and ate what Maggie had cooked.

Soon they were off to the airport. Driving Fred to the airport for his flight to Vegas early in the morning reminded Maggie of when she took him there for his flight to Hawaii years ago. In both cases, she did not want him to leave. But Fred was determined to go in both instances.

Fred took his carry-on bag and a larger piece of luggage to the nearest airline counter where an attendant checked his larger bag and gave him a boarding pass.

Then he said to his wife, "Bye, Mag. And remember, I'll be calling you each night at 9:00 your time from Vegas. And I'll see you again on Saturday. My plane is due to arrive at O'Hare shortly after noon."

"Okay, Fred. Be careful, and I look to hear from you tonight," Maggie replied. She kissed Fred goodbye and then left the terminal, returning to their house in Central Heights.

Fred was scheduled to spend the next three days in meetings with publisher executives, but each night at the appointed time, he would call his wife. His meeting ended at 8 p.m. just in time to phone Maggie with an hour's difference in time between Vegas and Chicago.

When Maggie returned home that morning, she had the remainder of the day open. She thought, *Oh, my, Fred. I'll try to find something to do around the house until I hear from you tonight.*

Because of the abundant snow cover outside, Maggie decided to remain at home all day until the phone call she anticipated from her husband later that night.

Although Maggie would miss Fred, she looked forward to a few days of relaxation. She did not take Fred seriously about going to the day care and checking on Mary. She trusted her niece to do an excellent job in her absence.

It was still early in the morning when Maggie decided to get back into bed to catch up on the sleep she missed by going to bed late and rising early. She got a second cup of coffee and then headed straight to her bed. She lay down to meditate on her current life, ready to drift off to sleep with her thoughts.

Just as she was about to nod off, the phone rang, and she answered. Not fully awake, she said, "Hello. Who am I talking with?"

"Maggie, it's me, Freddie."

"Freddie, why are you calling so early in the morning?" she asked.

"Maggie, you did say I could call anytime in the next few days. You *do* remember, don't you?"

"Oh, yeah, I remember saying that. Well, what do you want?" she asked abruptly.

Freddie replied, "Maggie, you said your husband wouldn't be there over the next several days. So, are you alone?"

"Yes, Freddie, I'll be here by myself until Saturday when Fred returns," she replied.

"Well, that's great. Because I want to see you."

"You want to see me? When?"

"I'd like to see you now!" Freddie replied.

"Right now? Right this minute?" she asked.

Before Freddie had a chance to answer, Maggie said, "Let me say this, Freddie: you already know my husband returned home late last night. Remember when you called? And I had to cut you off because he was coming into the house. I guess what I'm saying now, Freddie, is that I'm really sleepy."

Freddie responded, "Well, Maggie, that's good too. Because you could finish that sleep over here. I mean, I have a nice comfortable couch you could lie on to get the rest that you need."

After a brief pause, Freddie continued trying to convince her. "Oh, come on, Maggie. You don't have a lot of free time like this often. What do you say?"

Maggie replied, "Well, okay. Give me an hour and I'll be over by 11:00, she replied.

"Great! I'll be waiting for you. You know where to come. I live in the same place," he told her.

When Maggie arrived at Freddie's place, she saw he had a brand-new car, a bright red Firebird, sitting right there in the driveway. *Um, Freddie is moving up with this new vehicle*, she thought. She remembered his last car with the same license plate identification and the van they had taken to New York for their flight to Miami.

As Maggie approached Freddie's front door, she told herself that she would stay for only an hour or two as she had decided on the drive over.

Maggie's visit to Freddie's was a brief one as she had intended. For the next three days during Fred's absence, she repeated this visit. But subsequent trips took place in the evening at 6:00.

On Maggie's first evening visit to Freddie, she had mixed emotions; nonetheless, she slipped on some causal clothes and anticipated meeting the man she had been romantically involved with before her marriage to Fred. She felt a tinge of guilt about relinquishing her emotions to someone other than her husband. But she tried to justify it in her mind by telling herself how difficult it was to overcome the void in her life with Fred being away.

"Oh, well," she told herself, "it won't hurt seeing Freddie for an hour or so, and it'll eliminate some of the emptiness I'm feeling right now since Fred is away."

The time during Fred's absence from home came and went quickly for Maggie. Somehow, on the day Fred was due to return from Vegas, Maggie agreed to return to Freddie's place that Saturday afternoon—after her trip to the airport to pick up Fred shortly after noon.

Maggie met Fred at the gate and greeted him with a big hug.

"Fred, I'm so glad to see you."

"Hello, Mag. I'm glad those meetings are over and happy to be back. I never thought that publishing a book would be so complicated. It certainly wasn't like the first book I had published."

Maggie replied, "Well, I'm glad you're back."

"Let me tell you, Mag, those people are really involved with the marketing aspect of the publishing process. So hopefully all of this will pay off for me."

Maggie said, "I'm sure it will, Fred."

After the two greeted each other, Fred asked, "So, what have you been doing these last few days?"

Maggie replied, "Not too much of anything, Fred. And I've been thinking. Like you suggested before you left for Vegas, maybe I should get more involved with the day care."

When Fred heard Maggie's response, he then said with some confusion, "Well, Mag, why did you put it like that? Didn't you spend much of the time over there while I was away?" he asked.

She replied, "Well, yeah, Fred... I mean, no, I spent some time there. But I may need to be there even more in the coming weeks."

Maggie tried as best she could to find a way of avoiding any suggestion of what she was really doing a good portion of the time while Fred was away.

After they arrive home, the two spent the rest of the afternoon watching TV. About an hour before Maggie had agreed to visit Freddie at 6:00, she knew she needed to find some excuse for leaving the house at a time when she and Fred normally watched the local news together, so she told Fred she had to go to the grocery store to get some items and then visit the local mall.

"I'll be back a little later once I get the things I need," she said.

Fred replied, "Well, okay. But you know you'll miss the local news at 6:00, don't you?"

Maggie replied, "Yeah, but you can fill me in when I get back."

"Okay. I'll see you later."

Maggie's wayward spirit led her to be dishonest with Fred regarding her intentions. After Fred's return, it was more of a challenge for her to see Freddie for that one last time but she did it! That errant spirit within her prevailed.

Near the end of Maggie's visit with Freddie, he said, "Now, Maggie, it's been nice having you here this week. But next week will be different. I'll be away in Ames, Iowa, visiting my son, who is with his mother."

Maggie replied, "Well, Freddie, it's been grand these last few days. It certainly brought back memories of what it was like before between us. But, yeah, you need to go see your son. And who knows, your ex might reclaim some of that treasure you two had when you were together."

Freddie replied, "Not likely, Maggie. I think that bridge has been burned down."

Maggie realized the lateness of the hour and said to Freddie, "Well, let me be going now. Have a nice trip. I know you mentioned that you'll be over there for a whole week. You plan to stay in a hotel or something?"

"You got it, Maggie. There's a cheap place nearby where I can stay, but it's pretty nice."

Maggie said, "Speaking of nice, that new car you have is very nice—all bright and red. You can recognize it from a mile away."

Freddie replied, "Yeah, it's real nice, and it has a lot of power too. And I'll need it getting out there on the interstate." Freddie added, "Maggie, you know how fast people go on the highway."

"Yeah, I remember having to drive from south of Chicago to Flint to visit my parents."

Freddie laughed and said, "Yeah, I remember. You used to come here a lot of those weekends. I guess that was when you were supposed to have been at your parents' house, huh?"

"Oh, Freddie, you're making me feel so guilty!" she replied.

"Guilty? Guilty of what, Maggie? Satisfying your own desires?"

Before Maggie had a chance to respond to Freddie's latest comment, he continued, "I know one of those times you came by I could tell you really wanted to stay. But with that dream I had the night before you came by, I just couldn't bring myself to be with you then. You remember, Maggie?" he asked her.

"Oh, *do I* remember! Yes, I remember that night, Freddie. And when you rejected me—and for good reason let me tell you—I cried almost the whole way home. And when I finally got there, I found my husband was already sound asleep, and then I dozed off shortly after that.

"But then something unusual happened, Freddie. When I fell asleep, I apparently called out your name with Fred sleeping right there beside me. And, yeah, I believe he heard me! Anyway, the next morning, Fred told me he thought I was calling his name with that extra syllable on it. Yeah, Freddie, I guess I called out for you that night. Now, that was something I had to get myself out of. I know all this sounds ridiculous."

Freddie's response to what Maggie had told him was simply, "Wow!"

When Freddie gathered himself after what Maggie had just said, he told her, "Well, I guess it's good you were thinking about me in your sleep. Anyway, you know, Maggie, that drive I have tomorrow is over three hours. And when I return here next Friday after spending a few days with my son, I know I'll be extremely tired."

"Well, be careful driving," Maggie replied. "Remember that dream you told me about? Sometimes there's meaning to a dream."

"Yeah, I know," Freddie replied. "Well, Maggie, since I'll be away next week, maybe we can get together sometimes the following week. At any rate, I'll give you a call late on that Friday night when I get back, maybe at midnight. Yeah, I'll give you a call then."

"Well, make it late," Maggie responded. "My husband sometimes goes to bed early, and if that's the case, I won't have to worry about him seeing me on the phone. But midnight should be fine. He'll probably be sound asleep.

"Now, Freddie, don't make this a habit. Like I said, I'll need to spend more time at my day care. And remember, I'm a married woman now."

"Oh, I forgot that. At least I *want* to forget your marital status," Freddie replied in jest.

"Okay, bye, Freddie," she said, hastening the conclusion of their conversation.

"So long, Maggie."

Not understanding the reason behind his use of "so long," she replied, "Well, be careful." Then, the conversation ended.

Soon after leaving Freddie's place, Maggie arrived at her house and found that Fred was in bed already and asleep. She would retire soon herself. Maggie knew they would resume their weekly schedule on Sunday of going to church and having dinner afterwards, then socializing with the Manleys later in the evening. Maggie joined her husband to get the rest they both needed.

CHAPTER 6
Injured Spirit

Foundation Scripture: Numbers 32:23

"...Be sure your sin will find you out."

The week after Fred's return to Central Heights proved to be so different from the previous one for Maggie. No more daily trips to see Freddie at 6:00, and she no longer had to make up excuses for going out. Instead, she would be at home with Fred.

Fred wondered about Maggie's activities while he was in Vegas. He asked himself, "Why did Mag suddenly have so much shopping to do while I was away?" But he trusted his wife and assumed she felt the same way toward him when he was away for conferences relating to his career as an author and corporate meetings with Mojco.

As Fred reacquainted himself with home life after a few days away, he also resumed his duties at Mojco and continued to write in his spare time. He certainly had enough on his plate without worrying about what Maggie was doing.

Fred allowed Maggie to do whatever she wanted, whether managing her day care or planning trips to places like Bermuda and southern Florida or visiting her parents in Flint when they were alive.

For Fred, the week following his return from Vegas sped by with Maggie by his side every morning before work and in the evenings.

In a strange way, Maggie looked forward to hearing from Freddie at midnight when he returned that Friday night. As Fred slept beside her Friday night, she watched the clock, waiting for the call. Not hearing the phone ring at midnight, Maggie imagined he would wait until the next day to call. She grew sleepy and joined Fred in slumber.

When Maggie woke up early the next morning, her priority was to prepare a nice breakfast for her husband, but she still thought about why Freddie did not call her at midnight as he said he would. Maggie soon dismissed that idea and assumed he would call at some point during the day.

Both Maggie and Fred knew that the next day, Sunday, would be their usual ritual of attending church and having their weekly social gathering with the Manleys later in the evening.

After breakfast, Fred and Maggie relaxed most of the day. Midday came and went. About an hour before dinner, Maggie realized she still hadn't heard from Freddie. She finally accepted the fact that she might not hear from him that day. *Oh, well,* she thought. *I need to end this relationship with him anyway and concentrate on my husband.*

Finally, the Mints had dinner together. Afterward, Maggie asked Fred, "Hey, honey, could you unload the dishwasher?"

Fred could not refuse her request after the fine dinner she had prepared, so he did just that.

Maggie sat down to relax in her favorite recliner and began watching the 6:00 local news. *What a difference between now and the latter part of last week at this time,* Maggie thought, as she tried to get accustomed to being home again with Fred.

After Fred finished the dishes, he went into the living room and sat on the couch on the opposite side of the room from Maggie.

"Hey, Mag, come on over here and sit with me," he said. Maggie left the recliner and went to join her husband on the couch.

FIGURE 4 A Look at the News

When Maggie got there, sitting comfortably beside Fred, she said, "There! Am I close enough to you? Now we're all comfy and can enjoy TV. The news is getting ready to come on, so sit tight!" she admonished him.

"Okay," Fred said.

Their daily ritual of the local news felt familiar and routine. "Same old kind of stuff, Fred," Maggie said, hoping to see something that really interested her.

Her attention soon became drawn to a news story about a horrendous automobile accident—part of a multi-vehicle pileup on Interstate 80, the major thoroughfare from Chicago to Ames, Iowa. *That's the same highway that Freddie took while going to visit his son over in Ames*, Maggie thought.

Something among the wreckage caught Maggie's eye—a bright red vehicle just like the one she had seen at Freddie's. It was totally crushed.

"Oh, my, what a total mess with that accident, Fred! Look at all those mangled vehicles," she said. Even as she spoke, her eyes remained fixed on that red car.

"Yeah, that's a pretty bad accident all right. So many vehicles were involved," Fred said.

Maggie became more and more emotional about the situation, realizing that Freddie might be one of the victims in the accident she was seeing.

"Oh, my! Oh, my!" she shouted.

Fred noticed how intense his wife's response to the accident appeared.

"Mag, let's turn away from this station if it's getting you upset. It's not like you know someone involved in this accident," he said.

Maggie shook her head, and they continued to watch this news story. It was agonizing for Maggie to wait and find the identification of those motorists in the accident. Perhaps the condition of those involved in the accident would be revealed later on the Sunday edition of the 6:00 news. Maggie considered how she could get more information about the accident. Sure enough, the news ended that day without the names or the condition of the motorists involved being revealed.

Since Maggie had not received the information she wanted on Saturday's news, she thought maybe they could delay going to Gates and Courtney's house until after the 6:00 news on Sunday. *I'm sure by that time they'll have more information about the accident and about some of the victims,* she thought.

Maggie and Fred's usual TV lineup included a comedy show, but Fred noticed that his wife did not respond with laughter as she usually did. This prompted him to ask, "What's wrong, Mag? You usually are tickled to death over this comedy routine."

"I guess I'm just ready to go to bed," she replied.

All Maggie could think about was the prospect of Freddie being listed among the fatalities in that horrendous accident she had seen on TV.

Before too long, Maggie and Fred retired for the evening, and she did her best to put those thoughts to rest and go to sleep.

The following day on Sunday, as always they went to church and planned to go to the Manleys later that evening. Usually, they left at 6:00 to visit their friends, but Maggie tried to convince Fred to wait until later.

"Fred, lets' see the news at 6:00; then we can leave for Gates and Courtney's house afterwards. Maybe we can see who was involved in that terrible accident we saw yesterday."

Fred replied, "Well, okay, Mag. If you're that concerned about it, we can leave as soon as the news goes off."

So after dinner they relaxed a little in front of the television and tuned in to the 6:00 newscast. They agreed to leave for the Manleys after that.

"NEWS BULLETIN! Horrible Car Crash on Interstate 80 Takes the Life of Illinois State Senator Mike Mansfield."

At the beginning of the newscast, this bulletin appeared with the background showing the multi-vehicle pileup that Maggie had seen the previous day. "Oh, my!" Maggie gasped. "Senator Mansfield—I see him all the time on TV."

Fred said, "My, my! What do ya know! I didn't agree with some things he promoted, but I have the admit he was a hard-working politician." Then he continued, "Yeah, he was in the news quite a bit."

While Maggie felt sorry to hear the news of a popular state senator's demise, she was more concerned about the status of the person who was driving that bright red car. She dreaded the thought that her friend Freddie might have been killed. Visibly shaken by what she watched, her main concern was about Freddie. *Was he among those that perished along with Senator Mansfield in this accident?*

As the newscaster spoke about the senator's death—a rather lengthy discussion because he was so popular around the state—Maggie waited impatiently for the disclosure of others involved in the accident. The news anchor finally said that there were three other casualties in the pileup and also three who survived. Then he announced the names of the survivors.

The newscaster said, "Ladies and gentlemen, I have a list of the survivors of this terrible accident. They are all at the hospital downtown and are expected to have varying degrees of recovery."

He went on to give the names of those who survived.

Maggie's mind was unsettled between the possibility of hearing Freddie's name among those who were severely injured and those who had died. A terrible thought came to her: *What if Freddie survived the accident but would not be like he was before? Would he be a shell of who he once was, disabled for the rest of his life?*

But Freddie's name was not among the names of survivors. Maggie felt temporary relief. At least he wasn't debilitated for the rest of his life.

The other alternative had not yet made its way into her mind. She could not face the grim alternative outcome. It would be heart wrenching.

Could it be that Freddie is dead? The tears that appeared in her eyes when she first heard about the accident were now freely flowing down her cheeks.

Fred, who could not discern her thoughts, was prompted to say, "Oh, Mag, you are really affected by this accident, aren't you? Let me go get you some water."

While Fred was getting Maggie something to drink, the names of those who perished in the accident were called. Freddie's name was not among the first two. Maggie felt relief momentarily, telling herself that maybe the car she saw was not Freddie's after all.

Finally, the last name was called: Freddie Burroughs. Maggie cried out, "Oh, no! Oh, no! Freddie! Freddie is gone! Freddie's gone!" She said his name so loudly that Fred heard her from the kitchen.

"Mag, Mag! Are you all right in there?" Fred yelled.

Maggie shouted to him, "Fred, you know Freddie?" Her voice sounded urgent and strained as she continued, "Oh, Fred, come on in here. You can forget about that water!"

Carrying their glasses, Fred rushed back to where Maggie was. He said, "Okay, honey. I know you said forget the water, but here it is anyway. I think you really need it."

Maggie received the water and took a sip.

"There you go," Fred said. "The water should make you feel a little better. And did I hear you call the name of Freddie?"

No longer able to conceal the nature of what she had just witnessed, Maggie shared the details of what she saw on the news with Fred.

"You remember Sinbad's cousin who went down to south Florida with us during the summer? It's him! It's him! It's him in this terrible accident," Maggie shouted repeatedly at Fred. "Ooh! He's gone. Freddie's gone! He was listed as one of those who perished in this accident, Fred!"

"Yeah, Mag, I remember the guy," Fred said. "I remember him being with us in south Florida."

As he viewed a closeup of the accident on the news, Fred said, "Oh, my! That *is* a bad accident!" Fred continued, "As a matter of fact, wasn't he your partner down there as we took the ferry over to the

Island of Love? At least the way you described our trip over there in your dream while we were in Florida."

Maggie replied, "Yeah, that's him. Oh, he was such a good guy!"

Then Maggie caught herself. *How did Fred know that? It was only a dream.* Then she realized she must have revealed many of the details of the dream to everyone there, including Fred, during her birthday celebration back in Florida. But Maggie thought she had omitted the portion of the dream with Freddie on the ferry when she had described it to Fred. Maybe Fred found out when he talked with Freddie in casual conversation after her dream. She wondered if she actually had told Fred and everyone else that part of the dream.

Fred tried to calm Maggie as thoughts about the event flooded her mind.

"Now, Mag, go ahead and drink more of the water I gave you. It'll make you feel better."

"Okay," Maggie replied.

Fred continued, "Well, I really didn't know him—just casually met him. But everyone down there was friendly to each other. Apparently you knew him a little better than I did, Mag, the way you're carrying on like this."

As Maggie sat drinking her water, she seemed less overwhelmed with emotion.

"Mag, you seem to be doing a little better now. Everything will be fine. It's not like you knew the guy personally," Fred said, not realizing the closeness of their relationship.

With that comment from her husband, Maggie glanced at Fred briefly, as if to say *if you only knew.* She gazed downward again as tears reappeared in her eyes.

"Mag, why don't we stay home tonight and just go to bed," Fred said. "We really don't have to go to Gates and Courtney's house."

Maggie responded, "No, no, Fred! You know how dedicated we are to being together with the Manleys on Sunday evenings. I'll be fine. Let me go to the bathroom and freshen up a little, and I'll be ready to go in about ten minutes. I'll be fine; I promise," she repeated.

After Maggie wiped her eyes and reapplied a bit of makeup, they made the short trip to the Manley's house.

As the Mints arrived, Courtney welcomed them inside the house.

"Hello, Fred and Maggie; come on in!"

"Hey, that aroma is something else!" Fred commented. "What did you two cook that smells so good, Courtney?"

"Be patient, Fred; you'll see." After a brief pause, Courtney added, "Gates is grilling out on the deck. You know it's so beautiful outside this evening."

After a little while, Gates came in and greeted Maggie and Fred. "How are you two? You realize you're a little late, don't you?"

Fred replied, "Yeah, Gates. We were late getting here tonight because…"

Gates interrupted, "Hold on to that thought, Fred. I'll be back in a second."

Gates grabbed his coat and hat from the hall closet and then returned to rejoin the group. "Go ahead, Fred," he said. "What were you saying?"

Fred answered, "Well, Gates, I was gonna say that we stayed home and watched the evening news, which was the reason we were late."

"Watch the news?" Gates replied with a degree of wonderment. Then he continued, "You two never look at the news on a Sunday. You're usually with us, or at least on the way here."

"Well, Gates and Courtney, we did tonight," Fred replied. Then he continued in a more somber tone, saying, "And by the way, we have some sad news to bring you. Remember Freddie, Sinbad's cousin who was with us down there in Florida?"

Gates replied, "Yeah, I remember him. He didn't say much but I remember him."

"Well, he was killed yesterday in a car accident. And it's really affected Mag."

Gates and Courtney responded, "Oh my!"

Gates continued, "I'm devastated! We just saw him during the summer when we all went to Florida to celebrate Erin's position down there. Yeah, we're sorry to hear about that."

Courtney simply uttered, "My, my!" Then she looked down in silence.

Maggie added, "You remember the dream I had down in Florida before you all had that surprise birthday party for me? I dreamed he was my partner when we were on that ferry on the way to the Island of Love."

"Maggie, you're right. We never went to the island because of the storm, but you told us you dreamed about going on that trip. And you did it so well, so much in detail, it was as though all of us had gone," Gates acknowledged.

"Yeah, Gates, it *was* just a dream," Maggie said, "but I'm glad you got a lot out of my description. It seemed so real! I'll always remember that dream. And as far as the party is concerned, you all gave me such a nice celebration of my birthday, and even Fred was in on it, and Freddie was there too."

Then Fred said, "Yeah, Mag, you did tell us he was your partner when you dreamed about going on that ferry to the Island of Love. But beyond that, at least I didn't communicate with him much before the ferry we were scheduled to take."

"And, yeah, Freddie was there celebrating Erin like everyone else."

Fred left the room to go to the restroom.

After he left, Courtney turned to her friend and said, "Yeah, Maggie, we remember Freddie. He was a nice guy. Well, let me tell you, you just don't know when the end's gonna come. You just have to be ready, I guess."

Courtney fell into a brief silence and then continued, "That's why you should live life to the fullest every single day. We just don't know what tomorrow will bring. Like they say, tomorrow is not promised to you."

Maggie said with some emotion, "You know, Courtney and Gates, none of us know when the end is gonna come, but I think Freddie had some idea. And I say that because the last time I spoke to him we ended our communication with him saying to me, and I quote, 'So long.' I didn't understand the 'so long' expression at that time, but now I realize it was his way of telling me that we would never see each other again."

At that point Maggie's tears started flowing again.

Courtney said, "Wow! That's something, Maggie. It's what Gates would call 'Wonders of the Spirit.' Yeah, he says your spirit knows things like that. And sometimes you're led to reveal those things to others, like what Freddie apparently revealed to you—his own death."

"That's right, Maggie. God works in mysterious ways, His wonders to perform. And He performs those wonders more than you might think!" Gates said.

"Gates is right, Maggie. These things happen more often than we think, these wonders of the spirit as Gates puts it.... Well, anyway, I know he was a friend of yours. But it's good Fred is away from us right now and isn't seeing you become so emotional about another man."

Just as Courtney made that statement, Fred returned to the group. Having overheard some of what Courtney had just said, Fred asked, "What's this about another man, Courtney?"

Courtney responded, "Oh, it's nothing, Fred. But Gates *was* getting ready to make a point."

As Fred briefly turned his head away, Courtney nudged her husband to change the conversation. That gave Gates the opportunity to repeat what he had said to the ladies moments earlier.

"Well, Fred, I was telling Maggie that the scriptures talk about sometimes we may have premonitions about our own deaths. And I was saying that it's one of the 'Wonders of the Spirit' that I talk about often."

Courtney interrupted her husband, "Why, Gates, I've always wanted to ask you this question, and that is where does it say, 'Wonders of the Spirit' in the Bible?"

Gates replied, "I'm glad I have the Good Book on me, Courtney. Let me look it up. Just a minute." After briefly searching the scriptures, he said, "It's right here, in Second Corinthians, the first chapter and verses nine and ten. I'll read it to you, starting with the ninth verse. It says: 'But as it is written: Eye has not seen, nor ear heard, Nor have entered into the heart of man The things which God has prepared for those who love Him.'

"Now here's the part that relates to what I've been telling you. It says in the next verse, verse nine, 'But God has revealed them to us through His Spirit. For the Spirit searches all things, yes, the deep things of God.'"

Gates continued, "So, normally these spiritual truths have not entered the minds of people, because the subject of the workings of the spirit is not a part of common discussion. But these 'workings of the spirit' I'm talking about can be revealed to anyone who is receptive to receiving this kind of knowledge.

"Now let me tell you this, Courtney, and you too, Maggie and Fred, having premonitions is certainly what I would call deep things of God, those spiritual things I referred to. It's kinda like near-death experiences. You don't hear many people talking about that. Let's face it, death is never pleasant to talk about.

"But anyway, I interpret that tenth verse as saying that sometimes people *can* have an idea that the end is near, that is, to have a premonition about their own demise. And I believe this is just one example of the kind of 'deep things,' this verse of scripture is talking about. And that's one of the reasons I use the expression, 'Wonders of the Spirit.'

"I really believe that God sometimes speaks to us when we are about to go to Him—when we're ready to transition. So, it's not necessarily a sad thing—at least to the believer who is getting ready to make that leap."

Courtney seemed hesitant to accept the premonition idea Gates was promoting, so he added, "Let me get back to you, Courtney. Wonders of the spirit cover a lot of things that we don't necessarily understand, but that doesn't mean they are not true—even some things we don't like to talk about like the subject of death."

Without giving anyone a chance to respond, Gates tried to brighten everyone's mood, saying, "Now, listen, everybody. Let's cheer up. I'm sure we'll have a chance to mourn our friend with the family whenever final arrangements are complete."

"You've given us a lot of theological material to think about, Gates," Fred responded.

Gates replied, "Yeah, it is a lot, Fred. But speaking of arrangements, Maggie, I know you communicated with Sinbad when we were planning for our trip to Florida. Did you get any information about his next of kin? I'm sure someone close to Freddie will be making plans for a final service."

Trying to get over the intensity of her emotions, Maggie replied, "No, Gates. I don't know of anyone. He did say he had a wife and kid, but they are divorced now."

"Okay, Maggie, this is what I'll do," Gates suggested. "I can contact his cousin Sinbad after you contact his wife. But I'll do that only after I get permission from a known next of kin, and I guess that would be his wife or at least his former wife. Anyway, could you contact her?"

Maggie replied, "Well, I'll try. I know she lives in Ames, Iowa, and I can check to see if I could get her contact information and give her a call."

Gates responded, "Okay, Maggie. You do that, and based on what she tells you, you communicate that information to me; then I'll take it on myself to call down to Florida to inform Sinbad of what you tell me. From this line of communication, hopefully I can get a better idea on how to proceed as far as Freddie's final service."

Maggie replied, "That sounds like a plan, Gates."

The conversation had long since sidetracked Gates from the errand he planned to run. He said, "Listen you all. I know you're wondering why I have been talking to you with this jacket and a cap on. But I need to go to the store to get some more charcoal for the grill. You want to come with me, Fred?"

"Sure, I'll go with you, Gates."

"And as far as contacting Sinbad," Gates continued, "I'll wait until I get a word from you, Maggie, about his next of kin before I move forward."

"Okay, Gates," Maggie replied.

Gates then said to everyone, "Okay then. You girls can remain here while Fred and I go to the store. But we'll be back within the next hour."

Remembering the last time the fellows went to a store, Courtney said to them both, "You guys go ahead. Maggie and I will be fine. Just don't spend the time you took when you two went to that convenience store downtown."

"Oh, Courtney, why do you want to bring that up? We're outta here. Come on, Fred."

Now alone in the house, Courtney and Maggie ventured into the living room.

"Hey, Maggie, let's go and sit down a minute. I've been helping Gates and I need a breather. And I know you're an emotional wreck because of the death of your friend. You want some coffee or something?" Courtney asked.

"Yeah, Courtney, that would be fine."

"Okay then. Let me go in here and brew some. It won't take long."

Maggie sat in one of the recliners the Manleys had in their living room while Courtney was out of the room. She looked around at the familiar surroundings. It was a lovely room. Candle holders with small plants situated beside each of them stood on small shelves along the wall.

The Manley's home reminded Maggie so much of Freddie's place. He had plants galore just as Courtney did. Recalling this certainly didn't help Maggie's emotional state, and her feelings were still evident five minutes later when Courtney returned with the coffee.

Courtney noticed the tears building up in Maggie's eyes as she handed her the coffee. Without bringing up Maggie's obvious discomposure, Courtney said, "Here you go, Maggie. Drink some of this and you'll probably be refreshed. I know a cup does it for me."

Maggie replied, "Thanks, Courtney. You and Gates are always so inviting when Fred and I come over. Fred thought that maybe we should've stayed at home tonight because of the way the death of Freddie affected me. But I told him I wanted to come anyway."

No longer content to hold back her concern for Maggie, Courtney said, "Maggie, I noticed that even now you're getting emotional about the whole thing. It's strange, but I don't recall you getting this emotional about anyone else that you've known, not even your late husband John."

Courtney considered her words and added, "Well, I didn't mean for it to sound like it did, Maggie." But she was still concerned and asked rather bluntly, "Was there something special going on between you and Freddie?"

Maggie totally broke down and started crying with tears flowing everywhere. Finally, she said, "I'm sorry to be carrying on like this, but when you asked me that question, I just couldn't hold back any longer."

When Maggie regained her composure, she told her friend, "We've known each other for some time now, Courtney, and I feel I can tell you almost anything. And…"

Courtney interrupted, "Of course, you can, Maggie, and I want you to. It's not good to hold stuff inside; it just wears on you. Yeah, it's much better to bring things out in the open—of course with someone you can trust. And you can trust me, Maggie. Whatever you tell me will not leave this house."

Maggie replied to what Courtney said, "Well, thanks Courtney. But I'd appreciate it if you wouldn't even mention anything that we say to Gates."

"Well, okay, Maggie. If that's what you want. I know with his experience as a minister, he may be able to help you more than even I could, at least on a professional, even a spiritual level," Courtney replied. She continued, "But anyway, let me know what's on your mind."

After a brief pause to collect her thoughts, Maggie began by telling Courtney about the time before she met Gates. She said to her, "Courtney, you remember how it was between you and Gates when you two first met? If I remember, you said that you were just infatuated with him, looking so fine and debonair."

Courtney replied, "You got that right, girl. Just his physical presence made me give in to his advances. And let me tell you, he probably felt the same way about me. Yeah, it was love at first sight for the both of us, I suppose. Talk to him about it; he'll tell you. At least that's what he's told me!"

"Well, Courtney, I had those same feelings for Freddie long before I became married to Fred. In fact, it all started when I first moved to Detroit from Flint when I got a job at the church John was transferred to. It was my first time away from home, and I guess I was just excited being in the big city. I was just young and naïve I suppose in those days.

"My mother wasn't that excited about me moving away from Flint, but she knew John was going to accept his father's recommendation that he be transferred to a larger church, Faith Methodist in Detroit. While my mother didn't want me to leave home, she really wanted me to be with John, so she gave me her blessings when I left to work at his church. Of course, eventually we were married.

"Now, don't get me wrong. I really loved John. At least I loved his adoration of me, especially when he was in front of other people.

"Anyway, that's when I met Freddie. He just came on to me. And I guess, like you experienced with Gates, I was physically attracted to him—blown away, you might say. We met during the time I was at the law office, and we were both drawn to each other.

"At that time, John seemed to be so involved with his ministerial duties and receiving the acclaim of other people—so much that I felt neglected. And guess what, Courtney? Freddie came on the scene and immediately tried to hit on me. I'm sad to say now that it worked, because eventually he satisfied all the physical needs that I had at the time, especially with Fred living in Hawaii then.

"So, Courtney, we continued to have a relationship even after John's passing. Not only that, but Fred, who was the dream of my life at the time and still is by the way, had moved to Hawaii as you know. So, at that time it was just *Freddie and me,* and we continued to have a rather clandestine relationship. No one really knew we were secretly seeing each other. As I saw more and more of Freddie, I saw less of my parents, especially after Fred's returned from Hawaii and even after we were married."

Courtney saw tears beginning to fill Maggie's eyes again after that soliloquy.

"Okay, Maggie. Calm down now."

Maggie gathered herself and was able to continue. "I'm fine, Courtney. I just get so emotional every time I think about it.

"Anyway, as I continued those trips to Flint to see my parents, one time I decided to stop by Freddie's place in Detroit. My friend Sandra…"

Mentioning Sandra brought the sudden thought of her not knowing what had happened to Freddie. "You know, Courtney, as soon as I see Sandra, I'll have to tell her about Freddie. I sure don't look forward to that because I believe she was beginning to really like him ever since they first met at her recognition dinner as a new employee at the law firm."

Maggie returned to her original point. "Sorry to have digressed. Anyway, I had been going to my parent's house practically every weekend. But I knew Sandra would be there with them whenever they needed her if I was with Freddie.

"But you know, Courtney, I knew I was doing something wrong. I just felt helpless about it at the time."

Maggie again began to cry.

Maggie's pain was evident in her voice. Courtney wanted to comfort her somehow.

"Maggie, I really understand what you've been through. The only thing I can say is that there is always a battle going on between the spirit part of our being and the flesh part. And I'm afraid that it's a never-ending battle."

Courtney turned to the scriptures to provide some comfort to Maggie. "Remember in the scripture the Apostle Paul said that sometimes he was led to do things that were contrary to the spirit part of his being. Well, we're no different today! And I'm afraid it's a constant battle, like I said.

"Now, Maggie, I could read a lot of verses of scripture that address this topic, but I'll just say I interpret this as saying the more we focus on the spirit part of our being, the flesh part will continually diminish.

"You know as well as I do, Maggie, that the flesh is relentless, and anytime there's an opportunity for it to dominate your being, it's going to take it. The scripture tells us to give no place for evil in our minds. Apparently, Freddie gave you that place, that opportunity."

Maggie said, "Yeah, he provided me with an opportunity, Courtney, I guess an opportunity to do wrong. And I understand all of what you're saying. Remember, I was the wife of a minister for a while too, and John taught me a lot about the scriptures. But, Courtney, I guess it's just good to talk to someone, someone I can trust, about these kinds of issues."

Courtney replied, "Well, take the 'guess' out of it, girl. It's just good talking to somebody about certain problems you might have anyway, just to keep your sanity. You know this is an insane world we live in.

"But I know what you're saying. You can't talk to just anybody. So, yeah, you need to talk to someone you can trust who will not put all your business out there in the street.

"But you know, Maggie, I was in a similar situation when I first met Gates. I was attracted to that man based on his physical presence, and he certainly was relentless in his pursuit of me.

"Yeah, I'll tell you, if we're not careful, we all could very easily end up with an injured spirit. But remember, I'm here for you, Maggie."

Courtney continued, "Maggie, I know the guys will be back soon, so let me ask you this. Are you sure you're telling me everything about your issues involving Freddie?"

Maggie replied with much emotion, "Well, I've done a lot of things I'm not proud of, Courtney."

Courtney replied, "Okay, Maggie. Say no more. I understand, I think."

Courtney went over and gave Maggie a hug. As they embraced Courtney told her, "Well, all I can say is, that's what the Spirit is for— to comfort us in our time of need. And it sure sounds like you need that comfort now, Maggie.

"Just believe that God is there to help you, to pull you up, and not to condemn you. Like Gates says a lot, that's one of the Wonders of the Spirit—the forgiving nature that God has for us all. That should comfort us a lot in our time of need.

"And, you know, sometimes we all need comfort and mercy. That's what God is all about, giving us mercy and forgiveness. That's the reason for Jesus going to the cross and dying for all of us, because He knew that we would need it. We all make mistakes.

"Anyway, those are some of the major benefits of being a believer, having access to God's mercy. And let me tell you this, the scripture *does say* that the strong must bear the infirmities of the weak. At least that's how Gates quotes that scripture, and I forget where it is in the Bible.

"So hopefully, Maggie, I'm giving you some comfort now," Courtney said.

At that moment, as Courtney was hugging Maggie again, she looked up as into the heavens and said softly, "Yes, He's there to help us. And, yes, that's one of the 'Wonders of the Spirit.'"

At that point, the women heard a car drive up and knew that Gates and Fred had returned. Courtney pulled back from her embrace of Maggie and said, "Oh, I guess the fellows are back."

Maggie replied, "Let me run into the bathroom and freshen up a bit. I know my makeup is all over the place because of the tears."

Realizing Maggie was accurate in her assessment of her appearance, Courtney said, "Yeah, Maggie. You go do that."

Soon after that, the front door opened. Fred and Gates walked in and over to where Courtney was.

"We're back, Courtney," Gates said. "We're really going to have a good time this evening. We got the charcoal and I'll be able to finish cooking on the grill.

"By the way, where's Maggie?"

Courtney answered, "Oh, she's just gone to the bathroom. She'll be right out.

CHAPTER 7
Plans to Come Together

Foundation Scripture: Isaiah 1:18

"Come now, let us reason together, says the Lord. Though your sins are like scarlet, They shall be as white as snow; Though they are red like crimson, they shall be as wool."

After Fred and Gates had returned from the store, the Mints and Manleys had a typically enjoyable Sunday evening gathering.

On their way home that night, Fred said, "Mag, aren't you glad we went to the Manleys tonight instead of staying at home like you wanted?"

"Yeah, everything was fine, honey, except that it took longer than I expected for you two to go to the store and back, but I'll forgive you. Courtney and I talked about a lot of different things, so it wasn't like when you two went to the convenience store that night," Maggie said with a smile.

She continued, "And when you and Gates went out, Courtney and I had a good talk, which I think helped me a lot."

"That's good," Fred replied. "I know you two had a lot of woman's talk, didn't you?"

"Yeah, I guess you can call it that. Anyway, I'm glad you encouraged me to come out before we left home."

Maggie and Fred arrived home late that night. As they entered the front door, Fred said, "Mag, I know you're probably ready for bed."

"Yeah, Fred. I'm beat! But remember, I promised Gates that I would call Freddie's former wife to see if she knew about her ex passing and to see if she would be a part of the final arrangements for him."

"Oh, yeah!" Fred replied. "I do remember now that you mention it. But you know, it's so late you probably should wait till morning before you try to contact her."

"I guess you're right." Maggie gave it just a little more thought, then said, "Yeah, I can wait until early tomorrow."

The following morning came, and the first thing Maggie did upon rising was a trip to the kitchen to brew some coffee for herself and Fred. She didn't necessarily look forward to calling Freddie's former wife, but she made a promise to Gates the night before, so she went ahead and fulfilled that responsibility. She also wanted to call Sandra. But that would wait until later.

As she got the bag of coffee from the cupboard, she thought, *Fred is still asleep anyway, so I'll wait on brewing the coffee, and go ahead and make this call.* Maggie looked in the directory for Ames, Iowa, remembering that Freddie had mentioned that his wife and son had moved to that city and state. She focused on Freddie's last name and found Peggy Burroughs. She said to herself, "Okay. This is the only Burroughs I see in Ames, so it must be Freddie's ex. I guess I'll find out."

Maggie picked up the phone, hesitated a bit, then gained the nerve to dial the number. After several rings, someone answered.

"Hello. Who am I speaking with, and who would you like to speak to?"

Maggie was surprised by the male voice on the other end of the line. Momentarily, she thought, *Is she living alone? Or does she have a man living with her?*

Maggie quickly let such thoughts pass quickly and replied, "My name is Maggie. And I would like to speak with Peggy."

"Hold on a minute," the voice replied. Then he hollered, "Hey, Peg, someone's on the phone by the name of Maggie who wants to speak with ya."

Maggie heard a voice in the background say, "Okay, Butter Ball. Tell whoever it is I'll be right there."

Then the man told Maggie, "Hold on; she'll be here shortly."

After getting to the phone, the lady said tersely, "Who's speaking?"

Maggie replied, "I'm Maggie, an acquaintance of your former husband Freddie." Then she heard the woman say, "That damn man has another woman calling here."

After the lady realized Maggie probably heard her, in a more subdued, even dignified but louder voice, Peggy apologized, "Oh, I'm sorry. Hope you didn't hear that. But you're the fourth woman who's called here asking about that former husband of mine. You know, lady, he is such a player. That's why I left him. Any woman being with that man any length of time certainly deserves what she's got."

Peggy caught herself again talking about her problems and continued, "Oh, again I'm sorry, Miss. So what do ya want?"

After Maggie gathered herself, she said, "Well, Miss Burroughs…."

The woman interrupted her for a third time and said, "Don't call me that, Miss. I just had my last name changed yesterday. And I'd like to forget that name. Just call me Peggy."

Before Maggie could tell her why she was calling, Peggy added, "Now, let me ask you a question: Is he playing around with you now?"

Not knowing exactly how she should address the lady after she made those comments about changing her last name, Maggie responded, "No, uh, Peggy." Maggie continued and said bluntly, "I just wanted to call and let you know that Freddie was killed the other day in an automobile accident."

The tone of Peggy's voice suddenly changed when she heard this information from Maggie. She began to groan loudly, "Aw, aw, aw! What are you saying, Miss? Miss!"

Maggie said, "Just call me Maggie."

The lady then said, "Maggie, are you for real? The man's dead?"

Maggie replied, "Yeah, Peggy, I saw it on the news the day before yesterday."

Then Peggy said, "Maggie, I don't know what to say. Oh, my Freddie! My Freddie's gone! Aw, aw!" The lady continued to grieve right there over the phone with Maggie.

Maggie could feel the pain of Freddie's ex, although she couldn't figure out the divide between the unflattering remarks she had about him just a few moments earlier and her sensitive feelings of grief towards him now that she had learned he was dead.

Maggie ended up asking Peggy about final arrangements. "Peggy, are you expecting to be involved in any of the final arrangements that may be planned for Freddie?"

She answered, "No, child. I've divorced him and pretty much separated from his entire family. But, honey, please call me back and let me know when and where the funeral will be. I certainly want to give my final respects to the man I was with for some time."

Maggie said, "Sure, I'll let you know.

"Well, thanks, Peggy, for your time. Bye."

"Bye, child!" Peggy replied.

Before Maggie could hang up, Peggy uttered some last words. "Oh, my Freddie, my Freddie! Freddie's gone!"

Maggie finished listening to the lady's pain before ending the call. Afterwards, she took a few moments to just breathe and put aside the grief before brewing the coffee.

At least her task of contacting Freddie's ex was accomplished. Peggy had made her intentions clear about not participating in planning his final service but had a desire to attend the funeral.

Maggie could not figure out the lady's divided opinion of her former husband. Peggy seemed at first to be glad she was now released from Freddie, but, at the same time, she had positive feelings for him when she learned of his fate. Maggie didn't understand the lady's rollercoaster emotions.

Thankfully, she now had concrete information to give to Gates so it could be transmitted to Sinbad via a phone conversation.

At about the time she was having those thoughts, Fred walked into the kitchen and said, "Good morning, Mag. The aroma of that coffee brewing woke me up, I suppose. I can't wait to get a cup. I thought I heard you talking on the phone."

Maggie replied, "Yeah, Fred. I was able to contact Freddie's former wife, and we talked a little bit about whether she'd be involved in Freddie's final service, and she said she wouldn't be."

"Okay. So, you have some information to give Gates now," Fred responded.

"Yeah, Fred, I'll call him as soon as I have a cup of coffee. Let me throw some wheat bread on the portable grill and we can have some buttered toast to go along with our coffee."

"Sounds good to me," Fred replied. For the next few minutes they sat at the kitchen table, enjoying coffee and toast. They would not have a full-blown meal until later that day at lunch.

After breakfast, Fred went back to bed while Maggie prepared to give Gates a call. She asked Fred, "You goin' back to bed?"

"Yeah, I want to get a few more minutes of shuteye before starting my day. I think after I do that, I'll wash up and go out on the patio and do some writing."

"Well, okay. I'm going to give Gates a call now and tell him what Freddie's ex said," Maggie said.

"Okay, Mag. Let me know what he says," Fred replied.

"Yeah, I'll let you know. And Fred, once I call Gates and tell him everything, I'm going in the kitchen and start preparing lunch. It'll be a big one since we didn't eat much at breakfast."

Maggie called Gates, and after several rings Courtney finally answered. The two of them exchanged pleasantries, and then Courtney went to get Gates. After a brief wait, Gates answered.

"Hello, Maggie. I was looking forward to hearing from you. So, what did you find out?"

"Well, Gates, I was relieved to reach Freddie's ex so easily. Anyway, when I spoke with her, she said she didn't want to be involved in planning of his final service. She just wanted me to make her aware of when and where the funeral would be. I guess that means she'll be there; at least she wants to be.

"And one other thing I noticed, Gates, was that she wasn't very friendly. I guess the divorce and everything relating to it took a lot out of her. Anyway, that's some of what I can tell you about our conversation."

Gates replied, "Okay, Maggie, that's all I need to know. I'll call Sinbad to give him that information. I would suspect that he already knows about Freddie's passing by now and is in the process of making those final arrangements. I'll pass on your information. As far as his ex attending the service, I guess they'll figure that out, that is, Sinbad and the family down there in Florida.

"Anyway, I'll get back to you on what Sinbad has in mind about Freddie's final service. Like I said, I'm assuming he already knows about the accident. But thanks for the information about Freddie's ex, Maggie."

"You're welcome," Maggie replied. She added, "Gates, please let me know what the plans are for Freddie's service if you can get them. And tell Courtney I'll be talking with her soon. Bye!"

Before contacting Sinbad, Gates told Courtney about his conversation with Maggie, but he knew he needed to call Sinbad to deliver Maggie's information as soon as possible. As Gates had suspected, Sinbad knew about Freddie's death and was in the process of making the final arrangements.

When Gates got Sinbad on the phone, he said, "The reason I'm calling, Sinbad, is to first of all see if you know about your cousin Freddie."

Sinbad responded, "Yeah, I'm afraid I do. I know about the car crash he was in, and I know that he didn't survive. It's been very sad down here in Florida because of that news. I know you're a minister, Gates, so please keep us in your prayers."

"You certainly have that, Sinbad. My friend Maggie talked with his former wife recently and learned that she did not want to be involved in planning the final service. You know, we here in the Chicago and Detroit areas want to offer whatever help we can."

"I really appreciate the offer, Gates," Sinbad said. "Yeah, we knew Peggy wouldn't be involved. My understanding from what Freddie told me on several occasions was that she never was very friendly towards our family. Anyway, that's water over the dam, you might say."

Gates said, "Yeah, Maggie told me that Peggy wasn't that friendly when she spoke with her over the phone. Maggie *did* tell me that Peggy wants to come to the funeral though. And I don't know how that's going to turn out. Anyway, those are some of the things I got from Maggie about her conversation with your cousin's former wife."

"Well, be that as it may, let's talk more positive stuff," Sinbad said. "So far the planning for Freddie's final service has gone well."

Gates said, "You know, Sinbad, you were very gracious to all of us when we were down at your resort. We just wanted to share our condolences and, as I just mentioned, see if we can do anything for you up here where we are."

Sinbad replied, "Well, I'm glad you brought the possibility of you all helping us, Gates. And, yes, there *is* something all of you in Maggie's group can do. I know the focus now is on Freddie and making sure he gets a decent homegoing service. But given the circumstances, we may be able to kill two birds with one stone, you might say."

"Well, I'm interested in what you're talking about, Sinbad," Gates replied.

Then Sinbad said back to him, "Okay then, Gates. You all *could* do something that might go well beyond the service we have planned for Freddie. And I expect it to be successful—with help from you guys. And what I'm going to say you can communicate to Maggie and the others up there where you are, including the group from the New York area."

"Okay, okay, Sinbad. What is it? I'm anxious to hear what you have in mind," Gates said.

Sinbad answered, "Okay, let me give it to you straight. You know my colleague here at the resort, Bernie, is getting married."

"What?" Gates interjected with total surprise.

Sinbad continued, "Yeah, he and Erin have a wedding coming up."

Gates interjected, "So he and Erin are hooking up?"

Sinbad replied, "Yeah, Gates, and I know that Erin would want as many of you involved as possible. But I also know this is sudden, and she realizes that all of you can't come down on a moment's notice. And that's because the wedding is coming up in a couple of weeks. But I think the plan is to have all of you guys join us in Colorado for their so-called post-honeymoon at a resort that I have out there."

"Wow, Sinbad! I knew that Bernie and Erin were friends, but I didn't think it was *that* serious. I guess you never know about those things. But anyway, that's good news, and all of us up here will offer our congratulations, I'm sure. And inviting us to come along to help celebrate there—in Colorado? Now I can't wait to tell the others!" Gates said with enthusiasm.

"Thank you, Gates," Sinbad said. "You know, honeymoons are supposed to be private—just between the newly married couple. *I will* tell you this: they're going someplace just by themselves right after the wedding. And, Gates, you'd never guess where that might be."

Gates said, "Well, come on. Tell me Sinbad. Where *are* they going?"

Sinbad replied, "They're going to the Island of Love, Gates. You know, that place we didn't get to go to because of the hurricane when you guys were down here in Miami. Remember?"

Gates replied, "*Do* I remember? Of course I remember that, Sinbad. How can I forget? It was a grand experience for all of us, even though we didn't get a chance to go to the island. As you've already said, the hurricane derailed those plans. But at least we did something grand for Maggie; we ended up giving her a nice birthday party down there.

"And you know, Sinbad, Maggie *did* give us a lot of details of the dream *she* had where all of us *did* go to the Island of Love. And again, even in her dream, the way she described it, the hurricane curtailed our plans for participating in the activities you had planned for us there.

"But you know, Maggie gave us such a good description of going the island in her dream, it was almost as if we did go. But maybe *we will* get the opportunity to go for real at some point."

"Don't worry about that, Gates. Sure, there will be an opportunity for everybody to go there. But I'm focusing on Colorado right now," Sinbad replied.

Gates said, "Okay, Sinbad. I hear you loud and clear. Anyway, all of us up here talked about it for a while, the Island of Love, I mean, and wondered exactly what we were in for by going to this place. But as far as Bernie taking Erin on their honeymoon there—well, I'm sure they'll have a good time."

Gates, who had not gotten over hearing of Bernie and Erin getting married, continued, "Anyway, what do ya know? Those two are tying the knot! And as far as Colorado. I didn't know you had a resort there. But, listen, we send our congratulations to Erin and Bernie. I know everyone up here is just going to be so excited about *that* news, not to mention our being invited to be with them in Colorado. We sure need something to balance out all the sadness we've had since learning of Freddie's death."

Gates continued, "Let me say something else, Sinbad. I know Erin has probably talked to Maggie's friend Sandra about her getting married. And we know that she was Freddie's friend; at least it appeared that way on the trip to Florida."

Before Gates finished his thoughts, Sinbad said, "Well, Gates, give me Sandra's phone number, and I'll try to contact her myself and give her the news."

"Sure, Sinbad." Gates replied. "I'll text it to you when we get off the phone. Hopefully you'll have more success in reaching her than we've had. I know her best friend, Maggie, said she hadn't been able to reach her either. Our minds have been on Freddie since we found out about his passing and on learning the plans for his final service."

Sinbad replied, "I understand, Gates. And I sure would appreciate Sandra's number.

"And, Gates, a few of us will be up later this week to get everything together regarding Freddie's situation," Sinbad said. "It's Monday now and I think we can get things together down here by Thursday. We've booked a flight for that morning and will take off for Detroit then. Hopefully we'll complete much of the planning later that day.

"And something else, Gates, I've been coordinating with a couple of relatives *we* have in Detroit, so much of the leg work is being done by them. I guess you can tell Maggie and the others that a small group of us, resort workers and family members, will be staying in the area

Thursday night. We hope to complete all the business stuff related to Freddie's service on Friday. If we're not finished by then, we'll have all of Saturday to get everything done.

"We plan to have the service for Freddie on Sunday at a small Baptist church in town. But then on the following Monday, the plan is that we all come together to talk about the trip to Colorado. You might call it a mini family reunion or a retreat. So that's what the plan is on this end. We'll pack up and fly back to Florida early Tuesday morning."

Sinbad wanted to give Gates some encouragement. "And, oh, one more thing. Don't give up on having an opportunity to visit the Island of Love. I would still love you all to do that."

Gates replied, "Okay, Sinbad. I'll remember that. It certainly sounds like you have things in order, and I'll give Maggie a call when I hang up to give her an overview of everything we've talked about. I'm not sure if we'll see you when you all come up on Thursday because I know you'll be extremely busy while you're here. But we'll be at Freddie's service on Sunday."

Gates continued, "You know, speaking of Sunday, I think that day will be a grand opportunity for all of us to get together after the service. What do you think of that idea, Sinbad?"

"Yeah, Gates, I think we may be able to get together after the service on Sunday afternoon for a little bit—you know, just to hang out and chat with each other," Sinbad replied. "I may be able to talk a little bit about some of the plans we have for Colorado, although we'll reserve the details for Monday."

"Okay, Sinbad. Just let us know when the exact time you want everyone to get together with you guys that afternoon or later on in the evening the day of the service," Gates replied.

"Yeah, I will do that. And I'll get more into the details of the plans for Colorado the next day on Monday. Who knows! We may be able to finalize everything before we all take off for Florida on that

Tuesday. That would be great. That's what the plan is at least," Sinbad concluded.

Gates replied, "Okay, Sinbad. I'm really looking forward to that trip to Colorado, and I know the others will be too!"

"I'm glad to hear that, Gates!" Sinbad responded.

Before Gates ended the conversation with Sinbad, he said, "Well, Sinbad, let me assure you that I will mention everything we've talked about to Maggie, and I'm sure she'll tell Sandra. That is, unless you're able to contact her first.

"When either Sandra or Maggie is informed about what we've talked about, I'm sure one of those two will tell others in the group, including Katie and her son Wynn in New York as well as Sheri and her family in New Brunswick. All of them will probably be here for the service.

"If for some reason, Katie and Wynn and Sheri's clan in New Brunswick can't be here for the funeral on Sunday, I'm sure they would arrange being here on that Monday for the meeting concerning Colorado. It appeared to me that both these families enjoyed going to Florida, and I'm sure they wouldn't want to miss out going to Colorado for anything. Yeah, we'll get 'em here somehow."

Gates continued, "And one more thing, Sinbad, regarding that meeting on Monday after the service on Sunday, I know all of us will be trying to sort things out for our plans for Colorado, dealing with work schedules, school, things like that."

Gates concluded, "You know, Sinbad, there will be a lot going on over the next week as we plan for that trip. But we can do it," Gates assured him.

Before Sinbad could respond, Gates asked, "Now, Sinbad, you said that services would be at a small church in town—in Detroit, that is. Do you have your hotel reservations all set up?"

"Glad you asked, Gates," Sinbad replied. "The answer is yes. Everything is set for the Wingo Hotel downtown. It's not very far from the casino. A friend of mine is the hotel owner there, and he's taking care of all the accommodations, including the expenses for everyone in Maggie's group if you all happen to want to be near us in the hotel. We'll reserve five suites for you if you want to use them for any reason.

"Two of the five accommodations are for you and Courtney and for Maggie and Fred. This will allow you guys to stay in Detroit without having to go back and forth from Chicago. And Sandra could have the third suite. The other two are for your friends from the New York area. These five suites are in addition to the ones we've reserved for our group coming from Florida.

"So, you all are covered from the time we come up on Thursday until the following Tuesday when we return here to Miami, that is, if you need the accommodations I mentioned.

"Like I said, I know it's quite a drive going back and forth between Detroit and Chicago. But I'll let you all handle that. And don't worry if you decide not to use the suites. Just let me know. We can always find use for them."

"Sounds great!" Gates said. "Well, let me get off the phone, and I'll get with Maggie to fill her in on the details. And I'm sure we'll be talking more soon. You know the end of the week will be here before you know it. Well, have a nice flight to Detroit."

"Thank you, Gates! We're looking forward to it, even though it will be a sad occasion," Sinbad replied.

"Bye, Sinbad. And, yes, we all will be talking soon."

After Gates had finished his conversation with Sinbad, he considered all that he and Sinbad had discussed. *I can't wait to tell Courtney,* he thought. *I know she'll be right on the phone to tell Maggie. But I'll have to call Maggie myself to tell her the details. And maybe she can contact Sandra if she can find her. Soon all of us will know about Sinbad's plans.*

CHAPTER 8

Maggie Is Informed:
The Service

Foundation Scripture: Matthew 5:4

Blessed are those who mourn, for they shall be comforted.

Gates called Maggie to let her know about his phone conversation with Sinbad. After reaching her he shared that Sinbad had been notified of his cousin's death only minutes after the accident.

"Apparently, he was killed instantly," Gates explained. "And the authorities found papers in Freddie's vehicle with his name and information on next of kin. They were quite prompt in contacting Sinbad.

"Sinbad went on to say that they have everything in order down there in Florida as far as the planning of Freddie's funeral, which will be at Staples Baptist Church over in Detroit.

"And, Maggie, I'll give you the responsibility of contacting Sandra and our friends in New York and New Jersey. If they can't make it to the funeral on Sunday, hopefully they will come to the meeting on Monday for the planning of the Colorado trip."

Maggie had no knowledge of plans for a trip. She simply asked,

"Colorado trip?"

Gates responded, "Oh, I forgot! I *was* going to tell you, Maggie. Did you know Bernie and Erin are getting married?"

Maggie screamed right into the phone, "Wow! Heavens no! I didn't know that. Oh my! Erin's getting married? I can't wait to tell Sandra."

After she calmed down a little, Maggie continued, "But you know, Gates, I haven't heard from Sandra lately, and, who knows, she may already know."

More solemnly, Maggie said, "I think I'm back down to earth now. And while I'm just so excited for Erin and Bernie getting married, none of us can forget Freddie. And I'm not sure if Sandra knows. If she doesn't, it will be a complete shock when she finds out."

Maggie was a strange mix of sadness and excitement. "It's definitely a sad time, Gates," she added, "but I didn't know about the Colorado thing, and I'm still shocked about Erin getting married."

Gates replied, "Yes, she's tying the knot!"

"Anyway, Gates, I know the reason you called me concerns Freddie's passing. It sounds like Sinbad and his family down in Florida went ahead and finalized everything about Freddie's service."

"Yeah, I think they have things under control with regards to the funeral," Gates responded. "The final planning will be on Friday and Saturday before the Sunday service. They're going to fly into Detroit and arrive here on Thursday evening."

It was a lot of information for Maggie to absorb. But she still couldn't get over the Colorado trip. She said aloud to herself, "We're going to Colorado! We're going to Colorado!"

Realizing she was still on the phone, Maggie said, "Oh, sorry, Gates. I'm so excited I forgot I was on the phone."

Gates continued to share details from his conversation with Sinbad. He explained that the wedding was only two weeks away and would be followed by a honeymoon.

"Sinbad said the Colorado trip will be their *second* honeymoon about a month after they get married. That will give those of us up here in Chicago and Detroit enough time to plan for it. And that's what Sinbad wants to talk to all of us about on Monday, the day after the funeral. And he said to include our friends in New York and New Jersey."

"Well, that's really something," Maggie responded. "I guess we'll have to wait until then to get more information on it."

"That's right, Maggie," Gates agreed.

Gates went on to tell Maggie that Sinbad had booked suites at the hotel in Detroit for all their entire group, including the Manleys and Mints and their friends from New York and New Jersey.

Maggie was thrilled with the idea of joining the whole group and being a part of the honeymoon celebration in Colorado.

"So let me make sure this is not a dream, Gates. I did hear you right, didn't I? Sinbad's inviting us to go to Colorado with him?"

"No, it's not a dream, Maggie; it's for real!" Gates confirmed.

"Well, okay, Gates, I'll get with it and call Sandra right away and will make sure that Katie in New York and Sheri in New Jersey are notified."

Gates said, "Yeah, Maggie, see if you can reach Sandra especially. Seems like no one has seen her lately. Sinbad really wants everyone in our group to make the trip out to Colorado.

"I know how much you'd want Sandra here; she's been such a significant part of your family and meant so much to your parents, of course. I'll be praying that God will miraculously put you two together somehow prior to the service."

"Thanks, Gates. You don't know how much what you just said means to me," Maggie replied as tears began to form in her eyes.

Gates sensed her emotions over the phone. "It's okay, Maggie," he said.

"I'm fine, Gates," Maggie she assured him.

Gates continued, "I'm looking forward to everything that will come about in the next week. Of course, it still will be sad because of what happened to Freddie. Bye for now, Maggie. We'll talk again soon."

"Bye, Gates," Maggie replied to end the conversation.

Maggie and Gates did not speak again until the funeral on Sunday, which would be an early morning service.

As expected, Freddie's service was a sad occasion. A few of his family sat in the first several rows of the center section of the small Baptist church. Sinbad's Aunt Clara, a sister of his mother and Freddie's mother, as well as a few nieces and nephews were seated there.

Since Freddie wasn't a churchgoer, not much was said about him in the eulogy given by the pastor of the church. Given that his lifestyle included extramarital affairs, much of his life may not have been appropriate for accolades. At least that was the thinking of his former wife Peggy. But like most eulogies, some positive statements reflecting his life among his friends and relatives were shared.

Maggie had given Peggy the time and location of the service. As she sat across the aisle from Freddie's family, Peggy carried on quite a bit, crying and calling out Freddie's name repeatedly, expressing strong emotions about seeing her former husband no longer alive. Some, including Maggie, looked on at her in bewilderment. Given their phone conversation where Peggy expressed her thoughts about his limitations as a husband, Maggie had to wonder at her heightened emotions since his death.

Just prior to the beginning of the service, as Maggie was sitting in the back along with her friends, Sandra suddenly walked into the back of the building. As she quietly tiptoed into the sanctuary, she saw there was some space next to Maggie.

Maggie glimpsed Sandra out of the corner of her eye as she approached. After Sandra moved into position beside her, Maggie whispered, "Oh, Sandra, it's great to see you, girl. I was worried that you wouldn't make it. Come on and sit down right here; there's enough room. You can slide past me and sit next to Fred, and I'll stay here on the end next to the aisle."

Sandra replied, "Thank you, Maggie." After taking her seat and greeting Fred, she turned toward Maggie and said quietly, "I've been out of town a lot lately, Maggie, but Bernie called me, at the request of Sinbad from what I understand, and told me everything. And I was devastated."

"Well, you're here now. Yeah, it's been pretty sad for everybody, Sandra," Maggie replied.

The funeral was a short one. Family members were the first to exit the sanctuary at the end of the service. While standing at their seats, Maggie and the others in her group got a glimpse of Sinbad as the recessional started. Since Maggie stood next to the aisle, Sinbad and other family members approached her.

Sinbad stopped beside Maggie for a moment, holding up the recessional behind him, leaned over, and gently whispered in her ear. "Maggie, since the service is so early, we'll be able to meet later today at 2:00 in the lobby back at the hotel. I'll talk to you more when I see you outside the church shortly."

Not wanting to hold up the recessional any longer, Maggie simply nodded her head in agreement after which Sinbad continued in the recessional going toward the rear exit.

Maggie returned her attention to the remaining part of the recessional as family members marched out of the sanctuary. She knew her conference with Sinbad would be about the scheduled

Monday meeting. At that time, she assumed that Sinbad would mention Erin and Bernie's post-honeymoon celebration in Colorado to those invited to come with them.

Everyone eventually exited the church, and Maggie had a chance to speak with Sinbad briefly.

He said, "Maggie, it was good to see you." Not to disregard the others who were standing with her, he added, "And everyone here, I'm so pleased that you all paid your respects to my cousin today. Maggie, I'll talk to you more later.

"Now I want to tell everyone within the sound of my voice that you are well appreciated. Many of you are members of my family as well as our special travel group; that's what I'll call you, and you know who you are. I invited you down to Florida to help open my resort, and we'll soon travel to Colorado, which I'll give you the details later."

Sinbad saw Sandra standing beside Maggie, so he added a special greeting to her. "It's so good to see you, Sandra. I understand you've been missing throughout much of the planning for this service today, but I know how much Freddie meant to you. I'm just glad you're here."

"Likewise, Sinbad," Sandra responded.

With a louder voice, Sinbad said to others standing around him, "Before we leave, everybody, let me thank all of you again for attending my cousin's service. It means so much to me and to all of our family.

"And let me add this too: I understand our friends from New York and New Jersey haven't arrived yet, but Maggie told me that they would be here tomorrow morning in time for the 12:00 noon meeting.

"Except for the sadness of Freddie's passing, it feels like a wonderful reunion with those who helped me open my resort. I'll see many of you at the hotel shortly, and again thank all of you for coming."

It took a while for everyone to travel from the church where Freddie's final service was held to the Wingo Hotel. When they arrived at their lodgings, everyone congregated in the lobby, where Sinbad continued to express his appreciation for their attendance.

At that time, Sinbad finally had a few moments with Maggie by herself. He said, "I didn't get a chance to speak with you alone after the service like I wanted. But let me tell you how much I appreciate your organizing things up here, Maggie. And I was so happy to see Sandra. I remember you saying that you had not seen her lately."

Maggie replied, "Yeah, Sinbad, I was so happy to see her arrive at the church. You may have seen Sandra when she entered the sanctuary at the last moment before everything got started."

"Yes, I caught a glimpse of her coming in, and I was glad to speak to her after the service. Of course, you know since you were right there," Sinbad said.

She replied, "You're right. I *was* right there. Anyway, you know you have my support."

"Yes, I do. Thank you, Maggie. And I really appreciate that." He added, "I was able to talk with Sandra a little, but I would like to have more discussion with her. I'm sure I'll speak to her at some point before we head back to Florida on Tuesday.

"You know, there are so many people here now, both those in our group and those who are not. I would like to talk to as many as I can, especially those in our group."

Sinbad then proceeded to speak to some of the others who were gathered around. Soon they all would be in for a big surprise!

CHAPTER 9

Surprise Amidst Coming Together

Foundation Scripture: Luke 12:40

"Therefore you also be ready, for the Son of Man is coming at an hour you do not expect it."

After being at the Wingo Hotel for some time following Freddie's funeral, Sinbad and the rest of the group noticed Katie and Wynn walking through the front door. Sheri, Jeanie, and David were not far behind. Everyone was shocked that their friends had arrived a day earlier than expected.

Maggie was the first to greet them. She said to her old college roommate, "Katie, what in the world are you all doing here? I thought you wouldn't arrive until tomorrow morning before Sinbad's meeting."

Katie greeted them, saying, "Hello, Maggie. And it's good to see all of you. I know you're surprised to see us.

"Hello, everybody!" Sheri added.

Courtney said, "Like Maggie said, Katie, we're surprised to see you, but still we're glad you're here. It's just like old times when we all went down to Florida together. That's what Sinbad said before you walked in. And Sheri, David, and Jeanie, it's good to see you too!"

Sheri said, "Well, I'm just sorry that we missed Freddie's service. He was really a nice guy from what I could tell. And, Sinbad, all of us from New York and New Jersey give you and your family our condolences."

"Thank you, Sheri, and it's so good seeing all of you here," Sinbad said.

Addressing everyone, Katie said, "Like Sheri said, we're so sorry to have missed Freddie's service. But we can explain why we decided to come now instead of tomorrow as I had originally mentioned to Maggie.

"I know you all didn't expect us to come early like this, but David had talked with the administrator on his job, and an agreement was reached where he could be away for a day or two. So here we are! We're just thankful we were able to come here today. It's so good to know that we won't be rushed to make Sinbad's meeting tomorrow by leaving our area the same day–early in the morning."

David said, "Yeah, I was determined to make that meeting and to get firsthand information about the Colorado trip from Sinbad himself. Sheri called Katie to see if she would agree to leave early and make flight reservations for us to come here today, and she was able to, so as Sheri said, here we are!"

"Thank you so much, Katie, for making those airline reservations on such short notice," Sheri added, expressing her gratitude.

"Don't mention it, Sheri," Katie responded.

Sheri continued, "You know, everybody, I agree with David, I wanted to be here too to get firsthand information about our trip to Colorado. I'm really excited about it."

Katie said, "Well, I appreciate you, Courtney, for saying that everyone's glad we're here. And believe me, we are sure glad to be here with you guys too.

"And if anyone is wondering, no, it wasn't a problem getting air reservations on the spur of the moment. And thanks Sheri for calling and suggesting that I try to arrange the flight. I was able to book everyone's ticket to get us all here! Now we can spend the rest of the evening relaxed and well rested for your meeting tomorrow, Sinbad, instead of worrying about running through airports and being on the road on the same day of the meeting."

"I agree with you, Katie," David said. "It's better that we get to rest the night before the meeting. We wouldn't miss the Colorado trip for the world. That's why I made arrangements with my job to be here."

David turned to Sinbad and said, "Well, Sinbad, not to take away from what you're going to say tomorrow, but how many days will we be away?"

"We'll plan to be away for eight days between the time we leave Chicago on Tuesday, arrive in the Denver area, and return here to Chicago on the following Tuesday after an overnight stay in Chappell. But I'll give you the details tomorrow. I hope that answers your question, David."

"You did," David replied.

Sinbad continued, "And let me say it's so nice seeing you all. We just love our New Jersey connection. And, Katie, it's good to see you and Wynn from the Big Apple too.

"By the way, where are Wynn and Jeanie?" Sinbad added.

Sandra, who was standing close by, pointed to where the youngsters had separated themselves from the rest of the group.

"There they go over there," she said. "They just can't keep themselves away from one another."

Sinbad said, "Okay then. Leave 'em alone. They're having fun!

"Listen, you all. I know you're glad to see our friends from New York and New Jersey," Sinbad added loudly. "So, let's just continue to enjoy the day. We have a lot of serious things to go over tomorrow concerning our trip to Colorado.

"You know, everybody, we're having fun being together again, but today we need to remember Freddie as each of us continue to mourn our loss. I just want you to remember the fun we had in Florida. I expect our trip to Colorado will be twice as good. Just prepare to have a fun time out there. But I'm sure Freddie will be in the back of our minds while we're on this vacation."

During this period of togetherness after Freddie's final service, Maggie approached her college friend Katie and said, "Hey, girl, we need to sit together and catch up on some things a little later."

Katie replied, "Hey, we can do a little of that right now."

"Okay! I can go for that!"

While Maggie and Katie caught up on their time apart, other pairings were formed, including Sandra and Sheri, who had begun to reminisce about the time they spent together in Florida. Sandra stepped away from the group for a little while but soon returned.

Sinbad yelled across the room, "Hey, Maggie, this Florida delegation really appreciates your hospitality, and I'm talking about you guys from the Chicago-Detroit area as well as the New York City area."

Maggie responded, "Oh, come on, Sinbad; you're the one who's providing all the accommodations. We should be thanking *you*. And, besides, you're spearheading this trip to Colorado that we all are gonna take. For heaven's sake, you're the reason we're all together."

"Okay, Maggie," Sinbad responded. "The important thing is that we've all come together. And I'm especially thankful to the New Jersey group, Sheri, David, and Jeanie. You all surprised everybody by being here today. I know it took some effort to adjust your plans on such short notice. And I guess we need to thank Katie for that.

"And one more thing," Sinbad continued, "is everyone good with having that time free when we are ready to take the trip? In other words, hopefully you've been able to get away from your responsibilities at home."

Katie answered, "I was in the process of arranging to have free time for the Colorado trip long before we left New York City.

All of you know I'm a substitute teacher in our public schools in Staten Island, and I only need to let the administration know of my intentions.

"And you also know I'm a real estate agent, so I can pretty much work whenever I want. With these two jobs, it's just a beautiful situation to be in as far as getting time off.

"And as far as Wynn is concerned, he has already arranged his schedule for the trip."

Sinbad responded, "What you've said is great, Katie! I'm sure the rest of you have been making arrangements to have that free time too. Sheri, what about you all?" Sinbad asked.

"Don't worry about us. We'll be ready," Sheri replied. "As a matter of fact, when we return home, I'll be in communication with Katie about making plane reservations to come back here. And while we're at it, we'll book a return flight to New York so we won't have to drive back once we return to Chicago from Denver."

"Well, that was smart, Katie," Sinbad replied.

Sheri said, "And don't forget, David arranged things so we could get away at that time. I know we'll call the trip to Colorado a vacation, but David didn't mention that to his supervisors. That *is* right, David, isn't it?" Sheri asked.

"You got that right, Sheri!" David responded enthusiastically.

"Well, okay," Sinbad responded. "I see all of you have been making plans already for the trip; that's good!"

Gates entered the discussion. "So, David, like everyone else, I'm glad you're here. It's great the way things worked out so that you've been given clearance to be away from your job. You know at first you had a question as to whether you could have gotten off work to attend the meeting here tomorrow. But somehow you did it! Now that's what I call the 'Wonders of the Spirit!'"

"Well, I don't know about this 'Wonders of the Spirit' thing you keep talking about, Gates, but I do appreciate not having to go in tomorrow," David said. "As far as time off for the Colorado trip, I'll be on vacation then like Sheri said. I'm good to go!"

Gates replied, "Okay, David. I always look forward to talking with you, my friend. You're always direct and sincere when you speak and I like that."

David just stared at everyone after that remark.

Then Gates said, "Well, everybody, we still have a few hours where we can get into some interesting discussions here in the hotel lobby.

"Maggie and Fred went back to their suite but said they would return shortly. Sandra left too, but I see her coming back now. Anyway, when we finish down here in the lobby, we all can retire for the night, and get the rest we all will need for tomorrow."

When Sandra returned to the lobby after briefly going away from the group, Gates turned his attention to her. "I've noticed you over there, Sandra," he said, "and it's always nice seeing you. We haven't seen you in a while."

Sandra replied, "That's right, Gates. I had to step out for a moment, but I'm back now. And it's also good seeing you, and you too, Courtney. You know, I was telling Maggie that I've spent much of the last week across the river in Winsor at the casino. You know I'm enjoying the casino more and more these days. I guess it's a way for me to unwind, to get away, and to clear my mind.

"But anyway, I'm so glad I made it to Freddie's funeral. I was fortunate that Maggie had some room beside her where she was sitting, and I ended up beside her and next to Fred."

Fred said, "Yeah, Sandra, it was good you were in time for the service. I know you two had become close friends ever since he helped you from the stage that night at the event you invited us to.

"But, listen, I know Mag especially was concerned about you because she hadn't heard from you lately."

Maggie added, "Fred's right, Sandra. I was just hoping that you were told about Freddie's death.

"Like I said before, Maggie, Bernie called me and gave me the news, and I was devastated."

To brighten up the discussion a bit, Courtney said, "Now that everything is over, Freddie's service, I mean, it's good you're enjoying yourself, Sandra."

Gates said, "Yeah, I agree with Courtney. There's nothing wrong with going to the casino if that's what you enjoy. I know some of my colleagues in the ministry frown on someone going to a place like that, especially if you're professing to be a Christian. As a matter of fact, I've heard that going to the casino to gamble is just plain wrong, sinful, I mean. Some believe that it's just a part of the devil's work. But if you ask me, I think that judging someone for doing this or that without knowing their intentions, that's really the sin in my opinion.

"But, Sandra, just keep doing what you feel is right in your heart. That's the most important thing because that's where God's spirit is, the Holy Spirit, I mean. And don't worry. Whatever you might be doing that's not pleasing to God, you'll be convicted of it by that Holy Spirit."

Sandra replied, "Thanks, Gates, for that encouragement, and you too, Courtney.

"Well, I think I'll go to my suite and get some rest. Goodnight, everybody!" Sandra said to those assembled.

Gates said, "Well, Courtney and I are heading back to the room too."

Most of the others who were present followed the Manleys' lead and retired for the evening as well.

CHAPTER 10
More Discussions

Foundation Scripture: 1 Corinthians 12: 4,5,6

4 There are diversities of gifts, but the same spirit. 5 There are differences in ministries, but the same Lord. 6 And there are diversities of activities, but it is the same God who works all in all.

Sandra was the first one to enter the dining area the next morning. Gates arrived moments later.

"Good morning, Sandra. I see you're an early riser like me."

"Good morning to you, Gates. Yeah, I've always liked getting up early and starting my day. It's so refreshing at this time in the morning. To see the rising sun in the eastern sky and to hear the birds chirping away is just a relaxing experience to me. Anyway, I suppose you left Courtney in bed."

"Yeah, she's a real sleepyhead," Gates replied. "I agree with you about mornings. You know, I've heard when you witness nature it's like experiencing God firsthand. That is to say you're experiencing His creation."

"I guess that's why it's so tranquil because God is the essence of peace and tranquility. In my estimation, this is what brings you joy in the spirit. At least it does for me."

Just after Sandra made that last statement, they saw David enter the dining hall.

"Well, well, look who's here to join us, Sandra. It's David," Gates said.

As David approached them, he focused his attention on Sandra.

"I think I heard you say joy in the spirit, Sandra. It kinda sounds like what *you* talk about a lot, Gates, this 'Wonders of the Spirit' thing. I see some of that has rubbed off on my girl Sandra here."

Before Sandra had a chance to respond, Gates said, "Let me correct you, David. The spirit is *not* a thing; it's the third person in the Godhead."

"Well, excuse me, bro! No worries!"

"No, David! You shouldn't have any worries at all—if you're in the spirit!"

Not knowing exactly what to say after that, David simply stared into space.

David's response prompted Sandra to say, "There's nothing like a dope to liven things up!" Before David could respond, Sandra added with a smile, "Oh, just kidding, David."

While obviously embarrassed by Gate's and Sandra's attitude towards him, David said, "And you, Sandra, I assume you're doing okay."

"Yeah, David, I'm doing fine," she said firmly while retaining that smile.

Gates attempted to lighten up on the fun he and Sandra both were having with David, saying, "You know, David, we're just having fun around here. And I wasn't kidding yesterday when I said it's good to have you, Sheri, and Jeanie with us. You all really add spice to the group. Don't you think they do, Sandra?"

"Yeah, Sheri and Jeanie are really nice."

"Hey, Sandra, did you forget someone?" David asked, noting that she obviously omitted his name.

She said as she continued to smile, "You're okay too, David."

Turning away from David for a moment, Gates asked, "Hey, Sandra, we're all glad you were able to make Freddie's service. I understand you've been hiding over the last several days; at least Maggie thought so. I heard that you've been spending quite a bit of time over in Windsor at the casino."

"I have, Gates," Sandra replied. "It gives me a chance to unwind. It's not that I do a lot of gambling, but I really love the food and the shows. It's really entertaining."

David said, "Hey, Sandra, the difference between me and you is that I do like to gamble. I get a thrill from the prospects of winning. As they say, you can't win if you don't play. Wouldn't you agree, Gates? You've been around gambling in your past; you've told me so."

Gates replied, "Well, that's true, David. I was part owner of a casino back in Vegas. And you *do* have to play to win. The only thing is, though, that winning is not everything. In fact, it's only a mirage! That is to say when you win you only *think* you have something of value, and I'm talking about the money. But that's not the *most* valuable thing. That's why the scriptures talk about the deceitfulness of riches."

"There you go again, Gates, talking about what's in the scriptures," David replied.

Then Gates retorted, "Well, that's true, David. The best thing in the world is something *you can't buy* and can't see for that matter, and that's the Spirit of the living God. I mean, what the Lord gives you is free of charge. You only need to accept it. And let me tell you, it is good—better than money! Just look at Sandra—at how she's enjoying herself at the casino. And you haven't won a cent over there. Is that right, Sandra?"

"That is correct, Gates!" Sandra responded.

Gates continued, "Anyway, David, I understand that you love Las Vegas. And I recall you said that some churchgoers are not as genuine as they pretend to be, participating in activities like they have in Vegas."

David defended his statement by saying, "That's right, Gates! I said it! And I'm not taking it back. I think the Man above also wants you to be *honest* about your likes and dislikes."

Sheri, who had entered shortly after David, stood there listening to the conversation between Gates and David and could do nothing but laugh at the whole thing.

Sandra responded, "Well, Gates, you've never been shy about expressing your opinion. And, David, you grew up in New York City like me. At least I spent a good part of my young adult life there, so I know what you're saying about loving the things that are in the city—at least in Las Vegas. I've just moved beyond all that, so I know what Gates is talking about too."

Sandra continued, "Gates, you're unique as a minister because you've got a history of being around gambling. Now, most preachers I know *do* frown on going to the casino. But you know, Erin taught me a lot when I was first in Bermuda, and one of the things I learned was that God wants us to enjoy our life, and a large part of my life now is going to the casino over in Winsor across the river from Detroit."

Gates said, "I'm fine with that, Sandra, you going to the casino, I mean. I don't condemn you for that."

"Thanks, Gates. I appreciate you saying that," Sandra replied. "I know there's a casino right here next to the hotel, but it's not as large and as nice as the one in Winsor. And by the way there's less chance of me seeing someone I know over there. I mean, while everybody knows that Winsor is right across the river from downtown Detroit, I think a lot of people in this city are content with going to the casino near here where the hotel is, which is okay by me! Besides, the casino over in Windsor is not hard to get to; it's only a nice ten to fifteen-minute ferry ride away.

"And you know, Gates, the one time I *did* go to the casino near the hotel here, I saw one of the members of Faith Methodist where I work. And at that time, it seemed as though they were ashamed that I saw them, and who knows, they may have been just as surprised to see me there."

Sandra asked Gates a probing question. "Gates, let me ask you something since you're a minister. Why do a lot of Christians think there's a limit to where you can go and what activities you can participate in? In my opinion, some people try to put a limit on what you can enjoy because of their faith. I kinda agree with David on that point. I mean, there are a lot of things we as Christians can enjoy and still have a strong relationship with the Lord. Don't you think so, Gates?"

Gates answered, "Well, Sandra, some people are still tied to that fleshly lifestyle they may have had before they were converted, and now they feel guilty about participating in some of those things. Now, don't get me wrong; there are some things we should never go back to—at least pray to God that we never go back. But so often we as believers needlessly limit ourselves as to what we can enjoy when even the scripture says that all things were placed on the earth for our enjoyment.

"Amen to that!" David blurted out.

Gates responded, "I knew you'd say something like that, David. Anyway, Sandra, we just have to pray that we make the right decision in whatever we're doing and be led *by* the spirit, that is, by the Holy Spirit that's inside every believer."

"Even in someone like David?" Sandra said with a smile, looking at him.

Gates responded simply, "Yes, even someone like David!" Gates added, "No offense, David. Everything is good!"

David didn't know how to respond to that comment, so he continued looking into space.

"Courtney, what do you think about what we've been talking about? And while you digest that question, let me run to the restroom." Gates then excused himself.

At her husband's request, Courtney entered the discussion while Gates was away. She said, "Gates is right, Sandra. And you know that God is forgiving, so that if you happen to do something you think is wrong, just ask for forgiveness, and He will forgive you. Just accept His forgiveness and move on."

She added to David, "You know, David, that a lot of what Gates says is said in fun. Now, don't you be offended."

"Like Gates said, Courtney, everything is good!" David replied.

With Maggie and Sheri standing right there in their midst, Sandra said, "David, you know we're all about having fun. And I want to thank you, Courtney. You two have really made my spirit happy."

Then Sheri said, "Did you hear what Sandra said, David. You'd better listen!"

David said tersely, "No, Sheri. I don't have to listen, and I like Sandra. Let me go away for a smoke."

In response, Sheri shrugged her shoulders and said to Courtney and the others standing there, "Well, that's David for you."

As Gates had moments earlier, David excused himself from the group. David was not a spiritual person and had a lot of questions about all the religious talk going on. As he came near a window, he saw that it was open a little. In his mind, it was enough to let some of the smoke out of the area. He was conscious about the environment and didn't want others to be affected by the smoke.

With his legs crossed and torso leaning against the wall near that window, David began to smoke his cigarette while looking out the window. When he finished, he saw Gates, who was returning to the group from the restroom, and called him over as he approached.

"Hey, Gates, you got a minute?" he asked.

"Sure, David. What's on your mind?" Gates responded.

Then, in a lower tone of voice, almost in a whisper, David said, "Now, just between you and me—man to man—you *really* don't believe in a lot of that religion stuff that you were talking about earlier, do you?"

"Yeah, I do. I *really do* believe what I'm preaching about, David, because it comes from the heart. And God knows if we're real or not. And I know that expression 'from the heart' is not popular where I grew up. I mean, I grew on the rough side of town like you. And people know whether you're jiving or not. And let me...."

"Okay, man, you've made your point," David said realizing Gates was speaking in a way he could identify with because of his *own* background. Before Gates had a chance to finish, David tried to get him to answer the question posed more directly.

"Let me put it this way, Gates. I mean, having spirits inside of you and people not having any limits to what they can do to enjoy themselves? You really believe all that?" David asked.

"Well," Gates again tried to answer him with no success.

David attempted to make his own point by interrupting Gates again. "You know, Gates, in what little I know about the church and the Bible they teach from, I've always heard that you should follow the straight and narrow path, being strict in everything you do. You know what I mean? And I've heard some of you guys say that you don't have any limits to what you can do to enjoy yourself.

"You know when I was coming up, my mother used to be into this church thing. And, believe me, when I did anything wrong, she used to whip the living daylights out of me! Now, that woman really wanted me to stay on the straight and narrow, to follow the strict rules in the Bible, I suppose."

Gates finally got a word in and said, "Well, David, I hear what you're saying. Now can I ask you a question?"

"Sure, go ahead, man!" David answered with emphasis.

Gates did not answer David's question directly. He said, "I once had some of the same ideas as you have about that 'religious stuff' as you put it. But to answer your question, sure, there are guidelines that every believer should follow. But those guidelines are for our benefit, not to restrict us from having a good time.

"Remember, David, at one time I didn't even believe in a God. I was an atheist. But over time I learned some things I used to believe are just not true. Actually, there's only one thing I learned that *is* true, and that's Jesus, because not only was He a historical figure that actually lived and walked among the people of His day, He's also alive right now! I learned that not only is Jesus real and represents the truth, He *is* Truth. And…."

David cut Gates off once more, saying, "Yeah, Yeah, I knew Jesus' name would come up. You guys talk about Jesus all the time. Well, I just don't have that same feeling as others in the group do, and sometimes it shows in my actions and especially the way I say things.

"Gates, you've heard how Sheri complains about my language sometimes. She thinks I shouldn't use those 'bad words' as she calls them. But I'm just being me. You know what I'm saying? Now go ahead and finish your thought."

Gates said, "Well, David, it's not about your feelings as much as it is about what you say and do, but I know what you're saying. Remember, I've been where you are, not having any feelings about spiritual things. But what I've learned since I've been converted to the faith is that God is not so much concerned about our feelings as He is about how we respond to what He's asking us to do. And I know from observing your actions in the past that you have responded to help others in some way.

"And by the way, speaking of helping others, since we're having this discussion about Jesus, well, He helped all of us by giving of Himself on that cross."

"Okay, okay! You don't have to give me a Bible lesson," David replied. "Anyway, you said a lot there, minister, and I don't know what to say after all that."

Gates said, "Well, you really don't have to say anything, David. But you're telling me we talk about Jesus all the time. Well, the reason is that—and this is what I was gonna say before you cut me off—that Jesus *is* the end of the story. That's all I wanted to say. I mean, Jesus is it. He's the beginning and the end!"

Gates tried another approach in communicating with David about spiritual things, becoming analytical. He said, "Let me ask you a question, David."

As before, David interrupted him. "Yeah, go ahead with your question; I may learn something."

After that sarcastic remark, Gates asked, "Okay, David, tell me this: Can you preach—like a minister in a pulpit?"

David responded with disdain, "No! Hell, no! Not in a million years!"

Gates replied, "Well then, that's your spirit guiding you to say that. Your spirit knows that you do not have that talent."

David replied, "You're right, Gates. I don't have that kind of spirit and never will."

"Well, David, that's where you're wrong. Let me put it to you this way. When the air is calm, you never know when it's going to start swirling around, when the wind will start to blow. You know as well as I do that it will at some point. I mean, at some point the weather *will* change.

"Well, that's the way the spirit is. Since the spirit can't be seen, you don't know when it's going to hit you; it just does. At least that's what happened to me. And when it does, you'll know, just like I did.

"Anyway, David, don't worry about it. When the time is right, and the spirit hits you, you will know it. That's another 'Wonder of the Spirit.'"

David replied sarcastically, "Well, okay. You've said a mouthful. I will accept that if you say so."

Gates continued, "So do you see, David? You do have a spirit that is already inside of you! That's what led you to agree with me!"

Then David said, "Oh, come on, Gates. It can't be that simple. As simple as me agreeing with something like that."

Gates replied, "But it is that simple, David. Believe it or not!"

Gates went on, "David, you have to be drawn to God in some way, and He's using me to do that for you. Listen, the same thing happened to me. I was drawn to Him, and in my case it was my wife Courtney that did it.

"Courtney went with our friend Fred to this church in Hawaii, and after that experience she told me she was never the same again. And you know what? She transmitted all the positive spirit she had from that experience to me. That's how the spirit works—again what I call 'Wonders of the Spirit!'"

Gates added, "Listen, David, let me tell you this one last thing, and this was before I thought I had enough sense not to believe in God. I was a little boy, maybe no more than seven or eight years old. Well, during that time I had a problem in school. Never was a good learner back in those early years in elementary school. But to make a long story short, I found out what the problem was. I couldn't see; I mean, my vision was much less than 20/20.

"I sat in the back of most classrooms and couldn't see what the teacher was writing on the board. Well, that didn't help my self-image. But my mother ended up getting me eyeglasses, and a whole new world opened up for me. I could see! I started doing better in school and eventually went to college and did well after that, including becoming an owner of a hotel chain not to mention becoming a minister.

"My mother always said I would make something of myself. And you know what, David? I believed that. And because of the belief I had and because of my mother's faith in me, I became what she said I would be. I *did* go astray by becoming an atheist, but thanks to

Courtney I got back on the right track, and after that I continued to believe. I became a believer in these *spirits* you refer to them as.

"Now the same is true for you, David; at some point you will believe as I do, that God is real and you can have a relationship with Him. So don't worry about all the details. Just continue living and doing what you think you should do, and everything eventually will come to light. And in your case, it's Sheri that will likely lead you to the Truth.

"And remember this, we're all different as believers. I mean, we have different personalities, temperaments, persuasions, likes and dislikes, and I can go on and on. We have diverse gifts, but it's the same Spirit that gives us those gifts. And it's the same God we all believe in, who is sovereign over all of us, and He makes no distinctions except when we either obey or disobey Him. He's one Lord of us all. But He gives us free will to do and to act as we wish. It's up to us to follow His lead. So welcome to the club, David! Now, let's go!"

David replied, "That's some heavy stuff you're talking about, Gates. And, yeah, Sheri can get to be very spiritual sometimes, and maybe she can enlighten me on some of what you're saying. But, okay, I'm ready to go!"

Gates replied, "Okay, David, we're leaving. And hopefully your spiritual side will be strengthened because of Sheri. Like I said, and like you said you would do, just talk to her about some of these things sometimes. I'm sure she can shed some light on what I'm talking about so you might understand better."

David said, "You're a pretty interesting dude, you know, Preacher Gates! But we've delayed our leaving long enough. I guess now is a good point for us to stop this discussion, and I've long ago finished my smoke."

"I agree with you, David. We need to head back to the group," Gates said.

Gates and David walked over to where Courtney was. When they arrived, Sheri, Katie, and Maggie were standing together with her. Wynn and Jeanie were away from the group talking by themselves as usual.

David asked, "It's about time to for us to leave, Sheri; wouldn't you say?"

Sheri replied, "Well, you're right, David." Then she yelled out to get the attention of her daughter, who was standing with Wynn away from the group over in a corner of the room.

"Hey, Jeanie, we're ready to leave."

As Jeanie walked with Wynn and got closer to the group, Sheri said, "David's returned from having a smoke, and we need to be going."

Katie said to her son, "Hey, Wynn, it's time for us to leave too. We need to be rested for our meeting with Sinbad tomorrow."

"Oh, my!" Wynn commented.

CHAPTER 11
Sinbad Speaks

Foundation Scripture: John 10:4

And when he brings out his own sheep, he goes before them, and the sheep follow him. For they know his name.

On Monday morning, everyone gathered at 10:00 in the hotel lobby as was planned and prepared to have brunch. They were ready to eat and to hear Sinbad talk about their trip to Colorado. Before breakfast, everyone chatted with one another. Once the 11:00 hour came, they claimed their seats in the dining area, and soon everyone was served and enjoyed the food.

As the noon hour approached, members of the group anxiously awaited hearing what Sinbad had to tell them regarding their trip to Colorado. Sandra sat next to Maggie and had a brief conversation with her just before Sinbad's talk.

"You know, Maggie, I was told of Freddie's death by Bernie, who had given me a call at the request of Sinbad. When Bernie gave me the news, I just cried and cried all night long."

Maggie replied, "Well, you know now, Sandra, that you're among friends, and despite the sadness over the past few days, we're going to try to be more upbeat now that Freddie's service is over."

"Yeah, Maggie, I'll try to put it behind me, but I was a mess all during that service. I had come to like Freddie very much. He was so much a gentleman when he assisted me back to the table where you and Fred were after I gave my little talk that night. Of course, when we returned, you were still away from the table."

As Sandra discussed her time with Freddie, tears brimmed in her eyes. She got some tissue from her purse and then continued, "You know, Maggie, remembering Freddie on that night has me even more distraught over his passing. By the time of the service, I thought I had gotten control of my emotions.

"Maggie, we all supported each other yesterday at that service, and I think we all came together and got through it okay. That's what I love about our group; we're here for each other. And now I'm really looking forward to what Sinbad has to say about our trip to Colorado."

While Sandra was telling her close friend the emotions she had about the demise of Freddie, Maggie had her own thoughts about the times she had been with him on those weekends when she was supposed to be with her parents in Flint.

As noon approached, everyone finished eating and got ready to hear what Sinbad had to say. He arose from his seat and went to the podium to address the group about the specifics of going to Colorado.

"I'll be brief in my remarks, everybody. I just want to tell you again how much I appreciate you being here," Sinbad began. "Now about the trip, first of all, two vans will be rented to transport everyone from Detroit to Denver. Let me correct myself. Actually, we will be leaving together from Chicago. And I'll let Maggie tell you about the process of our getting the vans for the trip. Maggie, could you address the group about that?"

"Sure, Sinbad," Maggie answered. Then she stood and continued, "Let me first say that I've already talked to Sandra about this. She can leave Detroit the day before we all take off and get one of the rental vans we'll be using from Chicago. Fred will get the other.

"We all will be leaving from the Windy City. Fred and Sandra will get the rental vans sometime in the afternoon and bring them to our house so they'll be there the next morning. The vehicles will stay there overnight, and we all will be ready to leave first thing the next morning. And, Sandra, you can stay at our house overnight."

Sandra said, "That sounds good, Maggie. That means I won't have to drive all the way from Detroit to Chicago early that morning before we leave like I had first planned. Yeah, Maggie, that's a good idea to have me drive down the day before and help Fred pick up the vans as you said. It sounds like a plan to me. And by the way, when I do stay overnight at your house, I can sleep on the couch or just about anywhere."

Maggie replied, "Aw, girl! You don't have to sleep on no couch. You can stay in the extra bedroom we have. Anyway, I'll give it back to you, Sinbad."

"Okay, thanks for that information, Maggie. The morning of our leaving to go out west, we can leave the hotel where we're staying and come to your house. Then we all can start our trip out west from your place."

"But let me tell you, it's going to be cold, real cold, with a lot of snow too when we get to Colorado. So be sure to bring enough warm clothing.

"Now, let me give you a rundown on the timeline we'll be on, including our travel time out there and our return trip here. The whole trip is supposed to be for eight days and nights. We'll be leaving on a Tuesday very early in the morning; I'd say by 5:00 a.m. This means that we won't arrive in Denver until about 11:00 at night because of the 17 to 18-hour drive.

"Now the ideal time to arrive would be around 7:00 or 8:00, so to do that we'll need to make an overnight stop along the way, probably when we get to the end of our first main drag going west on Interstate 80 in western Iowa. Then we can get up Wednesday morning to complete the drive.

"After arriving in Denver in the early evening on Wednesday, we'll get a good night's rest at the hotel already reserved by Maggie and spend all day Thursday and through the weekend in Colorado before leaving on Monday morning. At that time, we'll start on our way back to Chicago and on Monday stay overnight at the same place where we lodged on the way to Colorado. From there, we'll finish the trip the next day on Tuesday.

"By leaving early Tuesday, we should be back in the Chicago area sometime later that day. That would include a stopover at a restaurant called Mickey's Diner, the first stop we anticipate making on the way out to Colorado. Maggie has done the research on a nice place to eat, and from what she's told me up to this point, this place might be the venue to patronize.

"Now that might seem to be quite a bit of time on the road, but think of it this way. We'll be together, and like I just said we'll stop occasionally, and at some of those times we may change drivers. It also will give you an opportunity to see the great Midwest from the highway. So, you're looking at two full days on the road going out to Colorado and the same coming back.

"But let me tell you, this time on the road will be well worth it once we get there; I promise you that!"

Sinbad continued, "Now all of you will have the time of your life out there in Colorado. You have been given all the particulars regarding preparation for the trip. And Lord knows we need it—not only to help celebrate the marriage of Erin and Bernie but also to get us over this time of sadness after the passing of my cousin Freddie. We will really miss him not being with us.

"Well, he'll be with us, in spirit. Like Gates says often, it's one of the 'Wonders of the Spirit' that our departed loved ones are still alive based on scripture, so let's try to get over this sadness."

You have in your possession packets that give an outline of everything I just mentioned, so refer to it often over the next three weeks. And if you're wondering, yes, when we get back down there in Florida after our time here now, we'll fly right back here to Detroit, or I should say Chicago; I guess that'll be more practical.

"As I think more about it, our flight definitely will be to O'Hare down there in Chicago. And after we return, we'll be with you for the duration of the trip as we make the drive out to Colorado. Some of you might say I'm insane for doing it, being on the road for that long of a period. But you only live once—at least in this physical life—so we need to take every opportunity to enjoy ourselves, to live life in abundance as Jesus admonished us to do."

"Hey, Sinbad. You've got a bunch of religious folks going on this trip," Gates said to him in response to his last statement. "And I hate to tell you, we really don't believe you live just one time in this life! We believe in a future life, a future existence beyond this present life we now have."

Courtney corrected him, "No, honey, we're not a bunch of religious folks; we're all actually quite spiritual who love the Lord. Besides, the scriptures do say that we live once in this physical life."

"Okay, Courtney. I stand corrected," Gates replied. "Sorry about that, Sinbad!" he added.

"Apology accepted," Sinbad answered. "Okay, you two, can I continue, please?" Sinbad said, partly in jest.

"You know, Gates, I appreciate you as a minister, but that was a good point your wife made. You continue to listen to that woman," Sinbad said with a smile.

"Okay, everybody, let me get back to what I was saying. We're gonna have a great time out in Colorado. And by the way, Erin and Bernie will be flying out to Denver a day early and will meet us when we get there. They'll be there at least a day before we arrive. Remember, our departure from Chicago is exactly one month from today.

"I want to make one last point. We'll have more time for discussion later this evening. I just have to go to my room and put on something that's more comfortable.

"Now, we'll be leaving the hotel tomorrow early in the morning at 7:00 to be at the airport in time for our flight back to Florida. But, remember, we'll be back in four weeks, so we'll have that much time to prepare for the trip. And we hope to see all of you again then.

"Well, that's all I have to say. Let's go out into the lobby and chat a little bit more."

With those words Sinbad ended his speech. Soon everyone departed the dining area and returned to the lobby.

The Florida group led by Sinbad, who had his friend Casey and two other cousins from south Florida with him, shared their last conversations with their relatives from the Detroit area who had helped in coordinating Freddie's service.

Sinbad and all the others soon returned to their rooms to get more rest and continue preparing to leave the next morning. Everyone would be on their own for dinner, and then later in the evening they would make final preparations for departure from the Motor City.

As other members of the group left the hotel lobby, Gates, Courtney, and Sinbad remained there to talk. Katie was with them too; Wynn had returned to the suite where he and his mother were staying.

Eventually everyone retired for the evening. After a night of rest, they went back home to start preparing for their much-anticipated trip to Colorado.

PART II: THE TRIP

CHAPTER 12
Onward Towards Colorado

Foundation Scripture: 2 Corinthians 5:7

For we walk by faith, not by sight.

The day before the big trip was a hectic one for almost everyone. Sinbad, his friend Casey, and his two cousins who lived in south Florida flew into O'Hare at midday. Upon his arrival, Sinbad immediately called Maggie.

"Maggie, how are you all doing? We just touched down and now are in the process of retrieving our luggage. You don't have to worry about us because the suites we reserved at the hotel are ready."

"I'm fine, Sinbad. Glad you all made it here safely. And it's good that your rooms are ready," Maggie replied. "We've been preparing for the trip on this end and are ready to go."

"That's good to hear," Sinbad said.

Maggie continued, "Sandra will be down from Detroit later this afternoon to meet Fred at the rental place, and they will pick up the two vans we'll be taking.

"And something else, Sinbad. Speaking of Sandra, we went over the details of the trip going from here to Colorado earlier in the week. And the groups from New York and New Jersey will be arriving later this afternoon, so everything has been going well as far as planning for the trip."

"That's good," Sinbad replied.

Maggie continued, "Like with all of you coming up from Florida, the group flying in from New York will be staying at the Wingo Hotel.

"Sinbad, I know you said you all could come to my house early in the morning and then leave for Colorado from here. But I've been thinking. Why don't all of us here at my house just come by and pick you up at the hotel? We can pick up the others who will fly in from New York too, since they are staying at the same hotel. Remember, we'll have the vans here. This way, you won't have to get up as early and drive all the way out here to our house in the suburbs. We can just bring the vans into downtown and pick you up from where you are staying and leave for Colorado from there.

"Remember, you'll be doing much of the driving at least at the beginning, and I think it's best that you be as fresh as possible. That means a lot of sleep, Sinbad!" she emphasized in a humorous and somewhat facetious manner.

"That's a great point, Maggie. I can drive for hours when I'm well rested. So, yeah, you all go ahead and get ready, and we'll be waiting for you when you get here, maybe around 4:30. Just give me a call to let me know when you arrive. This way we all can still start out on our trip westward by 5:00 as originally planned."

Maggie said, "Okay. Sounds like a plan. Meanwhile I'll let the group who will be flying in from New York know that we'll pick them up from the hotel too. I'll take care of that."

"Well, that's great, Maggie. I knew you would have everything covered up here," Sinbad replied. "As I told you earlier, and as you just acknowledged, Casey is with me along with my two cousins, Alphonso and Carlos.

"And you know I talked with Bernie and Erin yesterday; they're so excited about being married, and their honeymoon over to the

Island of Love went well. By the way, they'll be waiting for us when we get to Colorado.

"Anyway, I'm going to get off this phone and let you prepare for the people flying in from New York later today. And as soon as we get situated this evening, we're going to have dinner, probably at the hotel restaurant, and then go to bed in preparation for that long drive ahead of us."

"Okay, Sinbad, but remember, the group coming in from New York will be staying at the same hotel as you all, so we don't really have to plan for anything because we'll pick them up at the hotel too," Maggie replied, referring to Katie and clan flying in from the Big Apple.

"Okay, Sinbad. We'll see all of you there in the morning, I guess, in the hotel lobby. I'll give you your driving assignments when we arrive."

Before the phone conversation ended, Maggie added, "One more thing, Sinbad. I almost forgot. For your information, once we're on the road, we can stop some place after about an hour or so to have some breakfast. Then it'll be hopefully smooth sailing for the next several hours from that point. Of course, we can always stop a few minutes to refresh ourselves on occasion. But mainly we can just enjoy the ride."

Sinbad replied, "Sounds good to me, Maggie. And by the way, speaking of details. I mean, you're one detailed woman! You hear me? If you remember you mentioned one restaurant you're favorable towards as far as our first stop, a place called Mickey's Diner. But I know you're researching other possibilities too.

"I mean, you've even given details about people's seating arrangements for crying out loud. Usually when I travel with several people and I'm the driver, I just let everyone sit wherever they wish."

In a more serious tone, Sinbad said, "Anyway, I can give you the details of our stay in Colorado while we travel. It'll just be a schedule of activities over the days we're there, so don't worry; you won't have to digest everything before we leave. We'll have enough time to look at it while we're traveling, maybe during rest stops. Anyway, I think it'll be so exciting."

"Yeah, Sinbad, I'm looking forward to it. And don't worry about our first stop. I'm sure wherever we decide to stop and dine will be good.

"I'll be looking forward to seeing your friend Casey again too. And let me say this, it's so good to have Casey still with us. I mean, we almost lost him back in Florida when some of our people saved him from drowning. What am I saying? That was only in my dream, wasn't it? Oh, well, 'God is still good all the time, and all the time God is good,' as they say. And we all are looking forward to meeting your cousins for the first time."

"Great, Maggie, but as far as Casey still being with us, you can thank your husband Fred as well as David especially for saving him. And oh my, Freddie was there too," Sinbad said with much emotion. "Look at me carrying on about what was just a dream. I mean, you told it so well Maggie, in so much detail, it was almost as if we all made that trip over to the island. Well, I shouldn't be surprised because everything you do, including planning for this trip, is in much detail."

"Thank you for the compliment," Maggie said.

Sinbad recognized the need to end the call. "Oh, well, let me get off this phone. I feel the tears starting to build already. I miss that cousin of mine so much and am sorry that Freddie won't be with us on this trip. We'll see all of you in the morning, Maggie."

"Bye, Sinbad, we'll see you then," Maggie replied.

After her conversation with Sinbad ended, Maggie went to stand at the front door, waiting for Sandra and Fred to arrive with the vans they would take on the trip. As they drove up, Maggie said to herself, "Oh my! I'm amazed at the size of these vehicles. They're so high up off the ground!"

Once the vans were safely parked in the driveway, Maggie walked over and said, "Hey, Sandra. I'm sure glad you agreed to come over this evening to help Fred get these vans. I just said to myself how huge they are."

"Hello, Maggie. Yeah, I'm glad you suggested that we do this the day before our trip. At least for me, I won't have to worry about driving so early tomorrow morning to get over here from Detroit. And, yeah, the vans are pretty large," Sandra said.

Fred, who was standing next to Sandra, said, "Yeah, Mag, these vehicles are gigantic. They should be more than large enough to carry everyone who's going and then some."

Maggie cautioned, "Well, honey, remember that we'll need room for luggage and snacks as well, so I'm sure we'll be able to utilize every square inch of both vehicles. Anyway, you all can leave the vans where they are and come inside. I want to show you the seating arrangements that I've figured out."

After Fred, Maggie, and Sandra went inside, they entered the kitchen where Maggie had everything laid out before them on a table. She said, "Come over here, you two, and I'll show you what I have. By the way, I made some sandwiches for us to munch on while we're going over this."

"That's great, Maggie, because I'm sure hungry right about now," Sandra said.

"Let me get some juice to go along with these turkey sandwiches," Maggie added.

As Fred and Sandra situated themselves at the table, Maggie returned with a large pitcher of grape juice. They ate while reviewing the seating arrangements. Maggie handed each of them a copy of the seating chart she had made and kept the original.

"Okay, first I want to say that Sinbad gave me the responsibility of doing all the prep for the trip, including getting the van rentals and researching a suitable eating venue on our trip. But this part was all my idea. And again, thank you guys for picking the vans up," Maggie said.

Maggie continued, "Now, Sandra, I told you a lot of these plans earlier in the week. And you know a lot about what we intend to do too, Fred. Now, if you look at these sheets, you'll see who'll be driving and where people will be sitting.

"Fred, since you told me that the two vans are identical, it was easy to work out the seating."

Maggie continued, "So here we go. And by the way, I'll explain the same thing to Sinbad and his group and to Katie, Wynn, Sheri, Jeanie, and David when we see them tomorrow morning."

Maggie remembered, "Oh, and I forgot to tell you. They're not coming here. Sinbad and I discussed it, and we'll be picking them up at the hotel."

After Maggie finished speaking, Sandra commented, "Already I see something interesting in these seating arrangements, Maggie." After a brief pause, she continued, "But I'll let you go over it first before I say anything more."

Maggie proceeded to review her handiwork. "Okay, Sandra, what you see here in these diagrams are the two vans. The one on the left Sinbad will be driving, and the one to the right, Fred, you'll be driving this van. And by the way, I know I said earlier that the vans are identical, but they're obviously different in color, and that's good because everybody can easily get into the van that they're supposed to be in."

Sandra responded, "Yeah, Maggie, the way it looks, Sinbad's van will be the blue one and Fred's van will be red. That's simple enough."

"You're right, Sandra," Maggie agreed. "Now let me say this, despite that distinction, it doesn't mean that no one else on the trip will be driving. We're all good drivers, and all of us can take turns behind the wheel. Even Wynn, who has just started driving, will be available. It's just that Sinbad and you, Fred, will be our first drivers out the gate."

For clarification about the diagrams, Maggie added, "Keep in mind that you're looking at the vans from their tops. You'll have to imagine that the roof has been pulled away from each vehicle so that the seating arrangements of the occupants can be clearly seen from above.

"So, starting with the van Sinbad will be driving, the blue one, Casey will be sitting beside him, and his two cousins will be located directly behind them. Sandra, you and Katie will be in that third seat behind the driver, and in the seat behind them will be Sheri and David. There are pairs of empty seats in the back just in front of the storage area reserved for luggage. All the luggage for the people riding in this van should fit into this area.

"Now, to the right of the van Sinbad will be driving is the redone, the one that you, Fred, will be driving. As you can see, I'll be sitting beside you, honey, in the passenger seat. Courtney and Gates are located behind us, and then Jeanie and Wynn are behind them. I wanted to put the young people in the same seat because I knew they would want to be together.

"Since there will be fewer people riding in the red van, there are two pairs of empty seats in the back. The first pair can be used for our snacks. If someone gets the urge for a little something to eat, it's right here.

"We can stop briefly along the road and get some snacks to tide us over until we get to a rest stop where a wider array of snacks may be available. Better still, if there's a restaurant along the way, we can get off at an exit, take a little more time, and have a complete meal.

"Anyway, I call this the snack seat, and it will be reserved for a few light food items. And my cell phone will always be on, so if anyone in the other vehicle wants some snacks we have, then Sinbad can call me. Well, he could actually call Fred directly on a phone that was installed in the vehicles for the drivers. And, of course, Fred can tell me if anyone in Sinbad's van, the one you'll be riding in, Sandra, wants any snacks. We've already talked about that.

"The last pair of seats will be empty. Like in the other van, this large area in the very back of the vehicle is where luggage will be stored."

SINBAD'S VAN

(blue van)

Sinbad (Driver).................Casey	
Alphonso...........................Carlos	
Sandra...................................Katie	
Sheri.....................................David	
seat	*seat*

STORAGE

FRED'S VAN

(red van)

Fred (Driver)..............Mag	
Courtney...................Gates	
Jeanie.........................Wynn	
seat (SNACKS) *seat*	
seat	*seat*

STORAGE

FIGURE 5: Van Seating Arrangement to Colorado

When Maggie finished describing the diagram, she asked, "Okay, Sandra, you seemed to have a question about the seating arrangements?"

"Yeah, Maggie. First of all, and I know it's not the most important thing, but the van I'll be in doesn't have an area for snacks? Now why is that? Are you trying to starve us?" she asked jokingly.

Maggie answered facetiously, "Yeah, we're trying to make you all sit in that van and be good and hungry! Just kidding, of course! You will have an area for snacks, it just won't be as large as the one in our vehicle because your van has more people in it. You can always load up on snacks for your vehicle whenever we stop for a rest."

Then Sandra finally got to what she really wanted to express her concerns about. "Okay then. But there's something else that might be even more important, and it involves me, Maggie."

"Okay, Sandra, what might that be?" Maggie asked.

"Well, Maggie, I don't think it's a major issue, but I did notice that you have me in the same vehicle as that guy David, and you know some of our history," Sandra continued.

Before Sandra could finish, Maggie said, "Well, Sandra, if you have a big problem with that, we can always make a switch with someone in the other van."

"No. Let's just see how it'll work. I have two of Fred's books, and I'm sure I can spend much of my time reading, at least when I'm not talking with Katie, who is sitting beside me."

"Okay then. Just let me know if there's a problem," Maggie said.

* * *

Before bedtime that night, Maggie made one last call to her niece who ran the daycare; she wanted to make sure everything was okay before they took off. Her niece said everything was fine and that she would look after the business while Maggie was away.

Maggie went to sleep that night reassured that all would be well with the daycare while she was gone.

Everyone had a good night's sleep, arose early, and got themselves ready to leave.

Just before getting into one of the vans, Maggie asked Fred, "You sure you packed everything I placed on the bed in our room?"

"You know, Mag, there is a whole lot of stuff you're bringing that I hope you'll get to wear. But, yeah, I packed everything."

"Well, Fred, as long as I'm warm, that's the main thing. And I hope that you brought everything that you'll need," Maggie said.

Fred nodded his head, indicating that he did.

Sandra had already packed her things in the van she was assigned to for the trip and was set to drive the blue van to the hotel, so the three of them left the house and headed for the hotel. The scenery soon transitioned from suburban Central Heights to downtown.

Sinbad and the rest of the group waiting at the hotel had their belongings packed by 5:00 in the morning and were waiting when the vans arrived. Soon everyone was safely in their assigned vehicle. Fred, who was driving the lead van, motioned with his left arm out the window for Sinbad to follow him, so off they went, a caravan of two vehicles on their way to Colorado!

The two vans soon moved out of the downtown area and through the streets of west Chicago.

Maggie asked the occupants in her van, "Is everyone good in the back?"

Courtney said, "Maggie, we've been preparing all week for this day, and I'm sure Gates has loaded everything that we intended to bring, so, yes, we're all good."

Gates added, "Yeah, Courtney is right. I've gotten everything we need. By the way, Fred, the minute you get tired, just let me know, and I can take over."

After a while on the road, Maggie decided to make a personal call to Sandra, who was riding in the other van, to see how she was doing.

"Hello, Maggie. I'm doing well and I think everyone riding in this vehicle is fine too."

"That's great, Sandra," Maggie replied.

Before they finished their short conversation, Sandra said, "Maggie, I'm getting hungry! I'll be glad when we stop to eat."

"It will be a while, Sandra, before we have a meal, but we have plenty of snacks."

"Well, okay. I'll let you know if I want something," Sandra replied. With that, the conversation between the two ended.

Fred replied to Gates' earlier statement, saying, "It's going to be some time from now before I get tired, Gates. I feel pretty fresh. We'll see how I feel when we get to that first stop for breakfast. I may just let you take the wheel then. Thanks for offering me some relief though."

As Maggie continued looking ahead to the road in front of her, with a louder voice she asked the only other couple in the van, Jeanie and Wynn, how they were doing. When they did not answer, she decided to look behind her and saw they were sitting close to one another and deep in conversation about something.

Courtney, who noticed the same thing about the young couple, mumbled to her friend, "Don't worry about them; they're busy with each other, Maggie."

"I hear you, Courtney!" Maggie responded. She returned her attention to the road and quietly said to herself, "Oh, well. Anyway, look at this view; we're finally out of Chicago and into the rolling plains of the western part of the state."

Fred said, "Now that we're on the interstate, it should be smooth sailing going toward Des Moines. In about two hours, when we're almost there, we can stop to get that breakfast you were talking about, Mag. I overheard you talking to Sandra. My, that woman can eat! Anyway, you can call her again to let her know that we can stop for snacks at the next rest area if she needs something sooner. We have so many snacks in this van."

"Okay, Fred." Maggie proceeded to call Sandra to let her know of Fred's suggestion.

After Maggie's brief call, Fred said to his wife, "Don't worry about Jeanie and Wynn. Let's just leave those two love birds alone!"

"Oh, Fred, I had already forgotten about that." Maggie reassured him with emphasis.

Jeanie and Wynn overheard and responded to the adults'

comments with a giggle as they pointed their fingers at them in unison.

Maggie returned her attention to Fred and said, "I'm glad you brought breakfast up, Fred. When I called her on my cell, Sandra said she'll be glad when we stop and eat."

"Mag, I'm starting to get a little hungry myself! But like I said, we can stop and get some snacks if we have to."

"You know, Fred, riding tends to make people hungry. There's a very nice place just before we get to Des Moines, and it's probably the first decent place that we'll get to based on a list of places to eat shown on the map. Besides, I researched it before we left Chicago, and it has excellent food."

Gates, who was sitting directly behind Fred and Maggie, responded, "Good! I'm glad you have food in mind, you two. I talked with Sinbad earlier, and he said they were ready to eat *then*. So by now I'm sure they're really hungry."

Fred responded, "I spoke with Sinbad a little while ago, and he confirmed they're ready to eat. I let him know the approximate time we'll reach the diner Mag was talking about.

"I think you'll be satisfied with this place, Gates. It has a nice menu, and the prices are reasonable. I researched the place before we left Chicago," Maggie said. "Well, once we get there, get settled, and have some food in our stomachs, we'll be ready to hit the road again. From there, it'll be a straight shot down Interstate 80 until we get to a small place called Chappell on the other side of the state. Iowa is a large state. Now let me tell you, when we leave there, we'll need to exit onto a side road and travel south for another hour before we get to Interstate 70, which will lead us straight by a place called Manhattan, Kansas. And from there, it's still a good drive to Denver, but we should make it there before it gets too late."

Fred said, "You know, Mag, it's going to be a long drive. In order for us to arrive in Denver at a reasonable time, we'll have to stay overnight in the town you talked about. Chappell, you said?"

Maggie replied, "That's right, Fred, it's a small town out there on the high plains of west Iowa. I've made reservations for an overnight stay there just in case. And it does look like we'll need to.

"I've been told there are hardly any trees in that area, only short grasses and brush being blown around by the wind. And the thing is that, according to my map, there's hardly anything else around it as far as development is concerned.

"Anyway, after we leave Chappell the next morning, we can stop again when we get to Manhattan. We can eat there. We'll probably be good and hungry again about that time and ready for dinner.

"By the way, Manhattan is a college town right off the highway. We can keep an eye out for a good restaurant near there. But that's quite a ways down the road yet, and it will be a while before we get there, especially by staying overnight in Chappell. Any way you slice it, we'll have a ton of time left before we get there."

"You're right, Maggie. There's a lot of driving to be done before we get to Manhattan. Who knows, we may be on the road another 10, even fifteen hours," Gates said. "But again, Maggie, the GPS will get us there.

"Since you have your map, how far is it to Denver after we get to Manhattan?" Gates asked.

"Well, according to what I'm looking at here, it's a good distance," Maggie replied. "I'd say Denver is a good five or six hours away from that town of Manhattan. Hopefully, we'll get to Denver before it gets too late."

"Okay, Maggie." Gates replied. "No, we will get to Denver at a reasonable time if we stop in Chappell as our plans unfold. By this evening, it looks like we'll need to get situated in a hotel. This weather is no joke out here! And when we get there—to Chappell—Sinbad will have a chance to go over the week's activities with everybody."

"Yeah, Gates, Sinbad did say he would do that. Of course, we've all been taking a part in some of the planning for this trip all along, but there's nothing wrong with a little reinforcement," Maggie replied.

Gates responded, "Well, Sinbad and I had a brief telephone

conversation, and he gave some information in the limited amount of time we spoke."

Maggie replied, "Oh! That's good. I guess we'll get what we need to know from the both of you."

Maggie had printed a map and gotten directions before leaving Chicago, but Gates wanted to give her some practical advice.

"Now, Maggie, if you plug the address into the GPS, like I've already done, it'll direct us at every step of the trip, and ultimately it'll lead us to where we need to be in Denver."

"I know, Gates," Maggie said, "but I just like the idea of looking at a physical map, one you can unfold and write on. But do you know the most important thing? To me it's being able to see exactly where we are and where we're going."

Gates replied, "Well, okay. But you're doing a lot of useless work. You *do know* that you can see maps on the GPS."

"Yeah, I know that, Gates!" Maggie replied firmly. "But can you write on 'em?" she asked factiously.

Gates had no answer for Maggie on that point. He simply said, "You got me on that, Maggie." He then turned his attention to Fred and asked, "Hey, Fred, are you okay with driving so far?"

"I'm fine, Gates. But you should be more concerned about being schooled by my wife just now," Fred said with a grin.

"Okay, Fred! I can't win, not with both Mints ganging up on me."

With not much more said by Gates, Fred kept an eye on the vehicle behind them, the van that Sinbad was driving. It was still quite a distance until they would reach the restaurant near Des Moines.

After that, everyone was content viewing the countryside and waiting for their arrival at the diner. Maggie, however, had dozed off.

By almost three hours into the drive, most occupants in each vehicle other than the drivers were fast asleep. Getting up so early finally took its toll on everyone except Sinbad and Fred. Even Sandra, who had mentioned she was ready to stop and eat, had nodded off.

Fred and Sinbad remained alert and fresh at the wheel and safely drove their passengers to Mickey's Diner off Interstate 80, the restaurant Maggie had researched.

Maggie awakened about a mile before the exit for the diner and immediately asked Fred, "Is Sinbad's van still behind us?"

"Yes, he is, Mag," Fred answered.

Then she saw a sign saying: "Exit 24, Restaurant on Right, Ames 34 Miles."

The reference to Ames conjured up the memory of her conversation with Freddie's former wife Peggy, who now lived there. *Thank goodness I don't have to contend with that lady anymore*, Maggie thought to herself, recalling their unpleasant phone conversation.

In the vehicle Sinbad was driving, Sandra awoke to find everyone asleep except the driver. She yelled toward the front of the van, saying, "Hey, Sinbad, are you fine up there behind the wheel?"

"Yeah, Sandra, we're coming up to Mickey's Diner and, while most of you were asleep, Maggie called saying that Fred would make exit 24 in about ten minutes. I overheard you talking with Maggie on your cell phone earlier that you wanted to stop and eat. But I guess you dozed off."

"Yeah, I was ready to stop back then, but, like you said, I fell asleep and am just waking up now."

"Well, Sandra, and everyone, I hope you're ready to get out and refresh yourselves. I'm right behind Fred and his van, and we'll be stopping soon."

Unexpectedly, Sandra heard a voice directly behind her.

"Oh, Sandra, I had such a nice rest too," Sheri said.

Sandra believed Sheri was still asleep. Just short of being startled, she turned around and said, "Oh, Sheri, someone else is awake besides me—and the driver, of course." She glanced briefly at David, who was still asleep.

Sheri said, "Yeah, I just woke up."

David, who sat next to Sheri, began to awaken because of all the chatter.

When he opened his eyes, he asked somewhat incoherently, "Are we about… about at that restaurant? I'm really hungry."

Sheri replied, "Yeah, David, we're almost there. It'll be just a few minutes."

He gave Sandra a glance while taking a yawn, then turned his head and looked out the window.

As the vans took the exit off the interstate, it was clear that Mickey's Diner was the only establishment in the area although a sign *did* indicate a gas station was another mile up the road.

CHAPTER 13
Mickey's Diner

Foundation Scripture: 1 Corinthians 10:3,4

3 all ate the same spiritual food, 4 and drank the same spiritual drink. For they drank of that spiritual Rock that followed them, and that Rock was Christ.

Both vans came to a stop in front of Mickey's Diner, and everyone gradually exited the vehicles. When Sandra stepped off, she was particularly perceptive of her surroundings. Sandra had slept through the change of scenery during most of the drive to this point and was amazed at the rural surroundings of the Great Plains of east Iowa.

Sandra was accustomed to city life since she was a kid, particularly the streets of New York City as a young adult. Here, she saw only one building that housed the restaurant. It stood along what seemed to be a seldom used road. Farther up that road, another small structure was barely visible, a service station where Fred and Sinbad would go to refuel the vans.

Sandra continued to gaze beyond the back of the establishment. In the distance was what appeared to be miles and miles of desolate wasteland, a rolling landscape with hilly terrain continuing for as far as she could see. Even more striking to Sandra than the physical landscape was the eerie sound of the wind, which seemed to bring a calmness she could not readily explain.

Sandra said to Maggie, who was walking along with her, "I've never seen anything like this before, Maggie, being from the city and all. This place is just so open. You can see for miles. We're the only ones out here! And I'll tell you, the chill in the air makes me eager to get inside."

Maggie replied, "I think the patrons who are already inside feel the same way you do, Sandra. Just look out here. There are a few cars in the parking lot, so at least there are others inside now. Like you said, there's nothing going on here outside. But listen, Sandra, even though the sun is shining now, you can see dark clouds way down the interstate just above the horizon."

After a brief pause, Maggie continued, "But you know, Sandra, while it's bright out here it's also very cold. And that wind is making it feel that much colder.

"Anyway, based on my review of advertisements I saw back in Chicago before we left, this is about the only thing anywhere close to an eating place around here. But I told everybody in our van just before getting here that I researched this place before we left Chicago, and I found that the food appeared to be good."

"Well, that's great, Maggie, because I'm hungry!" Sandra replied.

"Hopefully you won't be disappointed," Maggie responded. "I'm sure there are more eating choices in Des Moines, the largest city in the area. But it's still over thirty miles away."

FIGURE 6: Mickey's Diner

"Oh, Maggie, thanks for your part in getting us here, but the place looks a little creepy to me. Well, we're here now and I'm hungry!"

Soon everyone entered the diner. As Wynn walked in, he said to his mother, "Mom, I kinda like this place. Listen to the music they're playing. It's the kind of country music I like; progressive country is what I've heard some refer to it as."

Fred and Sinbad had talked among themselves by phone about stopping at a service station about a mile or so farther up the road from the diner to refuel. After letting all the passengers off, they took the vehicles to that station. They agreed to eat and refresh themselves at the gas station, so when they returned to the diner, they anticipated that everyone would have eaten their breakfast, refreshed themselves, and be ready to hit the road again. However, after surveying the food that was available, Fred was prompted to suggest that he and Sinbad return to the diner and eat with the others.

"The food here just looks nasty to me," Fred said.

Sinbad agreed. "We can go back and eat with the group. We can refuel now and go back to the diner to eat. Nobody will have finished eating there by the time we get back."

So that's what they did.

Back at the diner, Jeanie commented on Wynn's love of country music.

"I still can't believe you like country music," she said, "being from New York City and all."

Wynn replied, "New Yorkers love all kinds of music. If you stay with me, you'll be listening to plenty of it," he said.

"Okay, Wynn. Don't rub it in." Jeanie replied.

Jeanie did not share Wynn's love of that kind of music but was willing to accept that one flaw about him. She overlooked that shortcoming because she really liked him and thought he was a nice guy.

The diner was a large restaurant and had TVs mounted on the wall everywhere. It made Sandra think of the many bars she had visited over the course of her life. With those days now largely behind her, like other patrons, she was content with viewing whatever was on the screen until their food arrived.

After orders had been placed but prior to everyone getting their food, a special announcement was made that interrupted regular programming. It said: "ALERT, ALERT: Storm System Brewing 50 Miles West of Here. Heavy Snow and Wind Expected."

"My, my! Looks like we're heading into bad weather, Fred," Sinbad said to his fellow driver at the front counter of the diner.

"Yeah, and I'm glad we're getting our food now. And it's looking good, not like what we saw up the road at that station."

Fred noticed an attendant and asked, "Sir, could our group get served as quickly as possible? We want to get back on the road as soon as we can. We're on our way to Denver."

The attendant answered, "Sure! I'll alert the staff and we'll take care of you all promptly. There's a section over here that's pretty clear of patrons right now, and you can be in that one area of the diner."

"That's great," Fred responded.

Soon after, a waiter instructed all who were in Maggie's group to take their seats in the area recommended to Fred by the attendant.

Both Sinbad and Fred went back to the diner's front counter where they sat when they first entered the building. Sinbad said, "Thanks for taking control there, Fred. Hopefully, now that everyone will be in one area of the diner, they will soon be fed; then we can be back on the road in a little while."

"Yeah, Sinbad, but we still need to go and get one last check of our tires before we get back on the interstate. I forgot to do that when we were at the station and refueled," Fred replied.

"You're right, Fred."

As Fred and Sinbad enjoyed hot coffee while waiting for their food, Sinbad mentioned, "Look outside, Fred. It's getting grayer out there by the minute. And the wind has picked up too."

Fred replied, "Yeah, we need to eat this food and head back to that service station to check the tires as soon as possible."

After a pause to sip on more coffee, Sinbad continued, "I sure don't look forward to running into all that weather down the road."

"Well, at least we got some good food here at the diner. The food we would've gotten back there at the station would have been terrible! And this coffee is really warming me up, and it tastes pretty good too!"

When the meal arrived, they quickly consumed most of what they had been served, knowing that soon they would have to leave and check tires at that gas station. They would be facing increasingly bad weather that had already begun. As they were about to finish, Sinbad said to Fred, "We probably need to leave here in a few minutes."

"You're right, Sinbad," Fred replied. "I'll be finished in a little bit; then we can go ahead and take the vans up there while the others finish up their food. It looks like some of them have just started to eat now."

"Good!" Sinbad replied. "I see the waitress bringing us more coffee now. That certainly should put a capper on this meal and will help us to stay alert later as we head down the road on the interstate. But now we can sip on that for a while, then you follow me to the station. I can take any food that I didn't get to finish here back with me in the van and finish eating at the wheel."

"I'm with you, Sinbad," Fred replied. Then he said, "We can go in maybe, say, five minutes? I think after we take the vans to that station, get the gas we need, and come back here, everyone should be close to finishing their meal. When they're done, they can wait for us in the lobby area before we board," Fred said.

Before they made the short trip up the road to refuel, they saw that some of the people in Maggie's group hadn't gotten their food yet. So Fred suggested they stay a little longer and went to sit with Maggie for a while.

"That's fine," Sinbad replied. "But come on back soon because, remember, the weather out there is not getting any better. In fact, it looks like it's getting worse as we speak!"

"Okay, Sinbad," Fred replied. "In about twenty minutes, I think everyone will be close to finishing their meals, and we can leave."

"Okay then. I'll be here," Sinbad said.

Fred came over to where Maggie was sitting alone at the only table available after everyone had been directed to the seating area. When he arrived, he asked, "Are you just getting your food, Mag?"

"Yeah, I think this waitress is coming by now to give me some of the items that I ordered."

"I'll sit here for a few minutes and keep you company since no one else is sitting with you," Fred said. "But Sinbad and I will need to go out to refuel pretty soon."

"Okay. I noticed that you two came back from the station kinda early. So you didn't stay to get the gas then?"

Fred answered, "No, we didn't. We were going to eat there, but the food didn't look good at all, so we decided to come back here to eat and then go back to get the gas afterward."

The waitress that Maggie thought was bringing her food continued to pass by their table and began serving Courtney and Gates, who were sitting at a table close by.

As the waitress walked past, Maggie saw her name tag said Peggy. Maggie immediately whispered to Fred, "Now, that's interesting, Fred. That waitress, I think I've talked to her before."

Maggie thought, *I wonder if that's the same lady I talked to over the phone, Freddie's ex. I remember her name was Peggy!*

After a little while, Fred stopped his brief discussion with Maggie, left the table, and returned to where Sinbad was. Soon they took the vans back to the service station.

The waitress finally arrived with Maggie's food.

"Thank you, Miss. The food looks really good!" Maggie said.

Rather bluntly, the waitress replied, "Yeah, we serve good food around here."

Maggie thanked the waitress for her service and began to eat what turned out to be a delicious breakfast of an assortment of foods.

As she ate, Maggie couldn't hold her curiosity any longer. The waitress passed by again to wait on another table no doubt. That's when Maggie stopped her.

"Excuse me, Miss. I don't want to hinder your work, but I see that your name is Peggy."

"Yeah, Miss, that's what they call me," she said and then proceeded to go to a nearby table without giving Maggie an opportunity to respond.

With that tone of voice, she certainly sounds like the woman I was talking to on the phone that day, Maggie thought. *And her attitude matches her voice! She didn't even stay to let me finish telling her what I wanted. She seems like the same abrasive woman I talked to on the phone that day!*

The waitress passed by again a few minutes later, and she apparently had more time to talk, having finished with the person she was serving. By that time, Fred had long gone with Sinbad to refuel the vans, so Maggie had a chance to talk to the lady alone for a while.

When the waitress stopped at her table, Maggie was relieved that she wasn't as abrasive as she had appeared earlier. Maybe she had felt rushed waiting on customers.

The waitress asked, "What are you doing sitting alone here at this table?"

Maggie answered, "Well, this was the only table available after everyone in my group came into the diner."

"Yeah, apparently the table I just waited on was people in your group. I overheard their conversation. This one man was talking about how the spirit of people rules their lives, a kind of 'wonder of the spirit,' he said. Now, I thought that was kinda weird. I mean, who comes to a restaurant and talks about spirits and stuff like that?"

Maggie briefly looked over at the table where Gates and Courtney sat and then returned her attention to the waitress.

"Well, Peggy, that man you're talking about is a minister, and he talks like that a lot."

"Well, holy hell! A minister, huh?"

Maggie was taken aback by the language the waitress used and simply replied, "Well, yeah. He's a minister."

In a softer voice so no one else could hear, Peggy said, "If you ask me, those preachers—all they want is yo' money!"

Then with a louder voice, Peggy said to Maggie, "You know, lady, after thinking about it, your voice sure does sound familiar."

Maggie replied, "Well, first I have to say that not all ministers are like that, wanting your money as you put it. Anyway, your voice sounds familiar too, and I bet you're the lady I talked to on the phone a while back who was Freddie's ex!"

Clearly surprised, Peggy shouted, "Oh, my God, *you are* that lady—the one I talked to about that husband of mine. I remember that! I never dreamed that I'd meet you. Oh! I miss that man so much! And that was such a sad service they had for him. Anyway, what brings you out here, Miss, almost in the middle of nowhere?"

Maggie replied, "Well, just call me Maggie."

"Okay, Maggie!" she said hesitantly, still being a little uncomfortable using her first name.

"I'm with this group," Maggie said pointing to the tables where her friends sat. "It's a special group because most of us have an affiliation to the church, and we're on our way to Denver. And the man you're talking about is kind of like our spiritual leader, being a minister and all."

"You mean you all believe in spirits and stuff like that?" Peggy asked.

Maggie replied, "Well, yeah, if you wanna put it that way."

Peggy responded, "Well, the only spirit I know about is that gin I drink every weekend."

"Um, that's interesting," Maggie said. "Anyway, we're going to a ski resort in the mountains of Colorado, and we decided to stop here because I read some advertisement I saw back in Chicago—that's where I'm from—that this place has excellent food."

Peggy replied, "Yeah, Maggie, we have good food here. And I'm the restaurant's manager. I usually work fifteen-hour days every day of the week. Do you hear me? Fifteen hours! And I'll tell you. I'm about good for nothing when I get to the house. That's why I can't wait to go home and have some of that gin. It really relaxes me."

Peggy continued, "You know, Maggie, I had a job like this one when I was in Detroit where I lived with Freddie. I was hardly ever at home then either. And when I *was* home, I was too tired to care for him, I guess. I suppose that's the reason why he played around so much, like I was telling you on the phone when we spoke. I just wasn't there for the man. There were times over the weekend where he didn't come home at all. To tell you the truth, I think he had a place on the side; just didn't tell me about it. Again, that gin saved the day!

"Anyway, to this day I believe that husband of mine, God rest his soul, was making out with some woman. That hussy! I'd sure like to meet her and give her a piece of my mind!"

Then the lady got over her vindictiveness about her former husband being with another woman, not realizing she was talking *to* that woman, that Maggie *was* the other woman.

After talking about who she believed her husband was seeing, Peggy began to change her persona towards Maggie, who tried to listen to her while enjoying the food the lady had just given her. The waitress then smiled and said, "You know, Maggie, if she ever were to come to this restaurant, and I happened to wait on her, I'd probably put something in her food! Sho would!"

The waitress made that comment just as Maggie was about to take another swallow of food. In response to Peggy's comment, Maggie threw up everything that had not yet been digested. Fragments of chewed food went all over the table, creating a mess!

Maggie was so embarrassed. Everyone in the area turned their heads to see what was happening. She looked around, ashamed by all the attention she was receiving, and said, "I'm all right, everybody. Some food I ate just went down the wrong way, and it came back up."

Gates, who was sitting at the table nearby, said, "Something didn't agree with you, Maggie?"

"I'm fine, Gates," Maggie assured him and the others.

She turned to Peggy and said, "Oh, I'm so sorry!"

Then she thought, *Oh, my! I wonder whether I should get another waitress.*

Before Maggie could finish that last thought, Peggy, who looked on in amazement, offered up a huge grin that showed her two front teeth were missing. She said, "Honey, you don't like your food?"

Maggie replied, "Oh, Peggy, like I said to Gates, the one I told you was a minister, I'm all right. But, no, the food is delicious.

Peggy said, "Here, take this towel and wipe yourself off."

Maggie took the towel, soiled and all, and awkwardly attempted to use portions of it that appeared to be clean. Without being totally truthful, Maggie then said, "I appreciate that."

Seeing that Maggie wasn't comfortable using the towel that had been given to her, Peggy called another waitress standing close by to lend a helping hand. "Hey, Jenny, come on over here and clean this mess up, will ya? Then go and get this lady another plate."

Jenny responded to Peggy's request, cleaned things up on the table as best she could, and then went to get Maggie the same order she had.

Peggy had returned her attention to Maggie, who continued to wipe off her clothes. "Let me finish what I was saying about that used-to-be husband of mine. I guess that was the reason I didn't get to go with him to south Florida. You know he used to go down there on occasion to his cousin's resort. And I wanted to go so bad but just didn't have the time. I just worked all the time, it seemed. And it's the same way now, working at this place. Well, at least they give me a two-week vacation during the summer, and the pay ain't bad either!

"But, girl! I pay for it though, working myself to the bone! Anyway, I'm glad to be talking to ya. And where's the man that was with you when I passed earlier waiting on another table?"

Maggie replied, "Oh, that's my husband. He's driving one of the vans we have, and he and another fellow went to refuel. And I don't know if you saw her or not, but my college roommate was sitting here for a while too."

Peggy replied, "No, I didn't recognize a lady sitting here. I guess I was too busy waiting tables. Well, I guess you haven't been here sitting alone the whole while. Anyway, you know this is a rough job, being the manager of a busy restaurant and being a waitress too sometimes.

"But listen. I don't want to give you all *my* problems. And you're fortunate to have a man in your life. And my life with Freddie was okay; I just didn't give him enough time, like I said. But now, I have a boo back at home where I live here. It's kind of funny, but I call him butterball and he calls me an abbreviated version my name, Peg. If I remember, he answered the phone when *you* called."

"Yeah, a man did answer the phone when I called you, Peggy," Maggie replied. "And I do remember him calling you Peg. That's interesting because my husband does the same. He calls me an abbreviation of my name, Mag. So do you mind if I call you Peggy?"

"No, not at all—like I told you two times already."

"Oh, sorry! I didn't mean to repeat myself," Maggie replied.

"No, don't apologize, girl! You know, after talking to you, I kinda like ya!"

Before Maggie had a chance to respond, Peggy said, "Anyway, I need to get on with life a little more and not work all the time. I have very few friends, Maggie, and while talking with you here, you're so cordial, I consider you a friend."

Maggie's initial reaction to that statement was to think, *I can understand why you don't have any friends given your attitude.* Maggie quickly made that a passing thought and suddenly became more sensitive to Peggy because of her history. Peggy's words about having few friends ended up almost bringing Maggie to tears.

Peggy went on, "Now, let me tell you, I have an Ames address, a bit south of the city of Des Moines, and it takes me about thirty minutes to get down here to the diner, fighting traffic and all. Feel free to gimme a call sometime like you did before.

"Well, I need to get going," Peggy said finally.

"Okay, Peggy. And thanks for the food, and thank you for having someone clean up the mess I made."

Peggy said, "Aw, hush your mouth, girl! You're good."

After listening to Peggy's personal business, Maggie felt great compassion for her and said, "Well, Peggy, I'm glad I got to meet you and to know you a little bit. But I think we're about to leave, and I know you need to return to work. Listen, thank you for inviting me to call you. If you ever have a need to call me, just do it—at least when I get back to Chicago. Here is my business card; it has my number on it. We'll be out in Denver for the next week at a ski resort, and it might not be the best time to reach me then."

Katie came to stand beside Maggie in preparation for leaving, and everyone else in their group started to walk toward the exit.

"Well, have a good time out there," Peggy said. "And who is this lady?"

Maggie went on to introduce Katie to her. "We go all the way back to college, Katie and me. I think I mentioned her to you a little while ago."

"Hello, Peggy," Katie greeted her.

"Katie, this is my new friend Peggy. And, Peggy, this is the lady I was telling you about that was with me here at the table earlier."

"So you two are college girls, huh?" Peggy asked. "I never got the chance to go to college. Anyway, I sure hope all of you have a nice trip."

As tears began to form in her eyes, Peggy said to Maggie, "And by the way, you can bring me back a snowman or at least a picture of one—a genuine Colorado snowman, one that you build yourself. We get a whole lotta snow around here during the winter but maybe not as much as where you're going. But the snowmen I've seen are bright and jolly. I guess that's how the people make 'em.

"Anyway, I *need* for my life to get brighter 'round here, much brighter, I'll tell you! Now, you say this is a church group. Maybe you'll bring back a word for me, a word from the Master up there!" Then she quickly added, "Oh, just kidding."

"No, you're not, Peggy! You're not kidding. We all need as much as we can get from the Lord!" Maggie hastily responded.

"Okay then, Maggie."

Peggy realized that it would be quite a while before she would see her new friend again. She said to Maggie, "I guess I wasn't kidding, Maggie. Like you said, I need *something* from the Lawd! Yeah, if God is real, I need for Him to speak to me somehow."

"And He will, Peggy. I'm sure of it!" Maggie replied.

Seeing that Peggy had gotten highly emotional, Maggie said, "You calm down now, Peggy. I know the emotions are high for you right now. I will be praying for you and Katie will too."

Katie said, "I sure will, Peggy."

"And remember, Peggy, God *can* speak to you because He *is* real, and He's concerned about you. He's concerned about your life," Maggie said, trying to comfort Peggy with those words.

Katie added, "Yeah, Peggy, God speaks to us all the time; it's just that we usually fail to listen *to Him*."

"Katie is right, Peggy," Maggie responded. "And another thing,

Peggy, I'll get you that snowman, at least a picture of one, a snowman that I'll build myself. I promise you that."

After that statement, Maggie gave Peggy a hug, looked her in the eyes, and said, "Bye now, Peggy."

As they embraced, Peggy whispered, "Bye, Maggie. I know God has spoken to me through you. And wait a minute. I have something for you."

Peggy returned to the back of the diner to get what looked like a roll of wrapping paper. She then went over to a nearby storage area and got an old portrait of the diner. When she returned to where Maggie and Katie were, Peggy gave both items to Maggie. She said, "Here. I want you to have this. It's something you can remember me by. You can wrap it up when you get the chance," Peggy added.

Maggie replied after viewing what she had been given, "No, Peggy! I can tell this is something valuable to this establishment; it looks like an authentic drawing of the diner. I can't take this!"

Peggy replied, "Yeah, it is, Maggie. It's a picture Freddie drew himself when he came here once. I guess he was trying to make up for all the indiscretions with those hussies I was telling you about. But I knew I wasn't going back to the man. I wanted to start a new life on my own. But I want you to have it; it's something you can remember me by—so you won't forget me."

"No! I won't forget you, Peggy," Maggie told her as tears began to form in her eyes. The tears were not just because of Peggy but also because the drawing reminded her of Freddie and the fact that she was the other woman Peggy was referring to.

But Peggy pressed the issue and said, "No, you go ahead and take it, Maggie, because that part of my life is over."

Hesitantly, Maggie did as Peggy requested and took the items. "Okay. I'll go ahead and take it, and I'll keep the wrapping paper too."

The two women embraced again and soon withdrew from one

another. After that emotional encounter, Maggie turned around and began to walk away, carrying the portrait in one hand and wrapping paper in the other. Maggie tried to conceal her emotions as much as possible. She found the strength to walk along with Katie and straightened herself out emotionally.

"Are you okay, Maggie?" Katie asked her as they continued their walk.

Maggie replied as strongly as she could under the conditions, "Yeah, I'll be fine, Katie."

"Well, okay. Let me take some of that off your hands," Katie said as she helped her friend by carrying the wrapping paper. They joined the other members of the group who had congregated near the exit.

As they waited for Sinbad and Fred to return, Katie said, "That's a talkative waitress, huh, Maggie?"

Maggie replied, "Yeah, Katie. She has an interesting history. When I first met her, I thought she was abrasive and unkind. Well, she really was! And she was really difficult to communicate with. But as I got to know her better, she really is a sweetie. She's just had a lot of problems in her life.

"I'm sorry I got so emotional there at the end," Maggie said.

"You're fine," Katie assured her.

Maggie omitted the part of her story that involved Peggy's late husband Freddie.

Everyone was waiting by the door when Sinbad and Fred returned to the diner. There was a sense that the weather was about to get even worse than it already was. It had been a sunny day with a scattering of clouds and strong winds when they arrived at the diner. Now the sky was blanketed with clouds, and the wind was howling.

Sinbad said to the group, "Is everyone ready to go?"

From their facial expressions, it was clear that they were anxious to get back on the road and head toward their destination. They didn't look forward to running into that storm, but their immediate focus was on at least getting to their next stop, which was a small town named Chappell.

Maggie saw Sheri, who was sitting in the back of the van Sinbad was driving, and said, "Hey, Sheri, could you take this wrapping paper and portrait and place it in the storage area behind where you and David are sitting?"

"Sure thing, Maggie," Sheri replied. "What is it?"

Maggie answered, "It's something the waitress gave me. I'll show it to everybody later."

When everyone had returned to their seats, Sheri did as Maggie asked her, placing Maggie's items in the back of the van.

Soon Maggie had comfortably resumed her place in the passenger seat beside Fred. She looked out the window thinking about the new friendship she had forged with Peggy. Then she saw what appeared to be her new friend standing inside the diner at the front door, looking out its window. It seemed to Maggie that Peggy didn't want her or any of the others to leave.

Maggie's focus remained on Peggy who continued to gaze out the small window of the front door. "So sad. That lady needs help," Maggie said to herself and offered up a prayer at the same time. "Lord, help her in some way."

Maggie thought back to what the minister had said at the morning church service before they attended the basketball game with the Manleys back in downtown Chicago. "We must go after the one that has gone astray instead of focusing our efforts on the ninety-nine, because we're all God's children, worthy of being found, despite our differences." Peggy certainly was different in Maggie's estimation, but she was worthy of being helped.

Maggie spent several minutes thinking about her experience at the diner, especially about her new friendship with Peggy, before gradually turning her attention to the group as they all began to continue their trip westward.

Everyone was content enjoying the ride until they reached that small western Iowa town; Chappell was still about five or six hours away. They wouldn't eat again until they reached that point on their journey. Before then, they would have a snowstorm to contend with.

CHAPTER 14
Stormy Weather

Foundation Scripture: Psalm 107:29

He calms the storm, So that its waves are still.

As the group journeyed westward on I-80 going toward Chappell, Sandra continued to marvel at the Great Plains' landscape. A few miles after they re-entered the interstate from that seldom-used road leading to Mickey's Diner, she was able to fully appreciate the physical surroundings. Miles and miles of rolling hills dotted an otherwise level landscape in all directions.

Sandra said, "Hey, Sinbad, there is absolutely nothing out here. I mean, you can look for what, maybe miles and miles without seeing any life, only brown brush, and high grasses as far as the eye can see."

"Sandra, look over to your left; you *can* see a herd of goats scampering across the plains," Sinbad said trying to brighten her outlook. "But, yeah, you're right. It's desolate all right. Nothing that much to see at all out there.

"Well, so long as we don't have a flat tire or something like that, I think we'll be okay," he added.

"And another thing. The radio reception out here is not good. There's only one station that comes in loud and clear, and it plays only country music. I'll bet Wynn would love this station. Let me call Fred and tell him about it."

After Sinbad called Fred, he said, "Hey, Fred, you all fine up there?"

"Yes, we're okay, Sinbad. And how about you guys back there?" Fred asked.

"Things are good here too, Fred," Sinbad replied. "Fred, turn on your radio. There's this country station that I think Wynn would love."

"Okay, Sinbad. I know the reception out here in the middle of nowhere is poor, but I'll try to get the station you're talking about. Once I get it, I'll just let him listen. I don't have to say anything. He'll like it, I'm sure."

When Fred finished the conversation, he returned his attention to the road and did what Sinbad had suggested. The only station he could find was the one that played country music. Wynn heard a selection and was so excited.

"This is great, Mr. Fred," Wynn said. "I love that station you just turned to."

Jeanie felt content just sitting beside Wynn. She didn't share his enjoyment of country music, but she liked him so much it didn't matter. She just sat there enjoying the ride. Those in Sinbad's van were happy to listen too.

Before Fred could respond to Wynn's excitement, a special announcement came on: "Bad weather expected in about 20 minutes. Several inches of snow and high winds in the forecast."

Fred said to Maggie, "Well, we're finally going into this bad weather that we heard in the TV forecast back at the diner. So long as the roads are clear, we'll be fine."

Maggie replied, "You know, Fred, the weather can really turn fast. While it was breezy back at the diner when we got there, the sun was shining clearly. But look at it now!

"I guess we should have known something was up because of the dark clouds that we saw far down the road when we left. Plus, at that time it was totally overcast, and there were even a few flurries. I guess it was that wind that brought all the bad weather in our direction."

Maggie was right. Even prior to the announcement of impending bad weather, the sky around the diner had transitioned from a bright sunny day to a heavy cloud bank moving in quickly. In a short while, the sky had become completely overcast, and a light snow had begun to fall. Fred reacted to the worsening weather situation by saying, "Oh, boy. Here it comes; that bad weather is definitely on its way!"

He continued, "And, Mag, a little while ago you *did* say that the breeze might be blowing some bad weather in our direction. Well, it looks like it's here. It's so dreary and gray now. And, Mag, I'm afraid it's only going to get worse."

Maggie replied, "Yeah, Fred, it kinda reminds me of Christmas time in back in Flint. You know we always have a white Christmas. Well, it's beginning to build up here already."

"Yeah, Mag, but the snow out here is different even from what it is in Chicago where I grew up. It comes down so rapidly here that before you know it, the whole ground is covered. And listen to that wind. I mean, the wind is howling, and the snow out there is beginning to drift almost totally in a horizontal direction. It's just different out here than what I'm used to back in Chicago," he reemphasized.

As they continued to ride westward and reminisce a little about their time growing up, the light snow that had been falling turned into a heavy blizzard. They were still quite a distance away from their destination of Chappell.

The wind gusts made the van waver from side to side, and it was a challenge for Fred to keep the vehicle on the road and in an upright position.

"You sure we shouldn't pull over, Fred?" Maggie asked.

"No, Mag," Fred replied. "Like I said before, being in Chicago all my life, I'm used to driving in the snow and wind."

While Maggie nervously sat in the front seat, Wynn and Jeanie seemed to be enjoying it all in the back.

"Mag, I'm going to call Sinbad and see how he's doing," Fred said. "I know he's from Florida and may not be used to driving in weather like this."

Fred and Sinbad discussed the deteriorating weather conditions.

"I know this weather is foreign to you, Sinbad. Are you okay?"

"Yeah, Fred, it's getting pretty bad out here. But I'm fine. The road is still not too bad yet," Sinbad replied.

FIGURE 7 Driving in a Snowstorm!

"But you know, Fred, we're still about three hours away from Chappell. At least we're on the interstate, and the road is pretty free of any snow cover—for right now anyway. Still, driving in these conditions can be a challenge to even the most experienced motorists, and I know you're experienced, being from Chicago."

"Yeah, hopefully we'll be able to make it to Chappell, but if this keeps up, I don't know," Fred replied. "Even if we make it there, I'm pretty sure we'll have to stay overnight, considering how the weather looks."

He added, "I know Mag said she reserved rooms in a hotel in that town, but I'll ask her to research some other lodgings there so we can get the best deal. The way it looks now, I'm sure it'll be too bad for us to continue down that side road from Chappell going toward Interstate 70 tonight."

The conversation ended with Sinbad supporting the idea of staying overnight in Chappell.

Once off the phone, Sinbad looked over at his friend Casey sitting beside him and saw that he was shivering.

"You cold, Case?" he asked.

Casey replied, "Well, it's getting cooler. I think that some air outside is seeping through someplace."

"I'll turn the heat up, and it'll get warmer in here soon," Sinbad replied.

Sinbad checked on his two cousins, Alphonso and Carlos, sitting behind them. Alphonso assured him they were fine.

"We'll just be glad when we get to Chappell," Alphonso added. "That is the name of the town, right? I think both me and Carlos had taken a nice nap!"

"Yeah, that's the place, Alphonso," Sinbad answered. "Chappell is another three hours away. It's 3:00 now, so we should be there by 6:00, barring any unforeseen difficulties. It's still daylight now, and visibility is not too bad. But in a few hours, nightfall will come, and it'll be a lot different out here.

"It looks like we'll be staying there in Chappell overnight because the weather is likely to get even worse. In fact, I'm pretty sure of it given the way it's looking outside."

Alphonso said, "Yeah, Sinbad, I know what you mean. My, my! You all see that brush being blown around by the wind, kicking up snow way over yonder in the distance?"

Katie, who was sitting next to Sandra behind Sinbad's cousins, responded, "Yeah, Alphonso, it's rough out there all right. And like you and Carlos, Sandra and I have been napping back here."

Sinbad responded, "Maybe it was good that you two were sleeping because that wind is ferocious—so much so that it was making the van sway a little bit. It's a wonder you were able to sleep through it all."

"Well, Sinbad," Katie interjected, "I've been awake, and noticed that these snow flurries are quickly causing the ground to turn totally white. And the bad thing is that it's getting harder and harder to see the road, wouldn't you say, Sandra?"

"You're right, Katie. I've had my attention on this book I'm reading, but yeah. You all see how it's blowing around in the air? That snow is really coming down now. It's getting to be so white all around us! Sinbad, Sandra's right. Even the road is beginning to get a large accumulation. I agree we have to stay overnight in Chappell."

Sinbad replied, "Well, I'm sure it too. We'll just have to wait to see exactly where we'll stop. I asked Fred to tell Maggie to find us a nice place there to stay overnight just in case. I think she's already made some reservations. It looks like there's no question about it now; we're gonna need to stop pretty soon."

In the rear seat just behind Sandra and Katie, Sheri had snuggled close to David while Sandra was absorbed in reading one of Fred's books.

Drivers Sinbad and Fred kept their vehicles safely on the road despite the inclement weather.

Fred said to his passengers, "Brace yourselves for bad weather for the next several miles."

Both vans traveled another hour on the interstate without any problems despite the increasing snowfall. The windswept flurries danced in circles around their vehicles, but the temperature had only dipped to just below freezing. As the late afternoon sun lowered toward the horizon, temperatures were certain to plummet into the night.

CHAPTER 15
Interruption!

Foundation Scripture: Psalm 91:15

He shall call upon Me, and I will answer him; I will be with him in trouble; I will deliver him and honor him.

The snow continued to fall, and the howling wind persisted as Maggie's group drove towards Colorado. About two hours away from Chappell, Fred heard a loud thump near the rear of the vehicle he was driving.

"Oh my, what in the world is that sound?" He quickly realized it came from one of the rear tires.

Maggie confirmed his worst fears, saying, "Fred, that sounds like the rear tire—on your side. I remember you saying that as long as we don't have a flat tire, we'll fine. Well, Fred, I'm pretty sure we have a flat tire! We're in the middle of nowhere, and it's storming out here—and getting darker!"

He could tell Maggie was in panic mode, so Fred said, "Now, now, Mag. Keep your composure. We'll still be fine. We just need to change that tire it if turns out that is the problem." Although he was not as composed as he pretended, Fred wanted to reassure his wife.

Fred wiped some sweat from his brow. "Anyway, Mag, as much as I hate to admit it, I think you're right. We do have a big problem right out here in the middle of the plains of west Iowa and in a blizzard to boot."

Despite Fred's efforts to retain his own composure in this obviously dangerous situation, he began to show his uneasiness.

Gates interjected, "Maggie is right. It sounds like the rear tire on the driver's side. Well, Fred, if it is, I'll see what I can do. I've changed a lot of tires in my time but never on a vehicle like this. This thing is huge!"

At that point Fred's cell phone rang. On the other end of the line, Sinbad said, "Hey, Fred. Did you know there's smoke coming up from the rear tire on your driver's side?"

"Yeah, Sinbad. Gates and I were just talking about it. But you say you saw smoke?" Fred asked with growing concern.

Sinbad replied, "Yeah, Fred. There's smoke coming from your rear tire."

"Oh my!" Fred responded louder than he had intended. His thoughts echoed his wife's initial worry. He added, "Hold on, Sinbad. Let me talk to Gates a minute."

Having overheard their conversation, Gates responded, "Okay, Fred. I heard everything. I guess what Sinbad saw confirms what we already knew—that we probably will have to change the rear tire. Anyway, tell Sinbad we're going to have to figure this thing out."

Fred returned his attention to Sinbad on the phone and said, "Okay, Sinbad, Gates and I discussed the situation a little while I placed you on hold. Sorry about that. We just need to figure out what to do now, so we'll keep you posted. Bye."

As Fred ended his phone conversation with Sinbad, he uttered a prayer in his mind: *Lord, help us in this situation. Like Mag said, we're in the middle of nowhere with a flat tire!*

160

By this time everyone in Fred's vehicle was awake and concerned about their predicament, hoping that things would be all right soon.

As Fred continued the drive, everyone knew that not before too long, they would have to stop to take care of the problem. Fred divided his attention between driving a vehicle with a badly damaged tire while talking to Gates. "I know one thing, and that is I'll be driving very slowly until we find a safe place to stop and change that tire."

Gates replied, "Yeah, you do that, Fred, but I don't know how much longer this van will be able to move with only three functional tires and one that is damaged."

Within a minute or two, he spotted a road sign that said, "Rest Stop Ahead—One Mile."

"Praise the Lord!" he blurted. "See, you all, it's only about a mile further up, and it'd be so much better to work on the tire there after we exit the interstate."

Gates replied, "I saw that sign. If we can make it to that rest stop, we can get out and change the tire safely. We sure don't won't to stop out here on the interstate. Changing a tire on the edge of the road with a huge vehicle like this would be too dangerous, especially with these weather conditions."

Fred added, "Well, Gates, we may not have a choice but to stop on the side of the interstate. But hopefully, we can make it to that rest stop. Then everybody can use the facilities as the tire is being changed."

Fred repeated more cautiously, "But I don't know. We may have to stop before then. That sound coming from the rear tire is not getting any better! I'm praying though that we make it to the exit.

"Well, Gates, I'm slowing down, not because I'm trying to but because I don't have a choice. We're practically riding on three wheels and a prayer. But I'm gonna keep my foot on the accelerator for as long as possible, and hopefully we'll be able to make it to the rest stop."

In the back seat, David and Sheri were feeling anxious like everyone else. David said, "Damn, Sheri, we're having tire problems with the other vehicle. Now, ain't that a bitch!"

"Now, David, watch your mouth, and let's keep a positive attitude about this," she implored.

As Fred's vehicle continued to decrease its speed, he said to himself–and to the vehicle, "Come on, baby. Let's make it just a little bit farther."

Soon Fred was able to guide the van onto the side road leading to the rest stop. The van slowly came to a complete stop on its own, just short of the parking area. But at least it drifted to an area to the side of the service road where there was enough room to pull over and change the tire. Miraculously, they all had made it to a safe place well off the interstate.

They still were at a distance from the building itself. It would be a long walk to the lobby of the facility where the restrooms were located. But at least Gates, Fred, and whomever else could work safely to replace the damaged tire. The wailing wind and driving snow would make it that much more difficult to complete the job.

Trudging through the snow and slush, the others had a difficult walk to the building, but no one complained. They were just glad to have a place to take shelter from the raging weather and to have that flat tire changed.

After both vans had stopped, Fred got out to check the condition of the rear tire. As he opened the door, he was met by a fierce wind, although the snow had abated. Shivering, Fred said, "Whew! It's really cold out here. At least it's not snowing as much as it was earlier."

Fred walked to the rear of the van where he met Sinbad, who had gotten out of the other van to assess the situation. While looking at the damaged tire, Fred said, "My, my! That tire is obviously beyond repair. It's totally blown out, Sinbad! Hopefully, we can get the spare and begin to change it.

Fred continued, "I'm glad you're here to help, Sinbad, because I know absolutely nothing about changing a tire on a van."

Sinbad replied, "Don't look at me, Fred; I've changed a lot of tires in my day but never dealt with a vehicle this large."

At that point Gates had gotten out of the van and approached the two men. He said, "My goodness! It sure is windy out here.

"Anyway, I overheard you two saying you don't have the knowledge to change a tire on a vehicle like this. Well, I worked in a mechanic's shop for ten years, so I think I can do it, but I'll need some help. Let me see whether the only other grown men with us can be of some help."

Sinbad said, "Well, Alphonso and Carlos have no knowledge of how to change a tire, so let's hope David does."

"Well then, I'll have to see if David can help," Gates replied.

As Gates turned around to go to the van, David was walking towards him and the disabled van, cursing up a storm.

"What the hell is going on here?" he said as he approached. "I heard that we might have a flat tire." As he looked at the damaged tire, David said, "Aw, shucks! Look at that thing; it's totally shot!" Then he informed the others, "Fellows, this type of van operates with what is called a booster spare, which is not very easy to get to. It's really a booger to change tires on this kind of vehicle, especially in this kind of weather, and it's so cold out here. I should've gotten my coat."

While having experience in changing tires, Gates had no knowledge whatsoever of what a booster spare tire was. He asked, "Booster spare tire? Exactly what is that, David?"

David explained, "Most vans like these have their spare tire under the rear, and there's this lever under the back seat that you need to use to lower it to the ground to replace the damaged tire. I've done this several times."

Gates said, "Well, you seem to know a lot about how to get the spare and put it on this type of van. That's what we need."

"Oh, yeah, preacher. Like I said, I've done lots of 'em. But we need to get going. Let me see what I can do."

"That's great, David. I guess it's you and me then. We have a job to do to get this van up and running again."

"A job to do, huh? Now what kind of knowledge *do you* have with cars, preacher?"

"Well, David, I haven't always been a minister, you know, and even before I accepted the call, I worked in the hotel business, and I also was a mechanic before that."

"Wait a minute. You were a what? A mechanic?" David laughed in disdain. "I just can't see you working on cars in a shop, preacher. You just don't look like a mechanic. You're going to have to prove it to me," David said.

"Okay, David, we'll have that opportunity. But the main thing now is to get this van up and going. But I have to admit this is the first time I've changed a tire on a vehicle like this. So you can teach me a lot."

"Well, well, lookie here! A mechanic telling a preacher what to do!" David stated facetiously. "Okay, I guess we need to stop yacking and start working on this thing. No need to stand out here getting cold and jabbing at one another."

David then asked, "Before we get started, I have one question for you. Don't we have other grown men on this trip that can help out? What about Fred and Sinbad? Can't they help?"

Gates replied, "I'm afraid they don't know much about maintaining cars, especially a big van like this."

Listening to their conversation, Fred added, "Yeah, David, I know how to drive this thing but never have been much on repairing one, especially a van as big as this one. You two go ahead and do what you have to do."

Sinbad said, "Yeah, Gates, you and David can work on the van. Fred and I can help the others get to and from the rest stop lobby. We can go into the lounging area and snack on something. It's been a few minutes since we've stopped, and I know everybody is eager to get out and stretch. You know it's a good walk from here to the building up there on that hill. We just have to navigate through all this snow and slush."

With everyone still seated in the vans, Fred and Sinbad returned to the vehicles they were driving to let their passengers know that Gates and David would be replacing the damaged tire.

Standing next to the front door of the van, Sinbad peeked inside and said, "Okay, everybody, Fred and I are going to help all of you get to the rest stop up there on the hill, so get ready for a little trek in the snow. David and Gates will take care of repairing the van while we're inside. One more thing: make sure you have enough on. It's cold out here," Sinbad stressed to those inside the vehicle.

Sheri said, "I hear you, Sinbad. I'll get David's coat because he left it when he went out to see what was going on."

"That's good, Sheri," Sinbad yelled back at her.

Bitter wind cut through their coats as the party exited and assembled near the front of the van.

Sinbad said, "Fortunately, it's not snowing too hard right now. Just be careful when we start our walk. It's very slippery out here, and we don't want anyone to fall."

Fred, who had already assisted those in his van to get out, agreed with Gates. "Yeah, be careful out here, and I hope all of you have enough on. Well, I guess it's too late to tell you that, because you're already out here now. Just kidding. You can go back in if you really need to. Is everybody fine?"

"Yes, let's go!" Maggie said.

After Sheri gave David his coat, she joined the entourage as they started to walk towards the rest stop facility. Some separated themselves into pairs, including Fred and Maggie, Sinbad and Casey, and Jeanie and Wynn. The others, including Sandra, Katie, Courtney, and Sheri, trailed behind.

Everyone covered up as best they could as the wind and flurries chilled them. Their time inside the rest stop offered a welcome reprieve before returning to their vans to continue the journey to Chappell, which was now only about an hour and a half away.

Finally, after walking through all the snow and slush, they arrived at the building, entering the comforting warmth of the lobby. It was a time to relax and warm themselves up and grab some food in the rest stop's diner.

The temperature hovered around freezing outside, and conditions were much less hospitable for David and Gates as they worked on the damaged tire.

While David and Gates replaced the tire, those inside the rest stop pondered continuing their journey when the affected van was again operable. Everyone agreed that they would get no further on the trip than Chappell, the next town, before stopping to wait out the storm.

Fred said, "Mag, you said you had already made reservations at a hotel in Chappell?"

"Yes, Fred. I made reservations for all of us," she replied.

Fred continued, "Well, I hope it's nice wherever it is that we're lodging tonight."

Maggie replied, "Yeah, Fred, it's real nice. It's the Ritz Colony Hotel. Because it's so nice, it's a little pricey. I mentioned the possibility of our staying overnight in Chappell to Courtney back when we had breakfast, and she seems to think that Gates can handle any extra expenses we might have. But, yeah, the Ritz Colony is a popular hotel chain in the Midwest."

Given the current weather conditions, everyone seemed content with spending the night there.

Overhearing what Maggie was saying, Courtney confirmed to Fred what she had already mentioned to Maggie earlier. "Oh, don't worry about the expense, Fred. Gates has it covered. He has so many connections in the hotel business it's not even funny!"

She continued, "And, Maggie, you did say the Ritz Colony, didn't you?"

Maggie replied, "That's right, Courtney. It was about the only thing I could find that wasn't all booked."

During their brief time at the rest stop, everyone grabbed a bite to eat, and all were ready to return to the vans once they got word that the tire had been replaced. They were confident that Gates and David would have the vans ready to hit the road again soon.

Gates and David did not disappoint anyone. The two men came into the lobby of the facility, and Gates announced, "Hey, everybody, we're all set to hit the road again."

They just couldn't wait until they arrived at the Ritz Colony and looked forward to a restful night before continuing their journey the next day. Besides, the sooner they could get off the road in these stormy conditions the better.

After their scheduled overnight stay at the hotel in Chappell, their next stop would be in Manhattan, Kansas, a small college town that Maggie had told everyone about. The plan was to have a brief layover at a local restaurant there to refresh themselves and then to continue their journey to the ultimate destination of Denver.

David's knowledge of the tire assembly on this type of van was mostly what got them up and running again. As Gates headed toward his vehicle where Fred was the driver, he did something David did not expect. He reached out for his hand and said, "David, without your help I don't know what we would've done. Thanks for your assistance."

As they shook hands, each one of them went into the diner of the rest stop to get some coffee for the road. Soon Fred and Sinbad had returned to the vans they were driving.

When David reached the van he and Sheri were assigned to, he found that everyone had claimed their seats. David stepped in and walked towards the back of the vehicle, giving a glance at Sandra. He continued past her until he approached Sheri in the back seat.

She said, "Oh, David, I'm so glad you were able to help. I'm so proud of you."

He replied, "Aw, it was nothing. Like I told Gates, that's something I've done lots of times as a mechanic."

Sitting with Katie just ahead of Sheri and David, Sandra succumbed to negative emotions about his sudden importance to the group as Sheri had expressed. Sandra had been nonattentive to things around her during the drive because she had been reading or asleep, but in this instance she couldn't help but think about Sheri's compliments toward David. Those comments generated contrary judgments within Sandra. She thought, *It's about time that man has done something useful.*

Despite Sandra's attitude towards David, perhaps justified by their history, everyone seemed to appreciate his efforts.

Soon both vans were back on the road. After traveling a few miles on the interstate, Fred said, "Well, Mag, we're only about an hour away from Chappell. So pretty soon we'll need to start looking at the signs that point us to the right exit for the hotel."

Because of the delay on their trip, the group was over two hours late arriving in Chappell. The blustery, gray clouds hanging low at twilight had given way to the blackness of night in the midwestern plains—without the assistance of a moon and starlit sky.

As the lead van Fred was driving took the exit for the group's lodging for the night, with Sinbad's van close behind, they soon approached the illuminated five-story hotel with a wide canopy attached to the front entrance. Its mostly glass structure glistened in the wintry midwestern nighttime sky and seemed inviting for everyone on this snowy night.

With both vehicles parked at the front entrance, protected from the driving snow beneath of that wide canopy, everyone got out and headed inside. Once in the lobby, they received their room assignments and began a night of solitude and rest.

FIGURE 8: The Approach to the Hotel In Chappell

CHAPTER 16
An Unplanned Overnight Stay

Foundation Scripture: Psalm 46:1,2,7

1 God is our refuge and strength, A very pleasant help in trouble. 2 Therefore we will not fear, even though the earth be removed, And though the mountains be carried into the midst of the sea. 7 The Lord of hosts is with us; The God of Jacob is our refuge.

At 8:00, they all arrived at the Ritz Colony Hotel for their unplanned overnight stay in western Iowa. Thankfully, Maggie had made reservations *just in case*, so the appropriate accommodations awaited them. On such a miserable night, the group was grateful to have a safe haven from the snowstorm.

After receiving their room assignments, they were told that dining services would end at 9:00, so they had little time to retrieve personal items from the vans, bring them to their rooms, and then return to the dining hall.

It had been a while since breakfast, and, since the dining area would soon be closing, everyone decided to go their own way for dinner and not come together as one group.

Katie said to Sandra, whose room was next to hers, "Hey, Sandra, come on and go with me to get a bite in the dining room. I know it will be closing soon, but we don't need to stay long."

Sandra replied, "Okay, Katie. I'm so tired though that I probably could fall asleep at the dinner table."

"I know what you mean," Katie said. "I guess you know where that boy of mine Wynn is. You can see him with Jeanie over there on the couch in the lobby. There's no telling how long they'll be there. But I'm going to bed once I eat a little something."

Sandra asked, "You must have a large room; I think you said Wynn is staying with you."

"Yeah, girl, and it's nice! It's good Maggie thought about the size of the accommodations when she made the reservations. We have two separate bedrooms, a living area, and a kitchenette," Katie told her.

"That's good Katie," Sandra replied. "As for me, I just have a room, a fairly large one, but it's just me, so it's more than enough room for a good night's sleep."

"Okay, Sandra. Let's go get that bite," Katie said. Off they went to the dining hall.

Sandra and Katie noticed other members of their party scattered around the dining room. After dinner, most everyone except Jeanie and Wynn returned to their rooms for the night. Courtney and Gates stayed longer than many of their friends but soon they, too, called it a night and headed toward their room. On the way Gates spotted David and Sheri, who also were just about to retire.

Gates said, "Hey, David, I know you and Sheri are headed to your suite, but why don't you and I go out here onto the enclosed patio and talk a little? It looks very comfortable out there with heaters and everything."

Gates pointed to the side of the building where a sheltered area provided a clear view of the snow.

He continued, "That will be almost like being outside but without having to experience the cold weather. I went over and peeked inside the area when we all came in, and I'll tell you, it's really nice. It has comfy chairs, a couch, and even a fireplace to go along with the heaters they have out there. And it has all the greenery you would want; I guess that helps to hold in the heat too."

"Sounds good," David responded.

David turned to Sheri, who was standing close by, and said, "Is that all right with you, Babe?"

"Sure, David. You and Gates go ahead and spend some quality time together."

Gates said, "Thanks, Sheri, for letting me steal your friend for a while." Gates added to his wife, "And, Courtney, we'll be out here for a while, and I will come to the room later."

"Okay, Gates," Courtney said. Then she turned toward Sheri and said, "Come on, Sheri. I'll walk you to your suite, and after that I'll go to our room and retire for the night."

"Okay, Courtney. See you later, David. You two have fun," Sheri said.

FIGURE 9 A Gates/David Discussion in the Enclosure

After a brief walk with Sheri to her suite, Courtney wished her a good night and went to her own quarters. Meanwhile, David and Gates headed to the outdoor enclosure to talk.

Gates and David were the only hotel guests in the lobby that were still up except for Wynn and Jeanie, who lingered there, still chatting with one another as they had been since arriving.

As they began to walk toward the outside patio, Gates said, "It's pretty quiet now. I'm just glad I'm not driving tomorrow."

After Gates and David took their seats on the patio, David responded to Gates' comment, saying, "I'm with you, buddy, about not driving. I drive enough when I'm home.

"And something else. You know, you're one weird dude, Gates. Most people are not that comfortable around me except for that Sandra. Yeah, she was real comfortable if you know what I mean!"

Slightly irritated by that remark, Gates replied, "Well, she may not have been as comfortable as you think; at least the spirit part of her wasn't. I mean, she's a changed woman."

"There you go again. Talking about this spirit stuff, Gates. Now, you and I have the same background, so tell me this. I know you're now a minister and all, but you really don't…I mean, you really don't believe a lot of that stuff, do you? I mean some of the stuff you preach about. Like heaven being a real place and dead people coming back to life—stuff like that."

Before Gates responded, David continued, "I mean, so many of the ministers I've seen are not *real*. Most of 'em are kind of deceiving if you ask me. They preach one thing and then turn around and do the opposite a lot of times."

Finally able to respond, Gates said, "Well, I'm glad you asked, David. Let me just say that I'm glad you put your feelings out there in the open. Believe it or not, that's exactly what I want to talk to you about—spiritual kinds of stuff as you put it."

"Oh, no! Here we go again," David interjected. "Are you gonna start preachin' to me, man? Because if you are, I'd rather be in the room getting some rest like the others."

"Hold on a minute, David! Are you gonna put me down like that—before we even get started?" Gates said. "Remember, man, I've already been where you are now, so I think you can learn a lot from what I have to tell ya," Gates added. "Come on over here and we can sit on this couch. I mean, it's further away from that fireplace, but it's more comfortable, plus we can still enjoy the heat coming from it while we look outside and see but not experience those wintry conditions."

"Okay!" David said. "You got my attention. But hold on! I don't want to get that close to you, to any man. I know you're not funny and all, but sometimes I like to keep my distance."

Then Gates replied, "Okay then, we can continue to sit in these two comfy chairs; we'll be closer to the fireplace, and we won't be sitting on the same piece of furniture."

"That'll work," David replied. "I love being near the fireplace!"

They changed locations and sat in the two separate chairs that were closer to the fireplace. After they returned to their seats, Gates went on to tell David a short story.

"You know, David, I saw in a movie once where there were these two guys, and one was the bad guy, a real bad guy. And the good guy, the other guy, wanted to talk to him and suggested that they sit by the fireplace. Well, the bad guy didn't take that idea too well because he had heard that fireplaces are romantic places, so he didn't want to sit there with another guy. And…"

Just before Gates was about to finish his story, David, who had heard enough, said, "Oh, no! I'll take your suggestion then. Let's move back over to the couch; it's farther away from the fireplace!"

Gates replied, "No, no, I'm just kidding! I knew you'd be kinda sensitive to that."

David replied, "You know, like I said, you're one weird dude."

"No, not weird. Just peculiar," Gates said. "That's what the scripture says about believers." Gates was referring to scripture in 1 Peter 2:9 about God's people being peculiar while being in the world and not being of the world.

Without any further discussion on that matter, both Gates and David remained in their two comfortable chairs near the fireplace.

A short while after everyone had checked into the hotel, the snowfall had picked up outside. "Look at that snow now," Gates said gazing out the transparent plastic covering that shielded them from the elements. "It's really coming down out there."

David replied, "Yeah, it's pretty neat the way it looks out there with the white flakes against the darker background of that forest of pine trees. I'm sure glad we're in here where it's warm and comfortable."

"Hey, David, I didn't know you had such an appreciation of nature," Gates said.

"Well, right about now I have even more appreciation of the heat coming from that fireplace. It's really putting out the warmth. You know, Gates, I'm kinda glad that you picked this place over here to sit. Yeah, this fireplace is all right."

The two men remained silent for a few moments, appreciating the heat on a wintry night. Finally, Gates said, "Tell me, David, how in the world did you and Sheri hook up?"

"Believe it or not, it was at a church gospel concert that a friend of mine had invited me to. I was sitting beside her and just struck up a conversation. I was surprised how friendly she was to a complete stranger. During a break, I asked her if we could meet the next day for a snack at a local soda shop in downtown New Brunswick, and she said yes! I was surprised that we ended up meeting, and the rest is history, you might say.

"But, you know, she now has this thing about getting married, and I'm not sure if I'm ready for that," David added.

David gazed out into the night and watched the snowflakes dancing in the wind. After a while, he said, "Okay, Gates. You wanted to tell me something. Well, what is it?"

"It's about what we were dealing with earlier today when we had that flat tire. You came in and solved the problem right there on the spot!"

"Don't give me all the credit, man. You were there too," David replied.

"Yeah, I know, but I just want to make a point. I don't know why you're so much against the church and everything, but I want you to know that you have a talent, a God-given talent. And you used it today. And that's all God wants. He wants us to recognize Him and then do what He tells us to do with the talents He has given us. And you know what, David? You satisfied both of those requirements to be a believer. You *do* recognize Him, don't you? I think I remember you saying as much before."

"Sure, I recognize the Man Upstairs. I do *believe* in God, man!" David insisted.

"Well, that's better than I was, because I didn't believe in God," Gates said. "In fact, I didn't believe God even existed—period! I was an atheist!"

"Um, you don't say," David responded.

Gates continued, "Anyway, I can prove what I'm saying—about the reality of God, that is—right from the scriptures.

"I'm sure you can, preacher," David responded with disdain.

Gates, who did not want to get into much detail because of David's limited knowledge of the Bible, went on, "Now, don't get me wrong. I'm not preaching to you, but what it says in the Good Book is that God is the giver of all life. And if we call His name, that is, recognize Him for who He is and do what He says, then He counts us as believers.

"If you don't believe me, then check this out. It's in two places in scripture. Now hear me out before you say anything because I can sense that you may be getting a little impatient."

David blurted out, "You're wrong, preacher. I'm listening."

"Okay then," Gates said. "In James, chapter four, verse eight, it says, and I quote, 'Draw near to God and He will draw near to you,' and you've done that simply by being willing to listen to what I'm saying. In a way you've drawn nearer to God."

Gates continued, "Now, the second thing is this: I'm gonna go to the Book of James again, but now I'm in chapter one, verse seventeen, where it says, 'Every good gift and every perfect gift is from above,' that is, from God, David. And He says that these gifts come down from the Father. The Father of lights, it says…."

"In other words, it's God who gives us the gifts we have. Now I could go into more detail, but I won't right now."

"Please don't!" David exclaimed.

Gates continued, "Anyway, David, God's saying that He's given you a gift. And the gift you have is working on vehicles like the one you worked on today. Heck, it's the gift of helping people. Remember what you did back in Florida when you saved Casey from drowning and how you got yourself into Maggie's room when she had already drowned?"

David retorted, "Now, wait a minute, man; even Maggie said that happened only in her dream. Don't give me credit for something that didn't really happen!"

Gates continued, "Okay. You got me on that. But you know? God is about solving problems, and He helped you with the talent He gave you, so that you could help us today. I mean, we couldn't have gotten it done without your help, your knowledge of working on vehicles like the ones we have. That's why we were able to leave that rest stop and get back on the road—because of your knowledge of how to change a tire on that type of vehicle. So, God helped us solve a problem by using you! That's right–God used *you* to help us, man. Now, what do ya think about that?"

"Well, it's something to think about," David answered.

"That's what I'm talking about! Think about it, man!" Gates said.

"Okay, okay! I'll think about then. I'll think about it. Is that all you had to tell me?" David asked.

"Yes, that's it. Now we can go to our rooms and get some rest. You know we still have a good drive ahead of us tomorrow."

Still sitting in his chair, David leaned over and said, "Okay, Gates. Now let me shake *your* hand. I'll see you in the morning."

With that, David got up and left Gates there in front of the fireplace, pondering what he had just told David *and* how he had responded. He had hoped to plant a seed perhaps and do some good.

Gates continued to sit there for another few minutes, contemplating what had happened over the past several hours. Then he saw Maggie come towards him.

"Hey, Maggie. What are you doing up? It's been a long day, and I thought that everyone would be in bed by now."

Maggie replied, "You know Fred is fast asleep, but I just couldn't go to sleep, so I decided to come out here and sit for a while. I just passed David, and I guess he's on his way to his suite with Sheri and Jeanie."

Gates replied, "Yeah, David and I were just sitting here talking about some things. Anyway, Maggie, you just go ahead and do what you were going to do. I think I'll retire for the night. You know we have a long drive ahead of us tomorrow, so don't stay out here too long."

"Yeah, I know what you're saying, Gates," Maggie agreed. "I think I'll just sit out here a few minutes in front of this fireplace and then go back to the room. After I get back, I think I'll be able to fall asleep pretty fast. But something is telling me that I should be here. I don't understand it, but I think I'll follow what my spirit is saying."

"Well, okay then, Maggie. We'll see you in the morning," Gates responded.

With that, Gates walked away. Maggie sat there staring at the fire, listening to the crackling sounds of the burning logs that provided a comforting warmth. The smooth jazz playing in the background helped her relax even more.

Maggie's thoughts went beyond the day's drive and the incident that occurred hours earlier on the interstate. Her mind traveled back to a more tranquil time at home back in Flint with her mother Mensie and her father Matthew. It was a glorious time, she thought, as she continued to gaze at the fire and felt its comforting effects. Maggie was mesmerized by the flames and imagined that her mother was speaking directly to her. She could almost hear Mensie say, "Little girl, live your life and live it abundantly."

Maggie sat there for another few minutes. Then she said, "Mama, I know you're not here. You've been gone for some time now, but it *seems* as though you're right here with me. Maggie heard a roll of thunder in the distance. *That's unusual*, she thought. *Thunder at this time of year during a snowstorm?*

While Maggie felt fatigued to the point where she knew slumber was near. She said to herself, "I take that thunder as a sign, Mama, that you're speaking to me. And more important than that, you're with me right now in the spirit. That's one of the 'Wonders of the Spirit' that Gates talks about a lot. Let me offer up a prayer:

"Lord God, you give us signs not only that you're near to us but also our loved ones who have passed on are with us too. I realize that we only have to pray that You will give us the insight to recognize reality in the spirit, to talk with and to be with our loved ones like I am with my mother right now."

Maggie felt comforted and ready for sleep, so she went to her room and retired for the night.

* * *

Everyone woke up the next morning fresh and ready to continue their journey to Denver. As they gathered in the lobby of the hotel after breakfast, Sinbad said, "I hope everybody had a good night's sleep and enjoyed breakfast. We're going to be on the road soon. And I want to tell you about a slight adjustment to our plans. The weather has gotten a lot better. All the wind, snow, and slush we had yesterday and into last night is gone. Well, maybe the slush is still with us and will be around for a while until it melts away. Anyway, now the sun is shining, and it's getting warmer.

"But getting back to what I really wanted to tell you, we can stop in Burlington to refuel and then, instead of having a meal together in some restaurant like we had planned, we can just grab some snacks and keep rolling."

Sinbad continued, "From here, it's only a two-hour drive to Burlington. I know highway 12 is not like the interstate; it's a much narrower road, so we'll be driving slower. But we'll get there. And when we do, it's another eight-hour drive to Denver."

Once we're on I-80, leaving early like we're doing, we probably get into Denver by late afternoon. I'd say around 5:00 or 6:00.

"Getting there at this time will give us enough time to unpack, have dinner, and rest a little. And I'll give everybody a revised schedule of activities for the week. I'm continuing to make some adjustments to it.

"I also got a little information about room assignments from Maggie, and I'll give you that too.

"So, here's the bottom line. When we make our stopover near Burlington, I'll make a print and give each one of you a copy of the schedule and contact info for everyone in the group, including Erin and Bernie. Maggie did some research and found the location of a printing shop in that city where I can get the copies, and it's near where we'll be staying."

Everyone listened and were in full agreement with Sinbad. They were so anxious to get to Denver and begin their vacation and particularly to see Erin and Bernie.

The travel from Chappell to Denver was uneventful. Late that morning, they stopped near Burlington for food and fuel and for Sinbad to make copies of scheduled activities.

Being so close to Erin on her first trip to Bermuda, during the stop in Burlington, Sandra gave her a call and was excited to talk with her again. It was a brief conversation, however.

After their initial greetings, Sandra said, "We stopped in a place called Burlington to grab a bite to eat, and now we're getting ready to hit the road again. We still have a way to go and should be there within eight hours. That's a day's drive.

"We don't have much time before we get back on the road. I just wanted to update you and hear your voice again," Sandra added.

"Well, Sandra, it's great hearing from you. When you arrive, maybe we can chat a little before we meet as a group."

"Okay, Erin. I'd like that. I'll contact you when we arrive. Give my regards to Bernie. We'll see you soon."

After their conversation ended, the group continued on their journey, exiting off the sideroad onto Interstate 70 heading toward Denver. After another several hours on the road, the group's travel from the Windy City to the Mile High City would be complete. Everyone looked forward to the real vacation to begin in the mountains of Colorado!

After about two hours, they passed Manhattan, where they had discussed stopping for food, but everyone agreed to continue and not delay getting to the Mile High City.

PART III: DENVER!

CHAPTER 17
Denver!

Foundation Scripture: Proverbs 20:27

The spirit of a man is the lamp of the Lord Searching all the inner depths of his heart.

"Denver, Colorado! We're finally here, Fred," Maggie said to her husband as they approached the city.

After eight hours riding from Burlington, the group approached Denver late on Wednesday afternoon as Sinbad had anticipated.

"Wow! Look at the mountains!" Maggie added. "The snow-covered mountains beyond the downtown area with all the skyscrapers in the foreground is a magnificent sight."

Sinbad and everyone in his van were equally impressed with the approach to the city. However, Sinbad was most concerned with keeping an eye on the van ahead of them, Fred's van, and making sure they would not lose them.

FIGURE 10: The Drive Into Denver: The Skyline and Mountains in the Background

Soon, both vans would arrive at the Santo Domingo Hotel, the host hotel for the group. The next order of business for everyone after getting established in their room was to relax and meet casually with one another, to become familiar with the premises, and review the plans Sinbad had made for the week's activities. The highlight for everyone would be reuniting with Erin and Bernie.

As Fred and Maggie entered the lobby of the hotel, she said, "I never dreamed it would be this beautiful. It's so clean. And those huge columns here in the lobby are so beautiful, and everything is modern, although I do see some antique furniture scattered about. But I think that is what makes this place something special—so modern and up to date with a touch of class with the antique furniture in places."

Fred replied, "It *is* nice, Mag. Unfortunately, to my understanding, we'll be here for only two nights, tonight and again on Sunday night before we take off on the road going back to Chicago the following Monday. Between tomorrow and Sunday, we'll be in the mountains. But I've heard it's nice up there too where we'll be staying until we come back here on Sunday."

Soon Fred and Maggie and other members of the group went to their rooms. Maggie said, "Fred, you know Sinbad mentioned he'd like for all of us to come together tonight at 9:00 to meet Erin and Bernie and to get the schedule of activities for the week. I think we're supposed to meet in the Ohio Room, a large conference area next to the lobby."

Fred replied, "Yeah, Mag, you're right. It's a little after 7:00 now. That gives us about two hours to get ready for that. But, you know, I think I'll lie down and take a nap."

"Okay, Fred. You go ahead and do that. You deserve it after all the driving you've done. I'm going downstairs to the first floor and see a little of this place, and who knows who I might run into. I might even take a peek in the conference room where we're supposed to have the meeting."

"Okay, Mag. I'll see you a little later," Fred replied.

With that, Maggie prepared to go down to the lobby and maybe even the conference room. At least her intent was to head in that direction.

* * *

The Ohio Room was the main gathering place for the evening. Erin and Bernie had arrived the day before, and Sinbad had given Erin the responsibility of preparing that room for his planned meeting. She utilized her experience as manager of the Bermuda resort in planning for formal events, especially the opening meeting. Sinbad wanted to take advantage of Erin's experience in managing special events. She made sure that the hotel's main conference room was appropriately configured for Sinbad's meeting.

As Erin put the finishing touches on the Ohio Room the day before the group's arrival, she said to herself, "Okay now. I think everything is the way it should be."

Erin realized the importance of giving Sinbad as much assistance as possible in helping him communicate the week's activities to others in the group. Arranging the seating in a way that would reflect Sinbad's preferences for the opening meeting was a top priority.

The room's configuration included a head table where Sinbad, his two cousins Alphonso and Carlos, and Erin and Bernie would be seated. A podium also was brought in and placed where Sinbad would speak.

The others participating in this meeting would sit at tables distributed around the room near the head table. Four tables with chairs were arranged behind the head table; these would be more than enough to accommodate everyone at the meeting.

Sinbad's cousins, Alphonso and Carlos, would coordinate other activities that would take place each day during their stay at the resort.

✦ ✦ ✦

Maggie headed downstairs as she said she would; Fred stayed back in their room to take his nap. As she stepped off the elevator, there was an unexpected surprise.

"Oh, my Lord! Erin and Bernie!" Maggie said in excitement as she saw the newlyweds.

"Hello, Maggie," Erin responded when she saw her friend. They embraced and said how much they missed each other.

Maggie then greeted Bernie and said to them both, "You know, I'm so happy for you two. I know you'll have a great marriage."

Erin replied, "Well, thank you, Maggie. I know any marriage is challenging, but I believe we'll make it work. Don't you think so, Bernie?"

Her new husband said with a smile, "Of course, honey. I wouldn't dare to disagree with you on that!"

"So, are you two going to your room?" Maggie asked them.

Erin responded, "You know, Maggie, we've been here for a day already, and do you know that girl of yours, Sandra, looked us up and called me? She was the first one in our group that I've heard from since we've been here; she called me. It must have been when you guys were on the road about eight hours ago.

"Anyway, we have a suite on the first floor, but she's on the second floor. She touched bases with me again, apparently right after she got in her room, and she gave me her room number. She reminded me of what we talked about on the phone earlier and said she looked forward to talking with me for a few minutes before we all come together at 9:00 for this meeting that Sinbad has arranged to have with everybody. So that's where I was headed—to Sandra's room."

Then Erin asked, "Why don't you come along, Maggie?"

"Of course, Erin. I thought you would never ask! I'd be glad to come along with you to Sandra's room. That would be even nicer than walking around on the first floor or maybe sitting alone in the lobby."

"Okay, Maggie, I'm glad you'll be coming with me. But Sandra and I agreed to meet in her room because our room is right beside Sinbad's room. I didn't want Sandra to come to our room, being right next to Sinbad, and for him to have an opportunity to see us. I don't think he expects Bernie and me to meet anyone from the group *before* his meeting at 9:00. And you know Sinbad. He wants to be precise about everything, and in this case *he* is the one who would want to meet with everyone for the first time.

"Anyway, I didn't want to take the chance of him seeing me with someone from the group *before* that meeting. I know it's crazy, but that's Sinbad for you."

Maggie replied, "I understand, Erin. And I do remember now when you two talked on the phone; it *was* about eight hours ago when we made a rest stop in this town called Burlington, and many of us made phone calls then. That's when Sandra mentioned that she had talked with you."

Erin responded, "Okay. Anyway, we can be finished with our little chatting session at least by 8:00, and then we can get ready for this meeting of everyone called by Sinbad at 9:00."

Erin continued, "Yeah, I can't wait for us to meet, which will be very soon. It's about 7:00 now, and we can reminisce till about that 8:00 hour.

"And by the way, Maggie, don't worry about Bernie. He's just here seeing me to the elevator; he is not going with me to her room, so it will be just you, me, and Sandra. Like I said, it'll be like old times with us chatting before going to that meeting."

Bernie interjected, "Yeah, Maggie. You go ahead with Erin because I'm going back to our room down here on the first floor and rest a little. I guess that's what Fred is doing now, huh, Maggie?"

"Yeah, as a matter of fact, he's taking a nap in our room on the second floor not too far away from Sandra's room," Maggie explained.

Bernie replied, "Okay then, let me go back to the room and take a snooze too. I'm sure you three have a lot to talk about."

Maggie replied, "Well, okay, you two. I guess I don't have a choice, do I? I wouldn't want you to go there by yourself when you've invited me to come along.

"I will tell you this much: while Fred is napping, my plan was to go to the lobby to see who I could see. But I can put that on hold.

When I get back to our room, I can tell Fred that I saw you two. Anyway, Erin, the three of us getting together again should be so much fun."

At that point Bernie went back to their room; Maggie, who was diverted from going to the lobby as she had planned, was ready to go with Erin to Sandra's room.

When Erin and Maggie arrived at Sandra's door, all it took was a couple of knocks from Erin, who was standing in front of Maggie, waiting for Sandra to answer. Sandra soon opened the door and greeted Erin. She gazed at her, then closed her eyes, all the while hugging her friend and then said, "Hello, Erin; it's great to see you!"

In her excitement to see Erin, Sandra didn't notice Maggie standing behind Erin. Sandra soon opened her eyes and saw Maggie; she shouted, "Oh my goodness! What a pleasant surprise, Maggie. I didn't expect to see you so soon. It seems like we've just gotten off the road.

"Anyway, welcome the both of you to my abode. Come on in," Sandra said.

"Thank you, Sandra," Erin responded. "Sandra, I saw Maggie getting off the elevator and I was shocked. That's when I invited her to come along with me to see you. You two have been the only ones I've talked to in our group since everyone's arrived here.

"As you know, Bernie and I arrived earlier on Monday. Anyway, notice I said our group because I consider being a part of you all and what you're about. I mean, while you know the Lord, you're so real and love to have fun. And that's me."

"Well, Erin, thanks for the compliment. But having fun has gotten me into lots of trouble, and both you *and* Maggie know that from my history…."

Sandra was ready to reply to what Erin had said, but then paused for a moment, looking down as if in shame. Then she continued, "At any rate, we can talk about what I *was* going to say over some tea.

"Well, don't just stand here at the door, you two. Come on in and take a seat. Even better, let's go out on the patio," Sandra said.

The three of them continued past the living area and went outside on a small patio overlooking the city.

After taking their seats in chairs beside a small table, Sandra said, "It's so fresh out here—much better than back in Detroit. And this view is magnificent with the downtown area and mountains in the background."

FIGURE 11: A Discussion from the Balcony

Sandra went on, "Well, before we get comfortable sitting here, I'll let you two talk a little while I go inside to get the tea and some cookies. I'll be right back."

Maggie and Erin sat there appreciating the view and beginning to chat while Sandra stepped away. Sandra soon returned with the treats she promised. She took her seat and asked her friends, "So how do you two like this hotel?"

"Gorgeous!" Erin replied.

Maggie said, "Amen to that!"

"Yeah, girls, it's very nice here. And this view is nice too," Sandra commented.

"Yeah, that's the first thing I told Fred about when we got here— how beautiful the hotel is and the city too." Maggie said. "In my opinion, it's just as nice as Sinbad's resort down in Florida," she continued.

Erin said, "Yes, I agree with the both of you. We have a nice suite down there on the first floor. As I told you on the phone, we're right beside Sinbad. He gave us the room assignments. I guess he got them from you, Maggie. Still, you can't beat the view up here."

Maggie responded, "Yeah, the hotel gave me all the details when I first made the reservation, but it didn't mention anything about the view. They *did* ask me about everyone who would be in our party, and I included you Erin because you and Bernie were already here. So, I definitely let them know that you are a part of our group. And I'm thankful to Sinbad for allowing me a part in doing the room assignments."

Erin then said, "Well, truth be told, Maggie, I wouldn't be surprised if Sinbad had more of a hand in those room assignments than you think. He has so many connections, you know. And he usually gets things done the way he wants them. But thank you, Maggie, for taking care of all that, even if Sinbad did have a hand in it."

Erin continued, "Anyway, regardless of how nice something is, it's always good to experience a new thing! And this is all new to me and Bernie."

Erin decided to change the tone of the conversation and asked, "Can I get a little spiritual on you girls?

Maggie answered, "Yes, by all means, Erin. What do you have to say?"

Erin responded, "Well, you know, I hadn't intended to say this, but it's interesting how the three of us came together. And the reason is that, Sandra, you had a hunger to get well physically when you first came to Bermuda. Heaven knows you tried everything else based on what you told me at the time. But you finally realized that you needed something greater than yourself if you were to survive the health problem you had.

"Well, when you made me aware of your health situation, I realized *that* was the reason you came to Bermuda. But you also told me about some of your history. And when I learned of the things that you've been through, I knew that your spirit as well as your physical health needed to be healed. Fortunately, you were receptive to my trying to help you, and we became lifelong friends! I just thank God for that."

With a bit of emotion, Erin added, "And, Sandra, your allowing me to help you was a key to me ending up in south Florida and becoming married to the man, I think, was made just for me, the man of my dreams if you will."

Sandra replied, "I guess I *did* play a part in you moving to south Florida. But let me tell you, Erin, you were a major factor in my receiving the help that I needed at the time. If it weren't for that, none of what you just described would have happened. Why, maybe you'd still be a single woman!"

Maggie got into the conversation. "Well, if you ask me, I think that both of you help each other. And like you said, Erin, that's another 'Wonder of the Spirit.' That is, how the three of us have come together like we have is nothing short of miraculous! And that's how God can work in our lives to make things right—that all things work together for the good, as the scripture states."

"Oh, yes, Maggie! The 'Wonders of the Spirit'!" Erin proclaimed with much emotion.

Sandra shouted, "You're right, Maggie." As Sandra turned toward her, she continued, "It is amazing how we came together like we did. I didn't know what to expect when I first got to Bermuda. I just knew I needed help from someplace. Then I met Erin! What a blessing!

"What I experienced back in Bermuda was the wisdom of this woman, Maggie. And I'll tell you again, it changed my life in several ways. I'm talking about physically and spiritually. And let me tell you, it changed my opinion on how I relate to men too. You see, Maggie, Erin was the key to me having a total transformation of my being."

"Sandra's giving you the credit, Erin, so don't shy away from it. Embrace it," Maggie admonished Erin.

But Erin provided a rebuttal, saying, "Don't give me *all* the credit. We all know the real reason why we got together back in Bermuda, Sandra, and why we're all together today with you, Maggie."

Maggie said, "You're right, Erin. I know what you're going to say. God is the one who has made all this possible. You just cannot ignore the spiritual element that has influenced all of us. There were just too many things that had to come together. Everything seems to have come together in perfect timing. And I know Sandra would agree with that," she added glancing at her.

"Amen to that, Maggie!" Sandra agreed.

Maggie turned back toward Erin and said, "Erin, you *do* deserve credit for the way Sandra turned her life around."

"Well, I'm just glad I was able to give Sandra some guidance, Maggie," Erin replied. "But I just hate to take all the credit, so I'll just have to disagree with you on that score, Maggie. As you just mentioned, it wasn't me who helped Sandra. It was really the Lord giving me the wisdom to say the right thing at the right time."

Erin then continued with her original thought. "Anyway, getting back to what I really was going to talk to you two about, and that was Sandra being receptive to receiving my help.

"You know, Maggie and Sandra, I think it's important to receive whatever God is trying to give us. Because we know that it's for our own good. And, Sandra, you were certainly receptive to me helping you when you came to Bermuda that first time. I mean, you were like a sponge, girl, soaking up everything I was telling you."

Sandra replied, "You're right, Erin. I *was* like a sponge. But if you think about it, I had no choice. I mean, I was so messed up, both physically and spiritually, that there was nowhere to go but up. And you sure did help me with the problems I had at the time. But as you said, we all know where the source of our help comes from.

"And by the way, that first time was the only time I was in Bermuda. You're probably thinking about the time I was there in Maggie's dream, the way she described it."

"Yeah, Sandra, Maggie gave such a vivid review of what she dreamed. It was as though I was actually there with her, and you and all the others in our group were there too," Erin said.

"But you know? Getting back to that source we were talking about, we all know that it's God who provides us with everything we need. And you sure needed a lot, and God provided it, didn't He, girl!" Erin proclaimed. She added, "But don't play yourself short! You had a part in that too, Sandra, because you were so receptive to me trying to help you. I'm just so glad I was used as a vessel to help you receive what you needed at the time. You know it's not difficult for any of us to do things on our own strength and not rely on that higher power. I'm just so glad that the Master is with us even in our limitations."

Then Erin asked Maggie, "Wouldn't you agree with that, Maggie? That we were led to come together in Bermuda by a higher power?"

Maggie responded, "I do agree, Erin. You're right! God did allow you two to come together. But then again, He allows everything to happen for His divine purpose. And the key is that the both of you had to respond to His presence. As you said, sometimes we're not as receptive to His voice as we should be, and because of it we suffer the consequences of *not* having His favor. But God does give us free will as individuals. That is to say, He doesn't make us do anything; we have to be receptive to Him; it's our choice.

"And it's obvious to me that you did respond, Sandra, and you too, Erin, during your time together in Bermuda; you two were placed together to help each other," Maggie said. "And that's the *only* way He can help us, and that is for us to open the door to our lives when He knocks, you might say.

"I only wish our other close friend, Courtney, were here because she would certainly mention how her husband Gates would say the hold circumstance of our coming together is one of the 'Wonders of the Spirit.'"

Maggie then decided to become more of a central part of the conversation. She thought about something more personal to her, of the time when she was intimately involved with Sinbad's cousin Freddie back in Detroit. She said to Erin, "All of what you're saying is true, Erin, but it doesn't release the bad feeling any of us have when we do something wrong. And I've had my share of doing wrong over the years."

Erin interrupted, "Well, Maggie, we all have done things displeasing to God. But that's why we have a Savior in Jesus; He came to earth to basically save us from ourselves. But both of you know that."

Erin turned toward Sandra and said, "But in your case, Sandra, when you first came to Bermuda, you needed help both physically and spiritually."

Erin continued, "Maggie, don't feel too bad about your shortcomings because we've all fallen short of what we should be. We only need to ask the Lord to forgive us and guide us in the right direction."

Maggie asked, "Well, Erin, how do you get rid of the terrible feeling, the guilt, that comes with doing wrong?

Erin said, "This might not be the answer you want, Maggie, but you don't, or I should say you won't necessarily get rid of it. My advice is to not worry about how you feel because you're likely not to get rid of the bad feeling associated with the guilt. You just do the best you can to not dwell on it and to avoid making the same mistakes in the future."

Erin continued to impart the wisdom she had to her friends, saying, "The beauty of all this, Maggie, and Sandra, this is for you too. All you have to do, is to ask God to help you and He will. You can depend on His help. And it doesn't matter how bad you might feel about a certain act that you think is displeasing to Him. You just have to trust that He's forgiven you and is actively working on your behalf in that situation."

Recognizing the time, Erin said to Sandra and Maggie, "Do you two realize we've been talking for about an hour? It's about 8:00 now. And the time of our meeting with Sinbad is in an hour. Like I said before, we can use the time between now and then to freshen up and prepare for that meeting, so I guess we should be going, Maggie," Erin said.

Maggie replied, "Yeah, you're right, Erin. I'm sure we'll get to talk some more before this trip is over."

Sandra said, "I'm so glad you two came up. Even though we talk often, Maggie, it's good for the both of us to be together and especially to be together with you, Erin, because I think we share a common bond, and that's how our histories are related."

Sandra continued, "And, Maggie, your mother will always be a part of this group, on a spiritual level. And my Lord, Maggie, I miss Mensie so much as well as your father Matthew."

"Yeah, Mama was my best friend," Maggie replied. "But I'll tell both of you, I still communicate with her every day. To me, she's still with us in spirit. At least she's with me. And you know how close I was to my father."

After those sentimental words, Maggie said, "Well, I guess we do need to be going, Erin."

"I guess you're right, Maggie," Erin replied. "And thanks, Sandra, for inviting me up, and I'm so glad you came up with me, Maggie."

Sandra replied, "You're more than welcome, Erin, and I'm sure we'll have a chance to talk more while we're on this vacation. And by the way, how is married life? We haven't talked to you at all about your new life with Bernie."

Erin said, "It's great! It's just another blessing. Well, not *just* another blessing; it's a *huge* blessing the way everything turned out. And what I mean by that is I wouldn't have had the opportunity to meet him without you guys. I mean, you two are the main reasons I ended up in south Florida with my position at Sinbad's resort. And I have more to say about that too."

Erin concluded her remarks by saying, "Well, we'll see you at the meeting, Sandra, in a few minutes."

Maggie confirmed, "Yeah, Sandra, as you know, everybody will be there."

"Okay, I'll see you two downstairs soon," Sandra said.

CHAPTER 18
Sinbad Speaks Again

Foundation Scripture: Ecclesiastes 3:1,7

1 To everything there is a season, A time for every purpose under heaven: 7 A time to tear, And a time to sew; A time to keep silence, And a time to speak..

The time of Sinbad's meeting had almost arrived. At about ten minutes before 9:00, everyone began to gather in the Ohio Room. They milled around conversing casually for a few minutes until Sinbad directed everyone to be seated and then addressed the group.

"Well, everybody, we're finally here. I know we thought about the possibility of being here a day earlier on Tuesday evening, but we really needed that overnight stay in Chappell, and we will still have plenty of time to get all our activities in, which I'll explain in just a little bit.

"I'm so glad to see all of you here. First off, let me thank my two cousins, Alphonso and Carlos, for being here to make sure everything goes smoothly. And I certainly don't want to forget my other cousin Freddie, whose final service we conducted last week back in Detroit. I know he's with us in spirit.

"I think we all know we're here this week to celebrate Erin and Bernie, who were recently married and are spending the second part of their honeymoon here in Denver with all of us. Well, we really won't be *in* Denver most of the time. We'll be in Echo Mountain only about a forty-minute drive from the city.

"As most of you know, the first part of their honeymoon was spent on the Island of Love back in south Florida. Now I know that might bring up sad memories of the time when all of you visited me at my Miami resort in celebration of Erin coming on board to work for us.

"As you know, we didn't get the chance to go to the island during your visit at that time because of the hurricane. But I will say that Maggie gave us a vivid description of a trip we all took there—in her dream!"

As Sinbad made that statement, there was a burst of laughter in the room. When everything calmed down, Sinbad continued, "Well, I know everyone got a big kick out of that, and I want to tell you, Maggie, please don't have any more dreams! And if you do, I hope that it's something more pleasant." The small group had another laugh, responding to Sinbad's comments, but it did not last long.

Sinbad quickly regained control of the room and said, "Listen, everybody, you all will have the opportunity again to visit that island *for real*. And as I've said before, it'll be a visit you won't soon forget. And by the way, I have some information on that before we leave the Denver area going back home.

"Now, let me warn you. Both Erin and Bernie have promised me that they will not mention to anyone anything about their visit to the island—absolutely nothing! And that's because I want it to be a complete surprise to everyone who will finally get to visit there one day, and one day soon, I might add."

"We're not in south Florida now, of course. We're here in Denver, a completely different environment from what we know about in south Florida. There's simply no comparison with Miami. And viewing the mountains from where we are here at the hotel is spectacular.

"Now let me say that I do love Miami and south Florida in general. It's a tropical environment with lots of waterways, lakes, and streams, and of course, there's always the beach and the Atlantic Ocean.

"But out here, you're about as far away from a tropical environment as you can get. And you know what? It will be even more of a drastic change once we get to our destination up in those mountains. That's what I want to talk to you about this evening—our time up there in the mountains.

"Yes, indeed! Soon we'll be heading to a cabin I have reserved in Echo Mountain. That's the name of the small town the resort is in. And let me tell you. We're going to play in one of the nicest ski resorts in the country. And that's what this meeting is about—to reveal what we have planned during the five days we're here in the area.

"But first, I want to recognize the couple of the hour, Mr. and Mrs. Bernie Mason. I want the new bride to speak; then the groom can say a word or two after she finishes *if* he wishes to do so. Erin, you go ahead a say something."

At that point Erin rose to her feet to speak to the small gathering. "Thank you, Sinbad, for everything that you have done to make this event possible. I really don't have much to say except that I'm so happy to see my friends from the Chicago/Detroit area as well as the New York/New Jersey region. I know we went to the Island of Love, but there's nothing like being together with you guys."

"You go, girl!" Katie shouted from the audience.

"All right, Katie. I see you out there!" Erin responded. She continued, "I'm so anxious to see Katie and all the rest of you during this vacation. I'm just so excited and looking forward to what this week will bring, so I'll end my remarks there. Bernie, do you want to say anything?" Erin asked her husband.

"No, I'll pass on that. I'm anxious to see the schedule too."

After Erin made her remarks, Sinbad started to review the week's activities with the group. "Thank you, Erin, for those comments.

"All right, everybody, here's the plan. And by the way, a summary of it was already in your seats; I hope you picked it up. Anyway, I'm looking at the same sheet, and, as you can see, we'll be doing something every day and evening that we're here in the area—except today when we are on our own.

"Now, everyone except for Erin and Bernie, who arrived here on Monday, got caught in a snowstorm, which is why we just got here today on Wednesday. But that's fine because we're all here now.

"Once we get to the mountains after leaving here tomorrow morning, it won't be long until we enter the town of Echo Mountain. The resort lodging site where we will be staying is Williams' Cabin. This facility will serve as our headquarters. For this reason, we will call it simply Headquarters.

"We will be staying there between tomorrow, Thursday, and Sunday when we return here. We'll spend three nights and will have two full days there, Friday and Saturday. Saturday night will be our last night there. We'll have two half days, one tomorrow on Thursday when we arrive there and a half day on Sunday when we come back here. We'll leave at about noon that day, heading back here to Denver, and will arrive at the hotel by 2:00 that afternoon.

"We will have something planned for each day of our stay in Echo Mountain except for Sunday when we return here. Now this is pretty simple, people. The first day of *scheduled* activities is on Thursday when we arrive at Echo Mountain, which should be early in the morning. We'll spend some time getting situated in our rooms in Williams' Cabin, have a small lunch, then plan to participate in our first activity that afternoon when we go on a cable lift tour at 2:00. It will take about thirty minutes to get to the cable lift site from Headquarters at Williams' Cabin. We'll be going in the vans that brought us here. Once we arrive at the Cable Lift Center, otherwise known as the CLC, we can anticipate a three-hour adventure from about 2:30 to 5:30. Then, we'll take the thirty-minute bus ride and arrive back at Williams' Cabin at 6:00 that day.

"Once we all return to the cabin, we'll have a chance to freshen up and prepare for dinner, which will be in the cabin's dining area at 7:30 on Thursday evening. We all should be finished by 9:00, and after that time you can congregate in groups and do whatever you want.

"Then on Friday we have a scheduled visit to Canyon Volcano where we will explore the surrounding area. In other words, we'll do a lot of hiking that day. Now, you should be prepared for that activity, so we'll need to get some hiking boots at the cabin's gift shop before we leave. Again, we'll do hiking on Friday starting at 10:00 in the morning, and we should return here to the cabin by 4:00. I would suggest that you get your footwear the day after we return from the cabin lift tour, which will be Friday, the day of our hiking tour. We'll be in the cabin the rest of that day ending with our social/dinner that evening at 7:00.

"Hopefully, the weather will cooperate because I heard that it's possible that a weather system will be coming through on Friday when we go hiking. But I think it's scheduled to arrive later in the day after we return to the cabin.

"Then on Saturday we'll be going skiing. Again, we'll leave at about 10:00. Now don't be afraid, especially if you've never been skiing before. I understand there'll be several trainers on hand to help anyone who needs it. But it should be exciting. You'll be able to see the views of this mountainous region close up. We'll be doing that all day, returning to the cabin by 3:00.

"But I will tell you this activity is optional. There may be those who decide to stay in the cabin resort area instead of skiing, and that's fine. But I strongly recommend it though. I mean, you don't get a chance to ski every day even in the northern part of the country where most of you are from. And we definitely can't do that in Florida. Anyway, I'll leave that up to you.

"Those who will go skiing should return to the cabin in time to freshen up a bit before dinner. It's not that far to the ski site from Williams' Cabin. Anyway, we'll come together again that Saturday evening. But this time dinner will be earlier at 5:00 in the main dining area of the cabin. We'll eat earlier so that you will have enough time to go back to your room and start packing Saturday night for our departure from Williams' Cabin the next day. Remember, Sunday is our second half-day. As I said, we'll leave at noon and should be back and well situated here at the hotel in Denver by 2:00.

"As I said earlier, you'll be on your own to eat and mingle with whomever and wherever you wish that afternoon and evening when we return here on Sunday. But be sure to pack everything before going to bed Sunday night because we want to leave Denver by early Monday morning; I'd say by no later than 8:00.

"The plan is to have an overnight stay again in Chappell that Monday night at the same hotel we stayed at on the way here during that snowstorm. You all remember," Sinbad said with a smile. "The plan is to then take off the next day on Tuesday for Chicago.

"I will say that we also plan to stop again at Mickey's Diner late that afternoon on Tuesday to eat and freshen up before we take the final leg of the trip back to Windy City. After the three-hour drive from the diner, we should arrive in Chicago by early evening on Tuesday.

"By the way, the longest time we'll have stopping on Tuesday will be at Mickey's Diner. I'm sure all of you remember that place! That was our first stop near Des Moines as you know. You may not want to remember when we ran into that snowstorm after we left the diner and had the tire problem on our way to Chappell on I-80.

"Anyway, there you have it. It's all in front of you on that sheet. But I'll be around if you have any questions.

"Again, I want to congratulate Erin and Bernie on their marriage and hope you two have many happy years together. This meeting is adjourned."

With that, everyone dispersed and went their separate ways, retiring to their rooms in anticipation of their morning trip to Echo Mountain and the adventure awaiting them.

CHAPTER 19
The Great Outdoors

Foundation Scripture: John 10:10

The thief does not come except to steal, and to kill, and to destroy. I have come that they may have life, and that they may have it more abundantly.

Thursday morning was clear and calm. Everyone packed their belongings in the two vans and were ready to roll to the resort where they would stay for the next several days. They would be there until midday on Sunday when they returned to the hotel in Denver.

A major difference between their sojourn to the event site in the mountains and their trip from Chicago to Denver was that Sinbad's cousins, Alphonso and Carlos, would be driving the vans. Alphonso replaced Fred in the red van, which was the lead vehicle. Carlos took over for Sinbad in driving the blue van.

<table>
<tr><td>ALPHONSO'S VAN
(Red Van)</td><td>CARLOS' VAN
(Blue Van)</td></tr>
<tr><td>Alphonso (Driver) ----Sandra
Courtney ---------------Gates
Maggie-------------------Fred
Jeanie --------------------Wynn</td><td>Carlos (Driver)---- Katie
Casey-------------- Sinbad
Winnie -----------------Ted
Sheri ----------------David</td></tr>
</table>

FIGURE 12

Vans Seating Arrangements to Cable Lift Center

After having breakfast in the hotel's dining area, the small caravan left with Bernie and Erin leading the way in their Jeep. The scenery swiftly shifted from metropolitan Denver to hilly suburban neighborhoods just west of the city; from there they began to enter the mountainous terrain of the Rockies within a matter of minutes.

Once in the Rockies, everyone witnessed the majestic views of the landscape. Even Wynn made a comment to Jeanie about the panorama. "Look, Jeanie; look down there. What a drop off!"

The young couple gazed out the window and witnessed the natural beauty of the area. But the potential dangers were acknowledged by Jeanie. "I just hope the vehicle stays on the road. It'd be such a long drop down into that ravine," she said.

"Don't worry about that, Jeanie," Wynn told her for encouragement.

Overhearing their discussion, Alphonso, the driver, attempted to put her at ease, saying, "Don't worry, Miss Jeanie. Wynn is right! Carlos and I have a lot of experience in driving, and we'll make sure all of you are safe."

FIGURE 13 The Ravine

"Amen, Alphonso!" shouted Gates, who was sitting with Courtney in the seat behind the driver. "Everyone will be safe, not just because of cautious drivers behind the wheel but also because of the road's guardrail, which provides a barrier from the steep embankment of the ravine beyond it," he continued.

Despite the concerns for safety, their drive through the mountains provided majestic views of the steep, snow-covered slopes dotted with pine, spruce, fir, and cottonwood trees. Beyond the ravine at the very bottom of the chasm was a rapidly flowing river amidst huge boulders which remained seemingly unaffected by the raging waters.

Wynn continued, "You know, Jeanie, I learned about this kind of landscape in my high school geography class."

"Oh really?" Jeanie replied, obviously impressed with his knowledge. Of course, most of the things Wynn did or said captivated her. They were just an agreeable, happy twosome.

There was other chattering going on among passengers in both vans, mostly about the physical landscape they were witnessing.

Finally, everyone arrived at Williams' Cabin, the ski resort headquarters located in the small community of Echo Mountain. As everyone exited the vehicles, they noticed the abundance of snow, which was much deeper than what they experienced back in Denver.

Everyone followed Bernie and Erin towards the building. After spending most of her adult life in a tropical setting, Erin was not familiar with such a scene. Even while growing up in New York City, she never saw this much snow. She had become so accustomed to the tropical environment of Bermuda and now of south Florida.

Erin made sure to take advantage of the snowy situation that was before her. As they continued to walk to the center, Erin decided to have some fun by lagging behind her husband, then picking up some snow and throwing a snowball at Bernie. Fortunately, he leaned to the side and avoided becoming a victim of his wife's antics. He then returned the favor by tossing a snowball of his own at his new bride, and he did not miss! Erin screamed as the snowball hit her jacket and scattered everywhere.

Maggie was walking with Fred behind the newlyweds along with the rest of the group. She said, "Oh, look at 'em, Fred. They're having so much fun, throwing snowballs and all. That's so sweet how they're expressing their love for one another."

Fred replied, "Now, Mag, they're still on their honeymoon, the second half of it, that is."

Maggie retorted, "Oh, Fred, don't be such a stiff! Lovers are not just for those recently married. You can have the fun they're having as you get older like us!"

Fred replied, "Are you calling us old, Mag?" Before she could answer, he quickly added, "Anyway, I'm not going to argue with you about that, Mag!"

Maggie replied, "Good! That's what I want to hear!"

Bernie and Erin were the first to enter the lobby. A receptionist greeted the couple followed soon by the others.

Erin said to her husband, "Bernie, this place is nice and so much different from the modern features of the hotel back in Denver."

"Yes, it is different. It has an antique, even homey, feel to it."

Soon everyone had entered the lobby. Sandra, who had come in with Katie, said, "Katie, I can't believe this place! It's so nice; it's a different kind of nice than what we experienced back at the hotel in Denver.

"Amen to that!" Katie said.

Three massive chandeliers were suspended from the ceiling, drawing the immediate attention of all who entered. Several gas-lit lamps lined the walls with paintings hanging between them, lending proof to Bernie's comment about the homey feel of the place.

The size of the chandeliers reflected the enormity of the facility— at least in the lobby area. The lobby adjoined a number of rooms housing various amenities. One room was filled with slot machines, another a restaurant, and still another was devoted to gaming machines.

Another feature that impressed Sandra and Katie was the presence of two large fireplaces on either side of the facility, which added to the ambiance. For the convenience of patrons, a large couch with several reclining chairs and an elongated table graced the area in front of each fireplace.

Once everyone had gotten accustomed to how nice the facility was, they were serviced by several clerks at the front desk who assisted them in claiming their living quarters.

Gates and Courtney were the first to be assigned their cabin, which was nearest to the lobby where everyone had assembled. Once they took the short walk from the front desk to their assigned living quarters, Courtney said, "My, my! What an interesting setup, Gates."

The small cabin where Courtney and Gates were lodged was supplied with two bunk beds, one on top of the other. The cabin contained a small kitchenet as well as a bathroom. A large window near the top of the cabin allowed for a view of the normally wintry conditions that prevailed outside—at least for the person who had the top bunk.

The Manleys seemed satisfied with the accommodations, although Courtney did question the inability to share the same bed with her husband, who would take the top bunk.

Like the hotel rooms back in Denver, their lodgings had been reserved prior to the group leaving for Colorado.

Since the group arrived early Thursday, everyone had the opportunity to spend the remainder of the morning adjusting to their new environment. All of their cabins resembled Gates and Courtney's living quarters. Wynn and Jeanie had separate cabins, and his mother Katie and Sandra shared a cabin.

After becoming situated, most looked forward to the first activity, the Cable Lift Tour, which was scheduled to begin after lunch at 2:00.

Shortly after 1:00 that afternoon, everyone began to prepare for the first activity, which would take place at the Cable Lift Center (CLC). After about thirty minutes, everyone gathered near a gift shop, waiting to be taken to the site. Maggie began talking to a lady standing beside her.

"Are you two going on the cable lift tour too?" Maggie asked the woman, who was standing by her male companion.

"We sure are. We're waiting on a taxi to take us there."

"The members of our group are going there in two vans that we have. You're welcome to come with us," Maggie said encouragingly.

"Well, that would be great if there's enough room for us," the lady said. "By the way, I'm Winnie and this is my friend Ted."

"Hello, Winnie and Ted," Maggie said. "Let me tell our driver to confirm everything."

Maggie walked a short distance to where Alphonso stood and asked him, "Hey, Alphonso, we have another couple who would like to join us. Will that be a problem to have an extra couple traveling with us in the van?"

"No! It will not be a problem at all, Miss Maggie. We have plenty of room," he answered. "Carlos and I are about to go and get the vans now. You can tell this couple that they can find a seat on either one of the vans we're taking."

Maggie returned to where Winnie was standing and said, "Everything is fine with you and your friend coming along with us. Alphonso, one of our drivers, just said there's plenty of room on either of the vans we have. And like I said, you're more than welcome to come with us."

Winnie replied, "Ted and I really appreciate you doing this. We're here from back east and will be returning to Boston tomorrow."

With that, everyone was set to go! The two vans were situated in front of the cabin ready to receive occupants. Since there were no assigned seats at this point, everyone took the spots they found open in the vans, and Maggie's new friends did the same.

Jeanie and Wynn were the first to board the van Alphonso was driving. They wanted to make sure they got to sit together. Jeanie left her folks David and Sheri in order to join Wynn.

"Mom, David, I'm going over there with Wynn," she said.

"We'll see you later then, Jeanie," Sheri said.

As Jeanie got nearer to Wynn, he said to her in a softer voice, "Come on, Jeanie; let's get in the blue van, the one we rode in when we got to Denver. I think we can get the same seats as we had before."

"Okay, Wynn, I'm following you," Jeanie replied. They headed straight to the back, and within no time they were in their seats.

Gates and Courtney soon joined them and sat just behind the front seat. Sinbad and Casey arrived later and sat just ahead of the young couple.

Sandra took the passenger seat beside Alphonso, the driver. She asked, "How are you doing, Alphonso?"

"I'm fine, Ms. Sandra," he replied. Then he said to the rest of the occupants, "We're about ready to take off people. Is everybody secure in their seats?"

Their response indicated that everyone was ready to go.

Jeanie's folks had boarded the other van driven by Carlos. Maggie and Fred were in this van along with Wynn's mother Katie, who rode in the front passenger seat beside Carlos. Maggie's new friends Winnie and Ted found seats near the back just ahead of Sheri and David who sat together in the very rear of the vehicle.

Erin and Bernie drove separately in the Jeep they had rented when they first arrived in Denver. They led the small caravan to the Cable Lift Center farther into the mountains.

Bernie, who was driving the Jeep, motioned to the drivers in the two vans by waving his left hand out the window. He spoke to all the occupants in both vehicles by way of a phone line that connected the audio system in the Jeep he was driving with each van.

"Hope everyone is ready because we're about to hit the road. Just remind your passengers to keep their belongings in front of them. Other than that, Alphonso and Carlos, just follow me," Bernie said.

The thirty-minute ride to the CLC was picturesque. To the right side of the moving vans, a mountain wall stood so high it was impossible to see beyond its apex. Passengers could only view the snow-covered surface scattered with trees and brush. To the left a dramatic downslope beyond the road railing led into the ravine below. At the base of the ravine, a rapidly flowing, rock filled stream was clearly in view.

The winding road and steep descent could have made the drive quite frightening. A driver's miscalculation could send them over the railing and tumbling down the mountainside. But the drivers assured everyone they were safe, and both Alphonso and Carlos encouraged their passengers to just sit back and enjoy the ride. The scenery, which included several miles of mountainous, snow-covered terrain, created spectacular views.

In Alphonso's van where Gates was one of the passengers, the scenery motivated him to make a comment. "You all, this area is just majestic in its beauty! It's the great outdoors that this ski country in Colorado is known for."

The drive from the resort to the CLC took about thirty minutes, enough time for everyone to enjoy the landscape. Just as everyone did when they arrived at the resort, occupants of the vans got out of the vehicles and trekked through even more snow and slush than they had experienced when they first arrived at Headquarters. Soon everyone would be in the CLC, and again there were amenities galore. But the group's focus was on the cable lift tour. Only two couples could go at any one time on a single cable car ride. From the origin of the CLC, the cable lift tour took a pre-determined path to their destination point. The ride lasted fifteen minutes; then, after about thirty minutes of surveying the scenery at the destination, the return trip took the same length of time. Upon the lift's return from the one-hour tour experience, two more couples awaited their excursion.

Jeanie and Wynn along with her folks, Sheri and David, were the first two couples to do the cable lift. The others had to wait at the CLC for their turn to board the cable car and start the next tour. They decided among themselves the order in which the couples would go on the tour before they left the cabin. Courtney, Gates, Maggie, and Fred were scheduled to go after's Sheri's crew returned from the tour.

Several other couples were waiting to go on the cable tour, including the couple that Maggie had befriended, Ted and Winnie, who would take the tour after Maggie, Fred, Courtney, and Gates.

The Mints and the Manleys would have about an hour's wait before they would go on the tour after Sheri's group returned. But everyone was patient inside the CLC, being serenaded by a live band with a female vocalist who graced a small stage.

In addition to live music, they were given their choice of food and drink. As tourists waited for their time to go on the lift, they enjoyed the conveniences that were available in the CLC.

Large windows offered patrons a view of the mountainous terrain that surrounded the facility. Though centrally heated, an open fireplace helped provide an ambiance accentuated by the stark contrast between the comforts within the facility and the harsh wintry conditions that prevailed outside.

The CLC was so accommodating that Sandra and Katie decided to remain inside and forgo taking the tour. They ended up doing what they thought was more relaxing, staying in the CLC, talking with each other, and enjoying the amenities.

The availability of live music and all the food and drink they wanted provided a perfect setup for people to sit, chat, and just enjoy the atmosphere. Like Sandra and Katie, Casey and Sinbad were among those who remained inside the CLC, not having signed up to go on the tour.

By the time Courtney, Gates, Maggie, and Fred got on the cable lift tour, the wind had picked up a bit but not so much to threaten the operation of the moving suspended cable cars. About ten minutes prior to the return of Sheri and the others in her car, the Mints and the Manleys made their way to the loading station dock on an extended patio.

As they left the comforts inside the center to meet the elements outside on the patio, Maggie lamented, "My goodness, it's cool out here, Courtney."

She and the others shivered as they stood on the large patio overlooking the scenic, snow-covered mountains and valleys.

As they waited for Jeanie, Wynn, and her folks to return from the tour, Fred said, "Yeah, Mag, it's cold, but I think we're wearing enough clothes to keep ourselves warm out here. But look at that view!"

Then he continued, "Look, Mag, here it comes. That cable car is almost here. And look at the youngsters. They seem to have enjoyed the tour."

Like Wynn and Jeanie, Sheri and her friend David seemed content with having successfully completed the tour as the cable car approached the loading station. The Mints and the Manleys were right there waiting for their turn.

Anyone standing on the patio could vaguely recognize a similar area at the point of destination where tourists could get off the cable car and walk around a little, taking advantage of even more of the natural beauty of the region.

FIGURE 14: The CLC loading station

Fred couldn't wait to get into the cable car and go on the tour.

As the cable lift car slowly drifted to the edge of the patio and came to a halt, Jeanie, Wynn, and her folks exited. David was the last to set foot back on the patio.

At that point Gates asked David, "Well, did you get scared, being that high off the ground?"

David replied, "Yeah, I was way up there near God Himself!"

Sheri rebuked her friend, saying, "Now, David, don't say that. It's so blasphemous."

"Oh, come on, girl. I don't even know what that word means," David responded.

David admitted having a little concern over how far it was between the cable lift and the ground once it left the boarding station. "You know Gates, I have to admit, it was quite a drop-off beyond this patio. But, naw, I wasn't scared."

"Okay, David, I know you say you weren't afraid," Gates replied. Then he turned toward Sheri and said, "And, Sheri, don't worry about David claiming to be near God. We all are learning something new about the faith—what to say and what not to say."

David retorted, "Well, look who I got defending me, the good ole minister himself!" As Gates looked on in amazement, David added, referring to Jeanie and Wynn, "Anyway, we should ask those young lovebirds over there what they thought about the tour. They were sitting right behind us, and I did hear Jeanie let out a scream or two when we were out there! Fortunately, the tour guide was with us to calm our nerves. And he was also good at telling us about the area we were viewing."

"Okay, David, thank you for easing my nerves a little bit, and I'll follow your advice about paying attention to the tour guide," Gates said. Gates continued, "And by the way, David, I wasn't defending you when you made that comment about being next to God. I was just telling you a spiritual truth."

David replied, "Okay, okay, preacher!"

As the young couple had gotten out of their cable car, Gates turned his attention to them and asked, "So how'd you guys like that tour?"

"It was great!" Wynn answered. "Well, Jeanie got a little nervous, but we're okay. You all should really enjoy the ride." Wynn and the others walked past them on the elevated patio and proceeded into the center. Just before entering, Wynn added, "I can't wait to get inside and play the video games!"

Both the Mints and the Manleys took their seats in the cable car as they were assisted by the tour guide. Soon they were off for an hour before returning.

* * *

Back at the CLC, Sandra and Katie sat at a table where cushioned chairs added to their comfort. Near one of the two fireplaces, the two of them sat listening to a female vocalist. The singer had introduced herself as Samone. Accompanied by a small band situated behind her, she sang smooth jazz on a stage near a corner of the lounge.

The jazz provided a soothing effect on everyone. Sandra and Katie just sat there remembering both the good and the bad times in their lives while listening to good music. After a while, the winds began to howl outside, competing with the entertainment. After a few selections, the band and the singer took a break, which drew more notice to the winds.

Sandra said to Katie, "I see Sheri and her friend and Jeanie and your son over there Katie. I just hope the winds are not too strong for Maggie and the rest of them who just got on the cable lift."

Katie said, "Well, Sandra, those things are supposed to be pretty sturdy. I've been told they can withstand a little wind. Still, they're so far away from the ground—literally. They're moving across a canyon of snow and ice! But the view is spectacular, I imagine."

Sandra wanted to change the tone of the conversation, so she said, "Let's leave the Mints and Manleys on their little tour and go back in time a little bit. You remember when we stayed at your house in Staten Island before that flight to Florida?"

"Girl, you know I remember that night," Katie responded. "We had such a good time just talking about ourselves and our excitement about that trip down to Florida to celebrate Erin's new position at Sinbad's resort."

"One of the things I remember most about that night was you discussing your ex and how he ran out on you," Sandra said.

"Yeah, girl. That mother… That *man* caused a lot of heartache and pain. That was the turning point in my life. After that, I had the responsibility of raising Wynn *alone*. And I became a single woman again at that time after I got a divorce from *that* situation."

Katie went on, "I guess that's the reason I haven't considered marriage as much as I have since that time. It's so hard to find the right man, a good man, and I'm sure he's out there *somewhere*."

Then Katie brought in the spiritual element, saying, "Well, Sandra, that's why you have to trust God in moving you in that direction—of marriage, I mean. But you know? There's a scripture that says you have not because you ask not, that is, ask for what you desire. And I think that scripture is in the beginning of James, the fourth chapter. You know sometimes I think you have to prove your faith by asking God boldly for what you want. And that's what starts the process of having your desires fulfilled.

"And I do think it's a process. He won't just dump stuff into your lap. What I'm saying is that, by asking God for something, it makes Him realize our trust, our total trust in His ability to help us. That's when He'll start to act on our behalf by making situations occur that will ultimately bring to us what we want. And keep in mind, by asking I'm not talking necessarily about making a verbal request. Sure, you can verbalize your prayer, tell God what you want, but it's just as effective believing that you will get what you desire. You know that's what God is all about, providing us with our desires. But only He knows what is really best for us, so we have to trust that He's working on our behalf."

Katie continued, "I realize, Sandra, it's a process, and we have to believe that process. And if we do, it's just a matter of time before our desires come to fruition."

Sandra replied, "Wow! That's pretty heavy, Katie. Anyway, I've certainly done that. I pray for a husband every day. But to this point the only thing I've been presented with is someone like David. Now, ain't that something?

"And let me tell you, he's already taken by Sheri. But the man *is* personable, a little bit too personable, even abrasive sometimes if you ask me. But for some reason, I think Sheri keeps him grounded—under control to some extent."

Katie replied, "Well, I guess you have a unique perspective as far as David is concerned. But anyway, Sandra, we're both in the same boat, I guess. I mean, we're both looking for husbands. Well, let me put it another way. It's not like I'm hard up to have a man in my life, but deep down inside that's what my desire is. And that's where God communicates with us—at that level in our spirit.

"That's one of the 'Wonders *of* the Spirit' that we can communicate with Him anywhere and anytime on that spiritual level. We don't have to be in a church, for example, to communicate with Him. I mean, we can be anywhere and still talk to the Master, even somewhere like the club, for example.

"We don't have that luxury with people for the most part, that is, communicating with them on a constant spiritual basis. Sometimes you know, people can be judgmental, so you have to be careful who you talk to these days. Now it's easy to communicate with them on purely a natural, physical level. But that doesn't produce the benefits we really want—our innermost desires being met. It only feeds our flesh, like with gossip, for example."

"I guess you have a point," Sandra replied.

Katie continued, "Yeah, there are very few people we can really trust to tell stuff to. That's why I treasure the relationship we have with the women in our group, especially Maggie. Now, I feel like we can tell that woman almost anything."

"Yeah, girl, I agree with you. Maggie is like that as are the other ladies in our group. I can attest to that because of my experience with Erin in Bermuda," Sandra said.

Katie continued, "Now, Sandra, I'm not saying people are bad because you communicate with them on just a physical level. But if you really want to make a change in your life, you have to get spiritual and talk with the Lord sometimes or at least with someone who really knows the Lord on that level."

"Amen to that," Sandra replied, remembering how she needed all the help she could get when she first went to Bermuda, and Erin supplied that help both spiritually and emotionally.

Katie continued, "And as for as David is concerned, Sandra, God may have allowed him to come across your path to fulfill some purpose."

She added, "Sandra, have you ever heard the expression, 'the proof is in the pudding?'"

"Sure, I've heard that expression," Sandra replied.

"Well, in this instance, you may have contributed to some positive change in David ever since that confrontation I had with him at dinner that night when I sat in his chair. Do you remember that?"

"*Do* I remember?" Sandra replied repeating the question sarcastically.

After thinking more about it, Sandra continued, "But wait a minute, Katie. Maggie told us all that as it occurred in her dream! Yeah, it was just a dream!"

"Well, Sandra, God does speak to us through dreams too, and it doesn't have to be our own dreams either. It could be someone else's dream—Maggie in this case. And that's another 'Wonder of the Spirit' Gates talks about often," Katie replied.

Katie went on, "But like I was saying, Sandra, people can give us only but so much. As good as their motivation and intentions might be sometimes, they can only deal with us on that superficial, physical level. And believe me, Sandra, the quality of that communication can change on a dime because, like I said before, we're all human.

"Actually, that is what happened with my husband. I dealt with him mainly on that superficial, physical level, and I was fine with that for a while. As a matter of fact, the man was really good on occasion. But of course, I eventually found out what his spirit was like, and that wasn't good.

"Anyway, Sandra, you have to admit, the scripture says that whatever you desire, just believe that you'll receive it, and eventually you'll have it. So I'm claiming it right now, girl! I've already received that husband of mine *in my spirit* because that's what I asked God for a long, long time ago. And, as the scripture says, He's not one to go back on His promises, at least promises to those who believe in Him.

"So, I got that man, girl! I just don't know what he looks like yet. Yeah, that prayer has already been answered in my spirit. And the good thing is that no one can take it away! And I think God will manifest this desire I have in His own good timing."

In response to all that Katie had said, Sandra said, "Yeah, you're right, Katie. You just have to keep on believing and not waiver, being double-minded, I think the scripture says."

"What you're saying is that we must keep the faith," Katie told her.

Sandra replied, "Okay, Katie; that's right. But what I really want to talk about is a biblical story I'm sure you're familiar with. And I want to bring it up because it reminds me of what you're talking about, having faith and everything, as you've just mentioned. And in the scripture, Jesus showed how faith works by cursing the fig tree. If you read that portion of scripture carefully, He intended for the disciples to hear it because He wanted to teach them a lesson about having faith, the kind of faith that can move a mountain, the way

He described it in the Gospel of Mark. The disciples were with Him at the time and heard the Lord curse that tree. But at the time, they saw nothing had changed about the tree. They probably thought that Jesus had lost it.

"Of course, based on my understanding of the sermon I heard on this subject, the disciples didn't think much of it until they came back by the fig tree a day later and found that it had withered up and died. To make a long story short, according to the story, the disciples saw that Jesus had accomplished what He set out to do by cursing the tree, which was the tree's inability to bear figs from the time Jesus had cursed it.

"As the story goes, Jesus took this opportunity to tell them that they too could have anything they wanted by speaking to a problem and believing that the problem will be resolved, just like the results He got by speaking to that fig tree."

Almost an hour had passed as Sandra and Katie talked, and the time was fast approaching for the cable lift with Maggie and her group to return to the center.

Sandra said, "We'll see Maggie, Fred, Courtney, and Gates come in any minute now, Katie."

Shortly after that, their four friends walked inside through the center's back entrance. As the Mints and Manleys entered, they came toward where Sandra and Katie were sitting, and it was not too long before a discussion ensued.

Katie said, "How was that tour, everybody?"

"Oh, it was great! A little windy but it sure was spectacular," Maggie said.

Courtney added, "Yeah, you two missed a nice tour. And like Maggie said, the views were amazing."

Gates then said, "Well, we have about another hour here because one of the last groups to go includes that couple who came with us, Ted and Winnie. They'll be gone for another hour. I see our new friends over there now, getting ready to go on the tour."

Fred said, "Gates, maybe you, me, and David can go over there and play the video machines while the women meet."

Courtney said, "That's a good idea, Fred! Maggie, you, Sandra, and I can try to get Sheri over here to sit down and talk about some things."

"Yeah, I know you two had a lot to talk about while we were gone. Now all of us can be included in the conversation."

"Okay, Maggie. Let me go over here and try to get Sheri to join us," Katie said.

Katie walked to the other the side of the room and met Sheri and her friend David. Then she said, "Sheri, hope you're having a good time. But why don't you come over here with us and we can talk a little? I think all the women in our group are there."

"That sounds great, Katie," Sheri replied. "Yeah, I saw you guys over there." She turned to David and said, "I guess you can go over there with the fellows, David. I see they're walking over to those video machines."

"Yeah, I'll manage," David responded.

David eventually went over to where the other men were, and Sheri joined Katie and the rest for a girls' discussion group.

When all the women were assembled, Katie said, "I must say it's great to have all the women together. We sure do have a lot of stories to share. Sandra and I told some of them when you all were on the tour. I just can't wait to hear more of these stories."

Sandra weighed in, "But keep in mind we have only one hour. We'll have to wait for the new couple that came with us to finish their tour. You know they'll be going back with us when they finish, so we're going to have to wait for them."

At that time, an announcement was made on the loud speaker:

"Ladies and gentlemen, I'm sorry to say that the center will be closing early today because there is a reported storm system headed our way. Those who had scheduled cable tours at this hour must reschedule. Sorry for the inconvenience."

"Oh my. That means Ted and Winnie won't get to go on their tour," Sandra said. "I know they were looking forward to that tour so much."

Katie said, "Well, maybe they can come back tomorrow."

Maggie responded, "No, Katie, Winnie told me when I first met them that today is their last day. They're heading back to Boston tomorrow, where they're from. Besides, who knows what the weather is going to be like tomorrow. I hope it won't affect any of our activities."

"Yeah, Maggie, I guess they can come another time," Katie said, "and speaking of time, what poor timing! Well, anyway, we'll get to go back to Headquarters an hour earlier at the time we had planned to come back before the new couple decided to come with us. Right, Maggie?"

"You're right, Katie." Maggie replied.

"Well, everybody, I guess Alphonso and Carlos will be rounding us all up to load the vans soon. We definitely don't won't to get caught in a blizzard in these mountains!"

CHAPTER 20
More Wonders of the Spirit

Foundation Scripture: 1 John 4:13

"By this we know that we abide in Him, and He in us, because He has given us His Spirit."

After their abbreviated stay at the Cable Lift Center (CLC), Bernie and Erin led the way back to ski headquarters. The two vehicles Alphonso and Carlos were driving followed the Jeep back to Headquarters.

Sinbad, who was sitting beside his friend Casey and just behind Carlos, the driver of the red van, decided to ask the couple from Boston, who were sitting directly behind him, a question.

"Are you two okay? I understand you were looking forward so much to going on that tour, but, of course, because of the weather everything had to be shut down."

The couple looked at each other, wondering who would answer. Then Winnie said, "Yes, Mr. Sinbad, it's very disappointing. But our flight leaves tomorrow morning, and our focus now is on getting back to the airport."

Sinbad said, "Well, I certainly understand that. But listen. You two are welcome to come down to Florida next summer when I invite everyone in Maggie's group to my resort. We were going to have something special this past summer but our friends Bernie and

Erin decided to tie the knot, so we scheduled this trip to Colorado to be a part of the second half of their honeymoon.

"Anyway, Maggie said that she had talked to you back at Headquarters even before we left there to come on this cable lift tour. Just get with her and I'm sure she'll be good with the idea of you two coming to Florida."

"Well, thank you very much, sir. We'll consider it," Winnie replied.

Sinbad added, "Well, don't just consider it. Start making plans for it! And like I said, get with Maggie, and she'll give you all the details about the accommodations, expenses, and so forth. And don't call me Mr. Sinbad; the name is Sinbad. I know you are good people."

Winnie replied, "Yes, sir. I mean, yes, Sinbad. Yes, I talked with Maggie just before we left Headquarters at Williams' Cabin to come to the Cable Lift Center earlier today."

Then Winnie turned toward Ted and said, "Well, Ted, I guess our summer vacation has already been planned for us."

He replied, "I guess you're right, Winnie."

Winnie returned her attention to Sinbad and said, "Sinbad, I'll give Maggie a call tomorrow morning before we leave for the airport. She gave me her cell number while we were standing there talking just before we boarded the van to come to the center."

Alphonso had become concerned about the weather as they drove back and decided to contact Carlos in the other van.

"Hey, Carlos," he said, "things look pretty good now except for the wind. It's picked up quite a bit and is really buffeting the van."

"You're right, Al," Carlos replied. "You can tell something is brewing out here. I think snowfall is only a threat for later today and tonight. But you know how it is in these mountains; weather systems can come on pretty fast, so you have to be prepared."

They agreed to slow down a little and be even more cautious.

When Alphonso had finished talking to Carlos, Maggie said, "Did I hear my name being called up there, Alphonso?"

Alphonso answered, "Yes, Miss Maggie. I was talking with Carlos, and I overheard the new couple riding in his van talking with Sinbad. It sounded like they agreed to come along on the trip to Florida he's gonna plan for you all next summer. And I asked Carlos to confirm what I thought I heard. According to him, Sinbad encouraged the couple to talk to you about that."

"Well, that's great," Maggie said. "I know they were disappointed by not going on the cable lift tour because of the coming weather."

Fred said, "It'll be good to have some fresh blood among us, that is, if they do decide to come with us to Florida."

When Gates heard Fred's response, he added, "Now, Fred, don't put doubts inside of Winnie and Ted about coming with us to Florida. You heard what Carlos said. Sinbad seems intent on having them come along. And I think that would be great if they came with us."

Courtney nodded her head in approval and said, "We can make this trip to Florida an annual event." Then she decided to correct her husband, saying, "Don't worry about Fred placing doubts in Winnie and Ted about going to Florida because they're in the other van; they can't hear us."

Gates responded, "Well, Alphonso certainly heard the discussion going on between Sinbad and the new couple who joined us about it, and they were not in the same van! You know this phone system is pretty sophisticated *and* sensitive. I mean, it's intended that the drivers listen to each other. But sometimes you can hear very clearly what others may be saying who are not in the same van.

"Anyway, our going to Florida is not a guarantee just because Sinbad said it. Everybody knows how he can change his mind sometimes. We were going to go this past summer, but you know what happened. Erin and Bernie got married and plans were changed; that's why we're out here in Colorado."

Courtney replied, "Well, I'm certainly glad it turned out the way it did. I'm enjoying this trip so much!"

As the vans followed Bernie and Erin to ski headquarters, Williams' Cabin, the wind continued to howl but the snowfall predicted had yet to arrive. After about twenty-five minutes, the vans following the Jeep Bernie was driving rolled up to the front entrance of the ski resort headquarters. Everyone got out with their travel bags and eventually returned to the cabin's lobby; most continued to their rooms, anticipating the next activity on the trip, which was the hiking excursion the next day, Friday.

Maggie, Courtney, and Sandra found themselves together in the lobby. Sandra said, "Hey, why don't we ladies stay here in the lobby and carry on the conversation we didn't get to have back at the Cable Lift Center because it closed early."

Both Maggie and Courtney nodded their heads in approval.

Courtney said, "Yeah, let's tell Sheri and Katie. I know they were far ahead of us because they got out of their van long before we did. I don't see them so they may have gone to their rooms already. I can give them a call."

"That's great!" Maggie replied. She added, "I see Katie and Sheri coming out of the dining area together. Let me go over there and tell them."

Maggie approached her two friends and said, "Hey, Katie and Sheri! We didn't see you and thought you had gone to your room."

Katie replied, "No, Maggie, I went into the restaurant with Sheri and her clan to see if we could get a bite to eat. But we didn't see anything we wanted, so we came back out into the lobby."

Maggie said, "Well, okay, Katie. Listen, I was talking with Courtney and Sandra about us ladies meeting in the lobby in about ten minutes. Why don't you two come and join us?"

Katie said, "Oh, yes, I'll be right there."

Sheri joined in and said, "That sounds good to me too."

Sheri then said to David and Jeanie, who were standing with her, "I'll be gone for a while, so, Jeanie, could you help David carry our things to the room? I'll just stay out here in the lobby."

Jeanie hesitantly agreed and said while looking at David, "Okay, Mom."

When David and Jeanie returned to their room with all their belongings, she decided to give Wynn a call. Jeanie paid little attention to her stepfather, which prompted David to ask, "What are you doing, Jeanie? We've just got here and haven't even had a chance to get comfortable, and you're already giving someone a call?"

Jeanie replied, "Now, David, I'm calling Wynn to see if he wants to meet with me. We'll probably meet in the lobby. You'll be fine here by yourself."

Then David said, "You know, Wynn's not the only one who wants to be with you."

Not knowing exactly what he meant by that last statement, Jeanie hastily dialed Wynn's number, continuing to glance back at David while making the call.

Wynn answered the phone and said, "Hello, Jeanie. Are you with your mom?"

She replied almost in a whisper, "No, Wynn. I'm here with David. Mom decided to stay in the lobby where she'll meet the other ladies shortly."

"You mean you're there alone in your room with that beast?" Wynn asked with concern in his voice.

At that moment, she glanced at David as if she didn't want him to hear her reply to Wynn. Jeanie ended up not answering her friend but instead told him, "Hey, Wynn, I can be outside on the bench in just a minute. I've seen heaters out there and they have a few chairs. It's kinda hidden on the side of the building. Do you know where it is?"

Wynn said, "Believe it or not, I'm here already, so come on—right now! I don't want you to be around that man too much!"

"Okay, Wynn," she said as she took another glance at David. Then, while looking at David with a menacing stare, she said, "I'll see you in a second."

After that brief phone conversation with Wynn, Jeanie finally told David, "When mom gets back, tell her I'm out with Wynn."

"Okay. I'll tell her that," David responded with the wink of an eye.

* * *

Most of the men in the group ended up in their living quarters while the women congregated in the lobby, as Sandra had suggested. Meanwhile, the wind had picked up considerably and light snowflakes could be seen outside through a huge window near where the ladies had begun to assemble.

"I'm so glad all of us decided to get together. You know, we're not together that often," Sandra said.

Maggie replied, "Well, Sandra, that's why these trips are so nice. We all can get together and talk about all sorts of things. It really revives my spirit, just like what happened when we all went to Florida. And, Sandra, I told you about the dream I had of taking a cruise to Bermuda. It was almost as though I was right there with you and everybody here."

"Well, Maggie, you *were* there with me *in spirit*. You and your family mean so much to me."

Katie said, "Maggie, you mean a lot to all of us."

Courtney got into the discussion as everyone now was seated comfortably near an open fireplace. She said, "Yeah, Maggie, you mean a lot to us. But what I was going to say is that Gates talks about this all the time—how we can form our own mental trip. So, Maggie, you *were* with Sandra in Bermuda through the dream you had.

"But we also can be someplace where we're not physically just by our spirit taking us there. I mean, that's what the term mental trip is all about, according to Gates. He calls it one of the 'Wonders of the Spirit,' visiting someplace without physically being there.

"Just think about it. How cool would it be to only think about being someplace where you're not physically, and then, bam, you're suddenly there in an instant—mentally, I mean! Yeah, to be there just by thinking about it. That's what Gates says our spirit will be like after our transition when we pass on from this life and into the next.

"It's very interesting how Gates describes it. He says that at this time of transition our spirit *will not* be tied to a physical body like it is now. He says the scripture promises we'll be like our Maker with the ability to be anywhere and everywhere at any time and at the same time. Now that's exciting to me, even though I certainly don't understand it. It's like what the scripture says and I think this is correct: *Eyes have not seen, nor ears heard, what God has prepared for us!* Now this may not be *exactly* what it says, and I'm not sure *where* it is in the scripture, but my spirit is telling that's what it'll be like after our transition. And I *do* trust that spirit, the Holy Spirit!"

Sandra interjected, "Yeah, Courtney. It is exciting all right. But I'm not ready for that experience right now! No, not quite yet!"

Katie added, "I agree, Courtney. The spirit part of us can lead to wonderful things happening. But this is what I want to know: Exactly what does Gates mean when he talks about a mental trip?"

Courtney replied, "Well, Katie, if you want me to repeat it, I will. According to that husband of mine, we all form images in our minds about everything. Some of those images we retain and some we get rid of. Gates even relates it to what professionals, you know, like psychologists and even geographers who study mental maps, talk about a lot. Yeah, I studied that in my college geography class. Anyway, I'm talking about professionals who study that kind of thing for a living. I mean those who study the nature of images that we form in our minds.

"Now what Gates says is that we all have the ability to retain information and to form images of that information as though we are really at some place or the other."

Courtney continued, "You know we all travel a lot. Now, if it's to an interesting place, somewhere we really enjoy going to, then we can bring these places up in our minds as though we're actually there physically.

"I know our physical body can never be someplace unless we travel to it in this present physical realm we live in. But you know, it's so strange saying that because everyone assumes when we go someplace our physical body has to travel to it. But according to Gates, that's not the only way we can get to a place; we can travel to it mentally—in our minds. That's the whole idea behind daydreaming, according to him.

"By daydreaming I think Gates meant that we can be in a totally different place mentally than where our physical bodies are at that time. I'm sure schoolteachers can relate to this concept with some of their students who may not be paying attention to what they're saying."

Katie interrupted, saying, "Hey, I remember when I was a kid, my teacher got on me a lot for doing that, Courtney. I mean, sometimes I had my mind on what I did the night before instead of on the lesson the teacher may have been giving that day, and apparently she could tell I was daydreaming. Yeah, I can relate to that! I remember in class one time the teacher asked me a question, and I just ignored her because I was thinking about something else."

"Yeah, Katie, that's exactly what I'm saying. Sometimes your mind can be somewhere other than where you may be physically at the time. It's in this way we can get to wherever we want to go simply by bringing it up in our spirit, by thinking about it. And it serves as immediate transportation to go where we desire to be."

Then Courtney said to Katie in jest, "But let me hasten to say, Katie, that's not a good idea in the classroom. You really needed to have been listening to your teacher."

Maggie said, "I know exactly what you mean, Courtney, because I felt that my first husband, John, daydreamed a lot. I mean, we had a good marriage, but sometimes I felt that, although he was with me physically, mentally he was somewhere else when we were together. And it was so frustrating at the time. Then I finally realized that I had my own issues, issues that may have contributed to me feeling that way. The sad thing is that at times I see some of the same traits in Fred."

Sandra said, "Come on, Maggie! Tell us what some of those 'issues' as you put it were?"

"Now, Sandra, I don't want to tell you everything—at least not now," Maggie replied.

Sandra responded, "Well, Maggie, you don't have to tell me. But let me tell *you* something. There are some places you *want* to be physically as well as mentally. And in my case, I'm talking about Bermuda." Then she began to fantasize, "I can see it now, being there on that beach and seeing the stars in the sky on that last night before my flight back home. It was a mesmerizing experience all right! But beyond that, it provided me with a sign that I was looking for to confirm my physical healing, and I got it!"

Katie added, "For me, everybody, it was really our trip to Florida that did it for me! I mean, I was so excited about going down there, and it turned out to be an experience I'll always remember. Especially that ferry ride to the Island of Love that we were supposed to have been going to, but we ended up not going because of the storm. And I'll tell all of you a secret: I was really expecting to find a man on that island! But it was not to be! I'm just fantasizing, you all, because you know we all went to the island only as a part of Maggie's dream.

"And speaking of Maggie, we did end up giving her a surprise birthday party."

"Oh, Katie, I love it the way you say I described the dream I had, but it was so real," Maggie said. "But can I interrupt you, Miss Katie?" Maggie asked jokingly, calling her name formally.

"Sure, *Miss* Maggie," Katie replied returning the favor in humor!

Maggie's response was "Well, Katie, I really appreciated that birthday party; it was awesome! Thanks to everybody for that. But listen, all of you, Katie and I used to carry on like this all the time when we were together back in college. Didn't we, Katie?"

"Yeah, Maggie. You were kind of like a leader back then, and even now in a lot of ways you're the leader of this group. Now what do you have to say?" Katie asked.

"Okay, Katie, don't put all my business out there in the street," Maggie said while giving her friend a smile. "You're right, Katie; you all know I described the dream I had going to the island. And it *was* so real."

Courtney said, "Yeah, Maggie, you made it seem like we all went to the island on the ferry with you that day. And talk about mental images—you sure gave us one on that imaginary voyage. It was almost as if we all had gone on that ferry with you!"

Maggie replied, "Let's forget about that dream for now. I was going to answer Katie's original question. And that is I think some of you already know this, but I've talked to Sinbad and guess what? He's invited us back to Florida next summer. And one of the things he said he would make sure we do, successfully this time, is to make it to the Island of Love."

"Oh, my! Oh, my! Are you kidding, Maggie?" Sheri shouted.

Before Maggie had a chance to answer, Sandra chimed in. "Wow, Sheri! I didn't know you were so eager to go back to Florida."

Sheri replied, "Yeah, you guys, I really loved going down there."

"Now, Sandra, let me answer Sheri's question," Maggie said. "Sheri, no, I'm not kidding! I really think Sinbad wants us all to come back down to Florida to his resort. I mean, the only reason we didn't go this past summer was because of Erin and Bernie getting married."

"Well, all I can say is that you all remember what Courtney was talking about earlier—about mental maps. And based on what she said, Sandra, at least what she said Gates had told her, we can experience a place like Florida in our own minds any time! All we have to do is just form a mental map or image of it in our minds."

Sandra continued, "Now let me just say, whether you even want a mental trip of where you've already been depends on if you enjoyed the trip or not. But I think we all loved going to Florida."

As Sandra thought about her time with David, she added, "Now, if for some reason you didn't enjoy where you were, you might not want to recall *that* experience, like the experience you said I had with David, Maggie? I mean, being cuddled up next to him and everything on that ferry is not what I call a pleasant experience except that it might have kept me warm, the way you told it, Maggie."

"Well, Sandra, I'm glad you brought that up because that's one of the 'Wonders of the Spirit,'" Courtney said. "Like I've told you before, I heard Gates talk about it a lot whenever he preaches. And that is our ability to keep or get rid of things we're thinking about. It's a matter of focus and of choice. It's our decision to recall something we've experienced if we want to, he says."

Courtney tried to explain further. "Let me put it this way. I think Gates is saying that within the spiritual realm, we're able to recall anything we want to and disregard or choose not to remember those negative experiences.

"And let me also tell you, girls, we experience this every day as we live in this world. What I'm saying is that we have the ability to remember what we want to remember, and those bad memories we usually simply choose to forget. But the challenge we have is that it's not easy to totally forget some things, especially the very bad or the very good experiences. They tend to stick out in our minds. But it's still our choice nonetheless to remember the things that are best for us to remember and to focus on those things."

Katie said, "Hey! That's what the scripture says. Right, girls? And that is we should think about only those positive things in life."

"Yeah, Katie," Courtney responded. "I've heard Gates say this is the key to anyone's happiness: to retain and focus on the good experiences and let go and try to forget the bad."

The main concern of the group gathered was on their shared experiences, trials, and tribulations as well as triumphs. While they discussed their various experiences, their focus was on the uniqueness of women's issues and how those issues had made them happy at any given moment in the past.

A break in the discussion occurred when Bernie and Erin entered through the front door.

Several in Maggie's group said in unison, "Hello, Erin and Bernie!"

Erin took the initiative to reply and said, "Hello, ladies. It looks like you all are having fun together."

Sandra said, "We are, Erin, so why don't you come join us?

"I'm glad you asked," Erin replied. "I think I will join you, girls, but just for a little while. Well, if that's okay with my new husband," she added in jest.

Bernie replied, "Are you kidding me, Erin? Of course, you should join these nice ladies! You go ahead, and I'll go to the room and get some rest."

Maggie said, "Yeah, Bernie, that's what Fred and most of the other men are doing now. They're back in their rooms, and I'm assuming they're resting.

"Okay, Maggie, and the rest of you girls too. You all continue to have a good time 'cause I'm headed to our room," Bernie assured them.

At that point, Erin joined the women to add insight into the many topics they were addressing.

Erin came over and sat in one of the few available seats and said to all of them, "So, what have you all been talking about?" Then she paused for a second and continued, "Wait a minute! Let me guess. Is it about men?"

Courtney said, "Yeah, Erin, we've been discussing relationships and how men sometimes disregard the significance of our feelings."

Erin joked with those assembled, "So did I get it right or what, girls?"

Katie said, "You sure did, Erin." Then she asked, "So how do you feel about this thing called a mental trip? We've been talking about that a lot too."

"Mental trip? Um." Erin pondered the idea briefly and then said, "That's interesting. Well, I know that it involves the mind, which is not very far away from a person's spiritual self."

"Uh-huh. That's exactly what we've been talking about, Erin—our spiritual body and how it's connected to our minds," Courtney replied.

Sandra added, "Yeah, Erin, I told everybody that my first time in Bermuda with you I was changed because of my introduction to the spiritual world. I remember like it was yesterday when you pointed out that God gives us signs sometimes to make us realize that He is still with us. And I sure did see those signs that night on the beach—at least the third and last sign I saw. My, my! All those stars, Erin, that we saw on that starlit night. And I really believe that was the key to my physical as well as spiritual healing, at least the key to my knowing and believing that *I would* be healed."

"Well, you all were talking about something that's very real, but sometimes it's difficult to fully identify in the world we live in today," Erin said. "I think the main thing is to be receptive to what the Master is trying to tell us at any given time, especially if it's an occasion when we desperately need divine guidance. And let me tell all of you, Sandra really needed help at that time; she was in a bad condition."

Erin went on, "And let me tell you all something else. If we are receptive and willing to be quiet and listen to the spirit within us, we'll get the direction we need as well as any physical and spiritual healing we desire—like what happened to you, Sandra, that time in Bermuda."

Erin continued, "Well, I hate to stop the fun, but if you all didn't know, the weather is really kicking up outside. Hopefully, we'll be able to get in our next activity, which is the hiking trip tomorrow. I'm going to my room now to get some rest and be ready for that.

"But you girls stay here for as long as you'd like. Yeah, Sandra and I did talk a lot when she came to Bermuda that time, her first time there."

Maggie said, "Erin, Sandra's told us. At least she told most of us about that experience. And I think we all should kinda follow what you're doing and make it to our rooms. We all need the rest too so we can enjoy the experience tomorrow. I've never been skiing before and I'm sure it'll be fun."

At that point, everyone seemed to agree with Maggie and started to disperse to their living quarters.

Before she left, Erin said to everyone, "Well, hopefully I'll get to talk to each of you more before we leave—whether it's here at the ski resort or back in Denver. But remember, what you're talking about is real, the spiritual world I mean, and I think there should be more discussions about the workings of the spirit in our personal life. And if we do, I think we'll see that spirit, the Holy Spirit, that is, in a different light. We'll begin to see the true 'Wonders of the Spirit.'"

CHAPTER 21
Overcoming

Foundation Scripture: Revelation 21:7

"He who overcomes shall inherit all things, and I will be his God and he shall be my son."

Everyone had finally retired for the night, looking forward to the long day on Friday, traversing the hiking trail near the volcano. Because of the weather, officials at Headquarters suggested not doing that activity, so group members were content enjoying the amenities within and surrounding the cabin. They changed their plans and decided on a much shorter trip to the ski slopes later on Friday instead of on Saturday as was previously scheduled.

The cancellation of the hike was a disappointment for everyone, but at the same time they wanted to be safe. Maggie was especially disappointed that the group would not be going on the hiking trail, but she was fine with taking the ski trip later in the day instead.

Figure 15: Williams' Cabin Lodging Accommodations

A more immediate concern for Maggie related to their lodgings.

"You know, Fred, I talked with Courtney back at the CLC about our living arrangements here at Williams' Cabin, and it's interesting that they also have two bunk beds, one on top of the other, just like we do. Oh, well!"

Fred replied, "Yeah, Mag, everything we need is right here, a kitchenet and restroom. It's very convenient. But I agree, it would've been better to have a single, larger bed. Anyway, I need to get some rest. I'll volunteer and climb up on the top bunk, and you can go ahead and take the bottom."

"Okay, Fred," Maggie replied.

Once they were situated for the night, Maggie looked up towards the upper bunk and said, "Hey, honey, one disadvantage of this bottom bunk is that you can't see what's going on outside. You can only hear what's happening with the weather."

Fred whispered, "Yeah, Mag, it's an effort to climb up here, but it does have that one advantage of seeing out the window. On this night you can see that it's snowing like crazy out there!"

"Well, at least I can hear the wind howling even though I can't see anything," Maggie replied. "And not only that, but this fireplace really adds to the ambiance of the room. I think it'll help me get to sleep.

"But listen, Fred, do you remember that night in Chappell on our way here how the wind just howled all night long? I didn't think it would have stopped snowing so soon when we left there the next morning. I mean, that was a pretty nasty snowstorm that we drove through on our way there. We barely made it to that town."

Fred replied, "Yeah, Mag, I think we were fortunate to have made it there. And to think that we considered driving all the way to Denver that day. That thought was total madness the way it turned out. But, yeah, tonight reminds me of the night when we did that stopover in Chappell. But let's hope just as it was there the next morning, tomorrow will be clear of all this weather we're having now. I just hope everything will work out for a nice ski excursion.

"According to the concierge, tomorrow it should take us only about ten to fifteen minutes to arrive at the ski destination from here. He said that the only challenge would be the main road, which he said is quite treacherous even in good weather.

"What concerns me most are the many curves in the road that he talked about not to mention several embankments with steep drop-offs to the side for almost the whole distance up there. He reminded me to alert the drivers to be careful."

"My, my, Fred! It sounds pretty scary, especially with the vans we have," Maggie said. "I mean, these vehicles are so high off the ground.

"Hey, Fred, I got an idea. You think Bernie would mind if I rode with Erin in the Jeep they have? And Bernie can take my seat and ride beside you. You know it's not going to be a long drive. Besides, by sitting together you two can have some men's talk, you know, like we ladies do."

"That's sounds okay, Mag," Fred replied. "You can ask him in the morning. He may be willing to do that. But as far as men's talk as you put it, usually we don't have a lot to say unless it's about sports or politics."

"Okay then," Maggie replied. "I really don't care what you and Bernie talk about. I'll just be glad to ride in something like that Jeep that's closer to the ground. It sure would be better than riding in the van, especially if there's bad weather. Maybe I'm being selfish, Fred, because no one else has asked for the privilege of riding in the Jeep. But I guess I'm having flashbacks to when I was riding with John when we had the accident that took his life."

"Well, I can understand that, Mag," Fred said. "But like I said, under the conditions you mentioned, I don't think he'd mind."

After Fred's reassurances, Maggie seemed to be more at ease. She only had to bring the idea up to Bernie in the morning. Both Fred and Maggie were now ready for sleep.

"Okay, Mag, you can talk to Bernie about that in the morning. I think we've talked enough, so good night!"

"Good night, honey," Maggie replied.

In a strange way, as Maggie lay there, the wind provided a serenity she had not felt since she saw that starlit sky through their bedroom skylight the first night home after returning from Bermuda in her dreams.

With the confidence that she would have a safer ride to the ski slopes in the Jeep, Maggie ended up spending a few moments thinking while Fred immediately went to sleep.

The wailing winds somehow had an exhilarating effect on Maggie. Since Fred had already fallen asleep leaving her alone with her thoughts, she allowed her mind to drift back to both the good and the bad times in her life. She even went back as far as the times she spent with her mother and father growing up in Flint.

Not only did Maggie reminisce about past times with her parents, she began pondering what they must be doing now that they both had been released from their physical bodies on earth. Maggie often wondered what heaven would be like. She remembered Pastor John Sr. so often preached about heaven back at Mark Methodist.

Somehow, the traditional story describing that wonderful place she often heard of in Bible class and in Sunday sermons left her with much to be desired. Yes, she heard the proclamation of streets of gold where the Saints will put on their golden slippers, dancing and praising God all day forever. Somehow this thought didn't enhance her expectation for or her anticipation of the afterlife.

Maggie desired a more clearly defined, substantive destination based on her efforts in *this life*, efforts that so far led to a dependence on Jesus and trusting His work of redemption for all mankind. In a strange way, as she lay there between being awake and in slumber, she thought that there must be more to heaven than she had been taught.

These thoughts led Maggie to a verse of scripture she learned as a child, Revelation 14:13. She didn't remember all the rather lengthy verse, so she got her Bible and began to read silently to avoid waking her husband. She whispered:

Then I heard a voice from heaven saying to me, "Write: 'Blessed are the dead who die in the Lord from now on.' "Yes," says the Spirit, "that they may rest from their labors, and their works follow them."

Despite her fatigue, a wave of confidence, a revelation, rose within her based on this verse of scripture. The words "…and their works follow them" resounded in her mind. She realized for the first time that the labor of her mother and father while on earth was not in vain. The product of their works followed them into that wonderful place where they were now.

The scripture Maggie recited spoke volumes to her because she interpreted the verse as an indication that not only *her* parents but also all other saints who had transitioned are now fulfilling their purpose in that place, a purpose that started and was fulfilled in their life here on the earth.

In Maggie's mind, the "product of their works" meant the type of spirit her parents had that led to the works they produced, the joy they brought to others. That is what the scripture says will last forever, the unseen spirit of a person's being. It is the type of spirit that is personified by what Galatians calls the fruit of the spirit, which includes love, peace, and joy.

As Maggie continued to meditate while lying there beneath her husband's bunk, she realized that, because of her faith, she was fulfilling her purpose now and would continue to fulfill that purpose in that wonderful place called heaven. She also realized her purpose started with their physical sojourn on earth, and she knew that she had an opportunity to fulfill that purpose in her life. The end result of accomplishing that purpose was to help others in some way.

As Maggie was taught back at Mark Methodist, she believed we are not saved by works; to the contrary, she accepted what the Bible says, that we are saved by grace with our trust in the Lord. But works *are* important, she surmised that night, because by our works we are able to help others. And that's what brings ultimate joy, helping someone else to fulfill their purpose.

Maggie believed that the saints who had transitioned continued to help others even now. And that's what, in her estimation, she could look forward to when *she* reached that wonderful place.

But the most important aspect of Maggie's train of thought was that she as well as her friends were destined for the same. Maggie became completely positive in her outlook for the future both in this life and in the next. *These are the Wonders of the Spirit*, she thought to herself.

As Maggie continued to lie on the bottom bunk, her thoughts led her to ponder her purpose further. *To fulfill that purpose, a purpose that involves what I do for others, I will have to look inward,* she thought.

At that point, Maggie couldn't help but think of Freddie and the wrongs she had done in her relationship with him. She also realized that to help others, she needed to overcome her own issues involving the flesh. Maggie thanked God every day for His help in doing that as well as His help in her progression generally in the Christian walk. In that moment, she silently said a brief prayer: "I pray, God, that You will continue to give me Your grace."

With that added knowledge and humility, she got her concordance and turned to all the scriptures that dealt with overcoming, and finally she came to Revelation 21:7. Again, she read the verse of scripture silently: "He who overcomes shall inherit all things, and I will be his God and he shall be my son."

Fatigue finally began to set in. Despite her efforts to stay awake and continue to receive even more of God's wisdom, she started to become drowsy. With a barely perceptible voice, she began to whisper repeatedly, "God help me to overcome, and I will inherit all things, all things, all things..." Then slumber finally overtook her.

CHAPTER 22
The Ski Excursion

Foundation Scripture: 1 Timothy 6:17

Command those who are rich in this present age not to be haughty, nor trust in uncertain riches but in the living God, who gives us richly all things to enjoy.

Everyone slept well that night despite the constant sound of the wind. For Maggie, it acted as a sedative, helping to create the joy of thankfulness in her being. She was grateful for the opportunity to witness a winter wonderland in the mountains of Colorado. While in that rather sedated state, she realized it was a chance to meditate on her blessings as well as to pray for herself and for others close to her. Those thoughts assisted her in having a restful night of slumber.

Friday was a new day, and the sun rose on a cold, crisp morning amidst clear skies.

After waking, Fred said, "Mag, Mag, wake up! It's already after 8:00, and we need to get going."

"What… What time did you say it was, Fred?" she asked as she struggled to awaken.

Fred repeated, "It's after 8:00, and we need to get dressed and get something to eat before we take off for the ski slopes. The vans are scheduled to leave at 10:00. And remember, you need to call Bernie to see if he's willing to have Erin give up her seat to you while she drives the Jeep with you sitting beside her."

"Oh, don't put it like that!" Maggie replied as she struggled to gain clarity. With a slight irritation in her voice, she said, "Let me go ahead and call him. Last night you seemed to be more positive, Fred."

"No, no! I'm sure he'll do it. But you need to call him now to let him know your plans."

After Bernie answered the phone, he asked, "How can I help you? But before you give me an answer, how did you two sleep last night with all the wind going on?"

"We slept well, Bernie. And I hope you and Erin had a restful night too," Maggie responded.

Before Bernie had a chance to give a reply, Maggie continued, "Anyway, Bernie, the reason I'm calling is to ask you a question."

"Go ahead, Maggie," Bernie encouraged her.

"Okay, Bernie. I'm wondering if you would be willing to exchange seats with me on our way to the ski slopes today. Let me explain. I would like to take Erin's seat in your Jeep. Now, I realize that would mean she would become the driver. You know what I'm saying? I understand it's not very far—maybe about a ten-minute drive?"

"Say no more! I know exactly what you mean," Bernie said. "There's no problem at all with Erin driving the Jeep and you taking her seat. You two should have fun riding together. And, yeah, it'll probably take a little longer than the ten minutes, more like at least fifteen. But get ready for adventure because there will be a lot to see along the roadside."

Maggie said, "Yeah, I know, Bernie. Fred told me that the concierge said it was an adventure, mainly because of the rugged landscape. But I can understand why it might take longer because the route to our destination provides such beautiful scenery; it's something that everyone should experience at least once."

"I hear you, Maggie," Bernie responded.

Maggie continued, "I was thinking too, Bernie, that with my history of being in an automobile accident, a very serious one, I might add, the last thing I need is an adventure—at least not while riding in a vehicle. Anyway, that's the reason I wanted to make the change I've been telling you about. I'd be seeing too much of the roadside as high up as the vans are. I'm sure the scenery would be great, but it'd be just too scary for me."

"Okay, Maggie, I understand," Bernie repeated. "So this is what I'll do. I will give Erin the keys just before we leave, and I'll go over and sit with Fred in the van he's riding in, taking your seat. There's no problem with Erin driving the short distance to the ski location. She drove the vehicle some our first day in Colorado before you all arrived. It's only about fifteen miles to where we're going. And like I said, it'll probably take longer than we expect because of all the snow possibly right on the road. I know Erin will be deliberate in her driving, which means going a lot slower than she would if the roads were better conditioned."

Bernie continued, "But you know, Maggie, this arrangement will give you two another chance to just talk and bond together, and I'll get a chance to talk to Fred. Maybe he can give me some pointers on how to have a successful marriage."

Maggie said, "Well, okay. That settles it. We'll see you and all the others at 10:00 near the front entrance of the building."

"Okay, Maggie. The Jeep we're driving plus the two vans will be ready to take all of us to that ski area in a little while," Bernie replied.

Before the conversation ended, Bernie reminded Maggie of something important. "Maggie, you and Fred need to be in the dining area by 9:30 so we can have at least thirty minutes for breakfast before loading up. We won't have an opportunity to eat again until dinner later tonight."

"Okay, Bernie. We'll see you in a little bit," Maggie told him.

* * *

The Jeep and two vans behind it were all lined up with the travelers eager to board them and go to do some skiing. At last, the wind had died down, so they were hopeful that the drive would be uneventful despite the treacherous road conditions.

Everyone would keep the same seats they had when they traveled to the CLC the day before except for Maggie, who planned to ride with Erin in the Jeep.

"I'm glad you agreed to have Bernie take my place in the van Erin; you know I told him about my desire to ride with you here in the Jeep."

"Maggie, when Bernie first told me about this, I told him I would love to have you riding with me," Erin replied. "It will be great having you to talk with for a few minutes. You know I always love talking with you. I'm disappointed that we're not going hiking as we had planned, but this will apparently be a lot safer, and we should have a lot of fun too!"

"I'll have to admit though, Maggie, I don't know how much talking we'll do because, from what I've been told, the views on the way there are spectacular, and I think both of us will be focused on that. But don't worry, my eyes will be fixed on the road since I'm driving. I don't plan to be spending a lot of time looking at what's around us. My focus now will be totally on the road, girl."

Maggie replied, "Well, I'm glad you're comfortable behind the wheel. And like I was telling Bernie, being in this vehicle, I'll be able to really enjoy that scenery because the Jeep is much closer to the ground, so it shouldn't be as scary."

"Well, yeah, it shouldn't be, Maggie," Erin said. "And I'll try not to drive very fast in order for us to take advantage of all the sites. Besides, we'll have all day to ski, so there's no reason to rush."

"You're right, Erin. It's clear right now, but according to the weather forecast another storm system is coming. It shouldn't affect us going there, but coming back should be interesting," Maggie said.

Back in the blue van, everyone seemed disappointed that Maggie was not a passenger on this short trip. Courtney, who had sat in front of Maggie, asked facetiously, because she knew about the switch, "Where is that girl of mine, Bernie?"

Bernie, who had replaced Maggie in her seat, said, "Well, Courtney, come on! You know the answer to that question; she wanted to make a change and ride in the Jeep. But what you may not know is the reason. Maggie told me she felt safer riding in the Jeep because it's closer to the ground."

"Oh, really?" Courtney replied.

Fred, who now was sitting beside Bernie, chimed in, "Yeah, Maggie talked about calling Bernie last night about making the change, but I encouraged her to wait until this morning.

"Well, I'm glad you did, Fred. I was beat last night!"

Gates said, "These vans *are* very high, but the views are really nice. At least, Bernie, now you and Fred can carry on a conversation, and I can put my two cents worth in too."

Bernie said, "Yeah, Gates, we'll be able to talk some on the way to the lodge. And, Fred, and you too, Gates, this will only be about a ten to fifteen-minute trip to the ski lodge, so we won't have a lot of time for discussion. But like you said, Gates, the views will be spectacular."

"I have an idea, you all," Fred said. "Before we start moving, why don't I take the wheel and drive with you sitting beside me, Bernie? How do you feel about that, Alphonso? Do you two up there in the front seat want to make the switch?" Fred asked.

"Sure thing, Mr. Fred, that is, if it's okay with Ms. Sandra here sitting beside me."

Sandra said, "No problem, Fred. Alphonso and I can go back to where you and Bernie are sitting now, and you two can come up here. I guess you want to keep an eye on your wife, huh?"

"Well, that would be an advantage of being up there, Sandra. But good! Thanks for agreeing," Fred replied. "And thank you too, Alphonso.

"You're welcome, Mr. Fred," he replied.

As they were making the switch, Fred said, "It won't take long to make this change, and then we'll be in the mountains pretty soon."

So Fred became the driver of the red van as he had been when the group was on their way to Colorado from Chicago.

Meanwhile, Wynn, who was sitting with Jeanie in the back, said, "You hear that, Jeanie? I can't wait till we get into those mountains."

While clear conditions prevailed earlier in the morning, clouds were now beginning to cover the skies. But that didn't deter the feeling of anticipation they all had for what was about to come.

THE JEEP

Erin (Driver) --------------------- Maggie

THE RED VAN

Fred (Driver) ---------------------- Bernie

Courtney ----------------------------- Gates

Alphonso -------------------------- Sandra

Jeanie -------------------------------- Wynn

THE BLUE VAN

Carlos (Driver) ----------------------Katie

Sinbad ------------------------------ Casey

Winnie -------------------------------Ted

Sheri ------------------------------- David

FIGURE 16
New Vehicle Seating Arrangement

The caravan slowly navigated through the curving, snow-covered mountain roads.

"Wow, Erin! Look at that scene just to your left," Maggie said.

The Jeep Erin was driving continued to inch forward to higher elevations, going at a snail's pace both because of treacherous road conditions and so that everyone could witness the panoramic view of the mountainous terrain. A light snow was falling as they made the journey, but it didn't interfere with the fantastic views.

"Maggie, the view is spectacular," Erin said. "But remember what I said earlier. Being the driver, I can afford only a glance at it. I think you'll agree that it'd be better that I concentrate on the road and get us safely to the ski lodge, so I'll let you enjoy the scenery, and I'll keep my attention ahead of me."

"Sure thing, Erin," Maggie replied. "Yeah, please keep your eyes on the road. The snow is falling but not hard enough for you to turn on the wipers, I guess."

"Yeah, Maggie, right now the snow is not the problem; it's the accumulation of the white stuff on the road that might be a growing concern, especially when we come back. But let's not think about that now."

"Listen, it sure doesn't take away from the setting around us," Erin said. "In fact, Maggie, I love the snow, always have. But we do have to worry about any more accumulation. The amount that you just mentioned on the road is only what they call a dusting. Now what it'll be like when we return to Headquarters later today is another story. But like I said, let's not worry about that now."

While Erin was careful driving, she couldn't help but notice the expansiveness of the view. She said, "Look way over yonder at those mountains in the distance, Maggie. Some of those locations must be over twenty miles from here. It's so beautiful."

Despite her amazement at the beauty, Erin remained aware of the potential danger. "Remember, Maggie," she said, "while the views are fantastic, I also realize that it can be dangerous. Don't worry though; I'll be careful going around these mountain curves."

Maggie replied, "Thanks for the assurance, Erin. I see what you mean. The view is amazing though. Listen, I guess you were referring to the drop-off beyond the railings over there being the dangerous part.

"That's right," Erin said.

"Well, we don't want to even think about veering off the road. That ravine down there must be hundreds of feet below deep. But what a view! I mean, those green pine trees and shrubbery with the snow providing a white background is something to behold—so picturesque."

After appreciating the beauty but also being aware of the danger, Erin said, "Okay, Maggie. We're coming up to another curve, so hang on!"

"Erin, you just continue to drive slowly," Maggie said. "Fortunately, the snow is not coming down that hard; otherwise, this trip would be much more challenging as a motorist. And I hope the drivers of those vans are doing okay."

* * *

Fred had taken the responsibility of driving the red van to the ski venue. As Sandra had mentioned, he wanted to keep an eye on the Jeep ahead of him that Maggie and Erin were in. While sitting beside Bernie in the front seat, Fred said, "Hey, Bernie, would you have believed the scenery of this place if you were not actually here to experience it?"

Bernie answered, "Well, Fred, I can believe it because my eyes are not lying to me. It's something I've never seen before! You just can't duplicate all this back in Florida or almost anywhere else for that matter. I don't think it ever even snows back there. At least you get snow in the winter up north where you all are," Bernie continued.

"I know what you mean, Bernie," Fred responded. "And to make it real, Bernie, we ran into a snowstorm while traveling out here to Colorado; we just made it to this small town in western Iowa called Chappell. You remember that. It definitely was an experience for everybody!"

Gates, who was sitting in the seat just behind Fred and Bernie, said, "Hey, Bernie, to change the subject a little, how is married life treating you?"

"It's been great, Gates. I'm just glad to be with you guys again. Maybe you can give me some secrets to your success in your marriage to Courtney, and you too, Fred; I don't want to slight you and Maggie!"

"No problem, Bernie. I'm willing to share," Fred said.

Courtney interrupted, "Well, Bernie, you can ask me *that* question about Gates and me. I can't speak for Fred and Maggie. And I'll give you the answer: it's communication. You have to be able to communicate with your partner."

"I agree with that," Gates said.

"Me too!" Fred agreed.

Bernie responded, "Okay then, that's some good advice. And I know when you and all the others come back down to Florida next summer, we can continue this discussion."

Sandra, who had been listening in on the discussion, offered her opinion from the seat behind Courtney and Gates. "I for one am looking forward to *that* trip. We had such a good time down there the last time, except for that hurricane, of course. And why don't you all give some love to us single people!"

Fred said, "Speaking of storms, this snow is coming down a little harder now, but hopefully things will be okay. And, Sandra, you know how you're appreciated by everyone!"

"Thank you, Fred," Sandra replied.

Bernie added, "Well, Sandra, I echo what Fred just said. But I want to transition into something else. You know Erin and I decided to come to Colorado not because of the *possibility* of storms—there's always *that* out here. We expected to see quite a bit of snowfall, something that you just don't see in Florida. So that's why Erin and I decided to come here, because it's so different from where we live. Of course, Sinbad having the resort out here is a major reason why we're here."

"Yeah, Bernie," Fred said. "We need to thank Sinbad for all the accommodations that we have out here. But as far as the snow, we get a lot of it in Chicago too, but it can't compare to what they get out here. The big advantage of being here is the mountainous scenery. I mean, Chicago is as flat as a pancake."

"Hey, listen, to change the tone of the conversation a little bit, the girls look like they're doing fine in the Jeep ahead of us," Fred said. "I'm sure Mag is satisfied being in that Jeep. Hopefully, she's not as afraid as I'm sure she would be if she sat in one of these huge vans. I mean, she seemed terrified as we began to move around these mountains when she was sitting with me."

"Well, Fred, they're right in front of us, and it appears as though they're fine. And the van behind us is keeping up, which is good," Bernie said.

Fred replied, "Well, Bernie, one reason I wanted to drive was to keep an eye on Erin and Maggie in that Jeep. I know you said your wife is a good driver, but I just feel more comfortable making sure they're okay. I know how dangerous it can be driving on the roads up here in these mountains."

"Yes, Fred, Erin is a good driver. I know because I've seen her in that vehicle of ours over the last few days. As I said earlier, Erin is as experienced as I am in driving the Jeep. They'll be fine," Bernie assured Fred. "These mountains can be terrifying all right! But you're in good hands with Fred at the wheel. No offense to you, Al, because you've done a great job driving too."

Bernie then asked, "Hey, Fred, is Carlos keeping up with us?"

"Yeah, they seem to be doing fine."

Fred added, "Well, everybody, we're almost at our destination.

Alphonso said, "Yeah, everybody, we can get ourselves ready for some skiing! We'll be able to actually go on some of these mountain peaks that we've been looking at over the last few minutes. It should be a lot of fun. And thank you, Bernie, for complimenting me on my driving."

"You're good," Bernie responded.

"Oh, goody, goody!" Jeanie shouted. "You hear that, Wynn? We're almost there!"

As Jeanie looked around at the ski slopes, she started to feel a bit overwhelmed. "Wynn, I've never skied before. I'm afraid," Jeanie said.

"Don't be afraid, Jeanie. I'll be here with you the whole time to keep you from falling."

"Well, okay. I'm just glad to be away from that David for a while," she muttered so that no one else could hear except Wynn.

"Hey now. Don't even think about him."

Everyone soon got out of their vehicles and stood in front of the lodge.

Wynn said to Jeanie, "Let's go over here and wait for the group to assemble. I think Mr. Bernie wants to tell us something."

The first thing Bernie did after everyone had arrived in the parking lot of the ski lodge was to see how Erin and Maggie were. They had just gotten out of the vehicle when he approached them.

"How was the drive, and are you two okay?" he asked.

"We had a good time riding together. Didn't we, Maggie?"

"We sure did! And we're fine, Bernie," Maggie answered with assurance. "And thanks, Fred, for agreeing with me to make the switch, and especially to you, Bernie, for being willing to do it. I was really able to enjoy the trip up here riding with Erin in the Jeep."

"No problem, Maggie," Bernie's replied.

Everyone in the group exited the vans and made their way into the lodge. It was a small venue but adequate.

After everyone had entered and gathered near the gift shop, Bernie went to the front of the group and spoke to them: "Hey, everybody, could I have your attention? I know you're excited to be here and we're all looking around at the amenities. But I just want to give some information on how you all should proceed now that we're finally here at the ski lodge. I hope all of you will have a good time on these slopes, but be careful; we don't need any injuries."

Bernie continued, "Anyway, you know early this morning it was cold but clear, but it actually began to snow on the short trip here. I first heard about that possibility on a weather forecast I saw before we left. Based on that forecast, the system should be a while before arriving where we are, but it may affect us before we leave the resort here in the mountains and return to Denver. As far as our excursion today, the only effects from that system would be an increase in snowfall later when we head back to Williams' Cabin."

"But listen, people, I'm from Florida and love the snow because we hardly ever see any of it down there. And how about that scenery on the way here? I mean, the views were spectacular. Fortunately, we have good drivers, including Fred here who made the switch with Alphonso, so we don't have much to worry about as far as safety on the road is concerned.

"But let's not go there, talking about the negative possibilities. Let's just stick with the positives. And speaking of the positives, this place is just majestic. As you look around, there's nothing but snow-covered mountain peaks and valleys for as far as the eye can see. But in between are the ski slopes, and that's what we'll be tackling today.

"Now, from what I've been told, the slope that we've been assigned to is one of the gentler slopes, not very steep. That's good because we're all beginners, and I don't want to see any accidents.

"Once we leave this area around the gift shop, we'll be going to the lodge's loading station to pick up our accessories. I've been told there is a large locker room where you can change, so once we do that just go out there and see what we can do. We all will be on our own, but there will be trainers to help you if you run into any problems. That's what they are there for—to help you.

"Now, Katie, because Wynn will be with Jeanie, you can partner with Sandra. I think everyone else will have someone with them. But as far as the trainers, they can easily be seen because they all will be dressed in red.

"One last thing. As I mentioned to many of you back at the hotel in Denver before we even arrived here in the mountains, Erin and I are so glad all of you could be here to help us celebrate our honeymoon. We're sorry we didn't do a lot of pre-planning for the wedding itself; that's why none of you from up north attended on such short notice; it was kind of a quick arrangement. But believe me, we'll make it up to you when you all come to Florida next summer—under the direction of Sinbad, of course. I think he told some of you about another visit to his resort.

"Anyway, I want you all to know that our time in Colorado is the *second part* of our honeymoon. As some of you already know, our two-part honeymoon started back in Florida with a visit to the Island of Love. Now, I know all of you didn't get a chance to go there when you were down last summer to celebrate Erin coming to work for us. But I've been told by Sinbad himself that he plans another trip to Florida for all of you, and at that time you *will* get the chance to visit the Island of Love. And believe me, when you go there, you will not be disappointed. I'd like to tell you about our trip there, but we promised Sinbad not to talk to any of you about it. I don't want to let the cat out of the bag, you might say. Just let me say this, it won't be for the faint of heart. It'll be something that you will never expect to see; I guarantee that.

"So enough about the Island of Love. Now, we'll have about three hours today to enjoy ourselves on the ski slopes. It's 2:00 now, and we'll have plenty of time on the slopes before we return to this spot at 5:30. Hopefully, we'll be ready to board the vehicles and return to Headquarters promptly at 6:00. That will give us enough time to make the short trip back and take an hour to recover from the excursion and get ready for dinner at 7:30. By the way, it'll be in the dining hall there. For now, let's have some fun, folks!"

CHAPTER 23
A Return To The Lodge?

Foundation Scripture: Psalm 46:1

God is our refuge and strength,
A very present help in trouble.

Everyone quickly changed into their ski garb and headed to the slopes. After about two hours of skiing, the two couples who were least likely to hang out together, the Manleys and Sheri and David, went back to the lodge.

After they returned inside, Courtney said, "Well, Sheri, I know we went out on the slopes together, but because of our ski assignments we were separated most of the time. So, how did you two do out there on the slopes?"

"It was a lot of fun, Courtney. I think the most significant part was that I overcame the fear of going down a mountainside so fast on skis. I was frightened at first. But it helped a lot that one of those trainers showed us how to slow down and stop when going downhill."

"And how about you, David?" Gates asked.

"We survived. But I have to admit, it was different. I think I like Florida better," he answered.

Gates replied, "Well, you know what they say, 'joy is in the variety of life,' at least when you're doing something different that you like to do."

Gates added, "Even in relationships, you have to create your own joy by finding new things that interest you and your partner. At least it works for Courtney and me."

Courtney, who was standing beside him, said simply, "I can vouch for that."

Over the next several minutes, the other couples returned to the lodge. Everyone returned their ski gear to the rental shop and walked into the front lobby to wait to board the vehicles for a return to Headquarters at Williams' Cabin.

By 5:00, everyone was ready to go back to the lodge and prepared to board the vans for a return trip to Williams' Cabin.

"Are you ready, Maggie?" Erin asked her as she stood in front of the gift shop.

"I am, Erin."

"And how did you do skiing out there?" Erin asked.

"It was great! It was a lot of fun, Erin. But I must tell you, Fred and I didn't go far, and he helped me stay on my feet."

"Well, that's good," Erin said.

Maggie replied, "While we had fun, I'll be glad to leave the ski lodge and get back to Headquarters, but I want some souvenirs from the gift shop before I leave. Just look at some of these items, Erin; you can't get any of these things from either Miami or Chicago or from Detroit for that matter."

Out of the corner of Maggie's eye, she saw a replica of a life-sized snowman. Maggie remembered how much Peggy had wanted a snowman.

"Erin, I see something that a waitress I befriended at the diner on the way here said she wanted me to get her. It's exactly what I think she wants! I've got to get this item for her, Erin. Based on the travel plans, we'll stop by the place where she works on our way back."

"Go ahead, Maggie; you do that, and get anything else you think you want from here. I got everything I wanted to take back from Colorado the first day we got to Denver," Erin said.

"Okay, Erin, I'll go with you and look for a while. But let me tell you, when we're all through here, I can't wait to get back to the cabin and just relax," Maggie said.

Maggie and Erin surveyed other items in the gift shop before they rejoined the group. Like everyone else, they were eager to get back to Headquarters once Maggie had her souvenirs.

Maggie continued to look around before purchasing what she knew she needed to get. After being with Maggie for a while, some of the other ladies in the group assembled near the front of the gift shop. Erin said to them, "Girls, let's get together later this evening once we get back to Headquarters and talk about our experiences."

Everyone agreed. Erin in particular looked forward to finding out if Maggie had gotten the snowman replica. When everyone met later, she got her answer.

Maggie was absorbed in viewing the different items that were available. She did more window shopping by herself before she rejoined the group.

Soon the group was together back in the lobby of the ski lodge ready to board the two vans. Led by Erin and Maggie in the Jeep, they started their journey back to Williams' Cabin.

Driving the red van that was directly behind the Jeep, Fred said to Bernie, "Finally, we're back on the road."

As they began their short trip back to Williams' Cabin, Fred asked Bernie, "Do you think Erin is okay driving back, Bernie? I know she did a good job driving to the ski lodge, but you know it's a little more treacherous out here now with much more accumulation of snow."

"Naw! She'll be fine. Just relax and enjoy the trip back," Bernie replied.

Back in the Jeep, Erin asked Maggie, "Did you return to the gift shop to get the picture of a snowman?"

Maggie said with much regret, "You know, Erin, I did not. I forgot all about it when I went about looking at other things. I got distracted, and I feel terrible because the waitress seemed so passionate about me getting a picture of a snowman; I guess with me in it. It would have been a good opportunity to do that.

"But, Erin, I just don't know the reason why she was so passionate about getting a snowman. I just don't know. But I guess she has her reasons. Anyway, I guess it was not to be."

"Well, Maggie, remember, everything happens for a reason."

"I think a more immediate concern for us is not a snowman but all the snow that's beginning to accumulate on the road; it sure has gotten worse out here with all the recent snowfall. You know, girl, it's really a mess out here," Erin said.

"You're right, Erin. We're getting some pretty bad weather now. And, yes, things happen for a reason. Everything will work out fine, I believe, so I'm not too concerned about not getting that snowman," Maggie replied.

"I'm glad you feel that way, Maggie. Now, with the wind blowing and all that snow, we can hardly see the terrain over the railing. Well, so much for that spectacular view," Erin said with disappointment.

Erin glanced back and forth from the road to her friend as she drove deliberately on the snowy road. She failed to return her attention to the road quickly enough as the Jeep came into an unanticipated curve. Erin quickly tried to steer the vehicle around the curve but overcorrected.

"Oh, my," she shouted. "Hang on, Maggie!"

In the van directly behind them, Fred and Bernie saw clearly that Erin was in trouble; the Jeep did not make the curve. Instead, it skidded straight ahead.

As the Jeep now spun out of control, Maggie shouted, "Oh, my God! We're in a skid! And we're headed straight toward that railing! Stop this vehicle, Erin! Stop!" Maggie shouted in desperation.

Erin knew well that the brake pedal should not be applied in a skid, especially on snow or ice, but in the heat of the moment she responded to Maggie's cries by applying just a little pressure to the brakes, hoping that it would be enough to at least slow down the vehicle. But that did not work, and the vehicle continued to skid forward.

Erin had no time to explain to Maggie what she was doing to prevent further skidding in the direction they were headed.

Maggie yelled, "Oh, that light! Oh, my God!" The last words Maggie heard Erin say were, "Hang on, Maggie."

By this time, the Jeep had approached the railing. Because of the vehicle's spin, it struck the railing on its side and subsequently flipped over and went into the ravine.

Fortunately, the Jeep landed in an upright position on its wheels, then rolled forward toward the steepest decline of the embankment; it stopped however, just short of the plunging drop-off beyond.

Back in the van, Fred was in panic mode. Bernie shouted, "Oh, my God, Fred, they're in trouble! No! Oh, my Lord! They've gone over the railing!"

Fred said, "Oh, no! It's horrible! I'm stopping and Carlos in the other van will stop too. Oh my! Bernie!"

Fred continued to shout, "We gotta do something, Bernie! Our wives are in there!"

Bernie tried to sound reassuring, but his own voice gave away the panic he felt inside. "Don't panic now, Fred! Just continue to slow down and stop like you said."

Only a few seconds passed before Fred stopped; they ended up on the side of the road near where the crash occurred.

Fred said, "Hey, Bernie, I'm gonna call 911. Maybe we can get some help here as soon as possible."

"That's a good move, Fred. You go ahead and do that," Bernie said. "I'll walk over there to take a closer look."

As Fred made the call, all the others got out of the vans and stood with him in the shivering cold near the railing where Erin and Maggie's Jeep had gone over. Everyone was hoping and praying that Maggie and Erin had not been seriously injured.

CHAPTER 24
The Vision

Foundation Scripture: Joel 2:28

"And it shall come to pass afterward That I will pour out My Spirit on all flesh; Your sons and your daughters shall prophesy, Your old men shall dream dreams, Your young men shall see visions."

Back in the now disabled Jeep, Maggie was aware she had just been in an accident, but she felt strange and somehow not fully present. She looked up and saw what appeared to be a ghost heading straight towards her. Maggie didn't believe in apparitions, but what she saw was so strange, even frightening.

When the figure got close enough to her, she realized that it was her mother. Suddenly, she wasn't afraid anymore.

"Hello, Mama. You look so beautiful," Maggie said. She gave Mensie a hug. To Maggie, her mother felt so soft and ethereal. What Maggie embraced felt more like a form made of mist than a physical body. As they held each other, her mother said, "You look beautiful too, Maggie."

There Maggie was between two worlds, the one where she saw her mother and the other where only moments earlier her companion in the Jeep, Erin, had begged her to hang on for dear life! It was then Maggie realized she was in a strange but peaceful new dimension.

As Maggie struggled between two dimensions, one physical and the other ethereal, the spiritual dimension won out, and she became totally immersed in her vision of her mother. They existed outside of time in a place of serenity where calm flooded their beings. In her physically unconscious state, Maggie experienced this spiritual realm.

During this period of tranquility, Mensie spoke to her daughter. "Now, look over here; I want to show you something." Mensie pointed toward a place that seemed to be a gathering of people in their home church, Mark Methodist, back in Flint.

In a few moments, Maggie replied, "Hey, Mama, I don't think I want to stay here. It's so sad. It's taking me back to Mark Methodist, and I think it's a funeral, and I used to hate going to those so much."

Mensie responded, "Yes, Maggie, it's a funeral all right. It's your own funeral!"

"What?" Maggie shouted.

Mensie said, "Yes, little one, I know. I know." She tenderly patted her daughter's back. "That's your body there in that box."

In a lower tone of voice, Maggie said, "Wait a minute. Let me go back and look a little closer." When she did, she continued, "Why, there's Erin looking over a dead body lying there in a casket."

Maggie felt bewildered and in denial about being the one lying there. She continued, "Erin seems so calm about everything, unlike many of the others. But despite her calmness, I see her shedding a tear, and she is a spiritually strong woman as I remember, Mama. Don't they all realize I'm in a place of peace and joy now, being here with you?"

Mensie responded, "Maggie, despite the strength of a believer, it's difficult to endure the passing of a loved one as your friends are now enduring in your absence in their physical existence. I mean, the physical body is easy to become acquainted with, to get used to over the years, without acknowledging the spirit that resides within it. Well, it's that spirit that constitutes the person's real being. In the physical dimension we're witnessing, sadness is a natural reaction to the loss of a loved one. Being sad and even distraught at such a loss is understandable in the physical world. But it's only your physical being that they are grieving."

"I understand, Mama, I think. But, oh, Mama! It's so sad."

After she calmed herself a little, Maggie said, "Wait a minute! There's Sandra, and for heaven's sake, I see Fred standing there over the casket and just crying his eyes out!"

"Yes, Maggie, there were a lot of emotions in your departure from physical life," Mensie said. "But Erin's reaction is so different from many others."

Maggie's mother tried to explain. "You see, Maggie, knowing that the person's spirit is with the Lord, as you are witnessing right here with me, helps a lot on those sad occasions. And let me tell you of a mystery: even now you're with them. But they are not aware of it."

"Well, Mama, little good it's doing them that I'm with them; all they see is my dead physical body lying there! But I understand the other part of what you're saying, that right now being with you, is *like* being with the Lord because we both have His spirit!"

"Yes, honey, you're with the Lord in the sense that in this dimension, we're all like Him, like His spirit as you said. It's in the Scriptures in 1 John 3:2."

Mensie continued to give her daughter inspiring information. She said, "Keep this in mind, Maggie, that same spirit can be within those in the natural, physical world by way of the Holy Spirit! And that's what brings all of us joy."

Maggie replied, "Yes, Mama. Speaking of joy, it's joyful here because I'm with you again, and I'll soon be with all those I've known in my natural life, at least those who have already transitioned. But the sad part is seeing those who haven't, my family, friends, and acquaintances at my service down there, Mama! Look at Fred! I've never seen Fred act like that, not even… Not even…."

"Yes, Maggie? Were you going to say something?" Mensie interjected.

"Well, Mama, even when we attended your funeral. Oh, I just can't say it."

Mensie tried to comfort her daughter, helping her by completing what she was going to say. "Okay, Maggie, you don't have to go there. You're talking about my final services. I know. We don't want to dwell on that."

Maggie replied, "But wait, Mama; it's not all sad."

"What do you mean?" Mensie asked.

"Well, I'm not sure about the time frame, but I can also see what they're doing after the service, after *my* service. Everyone is having a good time, eating, and laughing and carrying on. I almost feel like everyone has forgotten about me already. They're certainly happy, but being where I am right now with you, Mama, it's really making *me* sad."

"Okay, Maggie, we'll go somewhere that's pleasant. We don't have to stay here, little one," Mensie said addressing Maggie as she did often when she was a little girl. "Let's go someplace where there is no more sadness to experience a joyous occasion for you, Maggie. You'll be meeting your siblings. I know you're anxious to see them, especially that Sadie."

Mensie continued, "My, my! Was *she* some daughter! But believe me, Maggie, I loved all you children the same, and I know Matthew did too. But that Sadie, now she was a character all right!"

After Mensie expressed her thoughts about Maggie's closest sibling Sadie, she said, "And speaking of Matthew, you'll be seeing your father too!"

Before Maggie saw her immediate family, she met a woman named Priscilla. In the vision Maggie asked her, "Now, I don't know you, do I?"

Priscilla answered, "No, I never knew you personally while we were all down there on the earth, which is the reason you do not remember me. But we were on a cruise ship when I saw you and your friend. I guess he was your husband. You and some other friends of yours were all cruising to Bermuda."

"Oh, yeah! That was my husband. And I remember what you are describing. But, hey, wait a minute. That was only a dream!"

Priscilla said, "Well, dream or not, I remember it. And I recall you saying to your husband that all the people who were in line that day appeared so different. But I overheard someone say that God looked at them not based on their looks or personalities but on their spirit. And in that spirit, we're all connected, all the while retaining our individualities, whether we know each other or not. That is some of what I heard that day.

"Now, Maggie, we're able to connect in this wonderful spiritual realm even though we didn't cross paths in our physical existence except in that one instance, in that dream, of course!"

Maggie could only say, "Wow, Priscilla! It seems that I've always known you. We are so much like each other. I mean, we have such similar spirits. But like I said and you acknowledged, that was only a dream, although it seemed so real at the time," Maggie replied.

As Maggie and Priscilla continued to communicate in the spirit, Mensie said, "Yes, Priscilla, we're in a wondrous place.... But, Maggie, I want to say something about your final service we just witnessed. Well, that was over a thousand years ago, at least years in that dimension, the physical realm, when you were on earth as that event occurred, that is, when the van crashed."

Maggie responded, "What? A thousand years ago? And you were there, Mama? Why, it seemed that it was only moments ago when Erin told me to hang on for dear life when that accident occurred. I mean, it was like me being caught between two worlds. At that moment I was thrust into this dimension here with you, Mama, and, at the same time, I was apparently fighting there for my physical life!

And I do remember we headed toward the railing on the side of the road and struck it. That's when we apparently went over the railing, and then I blanked out."

Mensie replied, "Well, you're right, Maggie. For you, *it was* only moments ago. But since that time, perhaps in a fraction of a second, things changed, because when you blanked out, as you put it, time as you knew it ceased. That's when you immediately came to us, into the presence of Jesus and all of those who have passed on before—like Priscilla here."

"She's right, Maggie!" Priscilla responded. "Yes, your mother is so much like yourself, and I've enjoyed communicating with her as well in this dimension. It's like we're all one big, happy family, and that would include my folks that are here as well."

Maggie replied, "That's really something."

"Yes, that is something, Maggie," Mensie said. After a pause, she continued, "And I'll tell you another thing, I was there with you in that vehicle crash; in fact, I guided you into a transition from physical to spiritual life in this dimension. That was one of my assignments. You remember when you told your friend Erin that you had seen a light just before the crash? Well, that was me guiding you into this dimension; that was one of my assignments.

"Now, that's very exciting, Maggie, to have someone you knew who had transitioned from physical to God's spiritual life to usher you into this dimension! It was such a privilege for me.

"Let me explain something else, Maggie," Mensie continued. "You did more than just blank out, honey, as you put it. You transitioned into a brand new world! Yeah, the world we used to sing about all the time back at Mark Methodist Church. You did more than just blank out that day; you passed away, away from physical to a spiritual life.

"This is how wonderful it is, Maggie," Mensie said. "In that physical realm, your physical body was a focus, but your spirit was alive within you, the Holy Spirit. In that dimension, you could easily go back and forth in both dimensions, but then it was only your physical mind that acted as transportation. That's what happened when you were on the beach that time and communicated with me. Your mind allowed your spirit to connect with my spirit. Do you remember that?"

"Of course, I remember, Mama. That was a special time when I was on the beach. It took our friends, Courtney and Gates, who were lying on a beach chair at the time, calling my name to end my time with you," Maggie replied.

Mensie said, "Well, you were on the beach using your mind to connect your spirit with mine, but your friends were able to distract you. In this dimension, Maggie, the focus is on our spiritual body, so we don't have to worry about distractions like that. That's why we were able to simply move from that sad place where we could see your final service being performed to where we are now.

"The spirit makes it possible to move around without the limitations of being constrained by a physical body because we had been released from that body when we transitioned. But also we can go back to the physical body we had on earth, and we will when Christ returns to the earth at some point in the future. The time of that event no one knows but the Father as it says in the scriptures. But when that time comes, we'll be able to reconnect with our physical body, the body that perished, as explained in the Book of Revelation.

"Yes, Maggie, this is the wonderful place of joy and peace that we first learned about back at Mark Methodist. And you know what? You've only just gotten started."

Maggie could hardly respond after her mother's words. Finally, she said, "Wow! I guess that's the meaning of what I've heard during the latter part of that physical life of mine about the 'Wonders *of* the Spirit!'"

Mensie continued, "Yes, little one, the spirit *is* wonderful. And another thing, Maggie, is this: the world down there has been progressing since the time of your accident, the time of your transition. Centuries have passed. Time in this place is not like what we all thought of time in our past existence because everything here is new, as the scriptures said it would be.

"And you know what, little girl?" Mensie said addressing her daughter as she did often back home in Flint. "You get to see a panoramic view of all that, including the events that occurred just prior to your transition when you and your friends were on that ski trip to Colorado."

Maggie responded, "Oh, Mama, how I wish you were there with us. We had such a good time until the crash."

"Now wait a minute, little girl. I *was* there with all of you—at least when I wanted to be, which was pretty often I might add. I remember when you all went through that snowstorm there on the open plains of Iowa on your way to Denver, and I knew that you weren't going to make it to your destination at that time. Sure enough, you all had to stop in that little town called Chappell.

"And do you remember that night when you couldn't go to sleep, and you came into the lobby and sat in front of that fireplace? Well, I was right there with you, honey."

"Oh, Mama, I remember that night. It was so cold and snowy outside, and all of us in the group felt fortunate to have gotten to that hotel in Chappell. I guess everyone was so tired that they just went to bed. But I decided to stay up. And I remember seeing my friend Gates, who was up late too in that lobby, talking with his wife Courtney. I remember him trying to get me to go to bed, realizing we would be on the road again the next morning, but I just couldn't sleep, Mama. I told him that something was pulling me to sit in front of that fireplace, and I wanted to stay up a little longer. And I remember telling him that I just could not understand why I would want to be up at that late hour. I guess I wanted to just sit there and meditate.

"Anyway, I did feel your presence there, Mama," Maggie said to Mensie.

"You felt my presence there because *I was* there!" Mensie said. "I was with you, honey! And you know what? I felt you too that night, Maggie. I felt drawn to you and tried to draw you to me. That's why you said you felt a pull while you sat there. That was from me! I wanted to talk with you, little one, and impart some of the divine knowledge I had to share. Remember when I told you to live your life and live it more abundantly?"

Maggie replied, "I do remember that, Mama, that you were telling me to live an abundant life. And, yes, I also remember how I felt a pull that evening. Well, you've answered that question. So that was you, Mama, in spirit?"

"That's right, little one," Mensie answered. "That abundant life I was telling you about that God wants for all of His children is to have our desires met and to recognize Him as the provider of those desires."

"In other words, honey, praise is important, our praise of Him being a part of our lives, being the essence of our life. But what brings *Him* joy is to see *us* joyful. And let me tell you, honey, nothing brings us more joy than to have our inner desires met!

"Let me tell you this, Maggie. I viewed all the events that took place during that entire trip to Colorado and also at other times from this spiritual dimension where you are right now, so it may seem like yesterday to you, but, as the scripture says, one day with the Lord is like a thousand years and a thousand years as one day. It depends on your perspective. It was a long, long, time ago in the physical realm, but in the spirit, where you and I are now, it *was* yesterday. There's no limit or consideration of time here; everything is in the now and always new. These are just some of the 'Wonders of the Spirit' in *this* dimension.

"I'm telling you all this, Maggie, so you can gain an understanding about life. The truth is that in the physical realm God wants us to recognize that we live as a three-part being. We are a spirit, we have a soul, and, for a limited period, we live in a physical body while on the earth. Well, what you saw at your final service was the remains of your physical body. But you know now that your spirit is here with me and is alive and well!"

"Mama, after what you just said, I don't understand it, the process of me getting here as you described. But I can tell you this, I don't feel sad, not like I did when I viewed my own final service. That's because I'm here with you now, and I had missed you so much when you left us. And not just you, I missed Dad a lot too. I missed both of you so much in Colorado especially. Everybody had so much fun there. But you and Dad were always in the back of my mind."

Mensie interjected, "Well, you know, Maggie, that I was there in spirit. But I'm still learning. And there is so much work to be done still as well as a lot to learn in this dimension.

"But the beauty of it is that I will be working with the purpose of helping others like I did when I ushered you into this dimension when you blanked out from your accident. All the saints will know their assignments given to us by the Master Himself, Jesus the Christ. That day is still ahead of us when He returns to earth for a second time and establishes His kingdom there, and we will be with Him, as the scripture states. That's when our work really starts, and we'll be able to make use of that glorified, physical body right there on the earth to help others.

"And something else, Maggie, that I don't completely understand right now, but I don't think God is finished with His creation. The interesting thing is that we, you and I, as well as others who have overcome and qualify for the new government that God intents to establish right there on the earth will be trained to help those who are in their physical bodies on the earth. And the whole purpose of it will be for them to have the opportunity to receive the love of God that we've had the opportunity to receive during our physical lifetimes."

Maggie replied, "Mama, I certainly don't understand all that. It seems so, so unreal."

Mensie replied, "It's not meant for you to understand everything. That's why belief is so important. Just believe in Him who made you and me as well as all the humans in His creation, and ultimately everything *will* become new with the purpose of bringing joy to all of us. And not only that but we will come to understand all things.

"A lot of what I'm talking about is outlined right there in the Book of Revelation like pastor John Sr. taught us back at Mark Methodist.

"Yes, Maggie, we will be able to, first and foremost, help or lead others to the kingdom that will last forever! And in this new dimension, that's what we'll be doing when that day comes—when the whole world will be transformed.

"You know, Maggie, at that time, the time prior to Christ returning to the earth, life in the physical will still be going on; people will be carrying on their normal activities like working, partying, and everything. But did you know, little girl, that during the one thousand years since your accident there in Colorado, there was a pandemic that caused the whole country and many parts of the world to shut down?"

Maggie replied in shock, "What? Shut down? Now, what do you mean, Mama?" she asked with great concern in her voice.

Mensie replied, "Well, let me finish. I mean, you could hardly do anything, and everybody was going around wearing masks. It was an invisible virus that had spread throughout the whole world. Now, can you believe that?"

Maggie responded, "No, I can't, Mama. Everything was so normal when we had that accident in Colorado."

Mensie continued, "Well, let me finish. With people wearing those masks, it looked so strange. But that's what everybody had to do to survive this invisible virus. But I was able to see not only people's actions but also their thoughts, and no one dreamed that something like that would affect everything, the economy, sports and recreational activities, and even educational institutions. It was a big mess! I mean, even the churches were closed to their congregations coming together for a while. But that ultimately passed, and things went back to being normal again or at least to near normal."

Mensie appeared to be getting emotional at that point. It was as if her very faith had been challenged through the circumstances she had witnessed in the spirit.

Then she came out of it and said to Maggie defiantly, "But you know, Maggie, it says in the Bible that it will be that way—like what I described to you about this virus. And there are other things described in the scriptures that will take place during the so-called last days, the time just prior to Jesus returning to earth and setting up His kingdom. It says as much in the Book of Matthew. And you know what, Maggie? You and I, as well as others who have transitioned, will be with Him to help usher in that government. It was predicted even in Old Testament Scripture, Isaiah 9:6 and 7. Now that's something that we all can look forward to.

"Until then, we have our assignments like what I'm doing now with you, Maggie. At that time, all your friends will be here, including Erin, Sandra, Courtney, Fred, and all the others. It'll be an exciting time."

"Come with me now and let's see your father. Matthew has been doing quite well. You know how much he loved gardening, and he's been doing a lot of that. But you also know how much he cared for you.

"And don't forget about your sister Sadie as well as all your other siblings. They all are waiting to see you.

"And we'll have two surprises for you as well, and I'll go ahead and tell you. You'll be seeing Pastor Joe, the minister who started Mark Methodist back in Flint. You didn't know him because he was well before your time during that physical dimension on the earth. But I remember telling you about him when you were at home.

"But the exciting part is that you also will see his grandson, John Jr., your late husband. Now, isn't that exciting?"

"My, my! Oh, yes, I'm so thrilled," Maggie responded. "Yes, we did have some good times, as well as some challenging times, John Jr. and I, that is. But we both loved the Lord. And Pastor Joe, I've been told so much about him."

"Let's go and see all of 'em," Mensie said.

Mensie and Maggie went to that more pleasant place in Maggie's vision, where she saw Sadie as well as her other siblings. She felt overjoyed! She talked with Sadie and carried on as though they were still in high school playing in the band.

But the height of her joy came when she saw her father, Matthew. They had such a special relationship in the physical realm, even when her friend Sandra became more a part of her parent's lives.

After meeting the founder of Mark Methodist and reuniting with her first husband, Maggie would soon exit her vision but not before she saw another figure. She couldn't make out the person clearly at a distance, but as the figure got closer, she realized it was Peggy, the waitress she had befriended when her group traveled to Colorado.

"Hello, Maggie!" she said. Peggy grinned widely, showing all her teeth and none were missing. She wore a look of complete radiance and joy. Then inexplicably, she disappeared.

CHAPTER 25
Back to Reality

Foundation Scripture: Psalm 119:99

I have more understanding than all my teachers,
For your testimonies are my meditation.

Soon Maggie returned to the reality of her group's trip to Colorado, and the tragic accident she was in with Erin driving the Jeep. Maggie was fortunate that heavy brush kept the vehicle from tumbling farther down the embankment, which probably would have been fatal. But the collision could not prevent her from going unconscious upon impact.

Maggie did not know that emergency personnel had arrived at the scene—thanks to the foresight of Fred, who called 911 as he and Bernie watched in horror.

Still unconscious, Maggie and Erin were taken by ambulance to a local hospital for observation. While there, it was determined that neither had serious injuries. Only Maggie was detained because she had yet to regain consciousness. Erin, who had returned to a wakeful state, was released from the hospital and assisted back to the ski lodge.

While resting in her room with Bernie, Erin agonized about Maggie's condition because she was now aware that she had blanked out. The doctor's positive prognosis did not ease her worry.

Despite the relatively good report on their injuries, Maggie had not returned to her normal conscious self for some time. She remained at the local hospital being attended to by a physician, who assured Fred that she would be fine.

Everyone in Maggie's group had gone to the hospital where Maggie and Erin were treated and later that afternoon had returned to Headquarters, Williams' Cabin.

While still at the hospital, Maggie later regained consciousness, and, with assistance from medical personnel, was transported to her room in Williams' Cabin. After Maggie was back in the comfort of her bed at Headquarters, she needed to continue her rest and did so for the reminder of the Friday afternoon and into the night.

There was little activity for other members of the group that day; everyone was concerned about Maggie's extended period of unconsciousness. Nevertheless, the physician gave everyone assurance that they both would be fine. Erin had returned to her room with Bernie, and the other members of the group spent the remainder of the night in theirs.

Early Saturday morning, Maggie woke up feeling refreshed after a good night's sleep. She felt more fully awake than at any time since the accident.

Fred had just arisen himself and was happy to see Maggie awaken. When he got up, he had contacted their friends, who were all still deeply concerned about Maggie, and invited them to come to their room. As a result, Maggie found herself with a lot of company after she opened her eyes.

As his wife was gaining total clarity about her surroundings, Fred said to those around him, "She's coming around now, and soon you all will be able to talk to her. Just let her get her bearings."

"Thank goodness, Fred," Sandra said. The others seemed anxious to speak with Maggie as well.

Maggie, finally fully awake, recognized Fred, which prompted him to say, "Mag, Mag! You slept like a log last night. And all of us here were waiting for you to wake up! You were fortunate that the Jeep you were riding in with Erin didn't go beyond some brush, which kept it from tumbling further down that ravine. If that had happened, you probably would've been a goner and Erin too!"

"Fred is right, Maggie," Erin said. "Neither one of us would have been here if that Jeep had continued rolling. Instead, it stopped—in an upright position no less—and here we are! I'm just so glad God spared our lives!"

"Amen and hallelujah!" Gates shouted.

The accident now was history for both women, and Maggie was back to reality from the vision she had. Her only concern now was eating a nice breakfast she hoped Fred would get her.

"Fred, I'm hungry!" she said.

Fred was eager to fulfill his wife's request. "Okay, Mag. Your food will be ready soon."

Maggie couldn't wait to tell her friends of her spiritual adventure. It was so peaceful and joyful, and it enhanced her expectations of life after this earthly sojourn. Maggie rose up slightly and said faintly but clearly, "I have a testimony for all of you to meditate on, and later today you'll get it once I get my faculties back. I should be fine by then." Then she lowered herself back down into a more comfortable position.

So, there they were, all Maggie's friends, standing by her. Sandra, who was among those standing over her bed, said, "Maggie, we're just glad you're back with us. And you seem to be okay. Am I right about that?"

Maggie only nodded her head in the affirmative while still smiling. In a slightly stronger voice than before, she said, "You're right, Sandra. I feel fine considering the circumstances. All I want now, though, is a hot breakfast."

With that comment, Fred then gave her assurances again, saying, "Mag, that breakfast will be coming up right away."

The physician's orders back at the hospital were for Maggie to have some quiet time, so her friends soon left the room, and most of them went on to have breakfast themselves. The women of the group looked forward to the meeting they had planned among themselves later in the day after lunch. They were fortunate they had an unanticipated free day since the scheduled activity for the day, the skiing excursion, took place the previous day when the hiking trip was canceled because of the weather.

Maggie was eager to give everyone a glimpse of what she had experienced in her vision. She would have an opportunity at the lunch meeting to tell all of them the details of that wonderful place.

Later in the morning, the doctor who treated Maggie at the hospital made a visit to monitor her progress. Now alone with Maggie and Fred, the doctor told her to continue resting in bed for another two hours. "I'm going to leave, Maggie, but I'll return to see how you are later."

Maggie followed the doctor's orders and stayed in bed. With at least two more hours of rest in front of her, she eventually became anxious to get up and face the day, but Maggie abided by the doctor's orders and lay in bed. Fred was there to comfort her the whole time.

While Maggie continued to rest, she also looked forward to the late lunch meeting with her lady friends. She wanted to relive as much of the vision as she could remember with her friends at this meeting.

CHAPTER 26
A Shared Experience

Foundation Scripture: Hebrews 13:16

But do not forget to do good and to share, for with such sacrifices God is well pleased.

The fact that Saturday had become an open day for everyone turned out to be a blessing because it allowed Maggie to recuperate from her accident and meet with the women of the group to tell of her vision.

This "free" day also benefited Erin and Bernie, who had the time to obtain another rental vehicle for their remaining time in Colorado and their trip back to Florida.

Fred sat next to Maggie in bed as she reflected on the vision she had after the accident. Fred was deeply interested in knowing about the vision, and she was obliged to tell him about it.

"Oh, Fred, I realize I was in a terrible accident. But the vision seemed so real. I got to see my mother, and we talked a lot about how she was doing up there in heaven. It was such a divine place. She's been gone for some time now, but it was as though we never left each other."

As Maggie continued to give Fred as much detail of the vision as she could recall, Gates walked into their room.

He said, "Hello, you two. I just wanted to check to see how you were doing, Maggie."

"Thanks for coming by, Gates. I'm fine," Maggie replied.

"Yeah, Mag seems to be doing well, Gates," Fred confirmed.

"That's great, Maggie," Gates said. "Listen, I know you've had a rough day or two with that accident and all. But when all of us saw you a few minutes ago when you first woke up, you seemed to be doing okay considering the circumstances."

Maggie replied, "Yeah, Gates, it's almost as if I had a sound sleep, which I did. I had been pretty much out of it ever since the accident until I woke up this morning. Since then, I've been telling Fred about this dream, or you may call it a vision.

"Anyway, I was just telling him as you walked in about how I saw my funeral, and everyone was *so* sad. Afterwards, they seemed to have a good time though. But, of course, I was gone; at least my spirit had been released from my physical body just as I had been taught in church way back when I was a child at Mark Methodist.

"I told Fred that in the vision I was with Mama, and we were in such a sad place with me viewing my own funeral. I wanted to leave to go somewhere else that was more pleasant. And that's what we did; we went to a more pleasant, peaceful place in that heavenly dimension where I was, if you want to call it that."

Gates responded, "Maggie, we all know a funeral is always a sad event—everything about it. But I've found that people really want to get over the sadness, and so one formality of a final service is that after it's all over people come together to eat and socialize. A repast is what it's called. It's a way of helping loved ones to get over that sad experience."

"Do you mind if I share a story with you, a biblical story?" Gates asked.

"No, of course not! You can tell me your story, Gates. Go ahead!"

Gates said, "As a minister, it reminds me of the experience of Jesus when He was crucified, and he didn't even have a final service. They just placed His body in a tomb. Of course, we all know He didn't stay there; He arose. But the interesting thing is of all the people He came into contact within His earthly journey, only two women, Mary and Martha, were there with Him in this awful time. They stayed there by His body and were overwhelmed with sadness.

"Jesus' disciples, His trusted disciples, were not around at all. They were nowhere to be found. They ended up in a room having a little party among themselves about a week so after it was all over, thinking that Jesus was dead and gone. Well, He really was dead, and He really was gone. He went to the Father for His body to become glorified.

"But, Maggie, like in the vision you had of yourself, He laid there in that tomb, stone cold. Obviously, they didn't have caskets and other modern conveniences like we do today. But as the story goes, the disciples probably thought all they had been through with Him was for nothing, that it was all over. It was like when your family and friends you saw at your service, mourning over their loss, at least according to the vision you described.

"Again, back to the story... While you know Jesus *was* dead, in three days He resurrected. And after He ascended to heaven and His body glorified, Jesus later appeared to the disciples in that room as I said, and they all were amazed, even afraid, at first. Can you imagine seeing someone in person about a week or so after their final service and everything? You would be terrified too! Well, that's how the disciples felt.

"But they soon realized it was really Him; they saw the nail prints still on His body."

"And you know the story also includes one of them, Thomas, who was not there at the time. And when he was told what happened, he didn't believe it; he didn't believe that Jesus was alive. He just could not believe that a dead person could come back to life, although Jesus said as much during his ministry.

"Thomas did see Jesus a little later when He appeared in that same room again. This time, Thomas was with the disciples and saw Him for himself and that's when he believed.

"I said all that, Maggie, to remind you that we all go on with our lives when a loved one passes on, but that's not the end of our association with that person. One day, we will see them again, not in a natural, physical body like what we have now but in a glorified spiritual body like the one Jesus had that day when He appeared to the disciples in a room.

"And the vision you had was just another piece of evidence that you will see your mother again. At that time, it will not be a vision but a reality of the spiritual body you'll have *after* your transition from this physical existence on earth.

"And as far as the lady other than your mother you saw in your vision, the one you didn't know, Priscilla, she obviously had the same kind of spirit as you have now. In that spiritual realm, those with like spirits also will be able to connect with you even though they may not have had physical contact with you in this earthly realm prior to transition. That's the way it will be with everyone else who has a similar spirit; they will be able to connect and interact with one another!

"The spirit I'm talking about is not mystical at all; it's like the spiritual fruits that are described in scripture—like love, peace, and joy, the ones mentioned in Galatians. In other words, we'll be able to know each other because of those traits, those *fruits of the spirit.* Now, that's exciting! It's another 'Wonder of the Spirit' that I like talking about almost every time I deliver a sermon.

"And by the way, it's not like that here in the natural, physical world. I mean, sometimes we have to deal with people we'd rather not be around *because* their spirit is not like ours. You know who

I'm talking about—people with negative attitudes, for example. No one wants to be around a grouch, someone like that, except maybe another grouch."

"Oh, Gates, you're pretty funny; you know that?" Maggie commented.

Gates replied, "Okay, Maggie, it may be funny, but that's what you have in this world—all kinds of folks with their persuasions and proclivities."

Maggie replied, "Yeah, Gates, that is so inspiring. Those with like spirits being together and having fun, or I guess I should say, having the spiritual fruits that you talked about that's in scripture."

Gates added, "You're right, Maggie. In that dimension, you can say we'll have fun. You know, in this natural world, we have a distorted idea of what fun is. Anyway, it's more than that; it's beyond the level of having fun, you might say. It's like the scripture says, we'll have joy and peace, which are internal traits within every believer, traits that Christ Himself wants us to have—traits that will lead to an abundant life that we all desire. Anyway, I'm glad to make you feel a little better, Maggie."

Gates continued, "Let me turn my attention to you, Fred. The reason I came in here is to remind you that the men were talking about going out and surveying the area around the lodge. Do you want to come with us?"

"Thanks, Gates, but I think I'll take the time today to do some more writing and keep an eye on Mag," Fred said.

Gates replied, "Well, okay. I understand.

"And, Maggie, I know you and the ladies will be meeting for lunch later today, a rather late lunch, I might add. By that time, maybe you'll be able to venture out and join them. I'm sure Courtney will fill me in with all the other details of your vision that you will tell them about, so I'll see you two later."

When Gates left the room, Fred and Maggie were again alone. She continued to tell Fred about her vision. After a couple of hours, the physician called and told her that he would be there in ten minutes. By that time, Maggie was not interested in seeing a doctor; she was eager to start her day. She especially was looking forward to meeting with and telling the other ladies about the vision she had.

When the doctor came to monitor her progress, Maggie convinced him that she was fine.

"You look a lot better, Maggie," the physician said. "So, yes, I believe there's no reason for you to remain in your room as long as you don't try to do too much."

"Oh, no, doctor. I won't do too much at all," Maggie assured him.

With that assurance from Maggie, the physician felt he was no longer needed, so he prepared to leave.

"Mr. and Mrs. Mint, I'll be leaving now. But if you have any concerns, Maggie, just give me a buzz."

"Okay, doctor. Thank you for everything," Maggie told him.

After that meeting Maggie thought, *I'm so glad the doctor gave me permission to go outside.*

Maggie wanted to take maximum advantage of this vacation. She realized that soon they all would need to begin packing for the long trip back to Chicago on Monday morning.

After having breakfast in bed while talking with Fred about her vision, Maggie got up and prepared for the day. She proceeded to take a shower and get dressed. Meanwhile, Fred was preparing to go someplace to continue his writing.

A short time after that, Maggie went to the empty lobby and found a comfortable chair and just sat there, contemplating recent events. She was eager to meet with her lady friends at that late lunch and talk to them about her vision. She also planned to go out and wander in the snow after lunch.

Alone in the lobby except for an attendant behind the front desk, Maggie sat in front of the fireplace, feeling completely relaxed. She grabbed some coffee and Danish rolls which were on a table nearby and then just sat there staring at the fireplace and occasionally looking outside through a huge window at the lightly falling snow. Maggie felt particularly moved when she thought about talking with her mother in the vision and the joy it brought her; she could have stayed there forever.

FIGURE 17
Meditation by the Fireplace

As Maggie continued to sit there, sipping her cup of coffee, Erin arrived and stood in front of her. She said, "Maggie, how are you feeling?"

"Oh, hello, Erin. It's so wonderful to see you. We came through something major, didn't we?! I'm so glad to see you are okay!

"And thank you for asking about me. I'm fine now," Maggie said. After answering Erin's question, Maggie looked forward to sharing the joy of her vision with her friend. She continued, "Let me tell you, Erin…"

Then Maggie paused and said, "Just don't stand there, Erin. Have a seat!"

Erin sat on a couch as Maggie continued. "You know, I'm so glad to see you, Erin. It's good to be away from that hospital and back here at Headquarters. I guess the other ladies will be out later for the lunch they were talking about. For now, let me say this: I've already told Fred as much as I can remember of the vision I had. And what happened yesterday, the accident, I mean, seems so far in the distant past.

"After that accident, I must have blanked out, and that's when I had this vision. But I feel so much better, so much more alert now.

"It's interesting how in that vision, my mother said that a thousand years had passed since the accident we were in. But I told her it seemed like it was only moments earlier when I went unconscious because of the collision, and it was, of course. But according to my mother in the vision, a thousand years had passed.

"In that vision, Erin, time was altered, I believe, because I had transitioned into another dimension. It was a place that was strange, I'll tell you. For instance, my mother went into detail about how time is different in the afterlife as opposed to where we are now in this physical realm. It was interesting and quite inspiring at the same time."

After listening to Maggie, Erin began to give her own explanation. Erin said, "Let me tell you something, Maggie. God says in His word that He will wipe away all tears from our eyes. No death, pain, or sorrow will be there, and it sounds like the place where you were in your vision."

As Erin and Maggie continued to sit comfortably, Sandra, Courtney, and Katie walked through the lobby toward them. When they finally arrived, Courtney said, "Hello, you two. Have you been here long?"

Maggie replied, "Hey, you all. To answer your question, Courtney, we're fine. I've been sitting here for over an hour. Shortly after I got here, Erin showed up. I was telling her that I feel so much better. I can't wait to tell you all about my vision.

"Anyway, I'm just glad to be out of that hospital up on Echo Mountain. But they took good care of me, and I have no complaints. I'm just happy to be back here in Williams' Cabin—and conscious again!

"We're just sitting here talking, and, Sandra, you know how Erin can deliver so much wisdom. I've just been sitting here being inspired by her."

Erin interjected before she could finish, "No, Maggie. We've been inspiring each other. I've gotten so much from what you've been telling me about the vision you had."

Sandra continued, "Well, we sure want to hear about that vision too, Maggie."

"Yeah, Maggie, we sure do want to hear about it," Katie repeated.

Sandra added, "So I guess Courtney, Katie, and I have really been missing out on your discussion, huh?"

"No, Sandra! We'll certainly make up for that when we have our little ladies chat at lunch in a few minutes like we had planned to do," Erin said.

"Anyway, Erin, Maggie's right about you being an inspiration," Sandra replied. She repeated the sentiment, saying, "You're an inspiration to all of us and certainly to me with the experience I gained back in Bermuda.

"But getting back to Maggie's vision, I'm sure you'll fill all of us in at lunch on what we've missed with you here having talked with Erin. Right, Maggie?"

Maggie confirmed what Sandra had hoped, saying, "Of course, Sandra. 1 will share everything in that vision—at least what I can remember."

CHAPTER 27
Preparing to Leave

Foundation Scripture: Romans 8:28

And we know that all things work together for good to those who love God, to those who are the called according to *His* purpose.

As she had anticipated, Maggie met with all the ladies for lunch Saturday afternoon. They had a lively discussion about the vision she had. Shortly after lunch, they dispersed and went their separate ways in the cabin.

Later that Saturday evening, everyone, including the men who were in from their excursion outside Headquarters, came together again and were lounging around in the lobby. Most had already packed for their trip back to Denver this next day.

After Gates and David had returned, Courtney asked, "Since we didn't get to go hiking, did you two get the chance to venture out around the ski lodge today? I know it was a chance for you to see the snowy landscape of the Colorado mountains with the other fellows?"

Gates answered, "No, we weren't with 'em and ended up not spending a lot of time outside. We found a video arcade not too far from here and spent the day there, playing on the machines."

"And how was your lunch meeting? Gates asked.

Courtney answered, "It was fine. We listened to a lot of the vision Maggie had described to us. But I want to know more about what you guys did."

Gates replied, "Well, on the way back, we ran into Jeanie, and we told her where we'd been."

"Where was Wynn?" Sheri asked with great concern in her voice.

"You don't have anything to worry about, Sheri. Jeanie wasn't out there by herself. Your daughter said that Wynn had to make a trip to the restroom."

"Oh," Sheri responded.

Maggie said to everyone, "Well, I know where Fred was." She turned towards him and stated, "You spent the whole day writing on your next book; didn't you, Fred?"

"You're right, Mag. I've been writing all day."

"Well, okay!" Maggie replied simply. "I guess that leaves Bernie."

In response, Bernie said, "I was out for a while; then I came back to the room and relaxed there."

Maggie had grown concerned about Sheri's daughter and said, "Gates, I know you said Jeanie and Wynn were together, but where are they now? I don't see them anywhere, Katie."

Before Katie could answer, David said, "I'm sure she's out there some place with that dude."

"Well, I didn't ask you, David," Maggie said.

Sandra jumped into the discussion and responded, "Amen to that!"

Sandra then told everyone what she had noticed that apparently no one else was aware of. "Hey, don't you all see them partially secluded over there in that corner? Take a look; they're right over there." She pointed toward their general location.

Wynn and Jeanie were right there in everyone's midst, but only Sandra recognized them partially hidden from everyone else in a corner.

"Oh, wow! How could I have missed seeing them?" Maggie asked.

Katie said, "Sandra, thanks for making all of us aware of that. They've been together the whole day. Gates and David did see them when they were out; at least Gates saw Jeanie. But I need to go over there and break up their little get-together because we need to start getting ready for tomorrow's trip back down to Denver."

Sinbad said, "Katie's right. We need to start thinking about our trip back to Denver tomorrow. We'll leave at 2:00, two hours after the 12:00 noon departure as originally planned. That will give us enough time to finish our packing tonight and tomorrow morning before lunch. Beyond our getting ready to leave, Sunday morning could also be a time to relax for some, especially if you've already packed.

"We probably need to start that process soon—like right after we finish here. Once we're on the road tomorrow, it'll be only about thirty to forty minutes to drive back to the hotel in Denver. We'll be back in time to prepare for our closing dinner and social tomorrow evening starting at 6:00."

Sinbad continued, "Can you imagine? It's about time for us to leave Colorado!"

Bernie interjected, "Yeah, it's time to leave all right, but Erin and I are without our little Jeep. We'll need to pick up another vehicle from a rental back down in Denver."

Maggie said, "Well, it was my decision to ride in the Jeep with Erin and not in the van that caused all of this to happen; I mean the accident and all. I feel like it was due to my actions. If I had not been so afraid to ride in our van, then, Bernie, you would have been the one driving the Jeep instead of Erin, and maybe with you driving the accident would have been avoided."

Bernie said, "No, no, Maggie. You weren't the cause of the accident. And things may not have been any different if I were driving. You know, things just happen sometimes that we can't explain. Besides, Erin was just as good at driving that Jeep as I was."

"Okay, Bernie. I get it," Maggie replied.

Erin said, "Yeah, Maggie, sometimes things just happen that we can't explain."

Bernie continued, "Not only that Maggie, but everything that happened apparently was meant to be. All things turned out okay because we all seem to be fine now. Plus, the accident—and the vision you had—just added to the experience we've had out here."

Sinbad said, "Yes, that's true, Bernie. It was an experience and a miracle, I might add, that the Jeep didn't continue to plunge down that embankment into the ravine. If that had happened, we would be having a different conversation now. I mean, Maggie may not have survived to tell everyone about a vision, because she would have been gone. And that goes for you too, Erin. We all have a lot to be grateful for."

"But, you know, in the end I believe we all have a purpose, and I believe God will not allow any of us to leave this world without our purpose being fulfilled, whatever that purpose might be."

Gates chimed in, "Well, let me respond to what you two are talking about." He went on, "Bernie, sometimes we decide to do our own thing without consulting God about whether it is the best thing to do. In other words, sometimes we get out of God's purpose for us being here for whatever reason. But even in that instance, He eventually brings us back around to where we should be, so I understand what you're saying, Bernie, and you too, Sinbad. We are blessed to all be together, healthy and sound despite that experience with the accident."

The statement by Gates weighed on Maggie as she thought about the feelings she still had for Freddie, who had been tragically killed in an automobile accident. She felt that she definitely had gotten out of God's purpose for her with her relationship with him. Her distress about the matter was tempered, however, when she remembered what her mother used to say often, that we shouldn't cry over spilt milk.

As Maggie remained deep in thought, Gates directed additional comments to her, saying, "And, Maggie, Bernie *is* right from the standpoint that everything happens for a reason, a reason that may not have been revealed to us yet."

Maggie could only think that she had no intention of revealing her thoughts about her relationship with Freddie.

While the discussion between Sinbad and Gates brought negative images of her past to Maggie's mind, it also reminded Katie of her bad experience with her former husband and his infidelity.

Sinbad and Gates were unaware of the ramifications of their words to the experiences of both Maggie and Katie.

Sinbad had more practical thoughts in mind. "All you're saying is good, Gates and Bernie, but our purpose right now is to prepare to get back down to Denver. And I'm really looking forward to tomorrow's dinner and social. Bernie and Erin, I'm sorry that your Jeep got totaled, but there's enough room in the vans for you to ride back with us.

"Well, I'm going to call it a night and go and get some rest. By the way, the weather has thrown us behind schedule, so we'll have to spend tomorrow packing after we get back down to Denver."

Sinbad and his friend Casey retired for the evening. All the others in Maggie's group went to their rooms as well. They were now ready to leave the snowy environment of the Colorado mountains.

Sunday morning was bright and sunny without any snowfall for the first time since their arrival in the mountains. But there was plenty of snow cover on the ground from the constant snowfall from the previous two days of their being at the ski resort. With the increased temperatures and the bright sunlight, there would be less and less of the white stuff as the day progressed.

Maggie awakened that morning as she had the day before, still in wonderment at the vision she had. But she felt satisfied that she had communicated to Fred as well as to the group of ladies that met for lunch and to others the events she remembered in her vision. On this day, her desire was not to look back at the details of the vision but to look forward to the events that would take place later in the afternoon.

Maggie wanted to get out and experience all the snow that was around Headquarters before leaving this mountainous paradise later in the afternoon and heading back to the host hotel in Denver.

"Fred, I'm going to do something different today," Maggie said.

"Oh, what would that be?" Fred asked.

"I'm going to go out all by myself and just walk around Headquarters here and play in the snow. I might even be able to make a snowman. Maybe when I do that, I can have someone take a picture of me standing next to it. I know that waitress I befriended at the diner near Des Moines would appreciate it.

"With the sun being out so bright and all, the snow probably won't last long on the ground. But hopefully I'll be able to build a snowman before that happens. I'll be back later to finish my packing before we leave."

"Okay, Mag. I'll just stay in the room today and do some packing. But let's have some breakfast first," he said.

Fred and Maggie got dressed and ventured out to the lobby and then to the dining hall where they anticipated having a nice breakfast. They saw a few members of the group, but they were scattered about in different areas of the hall, apparently having some downtime among themselves. After a few minutes, Fred and Maggie had completed their meal.

"Okay, Fred, I'm gonna to take off. I'll see you a little later."

"Okay, Mag. Like I said, I'm going back to the room to do a little packing," Fred said. "And you need to come back to the room too to get dressed for the outside."

"You're right," Maggie responded.

After Maggie returned to their room and dressed for her sojourn outside, she walked back by the dining area and saw Sandra, who was sitting alone having her breakfast.

"Well, hello, Sandra," she said. "How are you doing this morning, and have you done your packing yet?"

"No, Maggie, I'm going to start packing in a few minutes. But to answer your first question, I'm fine. I see that everyone is having some time to themselves this morning. And I saw you and Fred over there earlier. I know Bernie and Erin are out on the patio, absorbing some of the morning sun. And before you and Fred came into the dining hall, Courtney and Gates were just finishing up their meal and had already left. I guess everyone is preparing for the trip back to Denver, for our planned departure at 2:00."

"Yeah, Sandra, I'm going outside now to spend some time in the snow. Hopefully, I can do everything I want to in a short period of time because I need to get back and finish what little packing I have myself," Maggie told her. "But I've always wanted to go out and play in the snow in a mountainous environment like we have here in Colorado. You know we get snow back in the Chicago and Detroit, but it's just not the same as it is out here, so I plan to take advantage of it. I told Fred I'd be back in the room later to finish my packing. You know, Sandra, I just might end up making a snowman out there! I'm so excited about that."

"Make sure you have fun, Maggie," Sandra said. "Why don't you sit down and have a cup of coffee with me? You can continue to relax for a few minutes before you head out."

"I would, Sandra, but something is telling me I should go ahead and go out there now, so I guess I should do that. Besides, Fred and I have already had our cup of coffee."

Sandra replied, "Well, okay. I wish you luck with building that snowman because with all the sun that's out this morning, it probably won't last very long. Anyway, I'll see you and everyone else at 2:00

when we board the vans and take off going back down to Denver. And by the way, I'm so glad that you seem fully recovered from your accident."

"Thank you, Sandra," Maggie said. Then she headed out the door to have her own little experience in the snowy Colorado mountains.

Sandra was getting ready to head to her room when she got a glance at David walking with Sheri. They had brief eye contact but nothing more than that. She then proceeded to her room to do some more packing.

Jeanie and Wynn had left the lobby and gone to the nearby gaming center.

"Lots of bells and whistles—that's what this place is all about," Wynn said to Jeanie as she tried her hand at one of the video arcades machines. "I never thought I would be encouraged by you to come to a place like this!"

"Oh, Wynn, you disrupted my concentration," Jeanie said. "Oh, well. I've lost this game—because of you, Wynn," she said in jest.

"You sure are having a lot of fun here, Jeanie," Wynn said. "How did you find out about this place anyway? We were having so much fun out there in the snow, but I guess when you tried to build that snowman and it didn't work, you saw this place as an alternative. Am I right about that?" he asked.

Jeanie replied, "Not exactly, Wynn. Believe it or not, I had a useful conversation with David yesterday when he talked about some of the men going on an excursion in these snowy mountains and told me that he and Mr. Gates ran across this place. He said when they arrived, they got hooked on some of the games and couldn't get away."

Wynn responded, "So you and your stepdad are on speaking terms now, I gather."

"I don't know about that!" Jeanie replied emphatically. "But I'm glad he pointed this place out to me; otherwise, we might not be here."

Wynn continued, "You know, Jeanie, I've noticed somewhat of a change in that man lately. Maybe it's because he's been hanging around Mr. Gates a lot. You do know he's a preacher. I guess those ministers can influence the worst of 'em. But I still wouldn't trust David being around you for any length of time. You know it's hard for a leopard to change its spots; that's what I've heard some of my mother's old friends say."

Jeanie replied, "Well, don't tell that to my mom. She thinks anybody can change if the spirit of the Lord comes on them."

"Yeah, Jeanie, but I think your mother's spirit is closely tied to your stepdad!" Wynn replied.

"Are you saying that my mother is not sincere, Wynn?" Jeanie asked him in a more serious tone.

"No, that's not it at all, Jeanie. I believe your mother is sincere, but again, like Ms. Erin says, the pull of the flesh is pretty strong, and that may be the problem with your mother as far as that guy David is concerned. In other words, she apparently likes your stepdad a lot—enough for her to remain with him."

"Okay, Wynn. I don't know why we're here talking about my mother and that stepdad of mine. Let's talk about something else."

At that moment, Jeanie was obviously displeased with what Wynn was saying about how her mother felt about her stepdad, although she realized that some of it was probably true.

"I think we should leave," she said.

"Okay! Let's go! We can go out the back door and play in the snow before it melts," Wynn said.

Just as they were about to head out the door, Jeanie suggested they change the nature of the conversation. She looked out the window near the front door and saw a figure headed in the direction of the gaming center, kicking snow up into the air with each step.

Upon closer inspection, Jeanie saw that the figure was Maggie. "Oh, my goodness! It's Ms. Maggie coming here."

"Well, well! What a coincidence. We were just talking about that lady! We're going to have some company, I guess," Wynn said.

Maggie entered the facility and got a glimpse of Wynn and Jeanie, so she went over to greet them.

"Hey, Wynn and Jeanie! I didn't expect to see you here. I see you two were headed towards the back exit," she said.

Wynn replied, "Hello, Ms. Maggie. We've been here for a while. But, yeah, we were heading out the back door when we saw you. We wanted to play in the snow some more. And we're surprised to see you coming!"

Maggie replied, "Well, Wynn, I was just out walking in the snow and saw this place, so I decided to check it out. What have you two been doing?"

Wynn answered, "Ms. Maggie, Jeanie tried to build a snowman but wasn't successful, so we saw this place and decided to come here to spend the day. At least we were able to take a snapshot of her standing by an artificial snowman in the gallery over there. Yeah, the gallery is one of the many amenities this place has."

Wynn continued, "Jeanie didn't want to do it, but I encouraged her to, so she went ahead and did it."

Jeanie added, "Yes, Ms. Maggie, I took that photo shoot. Well, actually, I took two of them, one of just the snowman, an artificial snowman, and the other one with me posing with it. I guess I was fortunate because that photo gallery closed down for the weekend right after my last picture was taken. We were going to leave them over there where the attendant is and come back to get them after we play in the snow for a while."

Maggie said, "That's interesting because I really would've wanted to at least take a photo with a snowman, even an artificial one. But the place is closed now?" Maggie asked.

"Yes, Ms. Maggie. I'm afraid it's closed now," Jeanie answered. "It won't reopen until Monday."

"Well, we'll be leaving early Monday morning going back to Chicago," Maggie said. "Oh, well, those are the breaks." Maggie sounded disappointed. "But anyway, Jeanie, we must have not been thinking to hope that a real snowman outside could last any amount of time with the sun shining the way it is out there."

Jeanie replied, "You're right, Ms. Maggie. It's so warm outside now that a snowman wouldn't last for long; it wouldn't take long for it to melt."

"But listen, Ms. Maggie, like I said, I took two pictures with the snowman at the gallery, and I certainly don't necessarily want the both of them. So why don't you take one? What do you think, Wynn?"

"Of course, Jeanie, why don't you give Ms. Maggie one of the pictures? I would like for you to keep the one with you in it though. What do you say, Ms. Maggie? Would you be okay with the picture of just the snowman in it? I'm sure Jeanie can write something beneath it that can really make it nicer," Wynn added.

Maggie replied, "Well, okay! But what would you write beneath it?"

Jeanie said, "I really don't know, but I'll think of something. We put the photos over there against the wall. I had planned to pick them up later. They're nice and large but small enough to take back in the van. I'll go over and get the one I'm not in and write something beneath it and give to you. Then take it to the copy shop over there and let them laminate it. It'll be nice and pretty when they complete the job, I'm sure. Then I'll let you see it when it's finished. After the final product is done, the way it'll look will be a surprise to you. I mean, both the picture and the phrase beneath it will be a surprise," Jeanie clarified.

"Okay, that'll be fine, Jeanie," Maggie replied. "Thank you so much for giving me one of your pictures, Jeanie."

Jeanie walked over to where she placed the photos and then went ahead and wrote something on a note pad. She planned to go to the copy shop and have the phrase transposed beneath the picture and then give it to Maggie. Later, she did just that and the phrase was written on the bottom of the photo in beautiful lettering.

While Jeanie was away, Wynn and Maggie talked with one another. Soon Jeanie returned with the laminated picture and phrase beneath, ready to present it to Maggie.

"I'm back, Ms. Maggie; now take a look at this and see what I had developed for you. And I hope you like it."

As Maggie unrolled the picture, she saw the image of a snowman and an expression beneath it that read, "A brighter-looking world awaits you!"

Maggie resisted the temptation of asking Jeanie what the phrase meant. She took the photo and said, "Thank you so much for the picture, Jeanie. And that expression you placed underneath it is so profound. I see that you had it laminated, but when I leave here I'm going to the gift shop to have it framed and then wrapped."

Maggie was so happy. Building a snowman was all she wanted on her excursion out into the snowy mountains of Colorado, but that didn't happen. This portrait of an artificial snowman would be good enough, the next best thing to a picture of herself standing next to a real one. What's more, there was such a profound statement beneath the photo! She only hoped that Peggy would like it.

Maggie thanked Jeanie for what both she and Wynn had done for her. "You two are so kind," she said. "You certainly made my day. I'm going back to Headquarters now and let you too have some more fun with what little time we have left. But remember, we'll be leaving at 2:00 today going back down to Denver, so you'll need to come back soon to do any packing you have left to do."

"Okay, Ms. Maggie. We're glad you're happy," Jeanie said.

"And we'll both be back at Headquarters soon," Wynn added.

With that, they departed from one another, and Maggie had her prize for the day.

The remaining time on this morning was uneventful for Maggie and her friends. She was still in recovery mode as her attending physician was keeping a close check on her by phone. Maggie figured that when everyone boarded the vans for their return to Denver later in the day, she would consider herself fully recovered from the accident she had. That experience in the mountains would soon be behind her.

She thought, *Thank goodness I don't have to see that physician again.* But she still realized that he was placed there for her good, which was a big help in her recovery.

It was just before 2:00 on Sunday when everyone gathered in the front lobby of Headquarters ready to return to their hotel in Denver to prepare themselves further for the trip back to Chicago first thing Monday morning.

For now, everyone's sights were set on the closing dinner and the social afterwards, beginning at 6:00 back at the Denver hotel.

The trip from the ski resort Headquarters was uneventful as they departed at the scheduled time. An hour later, the two vans arrived at the front entrance of the Santo Domingo Hotel where they were guests. Fortunately, Sinbad had made most of the preparations for both the dinner and the social before they left for the ski resort three days earlier. After their arrival, it would be just enough time for everyone to unpack, relax a little from the short trip through the mountains, and prepare for the evening's events.

Once safely in their rooms, Maggie said to Fred, "I think I'll take a little nap, Fred."

"Well, okay, Mag. But remember we don't have too much time," he told her. Then he said in jest, "And don't have any more dreams!"

"Aw, Fred," Maggie responded.

Fred continued, "Just kidding, Mag. As for me, I'm going to change clothes and look at the news on TV for a few minutes and then get ready for the evening."

After Maggie woke up from her nap, she spent a little time getting dressed and prepared for the dinner at 6:00.

Fred, who had already dressed, asked, "Are you ready to go, Mag?"

"I am, Fred, but let me go back into the bathroom and put on some makeup."

"Okay. I'll be near the door because I'm ready to leave," Fred said.

Soon after, Maggie and Fred left their room and in no time met up with Courtney and Gates, who were headed in the same direction.

Gates took the initiative to speak first. "Hey, you all. I hope you two got some rest. I say that because I believe we're in for a long night."

Fred answered, "Mag did, Gates. She took a nap almost as soon as we got to the room after we left the van with our belongings. But I'm ready and fresh—at least for now."

It was right at 6:00 when the Manleys and the Mints entered the dining hall. They were amazed that it had been transformed from an area designed for dining into a social venue for dancing and casual conversation. A stage had been erected intended to accommodate a small band and a female vocalist who had been advertised to perform.

Soon, Sinbad got up to formally address the group. He began, "I'm just so proud that everyone here had a grand time these last few days in the Colorado mountains. I'm also happy to be one of the co-hosts of the event with the other being Bernie. I want to thank all of you for being here to celebrate the second honeymoon of Bernie and Erin. We've had an exciting time. And speaking of excitement, this is especially true for Maggie, who is recovering from the accident with the Jeep. But she inspired many of us with her description of the vision she had not to mention with her recovery.

"It's time to leave now, but before we do that on Monday morning, we have the whole day left tomorrow to pack and to carry on any final communication among ourselves. I know I originally said we would leave on Monday, but I've decided to leave on Tuesday now because of the weather canceling our hiking trip together and Maggie's accident and recovery. We can still have our overnight stay in Chappell Tuesday night and our stop at Mickey's Diner on Wednesday before completing our trip back to Chicago. Our friends from the New York City will still be able to make their flight because I understand they made reservations for late Wednesday night, so the timing for that is great!

"As you know, once we get on those vans to head back to Chicago on Tuesday morning now, we'll be restricted in our movements and communication.

"Let me tell you, tonight is the night! And we're going to have a good time talking to one another and dancing as well as listening to good music. Of course, food and drink will continue to be available all during the evening."

The other thing I want to mention is that tomorrow, Monday, we'll be preparing for that Tuesday trip back to Chicago. By leaving early on Tuesday, we will have an overnight stopover in Chappell that night, as I said, then head towards Chicago the next morning on Wednesday. We should be back in Windy City by 9:00. So, instead of our having an eight-day trip on this vacation, we'll be away for nine with the extra day of Wednesday now included.

"Now, before we return to Chicago late Wednesday evening, we'll be stopping near Des Moines, Iowa, at the same restaurant we were at just before we ran into that storm on the way to Chappell. You all remember that, don't you, our experience getting to Chappell in west Iowa? I know you *do* remember! The place where we ate prior to that experience was Micky's Diner.

"So those are my thoughts, and I want you all to have a good time tonight! Thanks again for being here."

With those words Sinbad ended his talk, and everyone indeed had a good time that evening.

The next day on Monday would be a time of rest and packing, preparing to leave early Tuesday morning. That day finally arrived, and the group left the Denver hotel after a quick breakfast on their way back to Chicago.

Fred said to Maggie, "You know, Mag, except for occasional rest stops, I know we'll be staying overnight in Chappell again. But then tomorrow we'll be on our way back to Chicago after a stop at Mickey's Diner. That will be our last opportunity on the way back to relax a little bit and have a meal before getting back home. The weather forecast calls for clear conditions during the entire trip back."

Maggie responded, "Yeah, Fred, it's going to be a long trip, but because of the good weather forecast, it'll be without the drama we had with all that snow coming out here.

"Anyway, I can't wait to get to that diner after our overnight stay in Chappell. That's when I can give Peggy the picture of the snowman the kids gave to me."

After that comment, everyone hunkered down to a night of rest. Upon rising the next morning, they were ready to endure the long ride ahead of them. Nevertheless, they had memories galore of their vacation trip to Colorado.

PART IV:
THE RETURN HOME

CHAPTER 28
Going Home

Foundation Scripture: Psalm 84:3

Even the sparrow has found a home. And the swallow a nest for herself, Where she may lay her young – Even Your altars, O Lord of hosts, My King and my God.

With the loss of the Jeep, Bernie rented an SUV for the trip home to Florida. After members of Maggie's group said their goodbyes to the newlyweds, they all were off on their trip back east.

The newlyweds planned to have a one-night stopover in New Orleans then proceed to their destination the next day. For them, the honeymoon would continue in the Crescent City for at least one night. They wanted to enjoy a trip down Bourbon Street and a delicious Cajun meal.

Riding in the two vans, Maggie's group finally reached the interstate, going eastward towards their destination and their first stop in Chappell. As they exited the Denver metro area, Maggie decided to take one last glimpse of the city and mountains behind it. *So majestic*, she thought. As they drove away, the Denver skyline and the backdrop of the Rocky Mountains got smaller and smaller.

Maggie and the others left behind many stories of what had happened over the past few days in the Mile High City and in those mountains. All in the caravan of vehicles would share those stories with each other over the coming days, months, and even years.

Outside of occasional rest stops, the group had only two extended pauses to the trip. The first was an overnight stay in Chappell at the same hotel they lodged almost a week earlier. Then, the next day, they planned another brief break from travel at Mickey's Diner near Des Moines, Iowa, the first stop after they started out from Chicago a week earlier.

Everyone knew it would be a long trip. After the overnight stay in Chappell Tuesday night, they anticipated a brief stopover at the diner before continuing to Chicago on Wednesday evening.

The group made it to Chappell and had a pleasant stay overnight there. The next day provided an equally pleasant drive before arriving at the diner about 4:00 in the afternoon.

About thirty minutes away from the diner, Gates said, "Hey, Fred, there's the sign that says the restaurant we want to get to is off exit 24." Being weary from the long ride, he added, "Man, I'll be glad when we get there! I'm tired of being on the road. I just need to get out and stretch a little."

Fred tried to console Gates, saying, "It won't be long now, Gates. It's about twenty miles further down the road.

"You know, everybody, it seems such a long time ago since we were at this place last time, but it was just last Tuesday when we made it our first stop on the way to Colorado after we left Chicago," Fred added.

Courtney said, "Maggie, I know you're looking forward to seeing the waitress you were talking to when we were last here. Peggy, I think her name was?"

"You're right, Courtney. Peggy is her name. I think I've gained a new friend. And you know what? From the way she was talking, I think she'd like to become a part of our group. But we'll see."

Gates said, "Yeah, Maggie, I hope that happens. She seems to be a nice person. But it does seem like it was more than just one week ago when we were here. So much has occurred since then; not only what transpired out in Colorado but everything we experienced while traveling there, including the snowstorm and the flat tire. Everything that occurred, including your accident, Maggie, makes it seem like it was a much longer period since the last time we were at this diner. Don't you think so, Courtney?"

"Yeah, Gates, it seems like it's been ages ago since we were here last. But like the last time we *were* here, I'm really looking forward to the food *this* time around. I mean, the food at this place was really good," Courtney replied.

"Yeah, Courtney, the food was good. It's something we all can look forward to," Gates responded to his wife. "Maggie, just don't have food going down the wrong way," he added in jest, referring to the time she threw up while eating.

"No, Gates! I don't want to remember that," Maggie responded.

Then Gates returned his attention to the driver, "But, Fred, you know what happened when we left there the last time; we ran into a snowstorm. I mean, it was snowing all over the place. We were just fortunate to have made it to Chappell to stay overnight. I hate to bring up a negative, but that's the one thing I remember about this place—what happened after we left when we ran into the snowstorm and had the flat tire."

"Yeah, Gates, I remember running into all that snow, and having that flat was a scary experience," Courtney replied. "But what I remember the most is when Fred and Sinbad had to go and get fueled up at that gas station further up the road from the diner and how they said the food at that place was terrible. Yeah, it was the reason why they came back and ate with us."

As the group approached their last rest stop before continuing to Chicago, Fred made an announcement. He said to everyone in his van, and by radio to those in the van Sinbad was driving,

"Okay, everybody, we'll soon be stopping at the diner—maybe in about ten minutes. So be ready to take your jackets because it's still cool outside. In the meantime, after I finish with this call, I'll talk to you personally, Sinbad, and let you know when we're about ready to stop.

"So, Sinbad, how's everyone in your vehicle back there?"

"We're fine, Fred. Everyone is anxious to get out and stretch a little, and to have a decent meal," Sinbad replied.

"That sounds good," Fred said back to him. "Once we make this exit and go up the road to the diner, I'll try to find some empty parking spaces so that you can park your vehicle beside mine."

"Okay, Fred. We'll be seeing you in a little while," Sinbad said. The two drivers ended their conversation, and within minutes the vans had made the exit and were in the parking lot of Mickey's Diner.

CHAPTER 29
A Brighter Looking World

Foundation Scripture: John 3:16

For God so loved the world that He gave His only begotten Son, that whoever believes in Him should not perish but have everlasting life.

Maggie was about ready to get out of her van when she remembered her last time at the diner. It was so sad seeing Peggy gazing out the window of the front door in the lobby when the group was ready to take off, heading westward towards Colorado. It seemed like Peggy didn't want any of them to leave.

Maggie understood why Peggy probably felt as she did. Her sadness at that time was a result of what she had been through, Maggie thought. She had talked with Peggy and gained a lot of information about her history. She sympathized with what Peggy had been through, especially the time spent with her husband Freddie. It was even more emotional for Maggie given her own past relationship with him.

With these thoughts flooding her mind, Maggie said to Fred as they prepared to exit the vehicle, "Fred, this place brings back so many memories of our trip going to Colorado. I told you about the waitress who talked with me a lot when you and Sinbad had gone to refuel at the gas station further up the road from here."

Fred replied, "Yeah, Mag, based on what you told me, the lady really has problems. Too bad you didn't have a chance to take that picture of an actual snowman you said she wanted. It's a shame there wasn't enough snow for you to build it. But so much of the snow melted when it warmed up before we left."

"No, Fred, I was not able to make that snowman. But do you know what? I forgot to tell you, but I did get her a snowman—a picture of an artificial snowman that was in the arcade when I saw Jeanie and Wynn before I came back to headquarters. I got there too late for me to have a picture taken with me and *that* snowman because the shop had already closed.

"Thank God Wynn and Jeanie had taken an extra picture of it, and they gave one to me. I gladly received the picture from them and wrapped it up. Well, before I did that, Jeanie offered to place some expression on the bottom of it. At any rate, I had asked Sheri to put the picture, laminated and wrapped, in the back of the van where she was riding. Then I figured that there was more space in our van, so I ended up placing it in the back of our vehicle. Gates knows about it; he saw me place it there. Didn't you, Gates?"

Maggie looked behind her when she received no answer and saw that he and Courtney were asleep.

Maggie continued, "Anyway, Fred, I plan to give it to Peggy, the waitress I saw on our stop here the last time. I just hope I see her before we leave this time around. Now, let's go eat. I'm hungry!"

Soon everyone had walked into the diner to have a good meal and to relax a little before continuing their journey to the Windy City. The time was a little after 5:00 when everyone took their seats. They were hopeful to complete their meal by 6:00 and then make the three-hour drive to Chicago.

Maggie said to Fred after their order had been placed, "You know, Fred, that waitress I befriended when we were here last is not here now. I do remember her telling me she was the manager. If I recall, she works the evening shift, which doesn't start until 6:00. I remember her telling me that."

Fred replied, "Well, Mag, by 6:00 we'll be outta here and back on the road. Sinbad is intent on getting back by 9:00, and you know that it's a three-hour drive from here to Chicago.

"Well, I sure would like to give her the picture of the snowman I promised her. I had planned to give it to her before we left. I guess I could get it to her in the mail, but it would mean so much more to me if I could give it to her now—in person. Hopefully, I'll see her before we take off. I think she would appreciate it more too if I gave it to her personally."

As the 6:00 hour approached, everybody had finished their meals and were getting ready to hit the road again. Maggie noticed that Peggy had not arrived yet and was concerned about her getting the snowman portrait she had brought all the way from Colorado.

Maggie said to Fred, "You know, when we were here last, Peggy stressed to me how much she wanted me to get the picture for her while we were in Colorado. She said she wanted it as a souvenir. But I really think she wanted something—anything—from me to keep as evidence of our new friendship. What a difference in that lady from the time we first arrived here!"

Soon they had boarded the van and were ready to take off. Maggie was distraught that she was not able to get Peggy the picture of the snowman that she had brought from Colorado. But by the time the group left the diner, Peggy had not yet arrived.

Fred was about to give Sinbad, the driver of the van behind them, a signal that they were ready to leave. Then he noticed that the front tire on the driver's side of Sinbad's van was deflated a little. Fred sure didn't want any issues with a flat tire like they had experienced on their way *to* Colorado.

Fred then gave Sinbad a call on the vehicle phone. "Hey, Sinbad, did you know that the front tire on the driver's side of your vehicle might be going flat?"

"No, Fred. I didn't realize that. I'll get out now to check on it," Sinbad replied.

"Okay, Sinbad. I'll get out too and come back to survey the situation with that tire. It seems like everyone has taken their seats and is ready to go. But they'll have to wait a bit until we get this issue dealt with."

After Fred finished his conversation with Sinbad, Maggie said, "So you think we have another tire issue with that van, Fred?"

"It sure looks that way, Mag. You heard me tell Sinbad about what I saw."

Maggie replied, "Well, Fred, I hope we don't have to change it like we did before."

"I hope not either, Mag. We don't need that headache!" Fred replied.

"You got that right, Fred," Gates chimed in. "So you go ahead and do what you have to do to get us up and running again!"

With that encouragement, Fred said, "Okay, you all. Sit tight. I'll be right back."

Gates added, "Well, let me know, Fred, if there's anything I can do to help."

As Fred stepped off the van, he replied, "Well, Gates, you *can* offer up a prayer."

With that last statement, Fred and Sinbad headed back to the van behind him to survey the affected tire.

Maggie said, "Gates, we all will just have to sit here until Fred gets back. Hopefully he and Sinbad can deal with the problem, and we'll be on the road again soon."

Those last words from Maggie were difficult to express because she was still distraught because of not getting the snowman portrait to her new friend Peggy, who apparently had yet to arrive at work.

After about ten minutes, Fred returned to his van with discouraging news. "I have some bad news, everybody. We'll have to take Sinbad's van up to that service station to have some air pumped into the tire that's going flat. Hopefully, it'll be just a matter of putting more air into the tire. But hang tough until we get back. I'm gonna ride up there with him along with the other passengers in that van to the station. And hopefully, as I said, there's nothing serious going on."

Maggie, Courtney, and Gates seemed to lack the patience that Gates often preached about. Only Wynn and Jeanie, who were sitting in the back, seemed at ease about what was going on. They continued to carry on a conversation between themselves, laughing and having fun.

As Maggie sat there, she glanced out the window and stared at the diner's front door. That's where she had seen Peggy's sad countenance as the group left the diner going westward toward Colorado a week earlier. Maggie wondered if Peggy had now arrived at work yet. If so, maybe she would come to that front window again.

It was shortly after 6:00, the time when Peggy had informed Maggie that she would start her evening shift. As Maggie continued to focus on the front door, waiting for Fred to return with Sinbad's van, to her surprise an image appeared of someone standing there. Upon closer examination of the figure, Maggie realized who it was. She said to herself, "It's Peggy! It's Peggy!"

Realizing that it probably would be a few minutes before Fred and Sinbad returned from the station, Maggie turned around to tell Gates and Courtney, "Hey, I see Peggy standing there at the front door of the diner! I'm going over to speak to her before Fred and Sinbad get back."

Gates, who had just awakened from his nap, replied, "Okay, Maggie, but you'd better hurry because it probably won't take long for them to fix the problem; they only have to put air in that deflated tire. And whenever they get back, you know that Sinbad will want to hit the road."

With that comment from Gates, Maggie replied, "Okay, it won't take me long."

Maggie got out of the van and walked briskly toward the diner. Maggie was almost to the front door when it opened, and Peggy stepped outside and gave her a big hug.

"Oh, Maggie! I was afraid that all of you had left. Then I came to the door and saw only one of the vans. I thought maybe you might be on it. And sure enough here you are! When I saw you coming, I couldn't help but come outside and meet you. I'm so glad to see you, Maggie. I came to work late today because I got stuck in traffic up there near Des Moines."

"It's so good seeing you again too," Maggie said, smiling from ear to ear. "Yeah, we've been here for the last hour and have eaten and everything. And I was afraid that you wouldn't get to work before we left. But I'm so glad we got to see each other. We had to put leaving on hold because one of the vans needed air in a tire. That's why there's only one van here now. The other one is down the road at the gas station."

"Well, I hate that you all had that problem. But I'm glad you're still here so I got a chance to see you again," Peggy said.

Maggie turned and saw that Fred and Sinbad were returning from having the tire repaired. "I see that they're coming back now, and it looks like they got it fixed. But, oh, Peggy, the sad thing is that we're about to leave!"

Before Maggie could say anything else, she looked around and saw Gates walking towards her. "Oh, look, Peggy! That's my friend Gates coming, and he has a package with him." Then she remembered.

He had the wrapping for the portrait as well as the portrait itself that was given to her by Jeanie and Wynn. She hollered, "Oh my word! It's something I was going to give to you, but I had forgotten all about it."

Jeanie had wrapped the portrait in the back of the van for Maggie to give to Peggy, but in her excitement to see Peggy again, she had forgotten all about it until she saw Gates coming with it.

"Oh, Peggy, I almost forgot in all the excitement of seeing you again. But the fellow that's coming towards us is carrying something that I think you might want," Maggie said.

When Gates got to where the women were standing, he said, "Maggie, I realized that you forgot to get this when you left the vehicle, and I also knew how much you wanted to get it to…."

Seeing his hesitancy about calling her name, Peggy said, "The name is Peggy."

"Well, okay, Peggy," Gates said. "So here it is."

A momentary thought occurred to Gates as he said, "I'm sorry, Peggy. I really should give this to your friend Maggie and let *her* present it to you." He turned toward Maggie and said, "Here, Maggie, you take this, and I'll let you be the one to give it to Peggy here."

"Oh, thank you, Gates," Maggie responded.

Gates continued, "I'm going to head back to the van. But remember, Maggie, Sinbad and your husband are back from repairing the tire, and I know they're about ready to leave now. Nice meeting you, Peggy."

"Likewise," Peggy replied.

"Okay, Maggie, like I said I'm headed back to the van," Gates said.

"Okay, Gates. Walk over to the other van and tell Sinbad I'll be back in our vehicle shortly," Maggie said.

As Gates headed toward the vans, Maggie returned her attention to Peggy and said, "Peggy, I know you remember telling me to make a snowman while in Colorado and take a picture of it for you, but the weather started to get so warm just before we left that it made a lot of the snow melt, so I didn't get the chance to make a snowman and take a picture of me standing beside it for you. But I was fortunate enough to get a picture of a snowman nonetheless, an artificial version. So here it is. I hope it's okay. I believe you might like it. I sure hope so."

Maggie handed the package to Peggy who quickly unwrapped it. When she did and saw what it was, her emotions almost overwhelmed her. With tears in her eyes, she said, "Oh, Maggie, the picture is breathtaking—so beautiful. I knew you said we could talk over the phone after you got back to Chicago, but this is something I can place in my bedroom, and in a sense you'll always be there with me; I'll always have you close by, Maggie!"

Before being totally overcome with emotion, Peggy noticed that there was something written at the bottom of the picture. She said, "Wait a minute. What does it say at the bottom?"

When she took the time to read it, Peggy was equally overwhelmed with the message. It said, "A brighter-looking world awaits you!"

Maggie knew the phrase at the bottom of the picture was prophetic, based on the vision she had of Peggy. She was so beautiful and radiant in that heavenly dimension.

Back to reality, Peggy said to her friend, "Oh, Maggie, it says exactly what I've been hoping for some time now—for my life to get brighter. And that's exactly what it says. Maggie, thank you so much for thinking of that expression."

Before Peggy could offer any further appreciation to her new friend, Maggie said, "No, Peggy, I did not put that there. Someone else in our group did that."

"You mean, you didn't think of that expression; it just came out of the blue from someone in your group?" Peggy asked.

"You're exactly right, Peggy," Maggie admitted.

"That's weird. You know, Maggie, you once said that the minister friend you're with… What's his name? I forgot."

"Oh, you're talking about Gates," Maggie reminded her. "That was him who was just here and handed me the package with the picture in it."

Peggy continued, "Okay then. Well, as I was saying, once you said that Rev. Gates…"

Maggie interrupted her again. "No, Peggy, it's just Gates!"

"Okay! Once you said Gates preaches a lot about the 'Wonders of the Spirit.' It seems to me that the situation with how you got this picture of a snowman might be one of those wonders. I mean, for someone to come up with the perfect written statement that I've been thinking about for months, even years, is nothing short of miraculous!"

"Hey, Peggy, I hadn't thought of it quite like that! Girl, the way you're talking I think you're more spiritual than even *you* might think!"

Maggie continued, "Yeah, you're making me remember a preacher's sermon on the 'Wonders of the Spirit' that you're talking about. But I complained about it then because I didn't see his message being connected to people's practical experiences. That's what I told my husband Fred. But now I see what he was talking about, and that was securing that lost sheep that's out there—those that have gone astray."

Peggy replied, "Well, Maggie, I mentioned how miraculous that situation was of you getting the picture that I really needed. And I'll tell you, it was almost as if *I was found,* being that lost sheep found by you, Maggie!"

"Well, don't give me the credit, Peggy. It's all because of the Lord," Maggie emphasized.

Peggy responded, "Okay. I'll accept that, Maggie. I now realize what your minister friend was saying. Yeah, I guess a spiritual truth was revealed to me—from the Lord as you said. And deep down inside, Maggie, it's something that I've prayed about for some time, that my life be made brighter somehow. And, yeah, I guess that certainly is a 'Wonder of the Spirit'!"

"Well, all I can say, Peggy, is that *it was miraculous* how I got the picture in the first place. I mean, the person who gave me the picture had taken an extra photo. Otherwise, they wouldn't have had a picture to give me.

"And another thing, I wouldn't have had the opportunity to purchase a picture like that because the shop where they had the photo taken had just closed when I arrived! But some friends of mine had taken two pictures of an artificial snowman at this shop at the resort when I ran into them. That's when they gave me one of their pictures."

Maggie concluded, "And, Peggy, if I *had* gotten to that store before it had closed and purchased a picture like that, I would have never thought of an expression like the one our group member put on it.

"So, yeah, Peggy, everything about this scenario is just a wonder to behold; it shows the perfect timing of God."

After Maggie's last statement and before Peggy could respond, she heard a loud voice coming from the van, "Hey, Mag, Sinbad's getting on me about you hanging around here too long. Let's go!" Fred shouted.

"Okay, Fred, I'm coming," Maggie hollered.

Maggie leaned over and gave Peggy a big hug and said, "I really have to go now."

"Okay, Maggie. I understand. All I can say is that I feel God has spoken to me through you. That was one of the last things I said to you before all in your group left here the last time and headed toward Colorado. And I thank you for that, Maggie," Peggy said as the tears flowed down her cheeks.

The emotion of the moment was too much for Maggie, so with those last words from Peggy, she hugged her one more time and then turned and walked away.

Maggie returned to the van and sat beside Fred.

"Well, Mag," he said, "you finally made it. I guess you know by now that the tire has been fixed, and we're ready to roll!"

By this time, Peggy had returned inside the diner because the temperature outside was dropping quickly. But she remained at the front door, holding the portrait that Maggie had given her and looking out that window.

Now sitting in the front passenger seat, Maggie's mind was transfixed on that front door, gazing at Peggy. A week earlier, when she held that same stance, Peggy had looked so sad. Now, what Maggie saw in Peggy's countenance was a picture of joy.

Maggie knew that this time Peggy's tears were of joy at the prospect of a brighter future, largely because of Maggie's presence in Peggy's life. And tears began to fill Maggie's eyes as well, prompting her to say to herself and to God, "Thank you, Lord, for having answered my prayer, for revealing to me what the minister was talking about in his sermon that Sunday before left to go on this trip."

Maggie thought to herself, *The real "Wonder of the Spirit" that the minister spoke of did not occur just in Peggy's life but in my life too. Like Peggy, I was one of those lost sheep!*

She said quietly to herself, "My spirit sure has felt rejuvenated since meeting Peggy."

Sitting next to his wife, Fred asked her, "Mag, what's that you're muttering about over there?"

"Sorry, Fred. My mind was on Peggy and the conversation I had with her," Maggie replied.

"Don't worry about it, Mag. Remember I mentioned to you how Gates talked to me one time about how the spirit part of us may be somewhere else when our physical body might be right next to a person. Well, it's obvious now, Mag, that your spirit, that is your mind, is on that waitress."

Sitting behind the Mints and listening to their conversation, Gates said, "Yeah, Fred, I remember me telling you that and that being one of the 'Wonders of the Spirit.' I mean how two people's spirits can connect like that; it's a wonderful thing. And like in Maggie's case with that waitress, the two people don't even have to be together physically; they can be separated and still their spirits can connect.

"Yeah, their spirits can come together via the greatest mode of transport there is—the mind! And the great thing is that it's immediate, faster than any aircraft! Just think about the person, thing, or place, and you're right there with 'em."

Fred asked, "And how do they connect spiritually if they are apart physically, Gates?"

"Oh, come on, Fred! I just told you! Weren't you listening? It's through their mind. Two people can be separated from one another physically and yet be together as they think about the other person. And one other thing. Spirits can connect with the assistance of prayer. For example, God hears us when we pray on behalf of someone else; it doesn't matter if the two people are together physically or not.

"Remember, Maggie, when you were telling me how God answered the prayer I made when you were so worried that Sandra wouldn't make it to Freddie's funeral on time?"

"Oh, yeah, I do remember that, Gates," Maggie replied.

"Well, I did pray about it like I said. And you know what happened. She came there right on time and sat next to you just before the service started. Now, didn't she do that?"

Maggie replied, "You're right, Gates. Sandra did and apparently was the answer to the prayer you made. Yeah, it was amazing that Sandra came in just before the service as you told me you would pray for that to happen and it did!

"Yeah, I was an emotional wreck because of everything that was going on at the time. And Sandra being there was certainly one of my concerns.

"But getting back to Peggy, it really has been wonderful to connect with that lady. And I can truthfully say that we did connect mentally as well as physically. And I say that because I've been constantly thinking about that lady ever since we left the diner. And I guess the reason for that is that I know how she was before I *really* got to know her; she wasn't a very peasant person to be around.

"Since that time, however, Peggy and I have talked a lot on a personal level, and I've found she's a different person from what I perceived her to be at first. It's like she's gone through a total change in her spirit. And by that I mean I believe there was a spiritual transformation that took place in her life. Now to me that's a perfect description of the 'Wonders of the Spirit' phrase that you often talk about.

"And I'll tell you something else, Gates. Another wonder of it all is what Pastor Henry talked about that day in his sermon on the last Sunday before we took off on this trip—about helping that one lost sheep that has gone astray. Well, I feel that I've been able to help Peggy, given what she's been through. In a strange kind of way, Fred, I believe that I've been found too."

"You've been found, Mag?" Fred asked.

Maggie would not dare to tell him what she meant because it involved her own deliverance from the guilt associated with a previous transgression—with Freddie.

A challenge now for Maggie was to keep in contact with Peggy once she returned to her work at the day care center. She especially planned to notify her as the time approached for the group to begin preparations for their trip down to Sinbad's resort in Miami.

Finally, the caravan of two vehicles was back on the interstate, heading eastward towards Chicago. Everyone would soon be back home, although the delegation from New York and New Jersey had to continue their journey even farther eastward. But this time they would not drive back. Katie and Wynn and their friends from New

Brunswick had booked return flights to New York City before they left that area driving to Chicago for the trip out west.

Gates summarized everything that had transpired during the trip, highlighted by Maggie's vision as well as her gaining a new friend in Peggy. As Maggie continued to meditate while looking out the window at the plains of eastern Iowa, he said, "You know, Maggie, the joy we all seem to have now is not only about being on the road going back to Chicago but also your having gained a valuable friend. And let me tell you, true friends are hard to find these days!"

As Gates spoke those words, Maggie could not help but think about Peggy gazing through the entry door window and the look of joy she displayed as the vans drove away.

Maggie said, "It's experiences like these, Gates, that prompt me so often to think about the phrase you use, 'Wonders of the Spirit'!"

Gates replied simply, "Amen to that!

"And, Fred, I can say the same thing about the message we heard from Pastor Henry that Sunday at church before we left to come on this trip. Now, because of my experience with Peggy, I'm aware of how 'Wonders of the Spirit' are connected in a practical way to my own life," Maggie said as the tears rolled from her eyes.

As the caravan of two vans continued the journey, heading towards Chicago and points farther east, they would all soon be home again.

Puzzles

Wonders Puzzle Chapters 1 to 11

334

Chapters 1-11 Clues

ACROSS

1. Where Fred and Maggie first met.

3. Sinbad arrived at this hotel; location of his cousin's final service.

6. This trip represented Erin and Bernie's second one.

7. Hometown of Maggie's parents.

11. Invisible moisture in the air.

13. The number of days Sinbad said the group would be away on their trip.

15. The Mints' and Manleys' pastor.

16. Fred had a drink of this before he left for his flight.

17. A fireplace was in this area of the Mints' and Manleys' hotel.

19. Chicago is also known by this name.

20. Confirm flight reservations.

23. After dinner Fred was directed to this kitchen appliance.

24. King of Kings, and Lord of Lords.

26. Fred and Gate's beverage from concierge after returning from the store.

27. Fred had arranged to fly to this city with his publisher.

30. This activity was going on outside when everyone was having breakfast.

31. The group's first stop as they headed towards Colorado.

33. Aunt of Sinbad.

DOWN

2. Where Sandra often went for relaxation.

4. What Jesus offers for the life of a believer.

5. Courtney mentioned this course taken by Fred in college.

8. What Fred and Gates took advantage of returning from the store.

9. Hotel where the Mints and Manleys lodged.

10. Maggie moved to this city when she left home in Flint.

12. Gates had this in the bag when he and Fred returned from the store.

14. The name of Fred's corporate job.

18. The color of Freddie's car.

21. Maggie knew her from their college days.

22. A very sad occasion.

25. Another word for the church building.

28. The group drove to Colorado in this vehicle.

29. People do a lot of this in Las Vegas.

32. The name Fred called his wife.

Wonders Puzzle Chapters 12 to 16

Chapters 12-16 Clues

ACROSS

1. This was installed in both vans for drivers' communications.

2. Description of the vans.

3. The description of the breeze the group often witnessed while riding travelling along the plains of Iowa.

5. A terrible snowstorm.

9. The direction of the group's journey to Colorado.

10. David referred to Gates by this name when he was once talking to him.

14. The town where Fred and Maggie lived.

15. First establishment stop after leaving Chicago.

16. The kind of music that Wynn loved.

17. The kind of background music sometimes provided by the hotel.

18. What David referred to the Bible as.

19. This part of the vehicle needed to be fi xed before the group could continue their journey.

DOWN

1. 1Peter 2:9 says "ye are a chosen generation, a royal priesthood, a holy nation, a __________ people..."

4. Sinbad was from here.

6. The group was travelling on this type of highway.

7. Sheri and her family was from here.

8. An area in the extreme back of each van reserved for this.

11. The group's lodging hotel in Chappell.

12. A word that describes the area surrounding the diner that was the group's fi rst stop on their trip.

13. A geographic area of west Iowa.

Wonders Puzzle Chapters 17 to 25

Chapters 17-25 Clues

ACROSS

3. A mode of transport to the Island of Love.
4. The room where everyone came together after their arrival in Denver.
9. Alphonso's shortened name.
11. Another word for heaven.
12. An eating and social event that normally occurs after a funeral service.
14. The person Maggie befriended just prior to leaving for the mountain resort.
15. Another term for taking a picture.
16. The area where people waited to go on the cable lift car was the _______________ station.
18. Erin and Bernie's last name.
19. This is where the group spent most of their time in Colorado.
22. The fruit of the spirit are outlined in this Book of the Bible.
23. What Erin imparted to Sandra during her visit to Bermuda.
25. Images formed in our minds about travels to a place.
27. The Cable Lift Center was otherwise known as this.
28. The type of resort everyone was eager to visit.
30. Maggie called her mother by this name.
32. This is where Erin, Sandra, and Maggie decided to carry on their discussion.
33. The Mile High City.

DOWN

1. This person attended to Maggie during her recovery from the accident.
2. In her vision, Maggie saw this person when she did not know her in her physical life.
5. They were lying near the surface of the raging waters of the stream fl owing at the bottom of the ravine.
6. Something you want, deep down inside of your spirit.
7. The last Book of the Bible.
8. David referred to Wynn as this once.
10. The time of Sinbad's meeting with the group after their arrival in the hotel in Denver.
13. Maggie promised Peggy she would get her a portrait of this as a gift from her time in Colorado.
14. The name given to the cabin accommodation for the group.
17. Another name for William's Cabin.
20. Jesus' associates.
21. An invisible virus causes this to occur.
24. After the accident, Maggie struggled between two dimensions: one physical and the other _________.
26. A disciple who initially did not believe that Jesus had risen from the dead.
29. The name of the volcano the group had planned to visit.
31. The name of the mountain area where the resort was located.

Wonders Puzzle Chapters 26 to 29

Chapters 26-29 Clues

ACROSS

2. Van drivers didn't like this about the re-fueling service station.

4. This was Peggy's offi cial position at the diner.

5. This was the time that Peggy started her shift at the diner.

7. The snowman picture Maggie got was not real, like Peggy wanted, but was ______ .

8. This is what Gates told Fred he could do to help them change the vehicle's fl at tire.

9. This was what Wynn and Jeanie were having as the tire problem was being resolved.

10. Maggie and Peggy's action just prior to Maggie's return to the group in the van.

DOWN

1. This phrase has reference to lost sheep mentioned in the Bible.

3. New Orleans type of food.

4. Maggie's description to Peggy of how she got the portrait.

6. This was referred to by the number 24.

Author Bio

William Porter is an author and a book club host. His most recent novel, "Wonders of the Spirit," is the fifth in a series that presents spiritually focused, biblically based stories about people's experiences in everyday life. It is a continuation of the adventure that began with *Heaven Can't Wait, or Can it? Dreams of Love, Deceit, and Hope,* and followed by *Heaven Can't Wait, or Can it? THE SEQUEL, Heaven Can't Wait, or Can it? THE FRUITION,* and *For Heaven's Sake: THE DREAM CONTINUES.* The next novel in the series after the current work is anticipated in 2024."

Don't miss other volumes in the *Heaven Can't Wait or Can It?* series

Heaven Can't Wait or Can It? Dreams of Love, Deceit and Hope

This novel is the first in the series as lead character Maggie and her friends seek their "Heaven on Earth." However, while making their earthly journey, there are many pitfalls in pursuing this goal.

Heaven Can't Wait or Can It? The Sequel

This novel is a follow-up to the first in this series. Maggie and her friends continue the saga of trying to find "Heaven on Earth" while living in an imperfect world.

Heaven Can't Wait or Can It?
The Fruition

Maggie and her friends seek the fortunes of a happy life through relationships, adventure, and faith as they take a cruise from New York to Bermuda. Unfortunately, the trip did not go without conflict, danger, and misfortune.

For Heaven's Sake
The Dream Continues

A continuation of the dreams and desires Maggie expereinces as she and her friends traverse paths of personal realtionships.

9 781944 662837